SEIZED

A KIERAN YEATS MYSTERY

Linda J Wright

Published 2021
Printed in the United States of America
First Edition
ISBN 978-1-7323593-7-6
E-ISBN 978-1-7323593-8-3
Library of Congress Control Number: 2017930398

Cover Design by Bianca Gill
Cats Paw Books

For information, contact:

Cats Paw Books
630 Hickory Street NW
Suite 120-119
Albany, OR 97321
catspawbooks@mail.com

Kieran Yeats novels by Linda J Wright

Stolen (2018)

Sacrificed (2019)

Seized (2022)

Praise for
SEIZED: A Kieran Yeats Mystery (#3)

"Wright again follows animal crimes investigator Kieran Yeats, this time in Seized as she takes on the case of Captain Isobel "Izzy" Tremblay's kidnapped service dog, a labradoodle named Beatrice who helps her with PTSD. Izzy, a former Canadian Air Force pilot who was shot down and wounded over Iraq, survived while everyone else in her crew was killed. Now jihadists have followed Izzy to Canada, kidnapped her dog, and sent a ransom letter demanding money and telling Izzy "you must stay at home where all women should stay." As Yeats and her friend, retired RCMP constable Miranda Blake, investigate and try to get the dog back before it's too late, they uncover a dark world of terrorists, militants making IEDs, and dog fighters who use small dogs as bait.

There is beauty at the core of this novel, mainly in the relationship between Izzy and Beatrice, who "sleeps with her, wakes her up from nightmares, blocks strangers from coming too close to her in stores, goes to therapy with her." However, it's also a thriller about a rescue and about larger forces; the darkness Yeats and Blake uncover includes young Canadian men who "get sucked into that awful extremist mindset."

Yeats and Blake, as an almost buddy-cop duo, have great chemistry, and between constant dangers, discoveries, and a few Star Trek references, Seized: A Kieran Yeats Mystery is highly recommended."

– BookLife

"This fast-paced mystery weaves animal rights, rescue and activism in a way that keeps readers guessing and engaged. As narrated by Kieran Yeats, the voice is open and inviting, and the author's polished writing tyle and elegant prose work well. The story is populated by fleshed-out, memorable characters and its core themes of family, healing and optimism make it even more enjoyable."

– Readers' Favorite

"Another terrific entry in the Kieran Yeats series of animal rights mysteries. Each one of these is better than the last and I can't wait to see Number 4. I can't recall a series about animal issues which is as well-written, literate, and engrossing as this one. I love the characters even more than the solution of the mystery. Write on, Wright!"

– Safe Haven Humane Society, Albany, Oregon

Praise for
SACRIFICED: A Kieran Yeats Mystery (#2)

"*Sacrificed: A Kieran Yeats Mystery is a gripping story about animal rights and crime. I appreciated the skillful way in which Wright adds depth to the story through her own experience as an animal rights activist. And I loved Kieran's 'cadre' of people in her life: her adopted daughter Tris, and friends who love and support her. I also loved the way Wright weaves poetry and Kieran's Irish heritage into the story. A very enjoyable and thought-provoking mystery story for those who love animals.*"

– Saifunnissa Hassam, Readers' Favorite Reviewer

"*I found Sacrificed to be a powerful and completely authentic read. Author and animal activist Linda J Wright has written an entirely believable mystery which manages at the same time to be informative about the controversial subject of cosmetics testing on animals. Not only animal-loving readers, and mystery readers, but also readers who just love language will connect with Wright's clear-minded writing that includes moments of poetic prose.*"

– Trudi LoPreto, Readers' Favorite Reviewer

"*Mystery readers and animal lovers, especially advocates for their protection, humane treatment, and full inclusion in the world of living, conscious beings, will applaud the efforts of investigator Kieran Yeats in Linda J Wright's novel, Sacrificed. Wright's passionate advocacy for the helpless shines through in this novel, which is a solid, entertaining mystery with an animal rights message, a heart, and a terrific heroine named Kieran Yeats.*"

– Joel R. Dennesdedt for BookLife

"*A terrific follow-up to Stolen, Wright's first Kieran Yeats novel. She is establishing herself as a powerful voice for animal rights with this mystery series.*"

– Safe Haven Humane Society, Albany, Oregon

Praise for
STOLEN: A Kieran Yeats Mystery (#1)

"A superb series kickoff. Wright, who has been involved in animal advocacy for over 30 years, combines her passionate commitment to animal rights with a riveting whodunit that's not dependent on murder to sustain interest."

— Publishers Weekly (Starred Review)

"One of the best-reviewed books of 2018."

— *BookLife*

"A powerful tale of the rescue of pets stolen from an upscale Victoria, British Columbia neighborhood . . . the best animal book of this or any other year. A terrific story!"

— SafeHaven Humane Society, Albany, Oregon

"Wright's plot is taut and well-constructed. The story's bucolic setting on Vancouver Island had me wistfully considering relocation. I'm looking forward to reading about Kieran Yeats's other cases. Stolen: A Kieran Yeats Mystery is most highly recommended."

— Jack Magnus, Readers' Favorite Reviewer

"Stolen: A Kieran Yeats Mystery was a one I quickly got caught up in. The characters were all sharply defined and it was easy to identify, to empathize, and to root for all of them. The author used the story to raise awareness of the need for more protection for animals under the law, and I am always impressed, as a reader, when social issues are able to be promoted in fiction, without drawing away from the enjoyment of the story, and this author does it extremely well."

— Grant Leishman, Readers' Favorite Reviewer

"Linda J Wright has written an exciting mystery that will appeal to mystery readers and animal lovers alike. Through the story in Stolen, readers are introduced to some of the issues involved in using animals as research subjects, and the heartbreak animal owners face when their pets are stolen for such research. I look forward to reading more of Wright's books."

– Sandy Calkins, Librarian, Yachats, OR

"Stolen is a mystery that explores animal rights by giving us an honest look at the abuse animals often endure for profit. While containing some hard moments, the story is uplifting, has a terrific ending, and is told through Kieran Yeats's clear, passionate voice — that of investigator who fights to save animals."

– Liz Konkel, Readers' Favorite Reviewer

ABOUT THE AUTHOR

Linda J Wright is a Canadian citizen. Born in Ontario, she grew up in a military family, and spent part of her childhood in France. She lived in Victoria, British Columbia, before moving to Oregon, where she now lives with her partner and their spoiled-rotten cat. In the nineties, she was awarded three California Arts Council Artist-in-Residence grants to teach fiction writing to GATE high school students, and won a California Association of Teachers of English Excellence Award for those classes. She is the author of eleven novels. In 1992 she won the Lambda Literary Award for *Ninth Life: A Caitlin Reece Mystery* and in 2018 was a finalist for the Lambda Literary Award for *Stolen: A Kieran Yeats Mystery*.

An animal rights advocate, Linda has been involved in animal welfare for over thirty years. In 1990, she founded the rescue organization The Cat People, and served as its first president. Since then, she has served on the boards of several animal welfare organizations and has been a consultant to dozens of animal rescue/welfare groups. In 1999 she was part of the team that rescued Keiko the orca (the real Free Willy) and rehabilitated him in Newport, Oregon, setting him free off Iceland. She continues to advocate for animals through her writing.

You can see her books at Cats Paw Books'
website www.catspawbooks.com.

For Sheila Crandles

SUNDAY

CHAPTER 1

Ah, an April Sunday morning on Vancouver Island. A swirling of snowy plum blossoms; a gamboling of tweedy-backed grey squirrels; a lapping of lapis lazuli waves at the edge of Clover Point Park. What could go wrong on a day filled with such marvels?

I stood at the edge of the park, sipping coffee from a paper cup, watching Tristan, my blond, curly-haired adopted daughter, aim her digital camera at a puffy grey bird perched coyly on an evergreen branch. Tris had asserted knowledgeably that it was a Eurasian collared dove, and it did have a thin black ring around its neck, which might have been the eponymous collar. I smiled at Tris's ornithological earnestness: heck, the bird looked like a pigeon to me. It was even cooing. Hmmf. What did I know?

Today was Tristan's ninth birthday. Her new black long-sleeved T-shirt, a present from her nanny and tutor, Aliya, said GOLDFINCH WHISPERER under a photo Tris had taken in our backyard. The Junior Ornithologist and I planned to go stuff ourselves with blueberry pancakes and afterwards waddle to the wild bird store where Tris had her eye on a nifty transparent dome to keep the rain off her bird feeders. I recall I was smiling, feeling quite blissed out, looking forward to the afternoon.

But the best-laid plans, according to that canny Scot Robbie Burns, *gang aft agley*, right? In other words, often go straight to hell.

A white Bronco drove up and parked some distance away, on a little access path under the plum trees, and a tall, burly, sandy-haired guy got out. I couldn't see his face clearly but he was wearing jeans, a white polo shirt, and a navy windbreaker. And sunglasses. He opened the passenger-side door, took something out, then began walking purposefully in our direction. My metaphorical antennae twitched. Don't be paranoid, Yeats, I told myself. Surely even burly guys in sunglasses and jeans come to the park simply to amble in the spring sunshine. He came a little closer and I relaxed. It was my friend Mac, Detective Superintendent Alexander MacLeish of the Oak Bay Police Department. What? On a Sunday afternoon? I searched my mind in a spasm of frantic guilt. Had I forgotten to pay those parking tickets I'd been hoarding on my desk?

"Hey, Mac," I called to him. "You're all casualled out — a change from your in- office tweeds. And why are you not golfing? I thought that's how you passed your Sundays."

"Och, and I would be," he said, uncharacteristically solemn, removing his sunglasses and putting them in a pocket of his windbreaker. "But I have a wee matter to discuss with you."

"Oops, this sounds serious," I said. "And here I thought I'd successfully hidden from the world. Shut off my phone, left no forwarding address . . . that sort of thing. Oh, I imagine Aliya, that loose-lipped lass, told you where I was."

When I couldn't get him to crack a smile, I realized the wee matter that was troubling him was clearly nothing to be joked about.

"Let's sit," I said, indicating a bench behind us from which I could still keep track of Tris who was pursuing the collared whatsit as it fluttered from tree to tree.

"Kieran, what do you know about Iraq?" he asked.

"Well, not very much, apart from where it is." I pictured a map of the Mideast — Iraq, Iran, Saudi Arabia, Turkey, Syria. *What on earth was this all about?*

"Good enough," he said, smoothing his sandy moustache, a tell attesting to nerves.

"And do you know much about our mission in Iraq?"

"Canada's mission?"

He nodded, blue eyes serious.

"You know, Mac, I'm embarrassed to say I don't. Only that it's non-combat."

He sighed. "It is. And not everyone's in favor of it, even though it's our NATO commitment. We have only a few hundred troops stationed there. They're fulfilling an advisory role to Iraq's military operation against ISIL, or Daesh, as the locals call it. Our forces, they're part of Operation IMPACT."

"Uh huh," I said, completely mystified at this lesson in international politics.

He sighed. "Well, about a year ago, Operation IMPACT became one member short."

He reached into the brown envelope he was carrying and pulled out a photo of a woman with light brown hair pushed back behind her ears. She was standing in front of a large helicopter, a bleak landscape behind her, dressed in desert camouflage fatigues, smiling, exuding confidence.

"Captain Isobel Tremblay," he said with evident pride. "Izzy. Our niece. Her parents — Mary's brother and his wife — died in an accident some years ago. Their children, Louis and Isobel, were at the University in Toronto when it happened. They came to stay with us. Izzy had a difficult time, but she went back east to her four-year program. She graduated. Got her Bachelor of Aviation Technology. And later, her pilot's wings. In exchange, she had to serve seven years in the Air Force, but that's all she ever wanted to do anyhow. The Tremblays are a Canadian Air Force family," he explained. "Her dad didn't live to see her become a pilot, though. He would have been so proud."

"What about Louis?" I asked. "Did he go back to U of T?"

"Louis," Mac said. "Now there's a lost soul. I don't know why he didn't go back to school in Toronto. He never did explain it to us. Something was clearly amiss with him. Grief at losing his parents? Mary and I tried to help him, but he was difficult. We never had a son, you see, only daughters. So perhaps we didn't know how to talk to him. At any rate, after Izzy went back to school, he moped. It seemed his only interests were sleeping, eating, listening to strange music, playing video games, and reading obscure works of science fiction. We suggested delicately that he might want to volunteer somewhere, or go to school here in B.C. — U Vic or Camosun — or get a job, but none of those suggestions appealed to Louis." Mac shrugged. "He was depressed, of course. We worried about him, offered to help him find a therapist, but he wasn't interested. The last straw for us was when he skipped Izzy's graduation ceremony. The lad just couldn't be bothered coming to see his sister get her wings. We couldn't understand why."

Hmm, I thought. Maybe the why wasn't very mysterious. Maybe it was as simple as good old-fashioned jealousy. Izzy seemed to have been a pretty high achiever. Maybe she was a hard act to follow.

Mac continued. "Rightly, or wrongly, we decided to practice a little tough love and ask him to leave. His presence in our home was proving to be too disruptive. We offered to let him stay at our cabin near Deep Cove for a while, providing he got a job. He did — get a job, that is. But it didn't turn him around the way we hoped it would. No, he got a job as a restaurant busboy, joined a rock band, dealt marijuana, got into trouble with the law, went to jail, and then we lost touch with him. So did Izzy. He might still be in jail. I really don't know." He sighed. "Good heavens, Kieran. I'm embarrassing myself, rambling on. I rarely think about Louis's time with us. It's all come up for me because of what happened to Izzy."

"Oh," I said abruptly, recalling what he'd just told me about Operation IMPACT being one member short. "Izzy. She's not missing, is she?"

"No, thank God," he said. "Her Griffon, the helicopter she's standing in front of in the photo — she was one of the pilots, by the way — was shot down en route to somewhere in northern Iraq with medical supplies on board. She was the only survivor. Her copilot, the flight engineer, and the navigator all perished."

"Was it ISIL? Daesh?"

He nodded. "Yes. A mortar attack, she said. They'd learned the Griffon's flight path and were waiting in a ravine. They brought it down, stripped the interior of supplies, and systematically shot the crew members." He fell silent and I waited for him to continue. "Izzy was thrown out of her pilot's chair and ended up jammed under the controls. They shot her on the way out, as they did all the others, but only wounded her in the leg. They were in a hurry to get away, she said, and must have assumed she was dead." He shook his head. "She got off a distress call just before she went down, but it took the squadron over twelve hours to reach the Griffon. Bad country apparently. She spent a miserable twelve hours in that helicopter. It was horribly hot, she was wounded, and worried to death about her crew. One foot was stuck under the controls, so she couldn't move. She used her belt to fashion a tourniquet for her leg, but her crew, well, she couldn't get to them. When help arrived, they were all dead."

Poor Izzy. She must have a whopping case of survivor's guilt. "Where is she now, Mac?"

"Hmm?" he said, seeming to come back from very far away. "Oh. Here. In Victoria. She was in a military hospital back east for quite a while, and when she was released, Mary and I brought her here. We helped her get a quiet ground-floor apartment not too far from downtown. She's continuing her rehab here. Her leg is coming along nicely, she says."

"But?" I asked when he paused.

"But it's the psychological trauma she suffered that's, well, crippling her. Still. Mary found a nonprofit group that provides PTSD dogs to wounded veterans. They matched her up with Beatrice, a Labradoodle."

A PTSD dog? That was the first I'd heard about dogs helping veterans in that way. How interesting. I waited for Mac to continue.

"Izzy still has nightmares, still jumps at anything that sounds like a gunshot, still sees and hears the Griffon's rotors, still can't bear being in crowds that mill around her, still panics at the sound of Arabic being spoken, still spooks at the sight of dark-skinned, bearded men . . . that kind of thing. But the dog has made such a difference in her life. Beatrice sleeps with her, wakes her up from nightmares, blocks strangers from coming too close to her in stores, goes to therapy with her." He smiled in evident admiration for Beatrice.

"Until?" Why did I know there was going to be a bad end to this story?

"Until this." He reached into the brown envelope again and took out a single sheet of paper on which was handwritten, in block letters:

WE ARE DAESH. WE SEIZED YOUR DOG. BUT, HAPPINESS! YOU CAN BUY HER BACK. WE WANT $10,000. DO NOT TRY TO TRICK US OR YOUR DOG WILL MEET A FATE WORSE THAN DEATH. DO NOT CONTACT THE POLICE. YOU HAVE ONE WEEK TO GET THE MONEY. WE WILL CALL YOU SUNDAY EVENING AT FIVE O'CLOCK WITH INSTRUCTIONS.

YOU WILL FIGHT NO MORE AGAINST DAESH. NOW YOU MUST STAY AT HOME WHERE ALL WOMEN SHOULD STAY. REMEM-BER SINJAR.

LONG LIVE THE FIGHTERS!

"Oh, for cripes' sake!" I burst out. "Are we supposed to believe that some ISIL nitwits, what, followed Izzy here and are now punishing her for flying medical supplies to northern Iraq by kidnapping her *service dog*?" I huffed. "Hell, how do we know they even have her?"

He reached into the brown envelope again and handed me a round brass tag. BEATRICE, it said, with a phone number. Presumably Izzy's phone number.

"Okay, okay," I said. "They have her. Whoever they are. So this phone call is tonight?"

"Yes," he said, putting Izzy's photo, the ransom note, and Beatrice's ID tag back into the brown envelope. "Izzy followed their instructions and didn't contact us. But as the week went on, she got well and truly frightened for Beatrice. And she said she became convinced she wasn't doing the right thing. So she called me. She could scrape together the money, but she's frightened to death about the exchange. Should she trust them? Her instincts say not to. I agree."

"Brother," I said. "What was she going to do when they called?"

"Bluff, I suppose. Not a very good plan," he said.

"Not at all," I said. "Okay. I get it. She called you, you called me. But I have my phone off. So you're here."

"Kieran, I have to step away from this," he said. "I can't get involved. Not only is Izzy my niece, but the department doesn't chase lost dogs. Even ones whose owners are being extorted. Even when the ransom is as big as this one." He stuffed his hands into his windbreaker pockets, looking out to sea.

"Do I think Daesh is behind this?" he continued. "I think it's unlikely, but what do I know? If they are responsible though, dammit, they have their facts wrong. None of Canada's troops are involved in combat in Iraq. I'm surprised they don't know this. Or perhaps they're just angry that we're there at all. Nevertheless, if the note really came from them, and they're here, in this country, this needs to be kicked over to the RCMP."

I said nothing, sensing there was more. I didn't have long to wait.

"But I'm not going to do that. Not yet, anyhow. Neither am I going to do take this to the department, asking for a favor because Izzy is my niece."

"Wow, Mac," I said. "What do you have in mind? You can't do nothing."

He turned to me, eyebrows drawn together in a frown. "No, I can't. That's why I'm asking for your help."

"For?"

"Your help. Your professional help. I want to hire you to find Beatrice and bring her home to Izzy."

"Oh, Mac," I said, dismayed. "This might be way too big for me. What if you're wrong? What if Beatrice's captors *are* with Daesh, and they've discovered a new fundraising tactic — extortion — and this case really belongs with the RCMP? They have the resources to properly investigate something like this."

He nodded. "They do. But how long might that investigation take? And what happens to Beatrice in the meantime?"

"You have a point," I said. "But let's look at the other possibility. What if you handed the case to Oak Bay? What if they pulled out all the stops, treated this as more than just a lost dog case?"

He shook his head. "I'm doubtful, Kieran. Even with the big ransom demand — and you know as well as I do that extortion for that amount of money carries a pretty stiff penalty under the law — it's still a missing dog case. I know the department — hell's bells, I work there. I can predict how much attention the case will receive. It won't be placed on anyone's front burner. Time will go on, something more important will come up, leads might or might not be followed, the dog thief might get spooked, and Beatrice might well slip between the cracks. Besides, we're awash in fentanyl cases. Have been for years."

"Yeah," I said, agreeing with him. He was certainly right about the island's law enforcement entities drowning in drug investigations. "I get all that, Mac. And I'm flattered. You want to give the case to someone who'll care about it. Who won't put it on the back burner. Who'll stay focused on finding Beatrice."

But I felt a yammering of panic somewhere inside. Mac was my friend, but should I even be listening to his proposition? Weren't we talking about terrorists? Shouldn't I be kicking this job upstairs? I almost giggled: hell, I had no upstairs to kick it to.

I asked him, "But what if this someone starts turning over rocks and finds that Beatrice's captors really are with Daesh?"

Mac closed his eyes for a few beats, then opened them again. "Then this someone needs to tell me. And the information has to go to the RCMP. They're the right ones to handle things."

I didn't ask him the question that was on the tip of my tongue, but he answered it anyway.

"And I'll be the one to take it to them. Right after Beatrice's found," he said firmly.

I groaned. "If the dog thieves are with Daesh, keeping information from the RCMP, even for a short time, might not be wise."

"If Daesh is involved, the RCMP will get the information just as soon as Beatrice's safe," he said. I could see there was no budging him on this point. National security might have to take a back seat to dog rescue. *That might be a first*, I thought ruefully.

I said nothing, thinking this all over. I was humbled by my old friend's faith in me. What a role reversal this was — usually I came to Mac for help, asking him to bend the rules a little, to let me dot the i's and cross the t's another day. All in the service of justice, of course. But still . . .

"You can say no, Kieran," he said quietly. "I had to ask, but you don't have to agree."

He was right. I didn't. But what were friends for if not to have each other's back? I admit it took me a while to answer. Then I sighed. What the hell. "Okay. I'll take this on, Mac." Great choices, though. An Islamic terrorist cell, an extortionist gang, or . . . something else? Someone playing silly buggers?

"One thing," I said hopefully. "I know you said you had to step away from this case, but before you made that decision you didn't, ah, happen to send the note for prints, did you?"

"As a matter of fact, I did," he said. "I shouldn't have, but the forensics chappie owes me a favor." He shook his head. "No prints on it, though. Or the envelope it came in."

"So they were careful," I said. "Whoever they are. Well, prints would have been too much to hope for."

He said, "I can send you our dog theft files — complaints filed by citizens, suspects, action taken — but that's about all. They might provide you with someplace to start. As for the Daesh possibility . . ."

"I have a thought about that," I said. "Let me get my wits together. And I need to figure out what to do with the bird photographer. She was promised pancakes. And a visit to the wild bird store."

"Ah, yes," he said. "Well, I might just be able to help you there. I have grandchildren the age of young Tristan. I can act *in loco parentis.* Pancakes, wild bird store visits . . . I can handle those. And," he said, a twinkle in his eye, "I might show Tris the wild turkeys that live in a place known only to me."

"She'll swoon," I said. "And talk your leg off. You'll learn more than you ever wanted to know about the migratory patterns of the fox sparrow. And her latest passion — eBird, an ornithological online database run out of Cornell University. Apparently it's international. Tris is terribly impressed that she can learn about birds that people sight in Sri Lanka or Portugal. She regularly adds her Victoria bird sightings to the database."

"One other thing," Mac said. "Let me just add that I put in a phone call to a certain retired Royal Canadian Mounted Police constable. She's standing by. So to speak."

Ah, I thought. *He's worried that I might be offended.* Far from being offended, I entirely approved. "Good thinking," I told him. My friend, Miranda Blake, the retired RCMP constable in question, now ran an animal sanctuary up north near the ferry docks. If anyone knew anything about dog thieves, it would be Miranda. We'd worked an animal theft case some time ago, and she'd proved invaluable in helping me find and nail the suspects.

And she would certainly have thoughts about whether this could be a real threat from Daesh. Keeping track of terrorists in our country was, among other things, the business of the RCMP. If she didn't know, I was confident she would know someone who did.

"Did you happen to phone anyone else?" I asked, pretty sure of the answer to my question.

"Yes," he said. "Izzy. She's expecting you to call. I was hoping you'd get in touch with her, then maybe go over this afternoon and coach her on what to say when the bloody dog thief calls."

"Sure," I said. "So I'd better get started. Five o'clock isn't very far away."

"I really appreciate this, Kieran," Mac said. Then, "I'm quite aware that animal crimes investigation is your business. I know how much you charge — five hundred dollars a day. A thousand up front. I'm happy to pay your fee. Izzy isn't exactly flush with money. It's rather expensive being a wounded vet." He handed me the brown envelope. "You'll find a check inside, as well as the photo and the ransom note."

'To you from failing hands we throw the torch?' I tried not to think about those lines from the poem 'In Flanders Fields.' Daesh, I snorted to myself. Probably not. Probably a bunch of wispy-bearded druggies who'd read in the newspaper about the Griffon misadventure in Iraq, Izzy's PTSD, the animal nonprofit's gift of a service dog to Izzy, and thought up the dog theft plan one night after they'd popped a few greenies. 'LONG LIVE THE FIGHTERS' indeed.

"I'll just talk to Tris and then I'll take off," I said. Afterwards, I turned on my phone and called Miranda. Who was, apparently, standing by.

I took one last look at the ocean. Dark clouds had gathered to dim the bright day, which I considered entirely appropriate, and the sea had lost its lovely lapis lazuli sheen. Now it just looked sullen, fretful, and grey — a line of catspaws driven by wind rippling the surface.

Gang aft agley. Robbie Burns was right.

CHAPTER 2

"Honey, I'm home!" I called to my empty, silent house. No answer. Well, I expected none. Still . . .

Closing the door behind me, I hung my windbreaker on the hall tree, tossed the brown envelope Mac had given me onto the dining room table, and headed into the kitchen to make coffee. Coffee, that beverage of the gods, was always a good remedy for the megrims, and I sensed a few of them scaling the walls of my id. Before I began dwelling on what my friend veterinarian Zaira Lau, or Zee, called 'the scribblings of maudlin Irish depressives,' I decided to steal a march on all that and perk up my mood with some adenosine-receptor agonist. After all, even Wordsworth's "The World Is Too Much With Us" didn't stand a chance against a cup of good strong coffee.

"*Frrtt?*" a soprano feline voice inquired from the hall.

"*Frrtt* yourself, Jeoffry," I called back. "How's it going?"

A small, striped ribbon of a cat, half exotic Bengal and half common tabby, Jeoffry sauntered into the kitchen and twined around my ankles. "*Mmnn,*" he opined.

"It's going like that, eh," I replied, scooping him up into my arms.

He immediately stuck his cold, wet nose in my ear, which made me shiver and laugh in equal measure, and suddenly the megrims fled. None of us — neither I, Tristan, nor Zee — was certain how much Jeoffry could see. Maimed and half-blinded by an animal torturer, Jeoff had come to me as part of a case I'd undertaken last year and I hadn't had the heart to try to find him another home. Tristan loved him, I loved him, my big grey cat Trey loved him. End of discussion. The question of his sight still worried me, though. Fortunately, he could find his way to the kitchen and back, to the litter pan, to and from Tris's room, and to the best sunning spots (with Trey's help), so maybe my worrying was moot. Maybe his vision was akin to what a myopic sees without corrective lenses — color and light, but blurry shapes. He seemed happy, and that was the important thing.

I found the cats' treat container in the cupboard over the sink and poured a few bits of freeze-dried chicken into Jeoff's kibble bowl. He cocked his head, listening to the sound of falling treats, navigated unhesitatingly to the bowl, scarfed down the chicken, licked his chops, and set off back down the hall to Tris's room and the embrace of Trey, his beloved. Jeoff and Trey had been engaged in a feline bromance ever since his arrival chez Yeats, and neither of them strayed far from the embrace, or at least the presence, of each other. Ah, the strange forms love could take.

I poured coffee and took it and the brown envelope into my office, snapped on my desk lamp, hoping to further discourage those megrims, scanned and emailed the ransom note to Miranda, then sat down at my desk to gather my wits. Where to start with all this? I asked myself. Well, first things first, right? The impending phone call. A couple of hours still remained before I had to go collect Miranda and drive to Izzy's apartment, so I ought to concentrate on the call and leave everything else for later.

But I found myself unable to focus. I turned to look out my office window where rain streaked the glass like separate streams of tears, and wondered about my distractedness, which I was blaming on the megrims. Usually I'm pretty in touch with my feelings, but this afternoon I didn't seem to be. What had laid its hands on me? Was it this new case, Izzy's and Beatrice's plight? Was it Mac's evident distress? Was it the fact that work had interfered with my day with Tris?

Across my side yard, the just-in-bloom apple tree with its froths of pink blossoms, said clearly *spring*, and I thought back to the park and the plum trees in flower. And Tris's ruined birthday. Dammit. Was that the source of my distress? But maybe the day hadn't been ruined for Tris. Maybe she was enjoying herself with Mac and the turkeys. She probably was, I told myself. Tris was a surprisingly easy-to-please kid.

Not so long ago, she'd been an abused and neglected child, living in the woods north of Sidney with her animal-thieving grandfather — 'the old dog man,' as she contemptuously called him. And just down the road on the old guy's property lived drug-dealing Uncle Connor, and Connor's hangers-on friends, Peter and Stephanie. Tris had only described a few incidents about her life with those four, but the things she told me explained why she needed to protect herself by becoming a boy named Trouble.

When Peter had burned the kid's arm with his lighter to punish him/her for asking to have a pet, Tristan had become Trouble and bought an air pistol from Amazon to defend himself/herself. When Peter held a gun on a certain animal investigator named Yeats, Trouble unhesitatingly stepped out of the woods and demanded, 'Hands up!' And when Connor's off-again on-again girlfriend, the drugged-out Stephanie, had stolen eleven Bengal cats and thoughtlessly stockpiled them in a pen out in the rain behind her trailer, Trouble used the then-dead old dog man's credit card to call a cab and rescue them. The kid was not only resourceful, but bloody well fearless.

I think I fell in love with Trouble the instant he/she'd emerged from the forest behind Peter and, with no concern for his/her own life, distracted him, thereby saving mine. And later, when I learned that Trouble was actually a girl named Tristan, with not a relative to her name (apart from the soon-to-be incarcerated Connor), and no place to live apart from the old dead dog man's mold-covered, single-wide trailer, I was furious and heartsick. I didn't think twice. I invited her home, introduced her to the cats, fostered her, and eventually adopted her. I called her Sprout; she called me Kieran. She filled a Tristan-sized hole in my heart that I never knew I had.

I frowned a little as I wondered which birthday anyone had last celebrated with Tris. Well, the day wasn't over yet. Aliya was preparing a birthday dinner feast and guests were coming over. Tris and I had talked about the fact that her guests might want to bring presents, and this quite flummoxed her. She asked for time to think this over, and I suspected that she'd consulted with Jen Lau, Zee's fourteen-year-old daughter and my goddaughter, Tris's role model for social responsibility. A few days later, when the consultations were concluded, Tris told me that anyone who wanted to bring a birthday present should, instead, purchase supplies that the cats at Miranda's shelter might need, and that they should check with Miranda regarding brands of food and safe toys for cats. When she told me that, it was my turn to be flummoxed. And touched. I asked her if she was sure about her decision and she assured me she was. Cats needed presents, too, she said solemnly.

Okay, I thought. Maybe enough was enough. It was time to stop indulging my right brain and herd my left brain back to work. Besides, the sun wasn't yet over the yardarm — it was too early to pour whiskey. So I went out to the kitchen for another shot of coffee and thought about the upcoming phone call from the dog thief. It presented an opportunity. I mean, the guy would be right there, at the other end of the digital line. But dammit, so what? How could I use that situation? I had to admit, I didn't have a clue. But I knew someone who might.

Edgar Poe, my internet researcher, was, *mirabile dictu*, at the end of *his* phone. Or not. For all I knew he was really canoeing in the Malahat. Or brunching in Vancouver. Or admiring rhododendrons in the Butchart Gardens. I didn't expect him to answer — after all, it was Sunday — but he picked up.

"Hey, Edgar, you're there," I said, surprised.

"For you, Kieran my dear, I'm here even on the Lord's Day."

"Hmmf," I said derisively, but part of me was touched. The derisive part suspected that Edgar answered my calls in person because he found my jobs more intellectually stimulating than building firewalls for hospitals and airlines. But the part that was touched was, well, genuinely touched. Goodness, had we become friends? Digital pals? I'd never met Edgar in the flesh, but nevertheless, he and I went back years and years, to the time when he was a devil-may-care hacker and I a green attorney in the Crown Counsel's office. We'd both moved on from our original professions. Edgar, I suspected, had simply gathered together a gaggle of fellow hackers, morphed them into a respectable internet research company, named them Poe Enterprises, and offered their services to legitimate businesses. Their logo was a ruffled raven atop a computer; their motto, Nevermore; their clients, legion. All very cute. And lucrative.

I'd moved on to greener pastures also. Now I no longer argued in court for suitable punishment for animal abusers, no longer tried to wrest justice from a legal system that valued injured, maimed or dead plaintiffs with two legs more seriously than those with four. Now I interdicted, thwarted, stepped in before the cat was strangled, the horses starved, the rabbit microwaved, the dogs beaten to death. My work was sometimes exhausting, sometimes exhilarating, sometimes terrifying, but at least I could sleep at night. I no longer wept over the bodies of those for whom I was too late.

"How can I help?" Edgar asked.

I took a deep breath and launched into an abridged version of Izzy's and Beatrice's plight. "But it's this phone call," I said. "It's driving me mad. It's a gift, Edgar. He'll be right there, on the phone. And he'll leave a digital footprint."

"Indeed he will. And you're itching to get his number, aren't you?" he said.

"Yes, I am. And then I want to use the number to find the little bastard. Can you trace it? The number? I know zilch about tracing calls."

"Tracing calls. Hmm. Well, Captain Tremblay's phone will, of course, record the number the extortionist is calling from, but that will be useless to you."

"Oh yeah? Why?" I asked, dismayed.

"Because the call will most likely be made from a burner phone or a burner number."

"A burner — you mean not the caller's real number. Or phone."

"Sadly, yes."

"But even so, couldn't you . . . I don't even know the question to ask."

"Track him down? Beard him in his den? Run him to ground?"

Edgar, Edgar, this isn't the time for flights of fancy. "Yeah. Could you find him? Even from his burner number?"

"Probably. But it will take a while."

"How long is a while? Hours? Days?"

"Days. I'll have to liaise with a colleague at the cell phone service provider. Once I identify the provider, that is. There are, oh, a myriad of likely possibilities . . . Rogers, Bell, Telus, Freedom Mobile —"

"I get it," I said. "Lots and lots."

"And, depending on the carrier, I might or might not know a colleague willing to do the job. I might have to, ah, forge a new alliance."

"You have my Visa card," I reminded him.

"Indeed I do, and it's a continuing source of comfort to me. What did the Bard say? 'It is an ever-fixed mark that looks on tempests and is never shaken, the star to every wandering bark . . .'"

"Fooey. The Bard was talking about love there, Edgar. Not money. Although sometimes in your case the two *are* synonymous," I said testily. "I'm worried. Time is short. Don't be flighty."

"Oooo, you can be so cruel," he pouted. "But time *is* short, as you say. So 'once more unto the breach,' to quote the Bard again. The impending phone call."

"Thank you," I said.

"*De rien*," he said generously. "I've been pondering your Griffon pilot's plight as we've been speaking. Here's what she should do."

"Tell me."

"First, have Captain Tremblay record the call. Be very sure she does this. Then send it to me. Next, have her plead for time — as much time as she can. I'll need it to work on the origin of the call."

"And possibly forge a new alliance," I said.

"Exactly."

"I'm a tekkie dope," I admitted, "but can you give me the short course on how you'll connect the phone number with the dog thief? Can you ping it? I thought only the cops could ping numbers."

Edgar giggled. "Sweetie, there's no need to ping it. You've been watching too many cop shows on TV."

"Fat chance there," I said unrepentantly, unable to recall the last time I'd watched a cop show on TV. Or anything on TV for that matter, except *Jeopardy!*

"The real challenge won't be to locate the physical location of the call," Edgar said. "There are web-based GPS services to do that. For instance, you could use a GPS locator service to determine the location of my call right at this moment. But I might not be here for longer than, say, five minutes. I might be off to get a cappuccino."

"I see."

"So finding the physical location from which the call was made is not necessarily what you want. No, the chore will be to find the caller's real, billable cell phone number. You see, anyone can have a burner phone, or a burner number, or two, or six, or ten, but underneath them, rather like one of those nested Russian doll sets, lurks the cell phone owner's real number. And his real, billable account, and its history, all of which will have to be winkled out of the provider's database like reluctant oysters from their shells."

"And will this winkling provide a physical address?" I asked hopefully.

"It will," Edgar said. "Although we might find that the address is a post office box, or a business address, or a friend's address if your dog thief is a very shy boy."

"Crap. This sounds hopeless," I said, panicking. "What will we do then? If we end up with a real number, but no traceable address?"

"Ah," he said. "Fret not. That's when I perform my *legerdemain*. Untraceable is not a word in my vocabulary."

"I'm trying to be reassured," I told him. "Even though I can't imagine how you'll do what you say you'll do."

"Trust me," he said. "Have I ever failed you?"

"Actually, no," I told him. And he hadn't. The little ferret . . . he'd dug up the most remarkable things for me.

"There," he said. "QED. Be soothed. Just send me the recorded phone call, and the number, and I'll do the rest. But do have Captain Tremblay plead for time."

"You can count on it."

I ended the call, thinking over what Edgar had just told me. Okay, Miranda and I would need to persuade Izzy to record the call. That didn't seem difficult. But we'd also need to persuade her to beg. And that might be difficult. Was she a good beggar? I didn't know her. Before the call, we'd have to talk. What fairy tale could we concoct? Some difficulty acquiring the money seemed best. And could Izzy make this fiction believable? Could she put her concern for Beatrice aside long enough to tell an elaborate lie?

My gaze wandered to the ransom note on my desk, and I realized that I hadn't read it with the care it probably deserved. I'd skimmed it briefly when Mac had handed it to me in the park and hadn't looked at it again. So I picked it up and read it carefully this time. Every word. Twice. And thought with a sinking feeling that the note screamed out improbabilities. And questions. Why the single word 'happiness' after 'but'? Why did the author warn Izzy about further fighting in Iraq when the whole country knew our forces were not fighting? Why the transparently misogynistic statement about women remaining at home? What was Sinjar and why should Izzy remember it? What did he mean by 'a fate worse than death' for Beatrice? And who the hell were 'the fighters' who were supposed to, what, live long and prosper? I laced my hands behind my head, tilting my chair back, staring at the ceiling, thinking.

And quite apart from the questions the note suggested, it was the language that bothered me. The single would-be sentence 'But happiness!' was positively jarring. It seemed, well, foreign. I closed my eyes, willing the rusty cogs of memory to turn. And creakily, they did. What Izzy's ransom note reminded me of was the storied note accompanying the WannaCry virus that had terrorized the digital world back in May of 2017. That note was in English, but to a native English speaker like me, it sounded just 'off'. And it was.

Linguistic analysis of the WannaCry ransom note indicated that its author was not a native English speaker and, as time went on, the authorship of the note, and the virus, were traced to North Korea. Did I think the note sent to Izzy came from North Korea? No. Not at all. What was attempting to surface in my memory was the name of a University of Victoria professor, a forensic linguist, who had written an opinion piece for the local newspaper about the ransom note, predicting its authorship would be found to be North Korean. Indeed, her prediction was correct. Maybe, just maybe, I thought, she could take a look at the note on my desk and suggest its origin. Had it been written by a native Arabic speaker? Or a native English speaker posing as an Arabic speaker? Or? If she could put the Daesh possibility to rest, this case would be so much simpler. And less intimidating.

I turned on my laptop and, using Google to prowl the directory of the U Vic teaching staff, found the name of the linguistics professor more quickly than I expected. Metheny. Elizabeth Metheny. Uh huh. That was the name I remembered. Now what? Well, the directory provided an email address at the university. All right. I decided I would send Dr. Metheny an email. To Dr. Elizabeth Metheny, Professor of Linguistics, From Kieran Yeats, Animal Crimes Investigator. "A request for your assistance." Then I wrote a brief email message, summarizing the situation. I crossed my fingers, hoping that Izzy's plight might pique her interest, attaching my scan of the ransom note, and hoping that she wasn't on sabbatical, looked at her email regularly, and would get back to me sometime before the summer solstice. Whew. That was a heap of hoping.

I'd just turned off my laptop when a voice called from the kitchen, "Kieran?"

"Yup. In here," I replied.

A small woman with curly dark hair poked her head into my office. Aliya. As I recalled, she'd been grocery shopping for what she needed to prepare Tris's birthday dinner. Now she'd returned, probably bearing provisions.

"I saw your car in the driveway," she said. "What's up? I thought you and Tris would be gone for hours and hours. Pancake-eating, bird-feeder shopping. Is Tris in her room?"

"Nope. The best-laid plans and all that," I told her, outlining my meeting with Mac in the park, and the case I was now involved in. Aliya had been helpful with several of my other cases; I saw no need to shut her out of this one. Even though the villain of the piece might be a native Arabic speaker, as was she.

Aliya Hammam, her parents, her twin brother Samir, and their younger brothers Faisal and Simon — kids about Tris's age — had emigrated to Canada from Lebanon a couple of years ago. Aliya had finished her degree in computer science at Camosun College, moved out of her parents' house, and now ran her graphics and book cover design business from her home office in my renovated basement suite. I'd hired her as Tris's nanny and tutor months before her planned move, but once I knew that she was looking to relocate, had cleverly offered her my basement suite at a rent far more reasonable than anything she could have found in Oak Bay or greater Victoria. When she wasn't downstairs working, she was upstairs with Tris. Or me. Indeed, we ate meals together, most of them prepared by Aliya. Cooking has never been my long suit. Tris regarded her as one of the family, as did I.

"What a miserable, wretched thing to have done!" Aliya said heatedly. "Stealing a veteran's dog? And a PTSD dog at that. How's Izzy getting along, Kieran?"

"Not well, according to Mac. Miranda and I are due there soon. We'll find out. Say," I asked her, "refresh my memory. What's on the menu for dinner?"

"It's a Middle Eastern feast. Tris has become quite fond of it. It's vegan, it's exotic, it's tasty —"

"Ah yes, vegan," I said, raising an eyebrow. "This doesn't seem to be a phase she's growing out of, does it?"

"Nope," Aliya said. "Besides, going meatless is good for all of us. And for the environment, too."

"Hmmf, you sound like Jen Lau," I said. "Seeing Jen's MEAT IS MURDER sweatshirt is where this sortie into veganism all started. It was Tris's road-to-Damascus moment."

"Well, if the moment hadn't happened there, it might have happened at school," Aliya said. "Or in a discussion with one of her friends. Going meatless . . . it's not a fad anymore. It's one of the ways we can help the environment. We've turned too much of our world into a vast pasture for cows. A little less beef-eating would go a long way toward saving the planet."

"True enough. Just as long as she gets enough protein. Speaking of that, wasn't I supposed to bring something for dessert?" I asked. "This new case . . . it's driven most things out of my mind."

"Chocolate chip ice cream," Aliya said. "What time do you think you and Miranda will be done with Izzy? I can text you a reminder."

"That would be great," I said. "I feel like my head is full of scampering squirrels. Maybe around six? We should be on our way back here by then. I'll just stop somewhere and buy ice cream." I put the ransom note back in the brown envelope, preparing to take it with me to Miranda's.

"I'll leave you to feast preparations, then," I said. "Ten guests is a crowd — are you sure you're up to all that chopping?"

Aliya laughed. "When I lived with my parents, my mother and I prepared feasts for twice that number. Regularly. We Lebanese throw big dinner parties. So it's no problem."

"If you say so. Wow, all that cooking experience . . . maybe I should hire you," I teased.

"Go," Aliya laughed again. "And take a cold bag for the ice cream. There's one in the pantry."

I found the insulated cold bag, tucked it under my arm and, on my way to the front hall, paused and looked back to the kitchen. Aliya had turned on the light and the yellow-painted kitchen seemed to glow, a cheerful refuge from the gloomy, rainy afternoon outside. She'd switched on the radio in the kitchen as well, and a verse from an oldies song, Rick Nelson's 'Garden Party,' drifted to me:

People came from miles around, everyone was there
Yoko brought her walrus, there was magic in the air.

Well, there wouldn't be a walrus at Tris's dinner, but maybe ten guests, including Tris's best friend from school — a Syrian refugee kid named Dani — and Aliya's entertaining little brothers, would provide the magic. I doubted Tris had had a birthday party, attended by people who loved her, in years. If ever. She deserved one. Hell, everyone deserved one.

I closed the door quietly, leaving Aliya to her Middle Eastern feast preparation and Rick Nelson singing about his garden party. And magic.

CHAPTER 3

Under a barrage of on-again off-again rain, I pulled into the oak-ringed parking lot at The Sanctuary and sat for a minute, reluctant to race out into the weather. For how many days or parts of days had it been raining, anyhow? Not forty days and forty nights, yet, but it seemed to me, and to many Canadians, that it had been raining for far too long this spring. All of southern British Columbia was complaining. Especially the gardeners. In fact, this wasn't the first year that we'd had to suffer through onslaughts of rain. The sobering thought that this might no longer be the exception, but the rule, had occurred to many of us. Maybe, just maybe, these past few years' spring drenchings were harbingers, canaries in the coal mine, warnings of things to come.

I remembered a CBC story I'd heard the other day about Tuktuyaaqtuuq — an Inuit word which means, poetically, 'looks like a caribou' — the northernmost town in our country. Perched on the edge of the Arctic Ocean, Tuk's inhabitants are in a constant stew of worry because the sea is literally lapping at their front doors. Year after year, they've been losing three feet of land to the ocean, but this year, residents say, it's really, really serious.

They explained this at a town council meeting: "Someone needs to move our houses inland," they said. But so far, no moving had happened. Climate scientists at the meeting scratched their stubbled chins and explained the situation: as the Arctic ice melts — and it certainly is melting — the sea rises. What can we do?

"We understand what's happening. But we're losing our livelihood," the Tuk sealers and whalers explained. "We can no longer park our boats on the pebble beaches at our front doors, ready to set off at a moment's notice in pursuit of whales and seals. We've done this for hundreds of years. But no more. Why not? Because the pebble beaches are pretty much nonexistent. The sea has been gobbling them up, yard by yard, year after bloody year. And soon the sea will take our homes, too. It's literally at the front steps. Can no one do anything?"

So far, the answer has been no.

It's climate change, and it's killing Tuk. And the rest of northern Canada. The elk. The caribou. The polar bears who are invading northern Manitoba towns, eating out of garbage dumps, because they're starving, because the ice and the seals have just vanished. Who knew what else would perish as our world cooked, more Arctic ice melted, and we here on Vancouver Island, beleaguered by unseasonal drenching, cursed, checked our downspouts, and stocked up on rain gear?

And speaking of cooking, we were doing that, too. Not so long ago, the mercury soared to 105 in Toronto, and, as improbable as it seemed, our Arctic had suffered through a 90-degree heat wave. Elsewhere, people fried in 113-degree heat in Europe; and in India, over 100 people died when the thermometer hit 121. All this was enough to make me want to take to the couch with a bottle of Method and Madness Irish Whiskey. We were broiling ourselves here on this big blue marble. I forced my mind away from the rain, heat, the siren song of strong drink, and back to the business at hand.

Edgar would soon be launched on his job of ferreting out the dog thief's phone number; Elizabeth Metheny had my email and might decide my request merited attention; now Miranda and I needed to get into gear. I noticed that her yellow Jeep was parked in the lot, as was The Sanctuary's blue van, but apart from that, the parking lot was empty. That was odd, I thought. Usually a black Honda Civic belonging to Connie, Miranda's aunt and right-hand person, was parked there also. I shrugged. Maybe Connie was having a social life. A movie, a tai chi class, wine-tasting, a ballroom dancing lesson? Even sixty-somethings needed to kick up their heels.

Well, the parking lot wasn't completely empty, I noted. A motorcycle sat at the far end of the lot under the shelter of some oaks, a snazzy-looking red one, with a black helmet bungeed onto the seat. My only experience with motorbikes was as a passenger once in high school, a domestic felony for which I was grounded for two weeks. Entirely worth it, as I recalled. I wondered to whom this bike belonged. A volunteer? They usually parked in the back. A potential adopter? Miranda would never permit anyone to transport one of her adoptees in a carrier strapped to a motorcycle. Hmm. Well, I guessed I'd find out. Braving the rain, I splashed across the lot to the front door of the cedar-shingled two-story structure that housed Miranda's animal shelter.

Inside the lobby, Rowan Finnerman, a small, red-headed U Vic student, was on her hands and knees, dressed in jeans and a well-worn grey hoodie, building a cat tree. Ro and I had had quite an adventure last year, racing through a burning cosmetics testing lab with two cages of rabbits clasped in our arms, flames lapping at our heels. Strangely, that hadn't put Ro off animal rescue. She now had a part-time job at The Sanctuary as a fundraiser — her university major was nonprofit management — and had moved into one of the cottages on the considerable acreage Miranda owned behind the shelter. I had a feeling the motorcycle parked outside belonged to her. Feisty was definitely Ro's middle name.

"Hey, you," I said, greeting her, shedding my windbreaker and hanging it up on a hook on the wall by the door.

"Hey, you," she said back. "Kieran, do you know anything about carpentry?"

"Nope," I told her. "I'm useless with a hammer and nails. You seem to be doing a fine job, however."

"Not really," she said. "I'd rather be writing a grant proposal for cat trees than building them. But Miranda needs a couple right away, so . . ."

"So you're indulging her," said Miranda, laughing, appearing in the doorway leading to the hall. Tall, sturdy, with chin-length dark hair, and pale blue fighter-pilot eyes, Miranda had left the RCMP and the romance of the red serge and the Musical Ride for, of all things, animal rescue.

The case that had soured her on the RCMP was a dog theft case up-island, in which dozens of families had suddenly reported missing dogs. The community knew damned well that the dogs had been stolen for dog-fighting and expected the RCMP to do a proper investigation, shut down the dogfighting ring once and for all, and bring their pets home. However, the Force had done a sloppy, disinterested job, then covered up their inadequate efforts by asserting that coyotes had carried off the dogs. This despite the fact that coyotes hadn't been sighted in that neighborhood in years. Disgusted, Miranda turned in her spurs, so to speak, and never looked back. Now she coped with mange, fleas, ringworm, critter pee, and vomit, begged for money from charitable foundations, and was a better woman for it, she said. We'd had quite a few interesting adventures together since I'd met her, and I suspected this would prove to be another.

Today she was dressed in jeans and a faded blue RCMP sweatshirt — a memory of her time in the Force — a sartorial choice I always found curious.

"So I'm indulging the boss?" Ro chuckled. "Yup. Always."

"I see you're, um, standing by," I told Miranda. "So Mac reached you?"

"He sure did," she said. "I've been on the phone to an old RCMP contact. She's sending me some information on Daesh. Oh, nothing that would violate the Security of Information Act, but she claims it will be interesting nonetheless."

"Great," I said. "And Mac emailed me his file of the department's dog theft reports. I sent that on to you. I don't know if we'll get to it today but now we both have it. And, most important, I called in an order for sub sandwiches for all of us."

"Thank heavens," Ro said. "The carpentry department is starving."

As was I, having missed the pancake brunch. And the birthday feast wasn't until later.

"Where's Connie?" I asked, looking around. "I didn't see her car in the lot."

"Ha!" Miranda exclaimed. "If you can believe it, she's delivering that demon with feathers, Jimmy the doo-wop-singing parrot, to his new owner."

"Are you kidding me? Someone adopted the King of the F-bomb?" Jimmy, an African Grey Parrot, had languished at The Sanctuary for years. Prospective adopters were enchanted by his doo-wop playlist, but appalled by his language. There didn't seem to be a curse word Jimmy didn't know, and he gleefully ran through his *risqué* repertoire whenever adoption was imminent.

"Yup. A musician. A rock guitarist. He's looking forward to having Jimmy singing along with him at his gigs and warbling to him at home. And he doesn't care how foul Jimmy's mouth is, he says. Claims he swears like a sailor, too."

"Amazing. What did the Bard say? 'Let me not to the marriage of true minds admit impediments.' Or something like that. How does Connie feel about the adoption? I thought she'd become pretty fond of the little monster."

"Oh, yes and no. He was a handful. C'mon back," she said. "Ro, when those subs come, let us know?"

"Will do," Ro said.

In her office, Miranda settled into her usual place behind her desk, feet propped up on an open bottom drawer. I took a seat in the chair across from her, my feet propped on the windowsill.

"Alas, it's a little too early for the hard stuff," she said. "How about coffee though?" She gestured to the coffeemaker on a stand in the corner.

"Maybe when the subs come," I said. "Say, how's Ro working out?"

"Fantastic. Hiring that kid was the best thing I've done lately," she said. "She actually *likes* to write grant proposals. And she's good at it. Our new heating system ought to be called the Rowan Finnerman Memorial Keeping-Us-Cozy Unit. I forget the technical details," she admitted. "Anyhow, twenty-three thousand dollars, all paid for by a grant proposal. We can spend that money on the animals instead. I have a radical feline population control program in mind."

"Wow," I said. "Good for Ro."

"I made her a salaried employee after that coup," Miranda said. "True, only part-time, but she *does* need some hours in the day to work on finishing her degree. Seriously, having Ro fundraise will free me up to do some things I need to do. Some important things. Apart from the feline population control program, that is."

"Such as?" I asked, curious.

"Mac's call caught me in the middle of one of those things. Apart from reaching out to my RCMP contact, I'm afraid I haven't been able to give Beatrice and Izzy much thought. I'm too distracted."

"Hmm. Do you want to talk about the thing you got caught in the middle of?"

"Oh, well, maybe," she said. "For a bit. Then we need to talk about how to prepare Izzy for this phone call. I probably shouldn't say too much about my thing because talking will lead to fuming and fuming will lead to ranting. But it is going round and round in my head."

"Feel free to skip right to ranting, if you like," I said. "When have I ever held back from a good rant? And you always listen to me. But you're right. We need to think about the phone call. And I have a couple of things to tell you. I've been busy since I saw Mac. But fire away."

"Okay," she said. "Here's the thirty-second version of my current preoccupation. A few years ago, Connie and I started lobbying the pound seizure shelters on the island about changing their ways. I'd like us all to form a No Pets In Research coalition and present a unified front. Declare that our province's shelters decline to provide the research labs with cats and dogs for their vile and useless experiments."

"Wait," I said. "Pound seizure?"

"Yeah," she said, glowering. "Some shelters allow research labs to come in and buy their unadopted animals. Other shelters, certain municipal ones — or pounds as they were called in the old days — are required to do this. Hence the name 'pound seizure.'"

"For God's sake, Miranda!" I said. "That's —"

"Vile, I know," she said. "The rotten thing was, we had to give up on the coalition. There were three holdouts — shelters that just couldn't be talked out of selling their unadopted cats and dogs to labs. I'm fuming because if the coalition idea is going to fly, I have to revisit those shelters. Connie, Ro, and I have appointments this week. I have to prepare something reasonable to say to them, something persuasive, when what I'd really like to do is knock their heads together." She looked at her watch. "Anyhow, enough of that. It was more than thirty seconds. And I'm afraid it was ranting."

"It did seem a tad ranting-ish," I agreed.

"It was definitely ranting," she said. "So I better say no more on the subject. I can fill you in later on the wretched details if you're interested."

"Of course, I'm interested," I said. "Pound seizure? That's a new one on me. How about after the birthday party? You can resume fuming over a shot or two of Method and Madness Irish Whiskey. And lapse into more ranting if you like."

Ro knocked on the half-open office door and deposited a plastic bag with two sub sandwiches and two bottles of water on Miranda's desk. "Sounds heavy in here," she said. "You were ranting, boss. Should I close the door?"

"No, you can leave it open," Miranda said. "I'm done. And it was fuming, not ranting."

Ro gave me a quizzical look, shrugged, then took off back down the hall to the lobby.

"Barbarian," Miranda said to me, unwrapping her sub. "I appreciate the after-party offer, but Method and Madness indeed. Do you still have that bottle of Jack Daniels' Black Label that I brought over one night in desperation? *Scotch* whiskey," she said meaningfully.

"Uh huh," I said. "But what is it with you and Scotch whiskey anyhow? Blake isn't a Scottish surname. Or is it?"

"Fat lot you know," she replied, looking smug. "Actually it is. In the highlands when we wore kilts and spent our time loping through the heather after the king's deer, it was spelled *Blac* and it meant just that. Black. Dark one. See?" She sniffed. "You aren't the only one with an old country forbear. Even if your guy Yeats has a poem in every kid's English lit book. Why, the Blacs fought with Braveheart — you know, William Wallace — way back in the twelfth century."

"Really?" I asked, impressed.

"Nah, I made that up," she said. "I have zero idea about the Blacs and Braveheart. I just said that to twit you. William Butler Yeats, give me strength." She rolled her eyes.

"I can't help it if his maudlin Irish scribbling is famous," I said, laughing. "Although it's more like *two* poems in every kid's English lit book. Probably the oh-so-portentous 'The Second Coming' and that downer 'An Irish Airman Foresees His Death.' Okay, back to real life. Here's what I've been up to."

Between bites of sub sandwich — grilled vegetables, cheese, and Italian dressing — I filled Miranda in on my conversation with Edgar. "I hope Izzy is a good actress," I said. "She needs to make the dog thief give her more time. Edgar needs it for his, ah, research."

I'd emptied out the contents of the brown envelope onto Miranda's desk, and while she ate, she read the newspaper article about Izzy, Beatrice, our troops in Iraq, Operation IMPACT, and the downing of the Griffon.

"She sounds like a tough broad," Miranda said. "Twelve hours trapped in the Griffon in the desert heat, with a bullet in her leg, and her crew dead or dying around her? Brother. It was rotten luck that she got shot down." She looked up from the newspaper. "Although how Daesh learned about the Griffon's flight path is rather suspect, isn't it? Who blabbed? Usually mission details are pretty closely guarded."

I nodded. "I asked myself that question, too."

"Hmm. Makes you wonder if this nonsense about Daesh seizing Beatrice and sending the ransom note has some truth in it."

I groaned. "God, I hope not. I feel out of my depth already. Islamic jihadists. Ugh."

"Yeah, tell me about it," she agreed.

I said, "After my phone call with Edgar, I read the ransom note over more carefully than I did with Mac in the park. I know I emailed it to you and you've probably read it once, but take another look at it. Does anything seem, well, peculiar?"

Miranda settled back in her chair, took her time reading the note, then looked up at me. "How about everything?"

"Yeah," I said, relieved that Miranda, too, thought the note odd. "I called for help."

"You did? What do you mean?"

"I emailed a U Vic professor. Elizabeth Metheny. She's a forensic linguist. Back a few years ago, she identified the WannaCry virus ransom note as originating in North Korea. Wrote an article for the local newspaper about it. I thought she might be able to help out."

"Good thinking," Miranda said. "I hope . . . dammit, I hope this is just a case of garden-variety extortion. Some druggie who needs cash." She frowned. "Because if the dog thief is with Daesh, we have to hand this case over to the RCMP. You know that, right? They're way better equipped to run this guy to ground than we are. And they need to know there's at least one terrorist working right here in Victoria."

I shrugged. "Yeah, but here's the thing. If we come to the conclusion that Daesh is involved, well, of course we give our information to the RCMP. Actually, we give it to Mac and he'll give it to them. But . . ."

"But?"

"But Mac wants Beatrice out of harm's way first. Back with Izzy. He was very clear with me about that. He's afraid — and I think he's right — that Beatrice will just fall through the cracks if the case gets away from us. That's why he hasn't turned this over to his own department."

Miranda sighed and swiveled her desk chair to look out the window, clearly thinking. She was silent for a long moment, and finally I spoke up.

"I'd sure like you to help me, Miranda," I said, "but can you let Mac's wishes do the driving here? Will your conscience be okay with that? Doing things his way, well, it's not quite kosher, but . . ."

She said nothing and I was sure she was going to turn me down. Miranda and Mac went back years, as did Mac and I. But this? She swiveled her chair back to look at me.

"I bet *you* thought this over carefully, right?" she asked me.

"Well, sure," I said.

"What made you say yes?"

"One, Mac and I are friends. Two, he's looked the other way for me plenty of times. So I owe him. And three, I agree with him about Beatrice. Her abduction will just be a lost dog case to law enforcement. They'll go through the motions. Take a statement, file it . . ."

"That's what I think, too," Miranda said. "I just wanted to hear your reasons for saying yes."

"Whew," I said, relieved. "My palms are sweating. I thought for a moment you were going to go all by-the-book on me, Miz Blake."

"Nope, Miz Yeats. I left that book behind a while ago," she said. "So the plan is to get started digging, and cry uncle to Mac if we find ourselves with information that needs to go to the RCMP. *After* we find Beatrice. Right?"

"Right."

"Okay." She crumpled her sandwich wrapper and tossed it at the trash can. "Two points," she said. "Let's go talk to Izzy. We can do a little strategizing on the way. Want to drive? I should leave the Jeep here for Ro. Connie might go directly from Jimmy's new home to Tris's dinner party. I don't want Ro having to take her bike out in all this rain to join us."

"Sounds good. Grab your jacket. Let's go."

Driving to Izzy's apartment, we didn't do much strategizing. We agreed that our instructions to Izzy ought to be pretty simple: beg for time, lie about a delay in getting the money, and be convincing. After the phone call, we could ask questions. But we wanted her to stay focused on the phone call.

Besides, I had something else I wanted to talk over with Miranda.

"I want us to persuade Izzy that she needs to tell the dog thief to shoot a video of Beatrice," I said.

"To . . ."

"Shoot a video of Beatrice. And send it to Izzy's phone."

"Okay," she said slowly, nodding. "That would prove she's alive. I get it. Good thinking."

"I have another reason for wanting the video," I told her.

"You do? What?"

"Do you remember the Luka Magnotta case?" I asked.

"Not in detail," she said. "Only that he was a narcissistic little fruit loop celebrity wannabe who killed someone, videotaped it, put it online, and was eventually caught."

"Yeah, that was Magnotta. But I think people forget that the whole thing started with animal torture."

"Animal torture . . . really?" Miranda said.

"Yeah, Magnotta posted a video online called 'One boy, 2 kittens' showing him, well, killing kittens. It offended animal lovers greatly. Apparently in the dark corners of the internet there's an unwritten code of behavior called Rule Zero that goes like this: Don't Fuck With Cats."

"Wow. Good for those dark-corner-dwellers," she said.

"Anyhow, several people who saw the video formed an internet sleuthing group, called it Animal Beta Project, and chased Magnotta down the corridors of the internet for years. Along the way they tried to tell authorities that his animal killing was a rehearsal for killing a more important life form — a person — but their concerns were pooh-poohed."

"Sounds like law enforcement," Miranda muttered.

"Yeah, it does," I agreed. "Well the Beta Project people were right. Magnotta did kill someone. And videotaped it. Posted it online, too, if you can believe it."

"I think this is coming back to me," Miranda said. "Tell me more."

"The Animal Beta Project people formed a Facebook group — it was international, I think — and collected thousands of hours of video. Then they used the video footage to find Magnotta's identity. He'd used dozens of aliases over the years, but they eventually discovered his real name. Better than that, they found where he lived. Magnotta was so narcissistic and so arrogant that one of the videos he posted was of himself standing on the balcony of a high-rise."

"I remember that," Miranda said. "There was a gas station across the road from the apartment building, right? It showed up in the video."

"Right. A Petro-Canada gas station. Magnotta had already complained online that paparazzi were harassing him outside his Etobicoke apartment, so the sleuths used Google Earth to locate the gas station — there are only nine of them in Etobicoke — and then identified some of the other features of the view outside. They found him. Of course that wasn't the end of the story, but —"

"But I see what you're up to, you clever devil, you," Miranda said excitedly.

"Yup. If we can get the dog thief to shoot a video of Beatrice, it may serve two purposes. One, it will let us know she's alive, and two, he might just slip up and show us a bit of what's outside, something we can identify. Or something inside."

"I like this," she said.

"And maybe we can push Izzy into insisting that she get a video of Beatrice *daily*. With a copy of that day's *Victoria Times-Colonist* held up in front of her. After all, just because the dog's alive today doesn't mean she'll be alive tomorrow."

"Brilliant," Miranda said.

"Yes, it is, isn't it?" I agreed, chuckling. "Now let's go persuade Izzy of all this."

CHAPTER 4

Izzy's apartment was one half of a pleasant, one-story, off-white-painted duplex at the end of a short cul-de-sac not far from downtown. I spotted the black Toyota RAV Mac had told me she owned, and we pulled into the driveway behind it. The other half of Izzy's duplex had no car parked in the driveway and I wondered if the apartment was unoccupied. I'd have to ask Izzy. If there were neighbors living there, maybe they had seen something the night of the abduction.

"Nice quiet street," I said to Miranda. The duplexes were set back from the street with small, fenced-in lawns in front.

"Very nice," she commented. "Mac made a good choice."

Indeed there was only one other residence on the street — another duplex, with cars in the driveways, but no people out and about, no kids' toys in the yards, no junk piled up beside the houses. Well-kept residences. Across from the two duplexes was a lush eight-foot-high laurel hedge, which formed a green barrier between Izzy's street and what lay on the other side.

"What's on the next street over, I wonder," Miranda said as we stood in Izzy's driveway, looking around. The rain had subsided for the time being, leaving an oyster-colored sky dotted here and there with clouds the color of steel wool. Periodic rumbles off to the south suggested that we hadn't seen the last of today's fickle weather.

"A little strip mall," I told her. "The tenants are a title company, a CPA's office, an insurance agent, a financial planner, a couple of attorneys. Oh, and a convenience store, too." When Mac had told me Izzy's address, I had used Google Maps to look at this street, and the next one over. "Directly behind that hedge is a loading zone and a long parking lot that runs across the back of the strip mall. Probably for employees' cars."

"Look," Miranda said, pointing. "Gaps in the hedge there and there. I wonder if any of the businesses have a video camera trained on the back parking lot? The convenience store ought to have one. If we get lucky, maybe we can find some footage from the night Beatrice was abducted. And if we get very lucky, we might see something useful through one of the gaps in the hedge."

"Worth checking out," I said. I looked left, down to the end of the little street. "You know, I'm trying to picture how the abduction happened. The thief would have had to drive down this cul-de-sac, park, get out, walk over to Izzy's yard, persuade Beatrice to get in his car, then make a U-turn and drive back out. How did he persuade her?" I wondered aloud.

We walked up the driveway and around Izzy's short chain-link fence, letting ourselves into the front yard through a gate which fastened with a cranky, tight-fitting hasp. I closed the gate and fastened the hasp behind me.

"And for that matter, what was Beatrice doing out here in the yard in the wee hours of the morning, anyhow?" I said. "Mac told me that's when she was taken."

"Well, dogs have to go out to pee," Miranda said. "So . . . a doggie door?"

"Maybe," I said. "But how did the dog thief know what time Beatrice went out to pee at night? If she did. Or did he just wait outside in his car? Someone might have noticed him."

"Too risky," Miranda said. "Here's another question. Was the gate closed? I bet it was. So how did the dog thief open the gate without Beatrice barking her head off and waking Izzy up? Dogs are very protective of their owners' homes. I imagine Beatrice is even more so, as she's a service dog."

"There are too many things about this that don't make sense to me," I said. "But maybe I'm just being dense. I think the easiest way to get answers is to leave Izzy with a list of questions when we go. I'd like her to imagine the possible abduction scenario. She must have thought about it. And we need to know who's shown an interest in Beatrice, what Izzy's and Beatrice's daily routine was like, what they did in a typical week, who Izzy thinks might have grabbed Beatrice if the Daesh angle turns out to be nonsense."

"Leaving her with homework is good," Miranda agreed. "It will make her feel that the case is moving forward and she's part of it. After all, we're just here for the phone call. There's barely time for that before Tris's party. And I might go up-island with Connie and Ro tomorrow. If we can set it up, we'll be visiting those pound seizure shelters I told you about."

"Right," I said, recalling what she'd told me earlier. "No problem. I can pay Izzy a visit tomorrow morning. Review that homework with her."

"Good. Then maybe c'mon by The Sanctuary later in the afternoon. My RCMP contact should have gotten back to me by then. If not, I'll call her. You'll have talked to Izzy; I can look at the dog theft cases Mac emailed us; and maybe your Dr. Metheny will have replied to you. We can compare notes. Damn, I wish we could have gotten on this case earlier. But I guess I understand — Izzy was too spooked even to call Mac."

As we headed up the sidewalk toward the sheltered porch, I noted how well-tended the yard was. The grass had been recently cut. In a flowerbed in front of the porch, a neat row of three-foot-high red rhododendrons was just beginning to bloom. A six-foot-wide strip of blue indoor-outdoor carpeting had been tacked onto the three steps leading up to the front door, and another piece of blue carpeting had been laid out on the porch. Two comfy-looking wicker chairs with red and blue faux suede cushions sat on the blue carpet. Between the chairs was a glass-topped table; beside one was a stainless-steel dog bowl and a large dog bed with a cushion matching the cushions on the wicker chairs. Suspended from two hooks on the posts supporting the porch, pots of early red and purple fuchsia were already flowering. A six-foot rail basket held a profusion of begonia plants in every hue of pink, red, and orange. They looked a little wilted though. Some water would help, I thought. Well, Izzy had other things on her mind.

"Pretty," Miranda commented. "Izzy and Beatrice must have loved it here together. Bastard," she muttered.

I rang the bell, not knowing what to expect. A woman in distress, garments rent, hair in disarray, eyes bleary from weeping? After all, Mac had said Izzy was a mess. The woman who answered the door, however, was none of those things. Captain Isobel Tremblay was every bit as tall as Miranda, which probably made her just over five feet ten. And she seemed the opposite of distressed. Her jeans were crisp; her black T-shirt that said, in white, OPERATION IMPACT, was unwrinkled and tidily tucked into the faded jeans. Her hair, which was light brown, was shiny and tied back in a no-non-sense ponytail. Her eyes, which were dark blue, were neither bleary nor red from weeping. Izzy was no beauty, but hers was a face which could have, if not launched a thousand ships, certainly commanded them. She stood straight and unbowed in the face of the disasters that had overtaken her. But dark circles under her eyes hinted at sleepless nights spent worrying about Beatrice, and there was a haunted quality about those eyes that she couldn't quite hide. I felt for her. Fear will do that to you.

"Isobel Tremblay," she said, holding out her hand to me. "You can call me Izzy." I took her hand and we shook.

"Kieran Yeats," I said. "And my friend Miranda Blake."

They shook, too.

Izzy's mouth curved a little in a rueful smile. "You're the animal finders," she said. "Uncle Alex told me. Come on in." She closed the door behind us. "Be straight with me. Can you find Beatrice?"

"Yes," Miranda and I said together. All three of us laughed, which broke the ice. Then we got down to business.

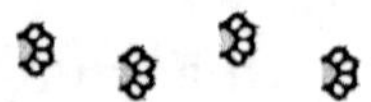

We hung up our jackets on a row of hooks just inside the front door, and sat down in the living room. I'd explained to Izzy earlier, when I talked to her on the phone, what we needed her to do, and she seemed okay with it.

"I can do all of that," Izzy called from the kitchen, where she was making coffee. "Snivel, beg for time — your idea about my RAV's fictitious buyer having trouble rounding up the money is a good one, Kieran. And I can be oh-so-worried, yet insistent, about having the thief take a daily video of Beatrice showing *The Victoria Times-Colonist* prominently. I could even cry a little at that point. It wouldn't take much. You know, it kills me to have to plead with this guy, but I'll do it. Anything to bring Beatrice back."

Limping a little — her gunshot wound evidently still bothered her — she brought three mugs of coffee into the living room and put them on the coffee table. Miranda and I settled back into a not-very-comfortable, newish-looking tweedy brown sofa, while Izzy took a seat on a brown and gold plaid armchair placed at ninety degrees to the couch. I wondered if Mac had furnished this apartment when he knew Izzy would be coming to Victoria for rehab — brown sofa, tan cushions, brown and gold plaid armchair, cream drapes — the colors looked drab, subdued. There was nothing vibrant in the living room, in contrast to the sitting area on the porch where the colors were vivid and alive. Oh well. If Mac had decorated, he'd done what he could. As I recalled, Mac's taste in haberdashery was so dismal that Mary selected his clothes.

Izzy's cell phone lay on the coffee table beside a pile of magazines — *Maclean's, Canadian Forum, Toronto Life, Canadian Geographic, Western Gardening* — and I glanced at them surreptitiously. I like looking at other people's magazines. Ditto their libraries. Seeing what they read says a lot about them, I think . . . or maybe I'm just nosy.

"It's five-fifteen," Izzy said, looking at her watch, her untouched coffee attesting to her nervousness. "He's late. What does that mean? Should we worry?"

"I don't think so," I said, although I was a little worried myself. "He'll call. After all, he wants the money, right?"

"Right," she agreed, nodding. But I could see the doubt in her eyes.

What I didn't tell Izzy was that this display of lateness by the dog thief was, in my opinion, quite calculated. *Oh, he'll call all right,* I thought. *But he wants you to know who's in charge. He wants you to worry. He wants you to suffer. Why?*

"So, are you all ready to record?" I asked her.

"Ready," she said. And at that precise moment, her phone rang. I smiled. 'O Canada' was her ringtone.

"You're on," I told her. *Be calm, be smart, be firm,* I urged silently. *Buy us time.*

Izzy picked up her phone. "Hello," she said, her voice suddenly sounding very un-Izzy-like — quavering, weak, weepy.

Miranda rolled her eyes and gave me a thumbs-up, and we vacated the couch for the kitchen, giving Izzy privacy for what we all hoped would be an Oscar-worthy performance.

I sat at Izzy's kitchen table with Miranda, looking around at the old-fashioned oak-paneled cupboard doors but the surprisingly modern granite countertop; the dated porcelain sink and faucets, but the state-of-the-art ceiling fixtures. The apartment seemed to be undergoing renovation one bit at a time, like a snake caught in the middle of shedding its skin. But it was clean and comfortable. And peaceful. I gave Mac full marks for finding Izzy something pleasant and out of the way, a cubbyhole where she could heal with Beatrice.

"What are your thoughts about the dog thief's being late with his call?" I asked Miranda, my voice pitched low.

"He's flexing his muscles. Showing her who's boss," Miranda said.

"Uh huh. I think so too."

"It feels personal," she added. "Like maybe he has a grudge against Izzy. I don't know." She sighed. "That argues against Daesh, doesn't it?"

"It does," I said. "Damn, but I'll be glad when we can rule Daesh in or out. I must admit, it's distracting. And intimidating. I'd prefer that the thief be a druggie needing money for greenies."

From the living room, we could hear Izzy's raised, teary voice. "Please!" she wailed. "Don't hurt her!"

"*Oy vey*," I said. "Sarah Bernhardt. Let's hope the jerk falls for this."

Then there was silence. Izzy came into the kitchen, crossed her arms, and stood in the doorway, looking stricken. "I could only get him to give me four more days to get the money."

"Okay," I told her, but my stomach clenched a little in apprehension. Only four days? "You did what you could. What about the video? Did he agree?"

"Once daily," she said. "Tomorrow morning, then Tuesday, Wednesday and Thursday mornings. Friday we're making the exchange. At noon. He said he'd call me in the morning with instructions. So no video that day."

"Hmmf," Miranda muttered.

"His voice sounded . . . like an alien was talking," Izzy said. "All deep and artificial and raspy."

"A voice-changing app," I told her. That was interesting, I thought. Was he afraid she'd recognize him?

"Okay," I said. "So he's given us four days? Fine. We'd better not waste time. Here's the number you need to call to forward the phone call," I told her, taking my phone out of my pocket. "It's my friend Edgar's number. I'm texting him to expect the file. He'll start to work tracing the call."

Izzy sat down at the kitchen table with us, frowning as she punched Edgar's number into her phone. Then she looked up at us and I could see in her eyes the panic she was struggling to hide.

"We're going to locate her, Izzy," I said. "As you remarked at the front door, we're the animal finders."

And then, suddenly, I just couldn't leave Izzy here alone with her homework assignment, despairing, missing Beatrice. Hell, why not ask her to come with us? I bet she hadn't been out of the house all week. I had no idea if this would be good or bad for someone suffering from PTSD, or even if she'd want to come along, but I thought I'd ask.

"We have to leave in a few minutes," I began. "Remember, I told you we had an engagement this evening?"

"Sure," she said, making an effort, sitting up straight, nodding briskly. No feeling abandoned for Captain Tremblay. No sirree. At least that was what she wanted us to think.

"So here's the thing," I told her. "It's my daughter's ninth birthday today. Mac — oops, your Uncle Alex — has been showing her the lairs of wild turkeys while I've been busy today. She fancies herself a great bird photographer. Anyhow, we're having a little party for her. A couple of friends her own age, some adults, a dog. The kids will probably watch DVDs after dinner — *The Jungle Book*, maybe *The Lion King*. I wondered, would you like to come along? It'll be Middle Eastern food and chocolate chip ice cream. Oh, and brownies. Pretty low-key, I think."

Izzy gave me a deer-in-the-headlights look and I realized that I'd probably stepped in something. Good one, Kieran.

"Thank you for the offer," she said. "I really appreciate it. More than you know. But . . ." She closed her eyes for a moment, then opened them, and I saw again the panic there. "I'm not good with groups yet. Ever since that day in the Griffon, well, I'm just not good with six or seven or eight people milling about. I'm working on that with my therapist. Or was."

"Was?" I asked.

"Oh, it can't be helped. I missed two sessions with her last week and I'll miss two more this week. Beatrice and I went together, you see," she explained, meeting my eyes with an embarrassed smile. "She actually sat in on the sessions with me. Put her head on my feet. I feel safer talking about things when she's there. Silly, I know." She looked away again, and I realized how much this must have cost her, admitting weakness to two strangers. Damn. I didn't know a thing about veterans' PTSD.

"No, it's not silly," I said. "Whatever works for you. If it's makes you feel better, it's fine."

Izzy nodded. Then she said, "I realize you two have to go. Kieran, you said you would leave questions for me to work on. I'll just go into my office and get a notebook."

When Izzy had disappeared into the back of the house, Miranda reached over and poked me in the ribs. "You big softie," she said. "That was nice. The dinner invitation."

"That was dumb," I muttered. "The dinner invitation. Of course she'd still be having trouble with groups. And our group? Laughing and talking? Kids possibly running around? Middle Eastern food? Whatever was I thinking? Anyhow, it's a damned shame she's missing therapy. And I certainly think she needs it more than ever now that Beatrice's fate is up in the air."

"Maybe we can help with that," Miranda said, smiling.

"Yeah? How?"

"Provide a chauffeur."

"A . . . who do you have in mind?"

"Ro."

"Ro?" I scoffed. "She can, what, whisk Izzy off to therapy on the back of her motorcycle? In the rain?"

Miranda raised an eyebrow. "Izzy does have a car. The RAV in the driveway."

"Say, she does, doesn't she?" I said. "That might work."

"Actually I have an even more brilliant idea," Miranda said.

"Uh oh," I said, alarmed.

"Yup. It's a doozie. I think Izzy needs a minder. What if Ro moved in with her for a bit? For protection. In case the dog thief, I don't know, pays her a visit one night. You can explain it. Speak investigator-ese to her."

"Ha, thanks," I said. "But what about Ro? I imagine babysitting a wounded Griffon pilot isn't in her job description."

"No, but once I explain this case to her, I think Ro will agree. After all, who would have guessed she'd *volunteer* to race through a flaming building to save rabbits' lives?"

"Indeed, who would've?" I said. "Okay, go ahead and ask her. If she says yes, I'll call Izzy later."

"Sorry to keep you waiting," Izzy said, reappearing from the back of the house. "I had to look a bit for a notebook. My office isn't really unpacked yet, even after all the months I've been here. I've felt too . . . scattered."

"I need to excuse myself to go make a phone call," Miranda said. "I'll just be in the living room."

Izzy and I sat at the kitchen table, I asking questions that needed answering, she writing them down. And then we were done.

"I'll be back tomorrow morning," I told her. "How about breakfast? I can bring it. I'll call first to make sure you're up."

She nodded, looking considerably more chipper than she had just after her chat with the extortionist.

"Can I ask you something?" she said.

"Sure," I replied, betting I knew what that something was.

"Well, Uncle Alex called you an animal crimes investigator."

"Uh huh."

"The cases you've worked on . . . how many have you solved?"

"All of them."

"Oh. Okay," she said, mollified. "Good. Good."

Pulling her spiral notebook over to me, I took her pen and wrote my phone number on the top of the first page.

"I'm going to call and check up on you in a couple of hours," I said. "But here's my number again. I want you to call me if you need to. Anytime. Not just tonight, but anytime. All right?"

"Okay," she said with a hint of what seemed to be a real smile. Her first since we'd arrived. Progress was being made.

"One thing I'm wondering about," I said, getting up from the table. "Does anyone live next door?"

"You mean right next door?"

"Yeah. Right beside you. There's no car in the driveway."

"Oh, well, yes. Mrs. Evans. Audrey. She's an odd duck. It's hard to guess her age — seventies? Eighties? Doesn't drive or own a car." She made a wry face. "She might have a bit of dementia, too. Her daughter comes by once a day, but really, I don't think Audrey should be living on her own. When I first moved here, she was able to walk over to the little convenience store — she used to take a shortcut through the hedge across the street. But several months ago she began getting lost coming back. So her daughter put a lock on the front gate." Izzy frowned. "About that time she developed an odd theory about the Air Force, too."

"Oh yeah?" I said. "What?"

"She believes the Air Force visits at night. Drops packages."

"Oops," I said. "That is odd. Maybe she took the information that you're an Air Force officer and scrambled it up with a package delivery company, like UPS. Their drivers wear uniforms. Hmm, do you get deliveries from Amazon?"

Izzy nodded. "Sure. And UPS brings them, of course. I do a lot of my shopping that way. I get deliveries at least once a week."

"Well, maybe that's it. She has the UPS guy's uniform and an Air Force uniform confused. I don't know how nighttime deliveries figure into Audrey's fantasy, though."

"It's all very strange, isn't it?" Izzy said. "And then there's the Green Man."

"Ai yi," I said.

Izzy nodded. "Yes. According to her, he comes through the hedge. At night."

"And you've told Audrey's daughter about all this."

"Sure. Not only Audrey's fantasy, but that it seems to upset her. One day, oh, about three weeks ago, well before Beatrice was abducted, she was quite agitated. She called to me from her yard to tell me that the night before, the Air Force had brought Beatrice a package and that the Green Man had come through the hedge and stood in the street outside my gate. She was very upset about this. I called her daughter that day. Anyhow," she said, looking sheepish, "I didn't mean to tell you all that. You just asked about who lived next door."

"Izzy, does this bother you?" I asked. I couldn't imagine that this next-door drama could be good for her mental health. *Ha*, I told myself. *Kieran Yeats, amateur psychiatrist.*

"Oh," Izzy said. "I see what you mean. But, no. None of this is a trigger for me. I'm just worried about Audrey. Leaving her alone with these strange ideas, locking the gate. That doesn't seem very responsible of her daughter. Or caring."

"No kidding," I said. Hmm, I thought. So there was a next-door neighbor. I definitely needed to talk to her. Even though she believed the Air Force dropped packages for Beatrice. Well, maybe she'd seen something that would be useful to the investigation, apart from her giggle-worthy fantasy of the package drop. Oh, and visits from the Green Man. I filed all this away to think about later in a hot bath.

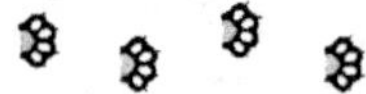

"Mac was right. Captain Tremblay is indeed a mess," I told Miranda as I backed my car out of Izzy's driveway and drove slowly down the cul-de-sac, turning left onto the main street, heading for the coast road and Oak Bay. "I hope we can help put Humpty Dumpty back together again. She's way depressed. And anxious. Putting up a good front, but . . ." I shook my head, merging into traffic. "God, Miranda, can you see Izzy flying Griffons again?"

"No, not with that leg. But I'd be surprised if she even wanted to, after what she's been through," Miranda said.

"You know, last year Zee was telling me about what a famous psychiatrist named Willard Gaylin said about depression. He believed it's caused by what he calls 'the loss of the loved object.'"

"That sure makes sense," Miranda said. "Look at the loved objects Izzy has lost. Her Griffon — and by that I mean the actual aircraft — three crew members who she was certainly close to, her career as a pilot, her mobility, and probably the Air Force. That's a lot of loss. And now, Beatrice's gone. No wonder she's a mess."

"Yeah, really," I agreed. As I turned onto Oak Bay Avenue, the rain started again, fat drops on my windshield. Perfect.

"What did Ro say about staying with Izzy?" I asked Miranda.

"Oh, she's up for it," Miranda said. "She's a good kid. Also, she smells adventure."

"God, I hope not," I said.

"Hey, where are you going?" Miranda asked as I signaled to turn off Oak Bay Avenue onto my street.

"Home."

"Nope. You need to get chocolate chip ice cream. You asked me to remind you. Drive on. Maybe turn in over there. They have yummy ice cream."

I groaned, pulling my car into the lot at Cold Comfort. "Can I buy a festive attitude here, too? I need to cheer up."

"Sure thing, Miz Yeats," she said. "I hear they're on sale."

"Thank heavens, Miz Blake. Should I buy two? I was thinking we could both use one."

"Bargain-basement festive attitudes," she said. "Irresistible. Sure. Buy two."

CHAPTER 5

At home, I parked behind what could have been a used-car dealership — Miranda's yellow Jeep (attesting to Ro's presence here), Connie's black Honda, Aliya's pea-green Nissan Leaf, Zee's sensible grey Caravan, Lawrence's dark green Range Rover. I had hardly closed my car door when Tris came running down the porch steps, slamming the front door behind her, a desperate look on her face.

"Uh oh," I murmured to Miranda. "This doesn't look good."

"I'll take the ice cream inside," she said.

"Kieran," Tris said, running up to me. She had pulled on a yellow anorak over the T-shirt she'd been wearing this afternoon, and the drizzle lay like little seed pearls on her jacket and in her mop of curly blond hair. "I thought you were never coming!"

"Hey, the ice cream was wily and elusive," I said, hoping to disarm her distress with humor. "It took all my guile and skill to hunt it down. All of Miranda's too." Sometimes light-heartedness worked to defuse Tris's emergencies. Not this time, though.

"No, Kieran," Tris said. "No joking now. You have to be serious."

"Okay, what's up?" I asked, putting an arm around her. "Too many people?"

"No, it's not that. It's . . . can we go around back? To the back porch?"

"Sure," I said, mystified, zipping my windbreaker up under my chin, shivering a little in the cold drizzle. "Is Dani inside?" I asked, worrying that Tris's best friend, a Syrian refugee girl in her class at school, had been unable to come to the birthday dinner.

"Yeah, she's here. C'mon now," she said, slipping out from under my arm. She hurried ahead of me, leading me around the side of the house, past the dripping apple trees, through the long grass, and up to the back porch steps. We'd both be needing dry socks and slippers, I thought as the wet grass soaked my sneakers.

Tris climbed the steps to the little enclosed porch — a mud room really — and opened the door. I followed.

"It's him," she said, leading me over to a seldom-used workbench and a small, brilliant, daffodil-yellow shape lying on it. A male goldfinch.

"Oh, Tris," I said. "What happened?"

"I don't know," she said as two enormous tears spilled from her eyes and ran down her cheeks. "I'm afraid it's climate change."

"Afraid it's —"

"Climate change. The weather's changed all over the world, y'know, and he might have, well, cooked, or frozen, or starved, or gotten sick. We're studying weather at school. And birds. Did you know that we've lost more than seventy-eight percent of the songbirds in North America? And the snowy owl in the Arctic? The tundra is warming. And we're about to lose the puffins because the sea is warming," she said, sounding desperate.

"No, honey, climate change didn't do this," I said gently. True, climate change and man-made depredation were devastating bird habitats, but the goldfinch here on Vancouver Island wasn't one of them.

"So tell me, how did you come to find this guy?" I asked her.

"Well, Mac and I brought the new plastic domes into the backyard to the apple trees. We were going to hang them up over the finch feeders, and that's when I noticed him." She angrily wiped the betraying tears from her eyes. I'd forgotten — Tris the toughie never cried.

"He was in the flowerbed. Just *lying* there," she said, stricken. "I picked him up, and Mac said to put him in here and talk to you. He said you'd know what to do."

Oh, thanks a lot, Mac, I thought.

Tris continued, "When I picked him up, well, he felt like nothing. Like he was just feathers. So light. What happened to him, Kieran?"

"Well, let's take a look," I said. I lifted the little bird up gently with two fingers, marveling at his canary yellowness, his black and white barred wings and tail, his jaunty black cap, his sharp orange beak. I slid him into my palm, and as I did so, his head lolled to one side. He'd clearly broken his neck. Life had fled from his body, leaving behind this bright shell. Heartbreakingly, from one of his open eyes, a drop of moisture like a tear had run down into the yellow feathers of his cheek.

I thought I understood why Tris felt heartsick . . . or perhaps these thoughts were mine alone. Why must beauty be with us for so short a time? Why, in the end, is a bright ember all that remains of it, an ember that we fan into a light in our memories, a light to hold off the darkness?

"I think he broke his neck, Tris. He probably flew into a window. Windows are like mirrors for birds — they see reflections of trees. It fools them. They think they're seeing the forest."

"Oh. I killed him then," Tris said, aghast, her blue eyes enormous. "I put one of the feeders on a pole right next to my bedroom window so I could see the birds close up."

"No, you didn't kill him, Sprout. He could have flown into any one of our windows." I searched my data banks for a remedy for bird strikes. "But we can prevent something like this from happening again."

"We can?" Tris asked, wanting to believe that I knew a fix for bird deaths. "Really? How?"

"Well, I think I read somewhere about decals that can be applied to windows," I said. "Apparently they've been UV treated so birds see them, but we see through them. What birds see are, oh, hawk outlines, instead of trees. They get scared and fly the other way."

"Yeah?" Tris said eagerly. "Can we get hawk decals? For all our back windows? Do you think the wild bird store downtown would have them?"

"We can find out," I said. "The store is closed now, but we can call tomorrow. We could go together after school and pick some up if you like."

"Okay," she said, wiping her tears away. "But what about him?"

Oh, lordy, I thought. *Let me say the right thing*. "We could return him to the earth. How would that be?"

"Like in *The Lion King*?" Tris asked with interest. "The circle of life?"

Having not seen the movie, I punted. "Sort of. We could —"

"Not just bury him," Tris said, sounding disappointed.

"Well, yes and no," I said. "Here's what I mean. A poet I read about once told a little story about her dog. She loved him very much, and when he died she wanted to remember him, so she planted a red rosebush in the garden. But she buried her dog underneath the rosebush first."

"Okay," Tris said, clearly trying to picture this.

"Then, when the rosebush bloomed every spring, the poet thought of her dog. You see, he lay in the earth underneath the bush, and little by little, he helped the rosebush grow." I took a deep breath, hoping I would explain the next part in a way Tris would understand. "She did this because everything on this earth is part of everything else, Tris. Your bird, if we placed him in the ground and planted a rosebush over the top of him, well . . ." I trailed off, not certain how to explain the last part. Chemical soup? Proteins in common? How could I express this in terms a nine-year-old would understand?

A look of delighted comprehension came into Tris's eyes. "I get it. Even though he's dead, he'd be helping the rosebush live. He'd become a part of it."

"Exactly," I said, relieved.

"And if it was a yellow rosebush," Tris went on, "a bright yellow one, well, we'd always think of the goldfinch. Kieran, can we do it?"

"Of course we can do it," I told her. I wasn't sure if she grasped exactly what I was getting at — that everything was indeed part of everything else — but maybe it was okay. For that matter, did I grasp it exactly? "So we have two things to think about, right? The decals and the rosebush."

"Right," she said, excited.

"We can go get the decals tomorrow, but we'd better look around for the right rosebush."

"Yeah. A really, really bright yellow one," she said.

"Maybe you and Aliya can do that," I suggested. "I'll be busy with my new case over the next couple of days, but you two could go rosebush shopping."

"What's your new case about?" Tris asked.

"Oh, just a lost dog," I said. Nothing much — Daesh, a wounded Griffon pilot, a $10,000 extortion demand.

"You won't get hurt like you did in your last case, will you?" she asked. "Something hit you in the head and you had to get stitches. Then you were kind of goofy for a while."

"I promise I won't be goofy," I told her solemnly.

Tris nodded, then, looking at the goldfinch as he lay in my palm, said, "What should we do with him until we can plant him under the rosebush?"

"Well, zoologists freeze their specimens," I told her. "In plastic baggies."

"Freeze . . . like in a freezer?"

"Uh huh."

"Oh. Could we —"

"Nope," I said. "Not a chance. Ours is full of food. I don't think it would be sanitary. But Aliya has a freezer in the little fridge downstairs in her apartment. She told me she just uses it for ice cubes. So maybe she could move the ice cubes upstairs and we can put the goldfinch in her freezer. I'll talk to her."

"Okay," Tris said, nodding. "Okay."

"Want to run inside for a baggie?"

She nodded. "Sure. But can I touch him one more time?"

"Of course."

She stroked him again with her index finger. "So soft. So pretty. And look at his feet. His claws. They're tiny. But they held him up on branches, didn't they?" She looked up from the goldfinch to me. "Since I've been on eBird and have been talking to other birdwatchers, I've been thinking, well, I might like to study birds. When I grow up."

"Hmm," I said. "You might want to become an ornithologist."

"And orni —"

"An ornithologist."

She nodded. "Okay. I'll look that up on Google. Could I study it at university?"

"Sure," I said. "You could enroll in a science program. Probably zoology. Then you'd study oh, the behavior and the physiology of birds, and maybe the conservation of their habitats." *Maybe zoology was a bad choice, though*, I thought. I remembered one of my roommates in college, a zoology major, talking about dissecting birds. I didn't think Tris would like that.

"Would that take a long time?" she asked.

"Probably four years after high school."

"Conservation," she said thoughtfully. "That means saving, doesn't it?"

"It does," I told her.

"I'd like to do that. Save birds," she said.

I had a sudden vision of Tris as a young university student chaining herself to a rock in front of some cattail swamp, joining arms with her fellow student conservationists from Save The Birds, trying to preserve the habitat of the blue-footed something-or-other, daring oncoming earth-moving equipment to bulldoze the swamp. I shuddered. Maybe conservation of bird species wouldn't be such a good field of study, either.

"You know, we learned in school that acres of the Amazon rain forest were cut down so a Burger King could be built," she said indignantly. "But I don't think that's right. Why do they need a Burger King in the Amazon? And then there were all those forest fires in the jungle. Where did the birds go?"

"Probably they flew away to other trees," I said soothingly.

She was quiet for a few moments, then asked in a small voice, "Kieran, there might not be too many birds left when I graduate from university. I should start helping them now."

My God, I thought, tears coming to my eyes. Only a kid in the latter part of this decade would have a thought like that. 'Will there be any world for me? Isn't there anything I can do about it now?' were really her questions. I felt bitterly ashamed of the mess we'd be leaving her.

"You are helping them, Tris," I told her. "Right here. The birds in our backyard. As for the others — it's sad and it's maddening and we should have done something to help them earlier, but we really can't do anything about the birds at the Burger King in the Amazon, or the snowy owl, or even the puffins. It's too late for them and it's our fault and we should be ashamed. But maybe all we can do is to help what we see going wrong right under our noses. Like you're doing. Making sure birds have enough to eat in the winter when food is scarce. Making sure their feeders are safe."

She nodded. "Okay. But there's more to do, isn't there?" she said, sounding panicked. "Not just for birds. Like . . . there's too much stuff in the ocean. Whales are getting tangled up in fishing nets. Sea turtles have plastic straws up their noses."

I sighed. I wanted to defuse Tris's panic and despair, to bring her back from the dying puffins and sea turtles to things she could do in her own backyard, so to speak. I was pretty sure she would feel better if she had some hands-on projects to occupy her thoughts and give her hope. Evidently taking care of birds was not going to be enough.

"Do you have, oh, something like a Save The Planet club at school? Where you talk about things kids can do to help the environment? Projects?"

"Well, no," Tris said. "Miss Linley talked to us about recycling our lunch stuff. Separating plastic and paper. And bringing our lunch in washable containers instead of plastic wrap that has to be thrown away."

"You know," I said, "I bet Jen has a Save The Planet club at her school. Maybe she could help you start one at yours?"

"Yeah? You think so?" Tris said. "We could talk about veganism, too. I could wear my Meat Is Murder sweatshirt."

Oh, please don't, I thought to myself. One step at a time. Baby steps.

"I'll ask Jen," Tris said. "And I could talk to Miss Linley, too. We could, you know, ban plastic straws from the cafeteria. I bet there are paper ones they could use instead."

"That's a really good idea," I told her. "There are probably dozens of things you could do." Just cool it with Meat Is Murder. It's a big jump from saying no to plastic straws to saying no to meat.

"Okay, what about the goldfinch?" I asked.

"I'll go in and get a freezer bag," Tris said.

"Put on dry socks and shoes when you get inside," I told her. "And wash your hands. Your face, too. It's all teary. I'll wash mine when I come in." *It wouldn't do to let the world know we'd been out here crying over a dead bird, now, would it?*

Tris put a hand on the kitchen doorknob, then paused, turning to look back at me over her shoulder. "Thanks, Kieran. You're pretty cool," she said. Then she went on into the house.

"You're pretty darned cool yourself, kiddo," I called softly after her.

Now it was my turn to sniffle and feel morose. And that was how Miranda found me when she came through the kitchen door. Sitting on the porch floor, holding the goldfinch, mourning the sea turtles with straws up their noses and the snowy owl and the puffins and the birds displaced to build the damned Amazon Burger King and the ones who'd died in the fires, and this particular bird and the hole in our hearts it had left when its bright beauty vanished. Oh, and the fact that my daughter thought I was cool.

"It's that bad is it?" Miranda asked, handing me a baggie. "Tris asked me to give you this."

"No, it's really all right," I told her, standing up, wiping my eyes.

"Ah," she said, as I tumbled the little body into the baggie. "Bird death. That's a tough one. Is Tris okay now?"

"Uh huh."

She raised an eyebrow. "Are you okay now?"

"Uh huh."

"Hmm, that's good, because, Houston, we have a problem."

CHAPTER 6

"A problem?" I asked Miranda as we headed for my office. "Only one?"

Dinner had been a great success — the Middle Eastern feast, the brownies and ice cream which Tris wanted instead of cake. The dishes had been cleared away; the kids were watching the DVD *The Jungle Book*; Aliya, Jen, and Lawrence were playing Scrabble at the dining room table (with Max, Lawrence's Belgian Malinois — a small, black-faced version of a German Shepherd — sleeping at Lawrence's feet); and Zee had excused herself to go back to her clinic to check on a cat recovering from surgery.

Ro and Connie followed us into my office, and I closed the door. I'd told Miranda she could fill them both in on this case, and she'd done so while I'd been outside on the back porch with Tris. They'd read the ransom note, too. I figured the more brains the merrier on this puzzle.

Connie, Miranda's no-nonsense aunt, was back from her parrot delivery, and I was happy to see her. Sixty-something, fearsomely intelligent and relentlessly practical, Connie had an impressive animal rights background, as well as a tekkie expertise that Miranda found indispensable. Today her irrepressibly bushy grey hair was tied back with a hank of festive turquoise wool, matched in hue by a turquoise cowl-neck sweater, black and white sneakers with turquoise laces, black jeans, and a pair of attractive dangling turquoise earrings. Hmm, I thought. Was the rock guitarist — Jimmy the foul-mouthed parrot's adopter — the reason for this sartorial splendor? I'd imagined him a callow youth of twenty, fond of John Mayer's guitar-playing, but perhaps he was a seasoned veteran of the music wars, a sexagenarian more devoted to the music of Eric Clapton. And perhaps a fan of the color turquoise. I smiled. Why not?

Ro put a paper plate with four brownies on my desk. "I liberated them from the kitchen," she said. "I'm ashamed of myself. Chocolate brownies rob me of good sense. I brought enough for all of us, though."

"So young, yet so wise," Connie said, peering approvingly at the brownies from over the rims of her silver-framed glasses. She took two folding chairs from where I'd stashed them behind a bookcase and set them up for her and Ro. I took a seat in my desk chair, and Miranda half-sat on a corner of my desk. "Now if only you'd brought coffee, too," Connie said.

Miranda said, "Here's the problem. Sylvie, my RCMP contact, got back to me while you were out on the porch earlier with Tris, Kieran."

"Good," I said. "You were going to ask her about Daesh activity here on the island. We were hoping she'd rule out Daesh as the author of the ransom note. What did she say?"

"Not what we wanted to hear. Apparently there are quite a few guys — their names are officially Canadian Extremist Travellers — with ties to Daesh here in this country. The RCMP has them under loose surveillance."

"Canadian . . . what?"

"Yeah, that's a new term for me since my time in the Force," she said. "So apparently these individuals are residents, or citizens, or visa holders who have traveled abroad, specifically to Syria or Iraq, to participate in extremist activity. And the RCMP defines extremist activity as not only participating in armed combat, but also radicalizing, recruiting, or financing extremist activity."

"Okay," I said, wondering how this had anything to do with Izzy and Beatrice.

"Apparently there are about sixty of them concentrated in metropolitan areas that the Force is keeping an eye on," she said. "They've traveled overseas, done whatever they went there to do, and are back. And some of them are right here on the island."

"Back to create havoc here, back to recruit others, or back . . . ?" I asked.

"Among other things, to raise money, Sylvie says," she said.

"For God's sake!" I yelled as the penny dropped. "They're raising money here, in Victoria, by kidnapping purebred *dogs* and holding them for ransom? Is Beatrice a test case? Really? Well, shit, it's nothing if not creative. Dammit. I was so hoping we were just dealing with druggies."

"And we might still be," Miranda said. "Sylvie just wanted us to be aware that we might not be. Also, she pointed out that the reference to Sinjar in the note may be meaningful."

"Yeah?" I said. "I figured it was the note-writer beating his chest about something or other that wasn't particularly important. I intended to Google it but haven't had time. What did Sylvie say about it?"

"Well, that's what convinced her that Daesh really might be involved in the Izzy and Beatrice affair. Apparently, Sinjar is a village in northern Iraq that was the site of a horrible slaughter a few years ago. Daesh massacred a group called the Yazidi there. Ethnic cleansing."

"Can I say something?" Ro asked. "I know a little bit about Sinjar and the Yazidi. I wondered about the reference when I read the ransom note."

"Sure, Ro. Go on," I told her.

"Well, I have a friend named Nadia. She's Iraqi. Yazidi. I met her at the assistance center downtown that's helping these women integrate into life in Canada. I'm a volunteer there — I teach English. Did you know that we took in twelve hundred Yazidi women? They're having a really tough time, though," Ro said sadly. "They cry every day for their friends or relatives left in the camps north of Sinjar — three hundred and fifty thousand women. And they scream every night in their sleep. Even the social workers can't help them much. Their trauma is that bad." She looked away, into a corner of my office, and I wondered just how much of a toll helping Nadia was taking on Ro.

"Anyhow," she went on, "Nadia told me that Daesh militants launched an attack on her village — Sinjar. The neighboring villages, too. They massacred the men all right, but they kidnapped the boys and women and girls.

The really awful thing about this is that the girls and women, all of them, were raped by Daesh fighters, then taken away to be used as sex slaves. Oh, there was a big multi-national push against Daesh after that, and it was supposedly defeated yadda yadda. Ha. But it wasn't. Despite what that guy in the White House claims," she said, clenching her fists. "So I wondered when I read in the note, 'Remember Sinjar,' that maybe it's a personal warning to Izzy that something might happen to her along the lines of what happened to the Yazidi women," she said.

"Rape, for God's sake!" Connie said. "He's threatening her with rape. It isn't bad enough to threaten Beatrice with 'a fate worse than death,' whatever the hell that might be, but he has to threaten Izzy, too."

"Maybe," I said. "But let's just slow down and think about this. Maybe the only reason he identified himself with Daesh and mentioned Sinjar was to terrify Izzy into silence. Maybe he's posturing. Assuming the persona of the bogeyman to scare Izzy half to death. Keep her quiet."

"It worked, didn't it?" Miranda said. "She didn't contact anyone."

"Not right away. But pretty soon her worry for Beatrice must have overcome her worry for herself. So she contacted Mac. And now we're involved. So the dog thief's threats didn't work. He doesn't know that, of course. Nor does he know that we're coming after him. So we may have a definite advantage here."

"I'm confused," Ro said. "You mean you think the extortionist *isn't* with Daesh?"

"I don't know. But I feel that the note-writer is a bit like the character in *Hamlet* who says, 'The lady doth protest too much, methinks.'"

"But if he isn't a Canadian Extremist Traveller, someone with Daesh, then who is he?" Ro asked. "And where is he? And whether he's with Daesh or not, how will we ever find him in time?"

"Good old-fashioned detective work," I told her. "However, that having been said, I don't think we can rule out the Daesh connection until we know more."

"I don't think so either," Miranda said. "I think we have to follow the trail of breadcrumbs until they either lead us to the witch's house, or they disappear."

"The witch's house?" Ro asked.

"A fairy tale," I told her. "Courtesy of the Brothers Grimm. One of the scarier ones."

Ro gave Miranda a spooked-horse look. "Um, okay. What do we do first? To rule out the Daesh angle."

Miranda said, "Sylvie dictated to me — she didn't want a paper trail on this — the names of the local guys on the RCMP's list. I think we should look at them. Kieran?"

"Yeah, definitely," I said. "As well, I think we should look at the list of dog-related complaints that Mac sent, too. Individuals who've been accused of dog theft by neighbors, been reported to the police, and who never had their cases investigated. And the people who lost dogs, too."

Miranda said, "Sadly, there's a thriving cottage industry in stealing designer dogs — doodles, French bulldogs, teacup poodles, handbag dogs — and advertising them for resale. And the thefts are rarely prosecuted."

"Why not?" asked Ro.

"Well, they're usually not even investigated," Miranda said. "The police don't follow up on dog cases."

"Yeah, okay, that's why we've got this case," Ro said. "I see."

"Among other reasons," I muttered.

"What do you want us to look for, Kieran?" Connie asked.

"Yeah, what?" I asked myself out loud. "Well, maybe someone on Mac's dog list who's recently developed an interest in Islam — I don't want to sound racist here — or traveled to the Middle East. Or someone from Sylvie's list who's, crap, I don't know, developed an interest in dogs. Started collecting teacup poodles. I don't know if looking at these individuals will rule Daesh in or out, but it's somewhere to start."

Miranda took a handwritten list out of her jeans pocket. "Here's Sylvie's list. Can you print out Mac's list, Kieran? Might as well get started."

"Sure," I said. "While I'm printing it, Ro, what about that coffee? It will go well with the pilfered brownies. Do you know where things are in the kitchen?"

"I'll go help her," Connie volunteered.

When Connie and Ro had disappeared into the kitchen, I said to Miranda, "You talked to Sylvie. What's your best guess?"

"About Daesh being involved?"

"Yeah."

"Oh, fifty-fifty."

"Hmm," I said.

"You sound skeptical," she said. "What's *your* best guess?"

"I can't quantify it," I said. "Either he's a garden-variety domestic asshole with an axe to grind against Izzy, someone who has read the newspapers, studied up on code words to frighten her, and thinks he can make a quick buck, or —"

"Or, Miz Yeats?"

"Or, Miz Blake, I'm wrong and he's a Canadian Extremist Traveller asshole with another kind of agenda. Raising money to help the cause of jihad by stealing purebred dogs, give me strength, and extorting their owners."

"Seems far-fetched, doesn't it?" Miranda said. Then, "Say, I wonder if we'd get any response if Connie posted the video, when we get it, on The Sanctuary's Twitter account, or Facebook page?"

"It can't hurt," I said. "Will you ask her to do it?"

"Sure. Just as soon as we get home."

"Crap," I said. "I wonder how many rocket launchers you can buy with ten thousand dollars?"

"Quite a few, I expect."

"And how the hell does the extortionist think he's going to get the money? Hundred-dollar bills left in a duffle bag in a busy location with Beatrice tied to a post outside in exchange?"

"Ha," Miranda said. "You've been reading too many espionage stories. That kind of thing rarely works. More likely he'll use a money mule. Maybe even someone in Nigeria. The country is rife with scams and money mules."

"Don't tell me anything about it," I groaned. "I'll stay awake all night fretting."

Miranda was quiet for a moment, then said, "I guess we'll sort it out. But when the dust settles and Beatrice is back at home with Izzy, munching her doggie treats, I'd sure like to hand the asshole over to Mac, and then the RCMP, for questioning about the implied threat in that note. Connie's right. Referencing Sinjar and what happened there — that's code for rape."

"I agree," I said, leaning back in my desk chair. Finding nothing inspirational on the ceiling, I decided to air a thought with Miranda, something that might explain what I saw as Izzy's near-paralysis about Beatrice's kidnapping. It didn't make sense to me that she had been frightened into silence. She was an Air Force officer, for cripes' sake. Maybe something else was going on.

"Miranda, remember that Izzy said that her Griffon was on a mission to northern Iraq? Their mission was to deliver medical supplies."

"Yeah."

"And remember she said she was having a hard time in therapy. That she was stuck?"

"Uh huh."

"So maybe she's stuck not only because the Griffon was shot down and the crew slaughtered, but also because they never got to this camp north of Sinjar that desperately needed the supplies they were carrying? Three hundred and fifty *thousand* women? That's a metropolis-sized amount of guilt. We have *cities* that big — London, Ontario. Gatineau, Quebec."

"When you put it that way . . . if it's true, no wonder Izzy can't sleep," Miranda said. "Or move forward in therapy. She must believe she let all those women down."

"You know, I'm glad that Ro is going to stay with Izzy," I said. "Maybe she can talk to her about her friend Nadia. Maybe it would be good for Izzy to hear about someone who was saved from that hellhole. It might make her feel better. Or not. Oh, shit, Miranda, is it too early for the hard stuff?"

I said goodbye to the guests, and left Aliya to see about urging Tris to get bathed, shampooed, and blown dry for school tomorrow. Then I gathered up Miranda's bottle of Scotch, my bottle of Method and Madness, and four glasses from the kitchen.

"For you, lassie," I said, depositing the bottle of Scotch whiskey on my desk.

"Och, and isn't it mother's milk?" she said.

"Your accent is truly awful," I told her. "Bet you wouldn't even have gotten hired as a tavern wench in *Braveheart*."

"She certainly wouldn't have," Connie sniffed. "I'll stick to coffee. I have to drive home."

"I assume someone's driving me to Izzy's, so I'll have some of *your* whiskey, boss," Ro told Miranda. "Scotch. Go ahead and pour it into the coffee, please."

"Okay, this is what we need to do," I told the others. "It's going to be a miserable time-consuming database slog. Ro, I see you have your iPad. I have mine. Connie, you can use my laptop. Miranda, I'll borrow Aliya's iPad for you. I'll give each of you my snoop services' user names and passwords. I have several accounts. We want to know all about everyone — the Extremist Travellers, as well as the people in Mac's dog files. Where they were born, where they went to school, where they're working, where they're living now, who they're married to, what their religion is, who their friends are. Everything. What are we looking for? Anything promising in any of these guys' profiles. Like I said earlier: did one of the dog files guys join a mosque? Start studying Arabic? Did one of the Extremist Travellers, oh, I don't know, join the Kennel Club? Put up a dog run in his yard? Or anything else hinky."

"Hinky?" Ro asked, raising an eyebrow.

"Yeah, it's a venerable but seldom-used investigative term," I told her, smiling. When she looked skeptical, I said, "Okay, weird, in other words."

Ro shrugged. "Sure. Let me have the URL of one of those snoop sites. And your info. And half the Extremist Traveller names."

"Miranda and I will split the dog lists," Connie said. "Should we send the files to your printer if we find anything, Kieran?"

"Yup," I said. "Let the slog begin."

CHAPTER 7

Connie and Ro worked in my office; Miranda and I worked at the dining room table, and four brownies, four mugs of coffee, three glasses of whiskey, and a few hours later, we had . . . something. Not what I had hoped for, but something. No one on Mac's dog list was an Extremist Traveller (that was a fatuous hope) or had recently taken a class in Arabic or joined a mosque. And no Extremist Traveller seemed to have any connection to the dog world.

"Now what?" Ro asked, joining us at the dining room table, followed by Connie. "I really hoped we'd find some overlap."

"Me too," I said. "But let's look at what we have. Connie?"

"Five hinky dog guys. One ran an illegal kennel. Two were the subjects of complaints from neighbors for noise violations — dogs barking after midnight. And two were accused of, well, stealing dogs. One from a neighbor. One from a dogwalker. There were actually charges filed against them. No great follow-up, of course. I think we need to go talk to these people. All of them."

"Agreed," I said. "Miranda?"

"Like Connie. Two midnight yappers. But here's a lead — one complaint by a neighbor about numerous dogs coming and going at a residence. Apparently, there was a lot of loading and unloading going on in the wee hours of the night."

"Sounds promising," I said. "Ro?"

"Well, this is interesting," she said. "Three Extremist Travellers with Canadian-sounding names. Nothing hinky except that it surprised me. I kind of thought Travellers would all have Arabic names."

"I can see why you'd think so but, sadly, it's not terribly unusual," Miranda said. "Young guys, native-born Canadians, sometimes get sucked into that awful extremist mindset. I think it's less a matter of ideology than a search for something to belong to — something that makes them feel valuable. It's so easy to get radicalized online. There are any number of sites where you can watch terrorist videos, or bomb-making videos, where rogue imams spout hate and jihad. Sadly, these guys don't realize they're being groomed. It's when the radicalized young men make multiple trips abroad, then return, that the RCMP gets worried, though. What have they learned? Will they be planting IEDs on Parliament Hill? Fertilizer bombs on the ferries? There's seemingly always a new way to deliver mayhem. And now, they're involved, as Sylvie said, in fundraising here to support Daesh's activities in the Middle East."

"Like stealing purebred dogs for ransom?" Connie commented in disgust.

"Maybe," Miranda said.

"Should we check those three out?" Ro asked.

"Is it your Spidey sense operating?" I teased Ro. "Or . . .?"

Ro looked embarrassed. "Oh, I don't know. It might be just their names. It seems so odd . . ."

"Hey, I'm not twitting you about your Spidey sense, Ro," I said. "I have my own loony genes. My famous forbear went all mystical in his later years — séances, table thumping, ghosts, the tarot. Sure, let's look at the three guys you found." I added, "As for me, I found two Travellers I think I'll take a look at. They have a downtown address and Arabic names. Mohammed Saleh and Aziz Amad."

"How will we divide these guys up?" Miranda asked. "Connie, Ro, I've been thinking that we probably should postpone our trip to the shelters up north. I think Izzy and Beatrice take precedence here."

"Darn it," Ro said. "I'm sorry we won't be going back to that shelter near Sidney. Evergreen Animal Refuge. I had the feeling that they were about to come around and join your coalition, Miranda. Stop selling unadopted animals to labs. I had some information for them — alternate sources of income. Charitable foundations." She shrugged. "Oh, well. That can keep. I just hope they can resist the temptation to say yes to the lab guys who are due at the end of the week." She continued, "You know, I could go look at the three Travellers with Canadian names in between helping Izzy with what she needs. Shopping, therapy, whatever. Those guys — they're not only local, they're all in one place. Roomies."

I hesitated for a long moment. Did I want Ro involved in more than a database search? These three young men had been flagged by the RCMP for a reason. Still . . . "As long as you just . . . observe," I cautioned Ro. "Take a look at where they live. But don't go knocking on their door. If you find anything suggestive, well, photos would be fine. Maybe talk to the neighbors. But be careful."

Ro nodded. "I will be."

"Maybe by the end of tomorrow we'll know if the dog list angle or the Daesh angle are boondoggles or something to be further pursued," I said. "Okay then. You've each got your lists. I don't know about you guys, but I'm fried. I can't sit upright any longer. God, it's after eleven. C'mon. Let's collapse in the living room."

"You know, I think I'm going to take off," Connie said. "I have to drive Miz Finnerman to Izzy's yet, then get back home. Don't see us out. We'll grab our jackets from the coat tree."

"I'm due at Izzy's for breakfast early tomorrow," I told Ro. "Should I bring you some, too? It'll be nothing more exciting than McDonald's, I'm afraid."

"That'd be great," she said. "Thanks. I'll find out from Izzy what her schedule is, and I can plan my Traveller-looking around what she has to do."

"And if the video of Beatrice comes in before I get there, send it to me?"

"Sure," she said. "Good night."

"Brother," Miranda said as the front door closed and we collapsed on the sofa together. We had each poured glasses of whiskey and brought them into the living room with us, and we sipped companionably. "Whatcha thinking about?" she asked me.

"Plan B," I told her. "Other breadcrumb trails. In case the dog angle or the Daesh angle poops out."

"Oh yeah?" Miranda said. "Like?"

"Okay, well, you know, maybe this is *my* Spidey sense, or my spooky forbear's genes, but the theft and the note still seem overwhelmingly personal to me."

"Because of the reference to Sinjar in the ransom note? Rape as punishment?" Miranda asked. "That brings us right back to Daesh, though, doesn't it?"

"Maybe," I said, thinking. "But I keep asking myself, who has Izzy pissed off? Who's sufficiently annoyed with her to do something like this? Who knows what would hurt her most?"

"Hmm," Miranda said. "Go on."

"I wonder about the Griffon crew's family members. Izzy might not be at the top of their hit parade. She lived; their loved ones didn't."

"True. Okay. Next?"

"Well, this is really pretty slimy, but what about the other veterans waiting for dogs? Was Izzy allowed to jump the line because she was in such bad shape? Could there be some simmering resentment there? A famous veteran, and one with PTSD . . . so what? Why does she get a dog and they don't?"

"Yeah, that is slimy. But possible."

"So maybe both groups of people — the Griffon crew's families, and the people waiting for service dogs — need to be checked out."

I sighed, Miranda sighed, and I thought, maybe Plan B could wait 'til tomorrow.

"Want to change the channel?" I asked Miranda. "Want to resume your rant?"

"My rant about —"

"About pound seizure. I owe you a chance to finish. Remember?"

"Hey, yeah. Well, ranting would certainly change the channel. And seeing as how Connie, Ro, and I are not going up north, maybe I will carp a little. After all, I need to keep the indignation fresh in my mind."

I said, "You were saying earlier that pound seizure shelters sell pets to research labs. Dogs and cats that people turned in, trusting that they'd be adopted? That seems pretty despicable."

"It is," she said. "Our most recent stats indicate that over a hundred thousand lost or abandoned dogs and five thousand cats were sold from pounds — municipal shelters — to research laboratories across Canada last year. And that's just in our country. Can you imagine what the situation is in the States?" She frowned. "I'm always up for a rant on this, but are you sure you want to hear about it now?"

"Sure," I said. "It'll take our minds off stolen Labradoodles. Midnight is always good for ranting, anyhow. I recall that you've listened to quite a few of my late-night complaints."

"Hmm. Okay. Well, it's beyond awful, Kieran. Most of the cats used in research labs' experiments — eighty-six percent of them — come from pounds. And over sixty-nine percent of the dogs. And here's another revolting fact," she added. "It's precisely those animals who are most adoptable that researchers tend to choose. They prefer docile, well-socialized, medium-sized animals — exactly the animals likely to be adopted."

She frowned fiercely. "It's an uphill battle. Private shelters are bad — like the one Ro mentioned, Evergreen Animal Refuge — but municipal shelters are worse. Fighting municipal governments that mandate shelters turn over pets for research? Making them change antiquated laws that are based on the premise that cats and dogs are nuisances to be controlled and therefore disposable? That's the rationale behind pound seizure, this outdated attitude toward companion animals. This, in spite of the fact that over seventy-five percent of our citizens, including the jerks in municipal government who enforce these outdated laws, keep pets. Talk about changing hearts and minds . . . it's bloody tiring, that's what it is."

"Thanks for putting your trip up north off for a bit to help out with this case," I said. "How are your plans coming along?"

"Well, Connie and Ro have made visits to several private shelters which participate in pound seizure. They've been trying to persuade the shelters that there are ways to earn money other than selling unadopted cats and dogs to labs." She laughed. "Ro has a plan. Every animal nonprofit's Holy Grail is mastering the grant proposal, right? But so few of them are successful at it. Ha. I should know. It's bloody difficult. But Ro's offered to teach the fundraising personnel at these shelters how to do it. Hands-on lessons on how to ask for money. Even offered to share with them her top-secret list of charitable foundations. If —" Miranda winked, "— they say no to the labs. She was almost there with Evergreen. But we can get back to them when Beatrice's found."

"Wow," I said. "What an offer. And what a devious mind our Miz Finnerman has! I hope other shelters are signing up to take lessons from her."

Miranda nodded. "Yes. Three. The others . . ." She waggled one hand. "They're thinking it over. Giving up an assured source of income for something uncertain scares them."

"What about the municipal shelters?" I asked.

"Well, we have law enforcement behind us now," she said. "Civil servants respond better to people in uniform, alas. In fact, Mac and I and one of his uniformed *protégés* will pay the municipal shelters a visit next month. This time around we'll also be taking a psychologist who's studied the devastating effects working in pound seizure shelters have on shelter personnel. And our fledgling No Pets In Research coalition has actually enlisted a researcher who's willing to call BS on research results produced by scared-to-death puppies and pussycats. We're attacking on all fronts."

She was quiet for a moment, clearly thinking, then said, "You know, one of the most persuasive arguments against pound seizure is that it undermines the public's faith in animal shelters. All shelters. Including ours. We don't want people to leave abandoned animals in ditches or at the side of the road because they're frightened they might end up in some researcher's lab. It's obscene!"

"But how are people to know, Miranda?" I asked. "Which shelters are we talking about? Private shelters, like yours? Well, not specifically yours, but you know what I mean. City or county-run facilities? People aren't sophisticated. They don't know enough to ask questions."

"No, they don't know," she said. "So we have to shut this whole practice down. Municipal shelters need to have a come-to-Jesus moment so citizens don't have to be frightened for the strays they rescue. And here's a last obscenity. What if a private shelter would rather take in the dollars paid to it from a research lab than hold the animal and allow its owners time to find it? Or check its microchip? Or implement a creative adoptions program? There are private shelters like that. I could name several. They're hellholes for animals — nothing but pass-throughs to the labs. Animals truly do go to a fate worse than death when they end up there."

She continued. "Those shelters rationalize their behavior by asserting that the lost dogs or cats who don't get adopted are going to be euthanized anyhow — and at some cost — so why not make a little money instead of spending it on euthanasia. I'm so looking forward to talking to this bunch of idiots again.

"Jesus!" she said. "I'd dearly love to see pound seizure banned, the laws mandating it revoked. And most of the animal community is with me. Then the bloody labs would be forced to re-evaluate their need for live animals. And their bogus experiments."

I held up the bottle of whiskey. "More Jameson's? Or coffee?"

"You know, I think I better switch to coffee," she said. "I'm going to have to drive home, too. Let me see if there's some left in the kitchen." When she came back with a mug, she said, "That's the last of it. Do you want some? We could make more."

I shook my head. "No thanks. I'll stick to Method and Madness."

Miranda sat back down on the couch, exhaling heavily. "Thank God one of the worst cruel and useless experiments has just been stopped — the kitten toxoplasmosis study in the States. But it's an example of what pound seizure makes possible. It should be made the poster child for animal porn. Imagine — an experiment with no purpose except its own self-perpetuation, and the jobs that it ensured year after year for researchers. Let's not forget that. That disgusting endeavor resulted in the deaths of thousands and thousands of cats and kittens over a thirty-seven-year period. Thirty-seven years! And how many cats and kittens died? The researchers shamefacedly admit that they didn't keep track. *They didn't keep track?* Of the lives they ended? And this fiasco cost the U.S. Department of Agriculture over twenty-two million dollars. I think that's why the plug was pulled on this experiment — the cost. What concerns me, though, is that the fucking USDA seized the cats and kittens from shelters. The numbers are staggering. And who knows how many similar projects are hidden away in our country?

"And," she said, "one of the most revolting parts of the experiment was the feeding of cats and kittens to each other. What the hell? Was this a cost-cutting measure? Cat cannibalism . . . who thought up that little horror?

"One last mini-rant before I call it a night," she said, "lest we think we're pure as the driven snow up here in Canada. Ontario, enlightened Ontario, site of our nation's capital, cauldron of the arts, home of countless institutes of higher learning, requires — actually *requires* — that shelters, any shelters, turn over animals to research institutions."

"You have to be joking! I didn't know that. Why —"

"Because Ontario is where most of our country's research institutions are located. Half the animal testing labs are housed in universities. I tell you, Kieran, this makes me ashamed to be a Canadian. If I lived in Ontario, I'd move. And British Columbia doesn't have much to brag about, either. A certain large mainland university is building a forty-five-hundred-square-foot research center that will use animals. All this was done under the radar until whistle-blowers let us know about it. And where do we think they'll get these animals from, hmm?"

She paused and I stared down into my glass. This was horrible. No wonder my friend needed to rant.

"Sorry," Miranda said. "I know I was yelling. I'll wake Tris up if I carry on. Here endeth the rant, though. God, I need to go. So what's first tomorrow?"

"Ah, yes, tomorrow. Well, we may have an ally in figuring out the note's authenticity." I explained that Edgar was on the trail of the dog thief's phone, and I was waiting to hear from Dr. Metheny, a forensics linguist at U Vic, and Miranda raised her eyebrows.

"Good for you," she said.

"If Dr. Metheny hasn't gotten back to me in the morning, I intend to go to the University and find her," I said. "And maybe we should both take a look at the video that the extortionist said he'd send. We may get lucky. It may be like the Luka Magnotta video."

I smiled a little, thinking of the anticipatory gleam in Connie's eyes about tomorrow's activities. "Do you think you could dissuade Connie from playing gumshoe? I have the feeling she's itching to pound the pavement."

Miranda laughed. "I have the same feeling, but I'll go hunt down the hinky dog people. Connie needs to put a request for information about the dog thefts on our Facebook page. Maybe Twitter, also. I know she'll be disappointed, but maybe I can appeal to her tekkie expertise."

"Thanks," I said. "I don't want to put her or Ro in harm's way. I'm even sorry I told Ro she could go look at where those three Travellers live. Anyhow, why don't I come round tomorrow afternoon? Maybe you, Ro, and I will have information to share. Ro will probably be at Izzy's but we can put her on speakerphone."

Miranda yawned hugely. "I definitely need to go home," she said. "Don't move. I'll see myself out and lock the door. See you tomorrow."

As soon as the door closed behind Miranda, I fell into a fit of serious fretting. Oh, I'd feigned coolness when I mentioned Plan B to Miranda, but really, I wasn't cool at all. I hadn't aired with her the zillion and one things I thought needed to be done apart from ruling in or out the hinky dog people and the Travellers. Checking out the Griffon crew's families? Talking to the group who ran the dogs-for-vets program? Yeah, those were two. But two of at least a dozen other things. I mentally ticked them off. Interviewing the no-doubt addled Audrey Evans about the Air Force's deliveries to Beatrice. And the Green Man. Talking to the owner of the convenience store to see if there was a video I could look at. In addition to hunting down the linguistic forensics expert, Dr. Metheny, if she hadn't gotten back to me in email.

"*Hein?*" said a small voice at my elbow.

I looked over to my right. Trey, my chubby grey cat, the Animal Crimes Investigator's Faithful Sidekick, had hopped up on the sofa and was looking at me with accusing green eyes. Missing me in bed, he'd evidently searched the house, located me here in the living room, and was now, wisely, suggesting that I call it a night and join him under my comforter where a certain amount of snuggling might not be unwelcome. The only survivor of a so-called benign learning experiment at a prestigious university in the east, Trey had been liberated by an animal rights group — friends of mine — and I had had unhesitatingly adopted him, bringing him west with me when I moved from Toronto to Victoria.

"Yeah, you're right," I told him. "Let me put my glass in the dishwasher and the whiskey in the kitchen cupboard. Go on into bed. I have to do one thing. I'll be there in a jiffy. Promise."

In Tris's room, the blue-green light of the lava lamp — her night light — had turned the space into a mysterious, undersea cave. I found it a little odd, but Tris liked it, claiming it was the Beatles' Octopus's Garden. Jeoffry lay curled at the bottom of Tris's bed and he purred as I reached down to pat him. She'd evidently thrown off her comforter, because it lay on the floor in a heap, leaving her wrapped in her top sheet, just her curly blond head visible on her pillow. Concerned that she'd be cold later in the night, I picked up the comforter and was just arranging it on her bed, when she asked sleepily, "Kieran?"

"Yeah, Sprout," I whispered. "I'm just fluffing your comforter. Everything's okay."

"I wanted to wait for you," she said, "but I fell asleep."

"Wait for me? What for?" I whispered.

"To open this," she said, sitting up and holding out something she had evidently fallen asleep with. "My present from you. It has a tag that says *'To Tristan from Kieran. With love.'*"

"Oh, honey," I said. "I thought you'd open it while you were watching *The Jungle Book*. When you opened the cat presents."

She shook her head. "No. Those were for the cats. This one was for me."

Oh, crap, I thought, feeling guilty that I hadn't realized how important my present might be to her. It'd been years since she'd lived with her grandmother and, earlier, her mother. Maybe she couldn't remember back to presents, if there'd been any. And after she came to live in the woods with her down-and-out remaining relatives, who in hell would have given her a present? The old dog man? Con? They barely knew she was alive. Her clothes were Con's hand-me-downs; her food, sandwiches from the market on the highway, purchased with change made from beer can recycling.

"Well, let's open it now," I said.

She carefully removed the wrapping paper, folded it, and put it aside. Then she held up the book, the hardback edition of *A Field Guide to the Birds of Vancouver Island*.

She was quiet, and I was afraid for a moment she didn't like it. I cleared my throat. "If you'd like a different guide, we can exchange it," I said. "The people at the wild bird store said this was the one to buy, so —"

"I love it," Tris said fiercely, clasping it to her chest. "I'll take it with me every day I go out birding."

I wasn't sure if that was the idea — I thought birders used field guides to check up on what they'd seen out in the marsh or the forest once they were back in the comfort of their living rooms, toasting their toes by the fire — but whatever Tris wanted was okay with me.

"How about settling down to sleep now?" I asked, putting the folded wrapping paper on the headboard of her bed. "Should I put the book up here as well?"

"No," she said definitely, wrapping herself in her top sheet again. "I want to keep it here with me."

I pulled the comforter up around her shoulders. "Was your birthday party fun?" I asked. "I'm sorry I was busy for part of it."

"I know. The case you're working on — the lost dog. My party was great, though. Especially the food. I liked the movie, too. Thanks, Kieran." She yawned, then said, "Can I ask you a question?"

"Sure."

"How many birthday parties can kids have?"

"How many —" Her question stopped me dead in my tracks. Then I got what she was asking me. What were the birthday party rules? Had she used up her quota of parties? Was this a one-off? Would she ever have another one?

"I tell you what," I said. "You can have a birthday party every year if you want one. That's what . . . parents . . . do for kids. They throw parties for them." God, that sounded odd: *parents*.

"Oh," she said, surprised. "Okay." She burrowed down in her comforter, hugging her field guide, presumably in case a bird flew by that required identification.

"Night, Kieran," she said.

"Night, Sprout," I replied, tucking her comforter firmly around her skinny shoulders. I pulled her door half-closed, and smiled sadly as I went across the hall into my bedroom. How many birthday parties? Oh, Tris. Lots and lots.

MONDAY

CHAPTER 8

When my phone buzzed at 5:23, I wasn't quite certain if I was alive, dead . . . or suspended in some ghastly intermediate state. I struggled awake from the dream which had imprisoned me — a Dante-esque nightmare of awakening in a dark wood where, as the poet says, the straight road had been lost, and he found himself in a dense and gnarled thicket with no way out. As the dream ebbed, I had a *frisson* of fear that this might be a message from my unconscious and that it wasn't Dante, but Kieran who was lost. Groggy, I knuckled sleep from my eyes, and sat on the edge of my bed, phone in hand.

The call was from my goddaughter, Jen. What? At 5:23 in the morning?

"Jen?" I said with more than a little alarm. "What's up?"

"Oh, Kieran, thank God you're there!" Jen exclaimed. "I have to talk to you. Can you come over?"

"Come over? Now? Jen, tell me what's going on. Has something happened? Are you all right? Is Zee all right?"

"Nothing's happened. Well, yes, something has. It's not mom, though. She's out on an emergency call. That's why I'm — oh, Kieran, I need you to come over. It's serious."

"Okay," I said, mystified. "I'm on my way."

I threw on a clean T-shirt and socks, struggled into some sweats I found on the rocking chair in the corner, stuffed my feet into sneakers, and stumbled into the bathroom where I washed my face, brushed my teeth, and ran a comb through my hair. After padding softly to my office, I wrote a note to Tris, taped it to her bedroom door, plucked my windbreaker from the coat tree, then let myself out the front door, texting Aliya so she wouldn't worry about my absence.

The sun was just rising as I turned onto the coast road leading north and I fell briefly under the spell of the gold and crimson light spilling onto the water, like 'shining from shook foil,' that famous image from Gerard Manley Hopkins' poem 'God's Grandeur.' The beauty of the ocean almost, almost, made up for the fact that living here in Victoria was becoming a PITA of traffic, people, and congestion — all the downsides of having been 'discovered.' From time to time I toyed with the idea of selling my house and moving north. Up the peninsula. Or even farther north, up-island. To Nanaimo maybe, a town of about 90,000, located 75 miles or so up the island's east coast. I loved Oak Bay — the marina, the fact that we were surrounded on three sides by ocean. But sometimes I wondered if I loved the Oak Bay that lived in my memory — a quaint little village of Tudor-inspired architecture, tea shops with scones as big as dinner plates, never a struggle for a parking place. Ah well. I had Tris to think of, and my tenants. I couldn't just pack the cats into my car, pull up stakes, and set off for Nanaimo. Still, the idea had a certain appeal.

What on earth could be going on with Jen? I wondered. She'd seemed all right last night. When we said goodbye — Aliya drove her home — she hadn't seemed in any way distressed. Or maybe I hadn't been paying attention. Well, I guessed I'd find out.

I pulled off the Pat Bay Highway at a little gravel road with the sign LAU, DVM, and drove slowly through Zee's hazelnut orchard — the trees bearing dangling, fuzzy green catkins — up to the long, low, cedar-shingled structure that served as both her home and clinic. Jen was waiting for me with the front door open, hands jammed into the pockets of her jeans.

"You're here," she said, relief plain on her face. It was clear she was distressed — her dark hair, which was usually gelled into fashionably spiky immobility, fell limply over her forehead. Things were serious when a fourteen-year-old girl neglected her coiffure. Even more mysteriously, she was dressed in worn, patched jeans tucked into black rubber boots and an old, faded navy sweatshirt with a turtleneck underneath it. Her mucking-out-the-barn clothes, if I remembered rightly. Certainly not going-to-school clothes and as far as I knew, today wasn't a school holiday. A smear of mud on one of Jen's cheeks completed the mystery as did mud on her boots and the knees of her jeans.

"Indeed I am here," I said a bit grumpily. "Wrenched heartlessly from my bed at five-thirty. I hope you have coffee brewing for me and a Golden Globe–worthy story. Let's go in."

"Um . . . don't hang up your windbreaker," Jen said once we were standing in the front hall, the door closed behind us. "I have mud on my boots so maybe you can help yourself to coffee — put it in a to-go mug? I made some for you — it's there in the coffeemaker on the counter. Then we can go over to the barn. Charlie's there."

"Charlie's there," I repeated. Charlie . . . Charlie . . . Jen's school friend Charlotte? "Sure," I said, filling a mug with coffee. "Let's go."

Jen led me along a narrow flagstone path, across the yard, and into the barn.

"Charlie!" she called, pushing open the sliding barn door. "It's me. Kieran's here. How is he?"

"Sicker, I think," said a girl with dark red braids, braces on her teeth, and a worried expression. She had come from somewhere inside the barn, and when she saw Jen, the two of them hugged. Charlie, too, was dressed in jeans, muddy boots, and a grubby sweatshirt. Who knew? Maybe they were devoting the day to mucking out the horse stalls. But what did this have to do with me?

"Okay, kids, what's up?" I asked, taking a big swig of coffee. "It's pretty early and I'm not in the best of moods most mornings. Also, I want to know what you two plan to do about school today. You're hardly dressed for it."

Silence.

"Tell her, Jen," Charlie said.

With a final hug from Charlie, Jen wiped her eyes, turned to me, and said, with a scared-to-death look on her face, "We stole a calf."

"You stole . . . a calf," I repeated. "As in, a baby cow? That kind of calf?"

Jen nodded miserably.

I sat down heavily on a nearby bale of hay, patting the hay beside me. The two girls sat down also, one on either side of me.

"Who did you steal it from?" I asked. "And why?"

"From the farm next door. Mortenson's," Jen said.

"He raises veal calves," Charlie said indignantly. "Well, not raises them specifically, but . . . you know . . . they're the male calves born to milkers. They're separated from their mothers, kept in pens in the dark, and fed some disgusting formula that keeps their meat white."

"We heard them crying," Jen said. "When they were separated, some time ago. It was awful, Kieran. The mothers cried, too. For days. We couldn't stand it. So we agreed we would do something about it. For one of them."

"Hmm," I said. "Did you talk this over at your school's club, by any chance? The vegan club?"

"Well, kind of," Jen said. "Each of us in the club agreed we would do an action project this spring."

"So this was your action project? Animal theft? Stealing Mortenson's property?"

Jen winced. "We didn't *plan* it. It just *happened.* And it was animal rescue, Kieran. We saved a life."

I sighed. She did have a point. A point that animal rescue always ran up against — the intersection of what was legal and what was moral. *Oh, Jen, what in hell am I to do with you? I can hardly tell you that what you and Charlotte did was okay. It was theft.*

As if she were reading my mind, Jen said, "I don't think it's right that Mortenson can make those calves suffer just because people want their meat a certain color. I think that's obscene. I mean, yeah, I don't agree with eating meat, but for God's sake leave the cows out in the pasture or wherever until it's time for them to be slaughtered. The way veal calves are treated . . . that's just horrible."

"How did you come to hear the calves and cows crying?" I asked Jen.

"We were out with the pony, riding," Jen said. "A while ago. On a Sunday morning. Over near Mortenson's farm. We might have trespassed a little, too," she added in a small voice. "We needed to see what was going on in his barn."

"Okay, so you realized he was raising veal calves, then what?"

"Then we decided we had to save one," she said.

"Brother," I said. "So the calf is back there in, what, one of the horse stalls?"

Jen nodded. "Yeah. He can't stand up."

"How did you get him over here?"

The girls looked at each other. "We put him on a tarp and dragged him," Charlie said. "Late last night. When Jen got back from Tris's party. I was sleeping over."

"Do you not think Mortenson will miss him?" I asked.

They nodded in unison. "Probably," Jen said. "But maybe not right away. That's why I called you."

I ran a hand through my hair in frustration. "Oh, Jen."

"Please don't be mad," Jen begged. "We don't have a clue what to do now. I guess we should have planned ahead, but we didn't. It kind of took us by surprise — if we were going to rescue the calf it had to be last night. We heard Mortenson talking. He was going to load the calves up this morning."

"Brother," I said again.

"What now?" Jen asked. Then, "You're not going to make us give him back, are you? Because we won't. And we don't feel guilty, either. Do we, Charlie?"

"Nope," Charlotte said loyally. "Not a bit."

"But we're scared," Jen said. "Mortenson, if he finds out . . . well, maybe we'll go to juvie jail. And when mom finds out, I'll probably be grounded for life. But we know we did the right thing."

I groaned.

Jen continued passionately, tears in her eyes, "And it *was* the right thing. At least this calf didn't have to lie in his own poop in Mortenson's stinking, crap-covered livestock truck for hours, scared to death, while he got carried away to be slaughtered. We saved his life." She wiped her eyes on her sweatshirt sleeve. "He deserves his life. Out in a pasture somewhere, under the sun and the sky, eating grass. Doing . . . whatever calves do."

She leaned against my shoulder, crying in earnest now, and I put my arm around her.

"You're brave kids," I said. "Both of you. You broke the law, but you did what you felt was right. And you did save a life." I thought for a moment, remembering another long-ago animal rescue, wondering if I should tell Jen the tale. What the heck, I decided, it might be instructive. I said, "I want to tell you a story. About an animal rescuer who wasn't as brave as you two. She listened to her head, not her heart."

"Oh yeah?" Jen said, sniffling. "Who?"

"Oh, a friend of mine," I said. "She was a researcher at a university in the east. She worked in an old Victorian house. Very . . . atmospheric. But it had a creepy basement no one ever went into. Or so she thought. One miserably hot August day there was a terrible smell coming from the basement. So she investigated. Way back in a corner, down a dark hall crammed with piled-up chairs, was a little room, oh, about twenty by twenty. The smell was coming from there."

"Kieran, you're scaring me," Jen said. "I wouldn't have gone down that hall."

"Me neither," Charlie said. "She was pretty brave. Your friend."

I squeezed Jen's shoulder. "No, she wasn't a brave person. But she had a bad feeling about the room in the basement. Something seemed to call to her. She had to find out what was in there. So she did."

"What was in the room?" Jen whispered.

"Cats," I said. "In stainless steel cages. Five of them."

"Oh, my God," Jen said. "And the smell?"

"Overflowing litter pans, and starving cats with URI. Some of them couldn't see for the pus in their eyes."

Jen looked stricken. "What did she do?"

"Filled their water dishes. Wiped the snot off their faces and the mucus out of their eyes. Ran out to the nearest convenience store and bought food and litter and garbage bags. Changed their litter. Then she went upstairs to her office and got on the phone."

"Whose cats were they?" Charlie asked.

"They belonged to the psychology department," I said. "They were just warehousing them there, before they went over to the department to be subjects in a so-called benign learning experiment. It took my friend a lot of phoning around over three days, but finally the department called her back. Apparently, the guy who was supposed to be looking after the cats went on vacation and neglected to tell the department."

"So the department sent someone to take care of the cats?" Jen said. "They did, didn't they? Once your friend reported them."

I shook my head. "No. It was Wednesday when she found out they were the psych department's cats. She really expected someone would come over to remove them, get them vet care, do something. But by the end of Thursday no one had come. So she called again. Emphasized that the cats were really sick, and had no food or water."

"But your friend was secretly giving them food and water, right?" Charlie asked.

"She was, but by that time it wasn't so secretly," I said. "She gave the psych department hell for leaving the cats in that condition."

"Good," Jen said. "And then?"

"And then on Friday about five o'clock the psych department called her up to tell her that if she didn't stop feeding the cats and didn't stop interfering, that the department chair would see to it that she lost her job."

"What? How could they do that?" Jen burst out, angry on my friend's behalf. "She was just trying to make them do the right thing. And what about the cats? The department was going to *leave them there* over the weekend? But they were *sick*! Who did they think would take care of them? So what did your friend do?"

"My friend . . . chose her job over the cats," I said. "She couldn't think of what to do with them. Vets' offices were closed. And she had two cats of her own."

"No!" Jen said. "She didn't just leave them!"

"No," I told her. "She called a friend who had contacts in an animal activist group. The animal activists went in on the weekend and took the cats. Stole them, actually. My friend left a door open for them."

"And the cats? Were they okay?"

I shook my head. "No. Four died. One survived. It was grotesque. The cats had name tags on their cages, well, number tags anyhow. In Spanish. They were *Uno, Dos, Trey, Cuatro,* and *Cinque.*"

"What happened to him? The one who survived?" Charlie asked.

"My friend adopted him," I said. "She took him with her when she moved from Toronto to Victoria."

Jen turned to look at me, and I saw first surprise, then comprehension widen her dark eyes. "Trey," she said softly. "The one who lived. That was Trey. Your Trey."

I cleared my throat. "My . . . friend . . ." I said, "was always haunted by what happened to those cats. Four living things died because of her inaction. Her cowardice. Her desire to keep her job. If she had only done something sooner." I shook my head. "You see, she let her left brain rule her right brain."

"Oh," Jen said.

"Whereas you girls, you let your right brains rule your left brains."

"I get it," Jen said, sniffling. "Your friend, Charlie and I . . . we needed both our brains to do the job right."

"Yeah," I said.

"But your friend," Jen said fiercely, "I don't think she was a coward!"

"Oh no?" I asked sadly. "But *she* did. And maybe still does. Okay," I sighed. "Here endeth the lesson. Now . . . what am I going to do with you two?"

I'm supposed to be your moral guide, Jen, dammit. Your godmother. What kind of guidance can I give you on this? I drank some more coffee, a headache growing somewhere behind my eyes.

"Do you want to see the calf?" Charlie asked timidly.

"No, thanks," I said. "I'm thinking." My goddaughter, the cattle rustler. And her faithful sidekick Charlie.

"Okay, here's what you're going to do. Who has her phone handy?"

"I do," Charlotte said eagerly, holding hers up.

"Okay, record this. One, you're going to call a large animal vet to pay an emergency call to the calf. Two, you're going to call Calista Russell at Farm Animal Rescue. Use my name. She owes me a favor. Don't say that, of course. Tell her you have a sick rescued calf that needs a place to live and needs transport. Three, you're going to use Google or whatever you need to in order to find out the market price for veal calves. Mortenson needs to be paid the value of the calf you stole. Get ready to send him a money order or an envelope full of cash. Four, you're going to talk to Connie about how to do responsible animal activism without worrying that you'll end up in juvie jail."

"How to use our right brains and our left brains together," Charlie said.

"Exactly," I agreed. "And five, Jen, you're going to explain things to your mother when she comes back. What you did — the theft — and what I've instructed you to do to make reparations."

Jen put her head in her hands. "Mom? She'll kill me. That's why I wanted this to be all done before she gets back. That's why I called you so early."

"All done?" I said. "This certainly won't be all done today. I doubt if the calf will be going anywhere for a couple of days. Maybe a week. He needs to get strong enough to stand on his own. You might be looking at several vet visits. And you, Charlie, I'd like you to accompany Jen when she confesses all this to Zee."

Charlie nodded, clearly miserable.

"Then, you're going to have to come clean to your own parents, Charlie."

"I'll go with you," Jen told her. "It'll be okay."

"And both of you are going to miss school today," I said. "An adult from each family needs to call the school and explain."

"Uh huh," they said in unison, sounding grim.

"Why does this feel like punishment?" Jen asked. "We were just trying to do the right thing."

"There's an old saying," I told them. "You may have to think about it for a while. It goes like this: 'No good deed goes unpunished.'"

"Ha," Jen said, after a moment. "I get it. Okay. Charlie and I will start phoning."

"And I'll talk to Zee," I said. "Maybe smooth the waters a little for you. Oh, you kids do have bank accounts, don't you?"

They nodded.

"Good, because you'll be paying for the large animal vet, transport to Calista's nonprofit, whatever she wants in the way of a contribution, and the market price of the veal calf. And if you run out of money, you'll have to think of where you can get more."

"No good deed," Jen muttered.

"Yup," I agreed. I got up to leave, brushing bits of hay off my pants.

"Kieran," Charlie asked, "your friend, the one who discovered the cats and thought she was a coward, what became of her?"

"Well, ironically, after having to choose between her job and the cats, she quit that job anyhow," I told her. "She felt sick at heart about the psychology department's neglectful behavior. And about cats — pet cats — being used in research."

"Oh," Charlie said. "So did she become an animal activist? Like the friend who rescued the cats?"

"Sort of," I equivocated.

"And does she still think she's a coward?"

"Some days," I said. "But she tells me she's working on that."

Zee and I sat at her scrubbed pine table in the kitchen, drinking Dragonwell green tea out of her favorite blue mugs. I would rather have had more coffee, but McDonald's was just down the road, and tea was evidently on the menu *chez* Lau this morning. When I told her about the calf theft, Zee erupted into a brief spate of what I imagined was cursing in her native language, then seemed to shift into autopilot. Making tea must be her go-to soothing activity, I thought. And today she was certainly agitated. She'd banged the teakettle in the sink, fumbled the container of tea leaves, dropped a mug on the counter, and finally managed to unite the tea leaves and water in a teapot, and put it and the mugs on the table. I had never been certain of Zee's ancestry — Chinese? Laotian? Vietnamese? Whichever it was, she commented again briefly in that language, then subsided, eyes closed, sipping tea.

"I hope I handled things with Jen more or less to your satisfaction," I said with more equanimity than I felt. Hell, maybe I'd been way too hard on the kid. All that money.

"You handled things well," Zee said. "Except for the part about not being grounded for the rest of her life. I'm mulling that over."

"Hmm," I said. "Don't be too hard on her. Jen might have to go out to mow lawns, or chop wood, or babysit, or deliver papers if her bank account runs dry. I figure she and Charlie are looking at about seven hundred dollars in expenses."

"*Phat dien*," she muttered.

Ah, I thought. Vietnamese.

"Perhaps this will teach Jen the price of intemperate action," Zee said.

"Mmm, perhaps," I replied. "It will certainly teach her something. Anyhow, I suggested she talk to Connie. She's an animal activist from way back — a veteran of Henry Spira's Revlon campaign in the States thirty years ago. Jen shows no sign of giving up animal activism for something tamer, like, oh, beading or choral singing, and if anyone knows how to talk to Jen sensibly about this, it's Connie."

Zee nodded.

"The kids will probably be over to talk to you soon," I said. "You'll have to call the school for Jen. And probably drive Charlie home. I need to go take care of another matter," I said, explaining the Beatrice affair briefly.

Zee raised her eyebrows. "You do lead the most interesting life," she said. "I suppose I should go over and take a look at the calf. Before the large animal vet arrives. There might be something I can do for the poor animal. Hydrate him, at least."

"Whatever you can do," I said. "I'm off to have breakfast with a Griffon pilot and her minder, maybe see a video, then interview a possibly dotty elderly lady who thinks the Air Force made special delivery drops to a service dog at night."

CHAPTER 9

I threaded my way through aggravatingly stop-and-start downtown traffic, my destination McDonald's. But before I ordered breakfast, I thought I ought to take a look at the address my snoop service had turned up for Mohammed Saleh and Aziz Amad. What? Here? I asked myself as I turned slowly off Quadra Street onto a narrow lane of warehouses. I drove slowly, looking for number 2011. Nope. Twenty-eleven was a vacant lot, populated by weeds and what looked like bricks fallen from a crumbling building directly east. A sign on the lot proclaimed it to be for sale, but I doubted if the owners were Mohammed and Aziz, that elusive duo of Extremist Travellers. Well, this was helpful, I fumed. I'd have to look more deeply into addresses for them, or even call the number on the For Sale sign, but first things first. Breakfast for Izzy, Ro, and me.

As I was about to pull out of McDonald's, my phone buzzed. Ro. She was sending me the video that the dog thief had sent Izzy, along with a text telling me all was well, Izzy was satisfied that Beatrice was safe, and that the two of them were on their way to Izzy's Monday morning therapy session.

"Fooey," I muttered, as I took a quick look at the video. I wanted a bigger screen than my phone afforded. Then I had an idea. Miranda had recently purchased a large monitor for The Sanctuary — it sat on Connie's desk. I forwarded the video to Connie along with a text telling her I intended to drop in. Miranda might still be looking at the hinky dog people but

Connie and I could examine the video together. I knew full well I was hoping for a Luka Magnotta breakthrough, as unlikely as that was, but still, I hoped.

That left me with three paper cups of coffee and three Egg McMuffins. Well, I hoped Audrey was hungry. I left my car in Audrey's parking place, vaulted the locked gate, McDonald's bag in hand, and with more than a little trepidation, knocked on her front door. To my surprise, she answered it at once — a small, thin woman with short, frizzy grey hair, and a pair of shrewd, bright blue eyes. Her violet-flowered muumuu was certainly a strange fashion choice, but it was neat and clean, and her lime green fuzzy slippers matched the leaves on the violet flowers. Audrey obviously took pride in her appearance — an odd appearance, but one she took pride in nonetheless.

"Can I help you?" she asked. "I'm sorry you had to jump the fence. It's locked to keep me in. Apparently I wander," she confided.

"I'm Kieran Yeats," I said. "A friend of Izzy's. I'm looking into Beatrice's disappearance. And I've been known to wander a bit myself," I confided in exchange. "In fact, a famous ancestor of mine wrote a poem about a man who wandered. Wandering is in our genes."

"Yeats, Yeats," she said, cocking her head to one side. "*That* Yeats? Indeed. I believe the poem you're referring to is 'The Song of Wandering Aengus.' Judy Collins made it into quite a successful folk song in the sixties. Called it 'Golden Apples of the Sun.'"

So much for Izzy's allegation of Audrey's dottiness, I thought. She was no dottier than I. To pull out of her memory the Judy Collins song and the Yeats poem that had inspired it? That took someone with most of her oars in the water. But what on earth were the Air Force's nighttime deliveries and the Green Man all about? Audrey and I had made friends over the Yeats poem and the Judy Collins song . . . so far so good. Maybe I could trade on that ephemeral friendship and use it to discover the truth.

I held up the McDonald's bag containing the sandwiches and coffee I'd bought for Ro, Izzy, and me. "Care for breakfast?"

She gave me a grateful smile. "Oh, yes! Come in, come in. I haven't eaten McDonald's food in, oh, I don't quite remember. Let's go into the kitchen. I can heat those breakfast sandwiches. And do I smell coffee?"

"Audrey, I want to ask you some questions about next door's dog," I said, as we were seated at her immaculately clean, off-white Formica-topped kitchen table, the Egg McMuffins and the coffee heating in her microwave. The apartment was the twin of Izzy's, but somehow crisper. Brighter. *The windows*, I thought. It was the windows. Izzy's were understandably covered with curtains. Audrey's were open to the sunshine.

"At last," she said. "I've been hoping *someone* would come and ask about Beatrice."

The microwave pinged, and Audrey retrieved the breakfast sandwiches and the coffee, placing them on the table, which she had set with paper plates and napkins from Subway. Almost before I had unwrapped my Egg McMuffin, Audrey had made short work of hers.

"Have another," I urged, and she did, devouring the second one with a similar amount of lip-smacking gusto. *Good lord*, I thought. "Maybe have this one, too," I said, handing her my half-unwrapped McMuffin. "I actually ate a little earlier," I fibbed.

"Well, if you don't mind," she said self-consciously. "But I think I'll just wrap it up again and save it for later."

Holy crap, I said to myself. This skinny little lady is famished. Audrey settled back with her coffee and I had a horrible feeling that the daily visits from the daughter that Izzy assured me took place might be, well, an exaggeration on the daughter's part. Or if not an exaggeration, then they were visits that didn't include homemade casseroles, or at least take-out. So much for filial affection.

Audrey was not dotty, as in demented, which is what I believed after my chat with Izzy. Instead, I found her to be . . . something else altogether. I'm sure at twenty, she was charmingly odd; at forty, delightfully unconventional; at sixty, engagingly eccentric. But now? Somehow we don't cut the elderly as much slack for weirdness as we do the young. They don't deserve the same romantic labels, apparently. But weirdness runs in my family. My famous forbear was a lifelong believer in ghosts, inuring me to the *outré*. Audrey and I got along fine.

"So," I said, sipping my coffee, "you wanted someone to come and talk to you about Beatrice?"

"Yes," she said. "I made notes on my nightly observations. About the Air Force's deliveries. Dates and times." She looked at me shrewdly. "Of course I know it wasn't the *real* Air Force that came at night. Not Izzy's Air Force. That was just my way of referring to it. Them. The little aircraft."

Aha. So the Air Force was not to be taken literally. Well, of course not. Audrey was someone who appreciated poetry. And song. The 'little aircraft' were metaphors. But metaphors for what? *Patience*, I told myself. This was a woman who remembered my great-uncle's poem about a little silver trout who had turned into a glimmering girl. With apple blossoms in her hair. *Patience, Kieran.*

"I'll just go into my bedroom and get my journal," she said. "Excuse me for a moment."

As soon as Audrey disappeared down the hall, I leaped to my feet and pulled open the fridge door. A suspicion was growing in my mind and I wanted to put it to rest. Or not. Inside the fridge was half a gallon of milk, a few cups of strawberry Jello, a jar of pickles, some ketchup, two dried-up cheese slices in an open package, a container of applesauce . . . and nothing else. The freezer held only two empty ice cube trays. Irked, I took a brief cruise through Audrey's cupboards and discovered three packets of microwaveable oatmeal, a mostly empty box of teabags, and half a box of crackers. Then I began to do a slow burn. Who the hell was this daughter? And did she not know that her mother was starving? I mentally pulled up the phone number of Gale Bradshaw — a friend of mine who ran a nonprofit downtown dedicated to helping seniors get the benefits and services they required. I vowed to call Gale as soon as I got back to my car.

"Here," Audrey said, putting a wire-bound notebook on the table. She opened it and turned it toward me. The first date was March sixth, and Audrey had noted:

4:22 a.m. Heard noises outside. Assumed it was the newspaper carrier turning around in the cul-de-sac and Beatrice going to fetch the paper. Looked out through the living room curtains. Beatrice was in the yard, looking up. A small Osprey was hovering over Izzy's yard. It dropped something. Beatrice went to investigate. Then she went up Izzy's steps and took the paper off the porch, pushed her way inside Izzy's front door and went in the house.

"An Osprey?" I asked.

"Yes, it's an Air Force plane," Audrey explained.

I could sense how much she had been wanting to talk to someone about all this. Dammit, why had no one dropped in to ask her questions? Because she had been labeled dotty. And who had attached that label to her anyhow? The daughter? Probably. Well, it had certainly stuck. I couldn't see Mac, for instance, bothering to go next door after Izzy had reported that Audrey, the one person who might have witnessed the abduction, was a fruit loop.

Audrey continued, "An Osprey resembles a helicopter in that it can take off vertically. But it has several rotors — not one big one like a helicopter."

"Wow," I said. "And this . . . thing . . . that floated into Izzy's yard looked like an Osprey, but it was smaller?"

"Yes," Audrey said, nodding excitedly.

Hmm, I thought. *Decidedly odd.* But I needed to ask questions about the dog.

"About Beatrice. She fetched the paper in the mornings?" I asked.

"Yes. Every morning," Audrey said.

"How did she get out? A doggie door?"

"No. Izzy had special hardware on her front door so Beatrice could open it if she couldn't. The nonprofit group that provided Beatrice installed it."

"If Izzy . . . couldn't?"

"Couldn't go to the door. Say, if she'd had a disabling episode." Audrey looked at me with sympathy in her eyes. "I know a bit about Izzy's history. She has flashbacks. I don't know if that's the right word. Izzy told me that sometimes she has to hide in the closet. With Beatrice. I guess sometimes her brain, or her memory, puts her back there at the scene of the Griffon crash. So even if she was able to phone for help, she wouldn't be able to go to the door. But Beatrice would."

"Ah," I said. "But why did Beatrice fetch the morning paper? Why couldn't Izzy get it later?"

"Oh, Izzy's nonprofit group thought it would be good for Beatrice to have jobs. So getting the paper became one of her jobs. Izzy told me this," Audrey said. "About Beatrice's jobs."

"Hmm. Audrey, who knew about this?" I asked. "About Beatrice going outside to get the paper every morning. About the special hardware that let her open the door."

"Well, me, of course," she said. "And I might have mentioned it to my daughter. And the newspaper carrier knew. She made it a point to throw the paper up onto the porch. So Beatrice wouldn't have to go down to the yard when it was raining. She thought it was so cute." Audrey chuckled. "And it was in *The Victoria Times-Colonist*, of course. A big story about Beatrice and Izzy and the nonprofit group, Paws For Patriots."

Give me strength, I thought. The whole city probably knew about Beatrice's early-morning activities.

"So starting March sixth, you saw this . . . delivery . . . take place every morning?"

"Yes," she said, looking mournfully into the depths of her now-empty coffee cup. I felt guilty for having finished my coffee, and vowed to at least make a pot of tea for her before I left. "Every morning until Beatrice disappeared. Well, almost every morning. I had the flu about two weeks ago and I missed a few days. Including the day that Beatrice actually vanished."

"And you told all this to Izzy?"

"I did," she said. "But I don't think Izzy really heard me."

Oh, Izzy heard you all right, I thought. But she discounted it. Attributed it to an old lady's dottiness. Admittedly, the little Ospreys were somewhat perplexing, but I was prepared to give Audrey the benefit of the doubt.

Audrey continued, "Izzy'd been having a very bad time right around then. We used to have tea together. But that was a while ago. Before Beatrice's abduction. And I know Izzy thinks I'm demented," she said, shame plain on her face. "My daughter Patricia probably told her that. Because that's what she told me. My own daughter! That I had dementia and she was going to lock the front gate for my own good. So I wouldn't wander off." She glared at me. "I didn't actually get *lost* going to the convenience store, Miz Yeats. I felt faint. Confused. And that's what I told Patricia. She was very vexed with me because Ajay — he's the store owner — called her. And she had to leave work to come and get me. But that's what it's like to get old, right? Make one mistake and you get an unpleasant label. And no one listens to you after that."

"I'm listening to you," I told her.

"You are listening, aren't you?" she said, gratitude in her eyes.

I felt furious. Audrey's confusion and feeling faint might have had a whole lot more to do with being half-starved and possibly hypoglycemic than it did with senescence. I was certainly going to report all this to Gale Bradshaw. And with any luck someone would come around with food for Audrey, maybe even as soon as this evening, and make a plan to take her shopping and stock her cupboards.

I glanced at Audrey. She certainly seemed sharp enough to me. She recalled the Judy Collins song written in, what, the sixties? And Yeats's poem. As well, she remembered in great narrative detail the nightly events leading up to Beatrice's disappearance. She even recorded them in her journal, for heaven's sake. And she hadn't gotten lost at the convenience store at all. Nope, this old lady was not senile. Just very, very odd. But, a small interior voice whispered to me: *What about the little Ospreys?*

"Okay, so tell me about the Ospreys," I asked. "Where did they come from?"

"Back behind the hedge," she said without hesitation.

"And you saw them pretty clearly?"

"Very clearly," she said. "There's a streetlight at the end of the cul-de-sac."

"And what did they do? The Ospreys?"

"They — well, one of them — rose up over the hedge, floated through the air, approached Izzy's yard, and hovered. About fifteen or twenty feet in the air. It buzzed a little. Then it floated down until it was, oh, six feet or so off the ground and dropped something. The first few times it did this, Beatrice stayed on the porch. I think she was frightened. After it left, she went over to investigate what it had dropped. Then she seemed to lose her fear and she'd wait for it. I could never see what it was that the little plane dropped, though. The fence was in the way. But whatever it was, Beatrice ate it."

"She *ate* it?" *Oh, brother. Really?* There was truth in there somewhere. But what in hell the Osprey was, and what it dropped, and why Beatrice ate it, was beyond me.

"You haven't asked about the Green Man," Audrey said reproachfully.

Oops. No, I hadn't. I'd been too caught up in the Ospreys.

"So tell me about the Green Man," I said. "What did he look like?"

"Well, he wasn't a little green man like a creature out of a science fiction story," she said testily. "I just call him that. It's easier to think about him that way."

Okay, I thought. Another metaphor? Maybe. But maybe not.

"He seemed to be about medium height. Dressed in black pants and a dark green . . . oh, you know, those things the kids wear. Like sweatshirts."

"Hoodies? Sweatshirts with hoods?"

"Exactly," she said. "A dark green hoodie. It had a little crest where the pocket would have been if hoodies had pockets."

"A crest. Could you make it out?"

She shook her head. "No. It was too small. And he had his back to the streetlight."

"And he came from . . ."

"The hedge," she said. "At least he came *through* the hedge. Right opposite Izzy's gate. And went back there."

"Was Beatrice frightened of him? Did she bark?"

"Beatrice isn't a barker. But she seemed wary at first. Then, after a few visits, she came over to the gate."

"Did she know him, do you think?" I asked.

"No, I don't think so," Audrey said. "She didn't wag her tail. I think dogs do that if they know you."

"What did the Green Man do?"

"Nothing," Audrey said. "He just stood outside the gate, looking at Beatrice. Then he went back through the hedge." She was silent for a moment, then said, "Miz Yeats, I wonder . . ."

"You wonder?"

"I wonder . . . could the Green Man have taken Beatrice? Somehow? Could the Ospreys have helped him?"

"I don't know," I said, patting her hand. Ospreys and Green Men. Ai yi. There were only so many possibilities here: one of us was loony, or both of us were loony, or neither of us was loony. Maybe I, too, was suffering from Metaphorical Thinking Disorder.

"Could the Green Man have taken Beatrice? I'm sure going to find out," I told her.

After phoning Gale Bradshaw, I sat in my car in Audrey's driveway, feeling very much relieved. Gale said her group would be happy to send someone out to assess Audrey's situation and to help her access government services, as well as any private services she might be eligible for. More to the point, someone would bring dinner! Audrey had given me the notebook in which she had kept track of the Ospreys and the Green Man's visits, and I paged through it idly before I started my car. As I reached the end of Audrey's journal entries, I noticed that she had drawn a picture and labeled it *Osprey*. I held it up in front of me, chuckling a little, until I realized what I was seeing.

"Holy crap!" I yelled.

Because Audrey's drawing wasn't of a small Osprey at all. It was an airplane-like craft all right — central body, four arms with rotors. But I'd seen one just like it last year. My friend Lawrence owned one. He used it to take aerial views of real estate. So what was it that Audrey had drawn?

"A drone," I exclaimed, comprehension dawning. "It's a bloody drone!"

CHAPTER 10

Faint with hunger, I fought the traffic back to McDonald's, ordered coffee and two breakfast sandwiches, then drove to a little fir-lined lake not far from U Vic. This tranquil spot had become my favorite soul-restoring, brain-unscrambling location — tidy, self-contained, still. Although I loved it, sometimes the ocean was just too immense, too borderless, too fretful. Probably 'Dover Beach' had scarred my impressionable undergrad soul, I thought. What was it that dour old Matthew Arnold said about the sea?

> *. . . you hear the grating roar*
> *Of pebbles which the waves draw back, and fling*
> *At their return, up the high strand,*
> *Begin, and cease, and then again begin,*
> *With tremulous cadence slow . . .*

I didn't want to contemplate roaring or flinging today. I wanted the wash of periwinkle blue sky above the dark firs, the barely rippled cobalt surface of the lake, the Vs left behind by a pair of Canada geese gliding like dreams over the water's surface. I wanted tranquility. I wanted peace. As I sat eating and drinking and thinking, I felt my blood pressure drop by about twenty points. Why didn't I do this more often? This was as good as meditation. Maybe it *was* meditation. I'd have to ask Zee about that. She was always urging meditation on me and had even given me a set of CDs by the Buddhist nun Pema Chodron. *How to Meditate*, I think the set was called. Alas, I hadn't even peeled off the cellophane wrapper. After a few minutes of lake therapy, I felt up to thinking about my case again.

So. A drone. Ingenious bastard. It did make sense. However, as I considered the mechanics of those post-midnight flights, I realized that the drone operator must have launched it from someplace close. My candidate was the little parking lot between the hedge and the backs of the businesses in the strip mall across from Izzy's and Audrey's. At 3 or 4 a.m. it would have been dark, deserted, and quiet — a perfect place for nighttime shenanigans. I bet the drone operator — I decided I was going to call him the Green Man — had parked his car in the lot, launched the drone, and watched on his iPad as Beatrice grew more and more accustomed to the appearance of the weird flying thing that dropped yummy treats. Dog biscuits? Something like that. Very damned clever.

I'd wondered earlier if the convenience store might have a camera trained on the parking lot. CCTV. Well, I'd ask the owner — Ajay, Audrey had called him. And if he did, maybe he'd be willing to let me have a look at the tape. If I got really lucky, maybe I'd see the Green Man's car. Now wouldn't that be sweet. And maybe, just maybe . . . a license plate? Even a partial plate. Hot dog . . . the possibilities were exciting. Down, girl, I told myself. Thank heavens for Audrey and her insomnia.

My phone buzzed, interrupting my thinking, and I picked it up, glancing curiously at the unfamiliar number.

"Miz Yeats?" a pleasant contralto voice inquired.

"This is Kieran Yeats," I replied.

"This is Elizabeth Metheny. You emailed me yesterday," the voice said. "I teach forensic linguistics at U Vic. You sent me an extortion note your client received. One supposedly written by Daesh."

"Of course," I said. "Dr. Metheny. Thanks for calling. I hope my sending you the note wasn't too much of an imposition."

"Not at all," she said. "Being asked to do some linguistics sleuthing is really very exciting. Puzzles like this one and the WannaCry virus ransom note don't come along every day. I emailed you a rather detailed explanation for my decision, but I thought I'd call you with the short version."

"Thanks," I said. "What do you think?"

"The note was definitely written by a native English speaker," she said firmly. "There's not a bit of doubt in my mind. But he wants you to *think* he's an Arabic speaker, someone associated with Daesh. Correct? He evidently has reasons of his own for making such an assertion."

"He does," I told her, recounting Izzy's Air Force background and the Griffon crash.

"I see," she said. "That explains his wanting to ally himself with Daesh. He's assuming the persona of the bogeyman."

"He's doing a good job," I said. "He has Captain Tremblay pretty frightened. But you're sure that whoever he is, and whether he's with Daesh or not, he's an English speaker?"

"Very sure. Oh, and that usage 'But happiness!' Really. That sounds like something that might have been pulled from the WannaCry virus note, but wasn't. No, the note-writer wants to terrify, in my opinion. Hence the reference to Sinjar. I had to look up that reference. That was vile of him, Miz Yeats."

"It certainly was," I said in disgust.

"I hope this has helped you," Dr. Metheny said.

"Well, at least we know who the note-writer *isn't*," I told her. "We do have a couple of Arabic speakers on our suspects list, and we can cross them off." I thought of my two Extremist Travellers, Mohammed and Aziz, the duo who supposedly lived in the vacant lot off Quadra. No need to pursue them now. "Thanks, Dr. Metheny. I'll look at your email when I get home."

"Call me if you have any questions about my interpretation," she said. "Oh, and one more thing."

"Yes?"

"Will you tell me how the dog abduction ends up? If — no, let's say when — you find her."

"I will," I promised, ending the call.

Okay, I thought. *Now we can concentrate on homegrown bad guys.*

Daesh devotees with Canadian names. I had a sudden twinge of concern for Ro. Should I have agreed to let her go investigate, even in a superficial way, the trio of Canadian-named Travellers she had found in our database? Dammit, last night she'd been eager, all four of us had been tired, and I hadn't wanted to play mother with her. Well, she'd assured us she'd be careful and just do the equivalent of a drive-by of the Travellers' home. I'd certainly be interested to hear what she found out . . . and then I planned to take over that angle of the investigation.

I took a last look at the little lake, started my Karmann Ghia, and drove back out onto the Pat Bay Highway heading north for The Sanctuary, vowing not to let the traffic ruffle my recently regained serenity. *Om.*

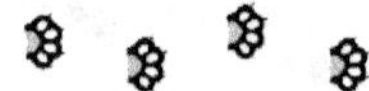

I parked in The Sanctuary's lot under a fir tree, crunched across the gravel, and was just reaching for the front doorknob when the door flew open and a tall, tanned man in a denim jacket and jeans barreled out, almost knocking me down. Quick as a cat, I jumped aside, and the tanned guy tugged on his Stetson (yes, he was really wearing a Stetson), gave me a glare, and hurried past me into the parking lot.

"Fooey on you, John Wayne," I groused, letting myself into The Sanctuary's reception area. "Who was that cowpoke?" I asked Connie, who was sorting papers at her desk.

She rolled her eyes. "The Lexus from Texas."

I burst out laughing. "The what?"

"Don't ask," she said. "It's —"

A series of wolf whistles interrupted us and I turned around, intending to administer a tongue-lashing to the whistler. But to my surprise, Jimmy the African Grey Parrot carried on whistling from atop his cage. "I thought he got adopted?" I said, incredulous.

"Adopted? For about twelve hours," Connie said. "Miranda, Ro, Robert the adopter, and I — we all thought it was a match made in heaven. But the beast rode Robert's Schnauzer around his apartment, chewed the cat's ear, defoliated several African Violets, and ruined a set of guitar strings. Singing manically all the while. Robert called this morning and I went over to reclaim him. I fear he's unadoptable," she said, giving Jimmy a glare from over the top of her rimless glasses.

"Wow," I said. "Cursing wasn't even an issue."

"Nope. I think he wants to be an only. No cats, no dogs, no fish, no plants . . . no competition."

"Fie on you," I told Jimmy.

> *Who's sorry now? Who's sorry now?*
> *Whose heart is aching for breaking each vow?*

Jimmy trilled, dancing on top of his cage.

"Well, it's not our hearts that are aching, birdbrain," I said. "That's a lame song choice, in my opinion. Unless you're trying to guilt Miranda and Connie for sending you away."

"I suspect that's just what he's up to," Connie said. "He'll probably never get adopted."

"You know, that might be what he wants," I said. "The wretch might have adopted *you*. He might sabotage every home you send him to."

> *I'm gonna stick like glue,*
> *Stick, because I'm stuck on you.*

Jimmy warbled, twirling, flapping his wings, then taking off out the open window. We could hear him continuing his song from a perch outside in his aviary.

"Omigod," I said. "He's channeling Elvis now!"

"Demon bird," Connie said indulgently, and I realized suddenly that she was actually happy to see Jimmy back. How odd — was she aware of her fondness for the feathered monster?

Ah well, I thought. What had Pascal, that seventeenth-century polymath said? 'The heart has its reasons that reason knows nothing of.'

Connie fussily adjusted her glasses then turned her gaze on me. "Don't you look fetching today," she said, raising her eyebrows.

I looked down self-consciously at my none-too-clean mismatched sweats and tugged my baseball cap a little more firmly over my case of bed head. "Yeah, well, I had to go hold Jen's hand at five-thirty this morning," I said. "She and her sidekick Charlie liberated a veal calf from the farm next door and stashed it in Zee's barn. Then they had a fit of oh-my-God-what-have-we-done and called me to sort things out."

"I'd like to say good for them," Connie said, "but I'm aware that I'm speaking to a former attorney."

"Indeed," I said heatedly. "There's so much wrong with what they did. One, it's theft, and two, it's theft and — oh, hell, I ended up aiding and abetting their craziness by telling them what they needed to do to play cleanup. And part of the cleanup involves educating themselves on how to strike meaningful blows for animals while staying out of jail." I gave Connie a hopeful look. "I was thinking that possibly you could mentor them on that. Especially the part about staying out of jail."

"Oh," Connie said, surprised. "Striking meaningful blows for animals while remaining unarrested. Hmm. You know, I'm involved with a group that's studying how best to publicize the new meat alternatives. The Incredibles and Beyonds. Plant-based products as well as lab-grown products. The girls could certainly come to a meeting. I wonder if that would be exciting enough for them, though."

"I think their craving for excitement is at a low ebb," I said. "Jen's going to call you. Please mention it to her. Maybe she and Charlie could enlist her school's Meat Is Murder squad into doing something less larcenous than cattle rustling." I shook my head. "I fear for those kids."

"I'll mention our meat-alternative initiative to Jen. Our group would be very excited to involve more young people." Connie gestured to the bookcase. "There's coffee over there. I'd offer you something stronger but I don't feel that I should pilfer the hard stuff from Miranda's desk drawer. Besides, it's barely one o'clock."

"I'll be okay," I said, stifling a yawn. "I need more perking up. Coffee will do just fine."

"I have your video cued," Connie said. "I moved the monitor into Miranda's office, so you'll have to look at it in there. I know you're hoping for a Luka Magnotta moment — Miranda told me that story. Who knows, we might get lucky."

Looking at her watch, she continued, "Our new intern will be here at any moment and I'll have to take her under my wing, so I'll be busy out here. Although I'd love to take a look at the video myself. Maybe I can set the young woman to printing out mailing labels and come in to take a peek." Connie sighed. "She was to be Ro's responsibility, but Ro's off being Izzy's minder. Ah well. Go on back. Grab some coffee on the way. There are some cheese Danishes there on the bookcase too. Help yourself."

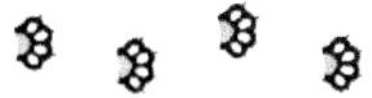

I sat at Miranda's desk and started the video playing. Against a green lawn, a chain-link fence in the background, sat Beatrice, a curly-coated, buff-colored dog of medium size, with melting chocolate brown eyes. A cross between yellow Labrador Retrievers and Standard Poodles, Labradoodles were calm, loyal, brave, and smart as whips. Perfect dogs for veterans. I realized this was the first I'd seen of her, as there were, strangely, no photos of Beatrice in Izzy's apartment. Well, maybe Izzy'd put them in a drawer after Beatrice had been abducted. Too painful? That made sense. I noticed Beatrice was panting a little, mouth open. Not knowing much about dogs, I had no idea what this meant. Thirst? Apprehension? She raised her head, presumably in response to someone's voice. Then, from off-camera, a figure dressed in a medium-green hoodie stepped forward and held a copy of this morning's *Victoria Times-Colonist* in front of Beatrice. I saw the newspaper clearly and the green-hoodied guy clearly also — but from the back, dammit. The bloody Green Man. Then the video stopped.

"Crap," I said. Well, it wasn't much, but he'd done what we asked him to. If it had been me, however, I would have videotaped Beatrice someplace indoors. Either he was very arrogant or very stupid. Because anyone seeing the video would not only see Beatrice, but also her surroundings. Where the hell was this taken? I wondered. Not someone's backyard. The fence was easily six feet high. And two strands of barbed wire ran menacingly along the top. Someone certainly didn't want anyone climbing — or jumping — over that fence. It looked formidable.

I finished my cheese Danish, sipped some more coffee, then started the video playing again. There was something else I wanted to look at, something out beyond the chain-link fence. When I got to what I wanted to see, I paused the video. Beatrice was blocking most of the screen, but what I'd noticed, what I wanted to look at more closely, was the white sign behind her. Well, half a white sign. With black lettering. But I couldn't make out what it said.

And just beyond the sign was something else. A truck. A black one, its back end peeking out from behind the sign. And part of a license plate. Again, too blurry to make out. I got up and paced Miranda's tiny office in frustration. Here it was — our Luka Magnotta moment, our Petro-Canada epiphany — and we were foiled. True, we had in theory three additional chances — tomorrow's, Wednesday's and Thursday's videos. But a nagging sense of urgency was making me anxious. I just had a bad feeling about this.

Pulling my cell phone out of the pocket of my sweats, I hesitated for a moment. Maybe she wasn't even in her home office. Maybe she had a deadline for one of her projects. Maybe . . . oh hell, I'd just ask. I needed tekkie help. I didn't even know if what I wanted was possible, but I knew who to ask. Aliya. Maybe she could get stills from the video, blow them up, make them sharper. If only we could get a few digits from that license plate, or a word or two from the sign. I texted Aliya, and to my relief, she texted me right back, telling me to send the video, saying she would get right on it, but promising nothing.

"Might be impossible," her last text said.

"I know," I agreed.

Then there was nothing else to do. I paced a little more, looked out the window, squared up the books in the bookcase, sat back down in Miranda's desk chair, thought briefly about getting more coffee, told myself I'd had enough, and then Miranda came through the office door.

"Nuts," she said, hanging her navy windbreaker up on a hook on the wall.

"No luck with the hinky dog people?" I asked.

"No luck. Three wasted hours. What are you watching?" she asked. "Oh, this morning's video of Beatrice, I bet." She stepped around the desk. "Start it playing for me?"

I did. She looked at it critically. "Short," she commented. "And maddening. Too damned bad about the sign and the truck."

"I sent the video on to Aliya. Maybe she can sharpen up those images. Say, what do you think about the fence?"

"It looks institutional," she said. "What do you think?"

"I think so, too," I said. "I don't think Beatrice is being held in the extortionist's home. Here," I said, getting up. "Sit. You're looming. It's making me nervous." I gave her back her chair, taking my usual seat in the corner by the window.

"Tell me how your morning went," she asked, leaning back, hands laced behind her head.

"Well," I said, and launched into my story about Audrey, the drone, and the Green Man.

"The Green Man — the guy on the video in the hoodie," Miranda said. "Beatrice's abductor. Good work, Sherlock."

"*De rien*, Watson," I replied.

"So the little turd seduced Beatrice with doggie treats, then when she was nice and docile, he just opened the gate and walked her into his car? Which was parked, where, in the cul-de-sac?"

"No, I don't think so," I said. "I think he probably left his vehicle on the other side of the hedge. There is another duplex in Izzy's little street. He probably wouldn't have wanted to draw attention to himself."

"Good point," she said.

"I'm going to talk to the businesses in that little strip mall," I said. "Especially the convenience store owner. We might get lucky. He might have some videotape. And I think I might like to recreate the nighttime drone activities. Lawrence has a drone. He might like to pay a midnight visit to the other side of the hedge with me. We could launch the drone and watch it on his iPad. Maybe I could even get Audrey to stand by and give us her opinion. I just want to be sure about all this."

"Hey, count me in," Miranda said. "The canvassing will go faster with two of us. And I'd like to be there for the drone-launching."

"Sure thing. I'll let you know what Lawrence says. Audrey, too. I'm getting antsy about all this, Miranda. I think we'd better canvass the strip-mall businesses tomorrow. And launch the drone tomorrow night," I said. "Oh, something else. I heard from Elizabeth Metheny. The forensic linguist. About the extortion note."

"Yeah?" Miranda said. "What did she think?"

"She's pretty definite that it was written by a native English speaker. Despite the scary Sinjar reference. Which, she thought, was gratuitous and probably made just to frighten Izzy. But," I said, "the note-writer, even though he's a native English speaker, might still be with Daesh. He might not be someone playing silly buggers."

"Crap, yes," Miranda said, looking glum.

"Cheer up," I said. "At least we know who the extortionist *isn't*."

"Yeah?" Miranda asked.

"Yeah. A hinky dog person or an Arabic-speaking Extremist Traveller."

"Yup," she said sarcastically. "That narrows the field, doesn't it?" She drummed her fingers on her desk, then said, "We need to get Connie to put this video on our Facebook page and send it out to our Twitter following. Luka Magnotta was caught by ordinary people on the internet. Maybe ordinary people can help us out. The green lawn, that fence, the white sign, the black truck — the combination might suggest something to someone. Let me ask her to do that."

As soon as she'd put her office phone down, her cell phone rang. She picked it up, and in mid-call, looked over at me, eyes wide.

"We'll be right there," she told the caller. "C'mon," she said to me, ending the call and getting to her feet.

"Where are we going?" I asked.

"The ER at Jubilee Hospital. That was Izzy."

"What the hell?" I asked, my stomach in free fall. "What happened?"

"Ro's been hurt," Miranda said. "Let's just go."

CHAPTER 11

In treatment room Number Seven, at the Royal Jubilee Hospital ER, Miranda and I looked on as Ro was being patched up. She had one leg of her jeans rolled up above her knee, and was having a nasty-looking dog bite on her calf attended to. She was, she claimed, just dandy. Even having broken her left arm falling down a fire escape hadn't fazed her, she asserted nonchalantly.

"I'm okay," she said, wincing as the dog bite was cleaned by a young, blond, female nurse in blue scrubs, who looked about twelve but seemed fearsomely competent.

"We don't usually suture these," the nurse explained to Ro. "Just try to keep it clean. We'll give you antibiotics to take home. Was the dog current on its rabies vaccination?"

Ro grinned, evidently deciding to be clever. "I didn't ask him. I was too busy running away."

The nurse, clearly unamused, gave Ro a baleful look and said, "Well, you'll have to fill out a dog bite report. It's the law. Then animal control will investigate. The dog will have to be impounded and observed for fourteen days if it hasn't had vaccinations. And you," she said, skewering Ro with a meaningful look, "may have to have rabies shots yourself. They aren't pleasant."

Ro bit her lip. "Oh yeah?"

"Oh yeah," the nurse said. "In any event, you'll have to have a tetanus shot before you leave."

"Shots," Ro grumbled. "I hate shots."

"Well," the nurse said, "maybe steer clear of strange dogs in future."

Ro raised an eyebrow, but wisely said nothing.

The nurse finished up with Ro's leg, left, and when the door had closed behind her, Ro muttered, "She's caring, isn't she? Nurse Ratched."

The door opened and Nurse Ratched came back with a wheelchair, announcing to Ro, "We're off to orthopedics now. You're going to get a nice cast on that arm."

"Swell," Ro said, then to us, "See you later, guys."

"We'll be in the waiting room," I told her. "Chin up."

An hour later, sitting on butt-numbing turquoise plastic chairs in the waiting room, I found myself getting seriously aggravated. About what, I wasn't exactly sure, but my ire was increasing by the second.

"I might strangle her," I said testily.

"Who? Nurse Ratched?" Miranda asked, looking up from her phone.

"No, Ro," I said.

"Nah, cut her some slack," Miranda said. "She's had a bad enough day. True, she assured us she was just going to look, but looking turned into sleuthing, didn't it?" She ticked off Ro's misadventures on her fingers: "Breaking and entering, an attack by a pit bull, a tumble down the fire escape, a broken arm —"

"Not to mention having to withstand the tender mercies of Nurse Ratched," I added. "Okay. I agree. She's had a bad day. Maybe I'm suffering from an attack of the guilts. After all, it's my fault —"

"Shhh," Miranda urged. Izzy was coming down the hall from a trip to the cafeteria, three coffees in a cardboard box. "Fault, schmault. Let's try to soft-pedal this. We don't want Izzy to get a galloping case of the guilts, too."

"You're right," I said. "I can flail myself in private."

"Drama queen," Miranda whispered to me, then, "Hey, Izzy."

"Hey, Miranda," Izzy replied, dispensing coffee. She looked more cheerful today than she had yesterday. Even her ponytail seemed perkier and her pale blue denim shirt was an improvement over yesterday's grim black Operation Impact T-shirt. All good signs, I thought.

"How did therapy go?" I asked her, trying to take her attention away from Ro's accident. The last thing I wanted was for her therapy to be sabotaged by ruminating over Ro's misadventure.

"Good," she said. "Really good. Margaret had two hours for me, so we talked for a long time. I did miss Beatrice in the session with me. But I'll see Margaret again later in the week. About Ro . . ."

"We talked to the nurse treating her," I said. "And to Ro. She'll be all right. As soon as she gets her arm casted, we can all leave. I thought you and Miranda could go in your RAV — she can drive — and I'll take Ro. In fact, you guys could go ahead."

Miranda gave me a thumbs-up.

"Sure," Izzy said. "But did Ro tell you what happened? All I know is she called me to come get her from that alley. She was sitting against a dumpster, holding her arm."

"We'll talk more when we get back to your place," I tap-danced.

"C'mon," Miranda said to Izzy. "Kieran will bring Ro. No need for us all to stay."

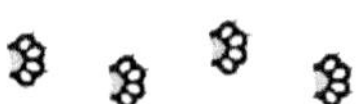

Ro, her left arm encased in a purple cast, leaned back in the passenger seat of my car and closed her eyes. She was holding her black hoodie, which evidently had to be removed for the arm-casting, and she shivered a little in her skimpy blue U Vic T- shirt. I turned on the car's heater for her.

"How was the shot?" I asked.

"It sucked," she told me. "Nurse Ratched is a sadist."

"You know, I could take you back to your cottage at The Sanctuary," I offered. "Connie could probably be prevailed upon to be Izzy's minder for tonight."

"No, I'll be okay," Ro said gamely. However, her freckles looked like crumbs on a white tablecloth, and her red hair stood up in tufts. A butterfly bandage sat just under her hairline, and a line of bloody scrapes marched down one cheek. "Nurse Ratched gave me a pain shot, too. In the butt." She glowered. "Toradol. And I have a prescription for extra-strength something-or-other and some antibiotics."

"We should get those filled," I said. Then, "What the hell happened, Ro? I thought you were just going to look at those three guys' house?"

"Yeah, well." She grimaced. "I was. So after I dropped Izzy off at therapy, I had two hours to kill. I drove to their place, a sort of second-floor loft thing, and got out to take a look around. I couldn't get inside the building through the front door, though — it requires a key — so I went around back. There is no back door, but there was a fire escape up to the second-floor window."

I groaned. "So you climbed up to, what, look in the window?"

Ro shrugged. "Yeah. Just to take a peek. At least that's what I intended to do."

"But . . ." I said.

"But I heard a dog barking. From somewhere inside the loft. Maybe a back bedroom."

"Ro, really?"

"Really. Cross my heart. I thought it might be Beatrice."

"Ai yi. So you opened the window? And climbed in?"

"Yeah. The window wasn't locked or anything. I just pushed it up and stepped inside."

"And then the dog attacked you?"

"Well, not at once. I have to admit that what I saw inside — there's one big room and I guess some smaller rooms in the back — sort of knocked thoughts of Beatrice out of my head."

"The suspense is killing me. What did you see?"

"A big table loaded with . . . Kieran, you may not believe me, but those guys, they're making IEDs in there."

"IEDs? What —"

"Improvised Explosive Devices. You know, like roadside bombs?"

"Ro, what? Are you sure?" Bombs? Is she serious? Here in Victoria. Maybe she's delusional. After all, she's just fallen down a fire escape and hit her head.

"Yeah, I'm sure. Remember last year I told you that my dad is an electrician? Well, he's also a contractor for the DND, the Department of National Defence. He's a bomb guy. He learned it in the army. Anyhow, when I lived at home, I found this all so fascinating that I researched it. I thought for a while that I might like to go into the army and be a demolitions specialist myself. But then my dad got two fingers blown off defusing a mailbox bomb. That's when I decided demolitions was a little too risky for me."

She continued. "So I know what those guys are making in there. The concept of an IED is simple. There are only five components: a switch, a fuse, a container, a charge, and a power source. IEDs are so basic they can be set off by a cell phone."

"Damn, Ro, how far along do you think these guys are?"

"Far," she said. "They seem to have just about everything they need — flashlight batteries for a power source, paint cans for containers, cheap cell phones, timers, switches, lengths of wire for fuses. Everything but the explosive. I guess they're still looking for that."

She went on. "They had a big map of Victoria up on the wall, with red circles drawn on it. That's when I got scared, Kieran, and started taking pictures. Anyhow, I knocked against the table where they had all this stuff laid out and that must've, I guess, alerted the dog to the fact that there was someone in the loft. That's when he came busting out of one of the back rooms," she said sheepishly.

She took a deep breath, and suddenly tough-talking Ro disappeared. Two tears trickled down her cheeks and she started shaking. I didn't know what to do, given that I was driving, so I reached over and ruffled her hair. She sniffled and wiped her nose on her hoodie sleeve. Reaching into the glove compartment, I found a package of tissues and handed it to her.

"Blow," I suggested.

"Thanks," she muttered.

She continued. "He just charged at me, barking his head off. A black and white dog. A pit bull, I think. He grabbed my leg and shook it, and I kicked him in the head and ran for the window. But I tripped on the windowsill getting out and sort of fell outside onto the fire escape. I slammed the window to keep the dog in, and then, well, I lost my balance and fell down the steps."

"How far did you fall, Ro?"

"Just two flights. Down to the alley. I kind of scrambled around behind a dumpster and then I called Izzy. Her therapy place wasn't far. Just three blocks away, so she was able to walk to the alley. I hope her bum leg didn't hurt her too much. But I couldn't think of what else to do."

"Damn," I said again. "What did you tell her when she got there?"

"Just that I heard barking, thought it might be Beatrice, went up to investigate, got attacked by a freaking guard dog, and fell down the fire escape."

"Nothing about the IED components?"

"No. I didn't think she needed to know."

"I think you're right."

"But I lost my phone," she said in exasperation. "Just after I called Izzy. I must have dropped it. I think I was having an oh-shit moment. We need it, though. It has all those pictures on it. It must be in the alley, near the fire escape. We need to tell Miranda's RCMP friend about these guys. Send her the photos I took," she concluded, looking a little desperate.

"We will," I said reassuringly. "We'll go get your phone, get that prescription filled, then meet Miranda and Izzy back at her place." I looked over at her. "Are you sure you're okay to stay the night with her?"

Ro laughed. "Yeah. I am. But I don't know who'll be holding whose hand."

"Don't worry," I said. "You can take turns. Let's go get that phone and your drugs."

Miranda had the presence of mind to pick up some sub sandwiches for Izzy and Ro, and when we'd settled them both in Izzy's kitchen, having a late lunch and drinking tea, I motioned for Miranda to come outside. We took seats on Izzy's wicker porch furniture, the afternoon sun in our eyes, and I filled Miranda in on the IEDs in the loft, the map on the wall, and the photos on Ro's phone.

"Holy moley," Miranda said, alarmed, "excuse me for a moment while I call Sylvie," and walked to the end of the porch. She was gone for a few moments, then returned, reporting, "I told Sylvie about Ro's photos. She wants to see them. I'll give her Sylvie's number in a bit and she can forward them."

"Now what?" I asked.

"Well, it's a little complicated," she said. "Technically, Ro broke the law when she entered that loft through the window. So the photos —"

"Fruit of the poison tree," I groaned. "They can't be used as evidence because they were obtained illegally."

"Yup," she said. "But Sylvie says her squad doesn't necessarily need them. All they need is to get into the loft, where they can see the IEDs for themselves. They'll take things from there."

"And how do they intend to do that?" I asked. "Get into the loft?"

"Well, Ro did hear a dog in distress, didn't she?" Miranda winked. "She knocked on the door downstairs, knocked on the window, feared for the dog's well-being —"

"Stepped inside, and was cruelly attacked for her concern," I supplied. "Brother, will this fairy tale fly?"

"Sylvie's talking to animal control right now," she said. "She wants to use the concern for the dog's welfare to gain legal access. But animal control has to sign off on that idea."

"Hmm," I said. "I can't see animal control saying no to the RCMP."

"Me neither," she said, "but this has to go down by the book. You can be sure the bomb-makers will get an attorney who will scream bloody murder. Sylvie's squad will accompany animal control to the loft. Then, while the animal control officer is checking the dog — and its vaccination records

—" I winced, hoping a set of rabies shots was not in Ro's future, "her squad will simply happen to notice the IED components. I don't think our three bomb-makers will stay unarrested for very many hours after that. Ro is quite a hero in Sylvie's book. The RCMP can't use her photos, but she may have prevented an attack in downtown Victoria. After all . . . The Parliament Buildings are right there. She's just sorry Ro had to get her leg chewed up in the process."

She broke off and we sat in silence for a few minutes, enjoying the sunshine.

"So we've come to the end of our suspects," I said, a cloud of depression settling over me. "The hinky dog people, the Canadian Extremist Travellers. Crap."

"It's a little surreal, isn't it?" Miranda said. "I mean, we saw — we can see — the guy in the video. We can see the lawn Beatrice is sitting on, and the fence around her, but we don't know where that is. It's a tease, dammit. If we could only reach into the damned video."

My phone buzzed at precisely that moment. Aliya.

"I have some stills to show you," the text read. "Also you'll want to look at the video on my monitor. Very interesting."

"Good work," I texted her back.

"That was Aliya," I told Miranda. "Apparently she's found some interesting things on the video. Want to look at them?"

"You bet," she said. "It's beginning to look as though the video may be our only lead, so sure, I want to look at them."

"I have to go get Tris from school and make a stop at the wild bird store," I said. "Why don't I drop you at The Sanctuary, take care of Tris, then meet you back at my house? Tris and I will probably pick up something for dinner, so feel free to come share with us."

She stood up, stretching. "Sounds good. I don't want to ascribe miraculous powers to that video, but I sure do want to see what Aliya's turned up."

"Me too," I said. "Let's hold a good thought for that."

CHAPTER 12

At the Oak Grove School — a long, low building in the middle of a grove of, unsurprisingly, Garry oaks — kids were being picked up by their parents (the Oak Grove School, alas, had no bus) and I joined the line of cars crawling up to the front door. Ordinarily I would have parked in the little lot and walked over to the front door to meet Tris, but I didn't want to embarrass her. I looked a fright and I knew it. Tris and Dani were waiting by what Tris called 'the big door' and she spotted me, waved, and hurried over to my car, Dani in tow. The two girls couldn't have looked more different, I thought in amusement. Dani, a Syrian refugee, was small, had beautiful café au lait skin and long, shiny black hair, and favored leggings worn under skirts or tunics. Today's leggings were dark blue, worn under a short tunic with blue and purple swirls. Tris was gangly, had a pale Celtic complexion (her parents were Scots-Irish) and unruly blond curls, and favored cargo pants with lots of pockets, topped with animal or bird print T-shirts. Today's cargo pants were khaki, and her T-shirt was green with a frolicking grey squirrel on the front, and the words SOMETIMES YOU FEEL LIKE A NUT below it in white.

"Hey, Dani," I said, rolling down the window.

"Hey, Kieran," Dani said, hanging back a little uncertainly.

"Can we give Dani a lift?" Tris asked, clearly worried. "Her mother can't come for her today. She's working in her new seamstress business. She told Dani to take the city bus home, but —"

"Of course we can give you a lift," I told Dani. "And that's terrific news about your mother's new business." I recalled that both Dani's refugee parents had been tailors in Aleppo, but only her father had been able to get work here in Canada. Dani had explained that it was her mother's English that had been holding her back, but evidently it had improved a lot.

"It's her own business," Dani said proudly. "Her very own. She rented the space underneath our apartment. She filled out all the forms and applications herself . . . well, the Refugee Centre lawyers helped a little, but she did most of it."

"That's quite an accomplishment," I said, wondering how Dani was going to get to and from school if her mother couldn't drive her. If she were my daughter, I certainly wouldn't want her riding the bus. The kid was about four feet tall and weighed maybe forty pounds. Would I let Tris ride the bus? Nope. Right after Dani and her parents were given asylum here in Canada, she had, according to Tris, called Canada a garden and its people flowers. But this garden, like all gardens, still grew its fair share of weeds.

"Jump in," I said, and the girls tossed their backpacks into the back seat.

"You'll have to sit in the back," Tris explained to Dani self-importantly. "You're still pretty small. I'm taller so I can sit in front."

"It's okay," Dani said, pulling out her iPod and putting in her earbuds. "I'll just listen to music."

We took a detour and dropped Dani off at her mother's shop — a location halfway between downtown and Oak Bay — and then turned west, negotiating our way through traffic to the wild bird store.

"Thanks for giving Dani a ride," Tris said. "She didn't let on but she's really scared. She doesn't want to ride the bus anymore."

"Oh, did something happen?" I asked.

"Yeah," Tris said. "A really bad thing. It's been happening for a week or so. Since her mother opened her shop and Dani's had to ride the bus. A creepy old man started sitting beside her. At first he just talked to her. She didn't answer back, she said — just listened to her iPod — and a couple of times she changed seats, but he changed seats with her." *Oh shit*, I thought. *I bet I know what's coming.* "So Friday when she was going home, he came and sat beside her and took her hand and put it, you know . . ."

"On his penis," I guessed.

"Yeah," Tris said indignantly. "When Dani got up to try to move away, he held her arm so she couldn't go. She missed her stop. Then today, on the way to school, he did the same thing."

I was angrier than I'd been in a long time. Oh, Dani. No wonder you didn't want to ride the bus.

"She got away . . . climbed over him . . . and got off," Tris continued. "But that was two stops before the school. Kieran?" Tris asked. "How does he know which bus she's getting on? It's pretty spooky, isn't it?"

"How does he know, Sprout?" I decided to tell her the dirty rotten truth. She wasn't too young to hear it. "Because he's waiting for her." *Because he's picked her out. She's his prey. He's like a wolf at a stream, zeroing in on the fawn he wants. And now that he's found his fawn, he'll never give her up.*

"Yeah, okay, but *why*?" Tris asked. "Why does he want to do that? Put her hand on his penis?"

"Because he's . . . disturbed. Sick. He gets satisfaction from doing things like that with little girls. Unfortunately, there are creeps like that in the world."

"So I'm going to ride the bus with her," Tris announced.

"Hold on, short stuff," I said. "Not in this lifetime." I decided to be straight with Tris. "This is a crime. It's not just something annoying that a creepy old man on the bus does. In the law it's called sexual abuse of a child. And the law takes this very seriously. He can be prosecuted and put in jail for what he's doing to Dani. It's very loyal of you to want to ride the bus with her, but what do you think you could do?"

"I don't know," Tris said miserably. "But I don't want her to be scared. We could sit together."

I looked over at Tris. "Scared is good, Tris. Scared is normal. Scared tells us to run away. And then tell someone. Wouldn't you have been scared if you'd have been Dani this morning? When the creepy man sat down beside you?" I asked her.

Tris shot me a give-me-strength look. "No way. I would have punched him out."

Ai yi, I thought. *She probably would have.* But Tris had dropped the creepy old child-molesting guy on the bus in my lap, so to speak, and now I felt compelled to do something about it.

"Okay, let's think about this," I told Tris. "We can certainly pick Dani up for school. I can do it when I drive, and Aliya can do it other mornings. And we can take her to her mother's shop after school. It's only ten minutes out of our way. It's no big deal."

"Really?" Tris said.

"Really," I replied. Then I realized, I needed to think about the rest of this. The creepy guy on the bus who likes to put little girls' hands on his penis? He's a menace. And when Aliya and I start driving Dani to and from school, when we deprive him of Dani, he'll do this to some other little girl. Some other kid will be scared. And scared might not even be the half of it. What happens when he follows some little girl off the bus, and around the corner onto a side street?

"Dani would never have told her mother about him," Tris said. "She'd worry, and Dani wouldn't want her to. She says her mother has enough to worry about with her new business. She just figured . . . well, I don't know what she figured. She was just crying and scared this morning. So I thought I'd tell you."

"Well, at least she told someone," I said. "You. And you told me. That was the right thing to do. Kids have to speak up about these things. They can't keep quiet. Then it's up to adults to do something about guys like that."

Tris nodded. "Can you do something about him, Kieran? The creepy old guy? Miranda could give you a hand," she added helpfully.

"Yeah, there are a couple of things we could do. But I need to think about this," I told her. Sure. Miranda and I will find the Daesh extortionist, bring Beatrice home . . . and then we'll take on the child molester on the bus. And leap tall buildings, too, I thought ruefully.

"Okay," she said trustingly.

"You could call Dani later and tell her that either Aliya or I will pick her up for school tomorrow. We probably ought to meet her mother, too, to re-assure her that we're regular people."

We drove along in silence, Tris humming a little, and I wondering when in hell I'd have time to explain this to Miranda, concoct a plan, then ride the bus and accost the creepy child molester. And we ought to do it soon — it would be best not to let too much time pass or the old guy might choose another bus, another route, another kid. I decided to let that problem rest for the time being.

"So I have a question for you," I asked Tris.

"Uh huh," Tris said curiously.

"Can I still call you Sprout? Now that you're nine. Older and wiser and sophisticated. A woman of the world."

Tris grinned. "Sure. I like Sprout."

"Okay," I said, privately relieved. I knew the day would come when Sprout would be an embarrassing name for Tris, but clearly that day hadn't come yet.

"Now I have a question for you," Tris said.

"I'm all ears. Go ahead."

"Well, how come so many of those oldie songs are about food? And don't really make sense?"

"About food?" I asked her. "I hadn't noticed."

"Yeah," Tris said solemnly. "Dani and I were sharing her earbuds and listening to songs at lunch and one of them said something like 'Every time you go away, you take a piece of meat with you.'"

I started giggling and thought I'd drive the car off the road. "That's a song by a guy named Paul Young. What he was actually saying was 'Every time you go away, you take a piece of *me* with you.' Me, not meat."

Tris started giggling too. "That's just weird. Everyone thinks it's meat, I bet. I thought maybe he was at a buffet."

"No, he's in looooove," I told her. "He's telling her she takes a piece of his heart away with her when she goes."

Tris rolled her eyes and groaned.

"Okay, next food song?" I asked her.

"The one that says 'I wanna hold your ham.'"

It was too much. I laughed until tears ran down my face.

"What, Kieran?" Tris said, giggling in anticipation of the right lyrics.

"That's a Beatles song. It really says: 'I wanna hold your *hand*.' Hand, not ham."

Tris shrieked with laughter. "People hear those songs all wrong, then!"

"Yeah, they do," I said, chuckling with laughter myself. "The misheard lines — they're called mondegreens. You can look the word up on Wikipedia. Got any more?"

"'She's got a chicken to fry, and she don't care,'" Tris said, snickering.

"Another Beatles song," I said. "It's 'She's got *a ticket to ride*,' not a chicken to fry," I said, wiping tears from my eyes.

"Did you hear songs wrong when you were a kid?" Tris asked when she'd recovered.

"No, not pop songs. But I heard Christmas carols and prayers wrong. That was when I was about your age and my parents made me go to church. There's a line in the Lord's Prayer that says, 'Surely goodness and mercy shall follow me all the days of my life,' but I heard it as, 'Surely Good Mrs. Murphy shall follow me all the days of my life.' I was quite worried about not being able to ditch Good Mrs. Murphy, whoever she was. I imagined her haunting me forever. I'd turn around and there she'd be!"

Tris laughed so hard she started snorting.

"And then there was the Undertoad," I told her. "He wasn't in a prayer, though. My parents always warned me to be careful of the Undertoad when we went swimming in the ocean. I was so freaked out about him that I never went in the water."

Tris's eyes were very wide. "What was the Undertoad really, Kieran?"

"It was the undertow. You know, the current of water under the surface that moves in a different direction from the surface current. It really might carry you away. But in my mind, it was a horrible warty monster. I think I was fifteen before I learned to swim. By that time, I believed the Undertoad might be lurking in any body of water. Certainly a swimming pool. Even the bathtub."

We drove along in companionable silence and I thought that it had been years since I'd laughed as hard as I just had with Tris. Damn, but I liked it.

"Aliya and I bought the rosebush," Tris said as we pulled up in front of the wild bird store. "A nice bright yellow one. It isn't blooming yet, but the man at the nursery showed us a picture."

"Great," I said. "My case should be wrapped up in a couple of days. Why don't you choose a spot for it and we'll plant it late one afternoon when you get home from school. Let's say, oh, Friday."

"Okay," she said. "After we get the hawk decals, can we go get dinner? It's my day to pick take-out."

"It is, isn't it," I said. "Let me think what might be yummy. Bouillabaisse? Vichyssoise? Cassoulet?"

"Nope," she said firmly.

"Ah, something Middle Eastern, then. Mannakoush? Halloumi? Tangine?"

"No, *silly.*"

"I'm stumped. What then?"

"Pizza!" she said. "Veggie pizza!"

"How could I have forgotten?" I said, theatrically smiting myself on the forehead. "Pizza it is, then."

CHAPTER 13

"How hard is it to become a Mountie?" Tris asked Miranda as we were finishing up our pizza. "Could I do it?"

"I thought you wanted to become an ornithologist," I said to Tris.

"Probably," Tris said, looking thoughtful. "But the Mounties could be Plan B."

"Well," Miranda said, winking at me behind Tris's back, "it's not hard. You have to marry your horse, though."

Tris's eyes flew open wide. "You do? Really?"

"Uh huh," Miranda said. "You have to live with him, eat with him, sleep with him, train with him. When the two of you perform in the Musical Ride, you have to be almost one. You don't even use the reins. You give him instructions with your knees."

"Wow," Tris said. "But marry him like in church?"

"Well, maybe not in church," Miranda equivocated. "And okay, maybe not really *marry* him, but you sure have to be prepared to live with him while the two of you are being trained. We just call it that in the Mounties. Marrying your horse," she said, smiling.

"Hmm, maybe I'll stick to birds." Tris stood up to clear the table. "I like horses, but that marrying stuff, it sounds like too much of a commitment."

I rolled my eyes. Commitment, indeed.

"Yeah, and what if you had a fight and wanted to break up," Aliya chimed in. "You'd have to divorce your horse."

Miranda went into the kitchen to help Tris with dishes. "Take my advice," she said. "Stick to birds. You don't have to check their hooves every day."

"Yeah, birds might be easier at that," Tris said. "Say, where did the Musical Ride come from, Miranda?"

"Let's see," Miranda said, rinsing dishes while Tris put them in the dishwasher. "The Ride dates back to the eighteen seventies, when the Northwest Mounted Police — that's what they were called then — was the only law on the prairies. They practically lived on horseback, and when they weren't chasing bad guys, riders would spend their days training and doing the same drills over and over again. It got pretty darned boring, so to break up the monotony, Force members started to do tricks on horseback and hold competitions among themselves. Then they started performing in public, and presto, the Musical Ride."

"Don't you miss it?" Tris asked. "Being a Mountie? The Musical Ride is awesome."

"Oh, sometimes I miss it," Miranda said. "Not often, though."

Tris nodded. "You like saving animals more, right? Finding them new homes. Seeing them happy."

"I do," Miranda said, drying her hands and closing the dishwasher. "Great pizza. Who made it? You, Tris?"

Tris giggled. "Nope. Kieran and I got it at that place called The Joint."

"Ready to do homework?" Aliya asked Tris. "The three of us are going downstairs to look at a video. Give us a holler if you need anything."

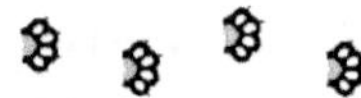

"Tris has become quite a chatterbox," I apologized to Miranda as we closed the door to Aliya's downstairs suite.

"Nah, she's just a normal nine-year-old," Miranda said. "I think all kids get chatty when homework looms. Marrying your horse and the Musical Ride are so much more interesting than, say, geometry. Or whatever nine-year-olds are studying these days."

"This nine-year-old is studying French grammar," Aliya said. "And not doing well. Conjugating irregular verbs has her stumped. I'm about to give in and show her the cheat sheet my father gave me to help me remember how to do it. Okay," she said, "c'mon over here to my desk. Grab a couple of folding chairs. I want to show you what I found on the video."

"This is quite a monitor," I said to Aliya as she took a seat at her desk and Miranda and I unfolded our chairs and sat behind her. "Is it new?"

"Yup," she said. "Twenty-seven inches. It's great for graphic design. I was able to see what's on the video pretty clearly. Look," she said, bringing it up on the screen.

"Wow," I said, "you can count every hair in Beatrice's coat."

"But," Aliya said in exasperation, "I can't sharpen the picture enough to see the license plate on that blasted truck that's just beyond the fence. And the truck is parked on an angle, so that doesn't help."

"The last number looks like a seven," Miranda said, bending forward. "What do you two think?"

"Mmm . . . it could be a one," I said.

"The truck's a RAM 3500," Aliya said. "Maybe your friend Edgar could trace the plate with that information — a seven or a one and the make of the truck? I know it's not much."

"It's something, though," I said. "Maybe he can. I'll ask him."

"I couldn't get anywhere with the sign though. It's still blurry. Sorry."

"Don't worry," I said. "I'll have Edgar get to work on the truck."

"But look here," Aliya said, "This is the really interesting thing. The guy in the video — look at his left hand. It's sort of trailing behind him as he steps forward. He has the newspaper in his right hand, and he holds that up in front of Beatrice. But he doesn't seem to know what to do with his left hand. I got a still from the video and blew it up. It's no clearer but it's bigger. What do you see? On his pinky finger?"

"A ring," I said. "Damn. A ring."

"It's a class ring, isn't it?" Miranda said excitedly. "A graduation ring."

"Uh huh, that's what I think," Aliya said.

I got up and peered closely at the photo. "It has a green stone in it," I said. "Well, it's glass of course, but that probably means the school's color is green. I had a ring like that when I graduated from the University of Toronto. I guess I thought I wanted to remember my undergrad days with jewelry," I said ruefully. "A blue glass stone. Anyhow, my ring had my graduation year on it."

"I can see something," Miranda said. "On the side of the ring, like you said. I bet it's his graduation year, too. But it's way too blurry."

"Damn," I said. "This is beyond frustrating."

"Well, there's tomorrow," Miranda said. "Maybe he'll obligingly hold up his hand in front of the camera. Or wave it around."

"Maybe," Aliya said, "but I thought I'd do a little work on this problem in the meantime. If his school color is green, it'll be on the college's website. So I made a list of B.C. schools, divided it into three parts and emailed each of you a third of the list. Each third contains about a dozen names. It seems there are plenty of colleges, universities, and trade schools in the province. I haven't worked on my third yet, but I will. As soon as I finish with Tris tonight."

"Hmm, more names than I would have thought," Miranda said. "Okay, I'll check out my list when I get home."

"I'll work on mine, too," I said. "And then . . . maybe, just maybe, if we can see his graduation year on his blasted ring tomorrow, and can identify the college, we can get a list of graduates. Edgar can definitely find that for us."

"And if Edgar can get anything from the truck's license plate, we might be able to correlate all this information," Miranda said. "I know I'm getting ahead of myself, but I feel encouraged. Aliya, you're a genius."

Aliya shrugged. "I have my moments."

"The Green Man," I said.

"The Green Man?" Aliya asked.

"His hoodie. It's green. He's evidently very proud of wherever he graduated from — proud enough to wear a ring and buy a commemorative hoodie. And I'll bet he bought the hoodie recently. Otherwise it would be as faded as Miranda's RCMP sweatshirt."

"Tut-tut," Miranda said. "That's called comfortably-broken-in, not faded."

A discouraging thought crossed my mind. "I sure as hell hope this isn't a high school graduation ring. We're assuming it's a college ring, but it might not be." An equally horrible thought followed on the heels of the first. "And we're assuming the guy attended school in this province. He might not have. He might have attended, say, community college in Inuvik."

"Well, we have to start somewhere," Miranda said. "Let's go down the B.C. college road first, using Aliya's list. If we're wrong, we can always do high schools. Or move on to other provinces."

"High school," I said, shuddering. "Was anyone ever so proud of graduating from high school that they would want to wear a ring to commemorate the event?"

"Only thick-skulled football players," Miranda said sarcastically.

"Tut, tut," I teased. Then I sighed. "I guess we've had our Luka Magnotta moment."

Miranda and I sat in my living room at opposite ends of my old comfy leather couch, sipping whiskey, our sock feet up on the coffee table. Some months ago I'd discontinued my practice of burning wood and installed the Pleasant Hearth Twenty-Inch Electric Fireplace Plus Grate from Amazon. Faux fire. No more guilt about carbon emissions. Best of all, the electric fireplace put out ersatz firelight as well as real heat. Firelight is necessary for us Celts. Over the centuries we've huddled over our sputtering peat fires, chanting, brooding, longing for the return of the light. It's in our genes. If I didn't have a fire to brood in front of, I'd feel, well, culturally dispossessed.

Miranda stared into the flames in silence, something clearly on her mind. I had a feeling I knew what it was — the Stetson-wearing guy who'd almost trampled me on his way out of The Sanctuary early this morning. The guy Connie had referred to as 'the Lexus from Texas.' An ex of Miranda's? Hmm.

I sipped a little whiskey and considered how to broach the subject. Pissed-off exes? Well, I'd had a couple. Did that qualify me as a member of the club?

After all, I batted for the other team, so to speak. But really, how much different could our experiences have been? Mine didn't wear Stetsons, though.

"Long day," I said, attempting a conversational foray, not one of my more brilliant ones. "I was up way too early."

"Me, too," Miranda said. Then, "Oh crap. Connie texted me that you ran into my ex, Lex. Almost literally. I apologize."

Whew. At least his name wasn't really Lexus. But 'my ex, Lex' was almost as giggle-worthy. "Don't apologize. It wasn't you who nearly ran me down. Besides, I'm nimble. Comes from all those years playing guard in college basketball. Is he really from Texas?"

"Yeah," Miranda said, sighing. "Dallas. He's a Texas Ranger. He came up to B.C. for training when I was in the RCMP. We spent a lot of time together and oh, well, you know . . . but things fell apart. He was a whole lot fonder of me than I was of him. Astonishingly, he won't let go. He's dropped in to The Sanctuary at least once a year for the past five years while he's visiting friends he made up here in the Force. Usually I'm not in the office, thank God. He tells his tales of unrequited love — and unanswered texts — to Connie, who is decidedly unsympathetic."

"It's like Jimmy the Parrot says. He's stuck on you." I laughed, hoping that levity was the right response.

"Five years is excessive," she said, frowning. "Five years is obsessional. Five years is, quite frankly, a little spooky. He truly needs to move on. What about you?" she asked. "Have any of your exes clung?"

"Have they clung? Well, Anne the attorney was pretty clingy. I met her when I was at the Crown Counsel's office. We were on again/off again for a couple of years, then, well, we weren't. She's asked me out a couple of times since, and mutual friends have resorted to quite transparent subterfuges to get us back together, but . . ."

"What went wrong?" Miranda asked.

"Oh, nothing specific," I said. "Things just . . . fizzled."

"Hmm, no sparks?" Miranda asked.

"No, it wasn't that. I guess we sparked intermittently. But I belatedly realized that Anne was deadly boring. Attorneys often are. Probably including me. When I left the Crown Counsel's office, I realized we didn't even have that to talk about. As well — and I might scandalize you here — I really like to wake up in my own bed alone. I'm too old for torrid bed-hopping affairs. Besides, now I have responsibilities."

"You bet," Miranda said. "Two cats, two tenants, and a daughter."

"And you know what?" I added. "I like them. The responsibilities."

"Amazing, isn't it, how our attitudes toward responsibilities change as we get older," Miranda said. "Mine changed when I turned forty. Tris asked me if I missed the Force. Well, really, I don't. I'd much rather work in animal rescue. Seeing them happy in new homes is pretty damned rewarding." She shrugged. "You know, sometimes I'm asked if animal rescue isn't burdensome, if the responsibilities don't weigh on me." She shook her head. "Nope. They don't."

I sipped a little more whiskey and said, "The curse of forty. I'm nipping at your heels, age-wise, friend. Maybe what comes over us is a new focus — a focus on having everything right."

"Having everything right," Miranda said. "A great line."

"It is, isn't it?" I said. "I wish I'd coined that phrase. It's the title of an essay by Kim Stafford, son of the Oregon Poet Laureate William Stafford. It comes from the Kwakiutl, the indigenous people of our province. Kim Stafford is a poet, too, so naturally he loves words, although I think his essays are much better than his poems. Anyhow, in the eighties he spent time here, on the island, studying the Kwakiutl language. It's very poetic. For instance, we call this island's capital Victoria, naming it for a queen; they called it 'Where Salmon Gather.' They called a certain bend in the river 'Insufficient Canoe.' A place-name for them isn't something that is, but something that happens."

I went on, "There was a word that really moved Stafford, something called *helade*. It's the Kwakiutl word for a meadow, a place at the mouth of a river, a place where people come together and gather berries in summer, and dance and trade stories in winter. Berries by summer, stories by winter."

"Ah," said Miranda. "A place where they had all they needed. I bet they called it 'Having Everything Right.'"

"They did," I said. "Stafford ended his essay by saying that what he was seeking was his own home, a place where *he* could have everything right." I was silent for a minute, then continued. "I guess that's what I've been looking for, too. A place like that. And people to put in it. People to eat berries with. People to trade stories with."

"Aliya. And Zee and Jen. And Helen. And Tris," Miranda said.

"And Lawrence," I said. "And Connie. And you, too."

"Shucks, Miz Yeats, you might make me cry," she said. After a bit, she said, "Remarkable that the people who we once thought might be our life companions . . . dropped away. Or we moved on from them. Anne. And Lex. It's kind of sad, isn't it?"

"Sad? A little. But we'll undoubtedly meet other Annes or Lexes." I smiled. "Or, better yet, their two-point-oh versions."

"So you're not closing the door on the 'L' word?" Miranda teased.

"Not at all," I said. "But there are plenty of other kinds of love besides romantic love or *eros.* The ancient Greeks regarded *eros* with great suspicion, you know. They thought it the least reliable and satisfying of all the loves. I think that, having arrived at my mature years, I'm more open to other kinds of love. *Storge*, which means love of family. *Filia*, love of your friends. *Pragma*, that love that supersedes *eros* in a relationship."

"Your mature years," Miranda scoffed. "You're hardly doddering." She yawned and put her glass down on the coffee table.

What time was it anyhow? I looked at my watch. Eleven-ish. Late, but there was still time to bring up another subject I wanted to air with her. Dani. I outlined what Tris had told me about Dani and the scary old child-molesting guy on the bus, how I had driven her home, and how I had promised Tris that I would do something about the creep.

"That fucking pervert!" Miranda exploded.

"Yeah, exactly," I agreed. "I go back and forth between wanting to cry at what Dani had to go through — she was probably panicked and scared to death — and wanting to kill the bastard. She's so little, Miranda. Well, you met her yesterday."

"Yeah, she is little," Miranda said. "Probably one of the reasons the old guy picked on her. Do you have something appropriate in mind for him?" she asked.

"The vague outlines of something," I said. "I wanted to know if you were interested in joining me in that something. I think we'll have to involve Mac also."

"You bet I'm interested," she said. "How's Dani doing?"

"Well, I didn't get a chance to talk to her," I said. "Tris told me this after I'd dropped her off at her mother's shop."

"Hmm," she said. "Whatever you and Mac and I do, I think it's important that one of us — you, probably, as she knows you — talks to her. About how what happened is not her fault, that she was a brave kid to tell someone, and that law enforcement is going to use her information to get the creep off the streets. I only had one experience like this with a minor child, but our protocol involved that kind of talking. I'd volunteer to do it, but she knows you, not me."

"I'm sure she's worried about her family's refugee status, too," I said. "Maybe Mac has to reassure her — and her parents, as well — that their refugee status will absolutely not be affected. That we're all Canadians together — refugees and immigrants as well as citizens — and that the law is for everyone."

"Good point," Miranda said. "You know, Mac's department has a child advocacy officer. Dani will have to give a deposition, but it's done by videotape. It's not a scary process at all. I've been in the interview room and it's kid-friendly. Colorful. Bright and cheery. Lots of stuffed animals . . . crayons and paper, too. She — or her parents — might want you to be with her, though."

"I can do that," I said. "Whatever would make things easier for the kid. I'll let you know what I have in mind for the pervert just as soon as I have more than forty-five seconds to think about it," I said. "I envision a sting and hope that Dani will agree to ride the bus one more time. With both of us along. But we can't let too much time pass. Once the guy realizes Dani isn't riding the bus anymore, he may move to another route. And another little girl."

"Gotcha," she said.

"Thanks, Miranda," I said, and this time I yawned. *Brother*, I thought. It had been an awfully long day.

"Shall I come get you tomorrow?" I asked. "We can go strip-mall business canvassing. As the British say, 'I'll come knock you up.' But only if you have coffee waiting."

Miranda threw back her head and laughed. "They do say that, don't they? And I'll have coffee ready, no worries." Putting her glass down on the coffee table, she stood up, stretching. "I wonder what the Kwakiutl would call our pursuit of Beatrice? If 'Insufficient Canoe' is really about tipping over in the rapids, what would seeking Beatrice be called?"

"Hmm, 'Curly-Coated Bown Dog Wanders'?"

"Maybe," she said. "Maybe. See you tomorrow."

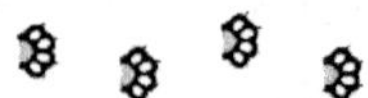

After I'd walked Miranda to the door, locked it, and put our glasses in the dishwasher, I thought fondly of a hot bath, then decided, nah, I was so tired I'd probably drown. I wandered on down the hall, turning off lights as I went, pausing in Tris's doorway. She was wrapped in her comforter in the aqua glow of her lava lamp; Jeoffry, curled at the foot of her bed. He raised his head as he saw me and opened his golden eyes. As he did so, lines from the poem 'My Cat Jeoffry' came to my mind, lines written by Christopher Smart, the so-called madman who, imprisoned in Bedlam in the eighteenth century, wrote so affectingly about his own cat:

> *For he keeps the Lord's watch in the night*
> *against the adversary;*
> *For he counteracts the powers of darkness*
> *by his electrical skin and glaring eyes.*

"Good boy, Jeoffry," I whispered. "You keep watch."

In my bedroom, I sat on the edge of my bed, shedding my socks and pulling my sweatshirt off over my head. A lump under my comforter attested to the presence of Trey and I smiled, looking forward to finding the furry footwarmer with my toes. I put my phone on the bedside table, then realized, nope, I still had one pre-bedtime task. But before I could get to it, however, my phone buzzed. Aliya.

"I've got it!" she said excitedly.

"Okay," I said, laughing. "Which *it* have you got?"

"The dog thief's graduation year. I fooled with the photo, turned it black and white, upped the contrast — oh, you don't need to know about that — and got a better look at the side of the ring. The year is there, just like you said yours was."

"Miranda said you were a genius," I told her. "I'm dying of suspense. And the year is?"

"Two thousand and four," she said. "I'm absolutely sure."

"Well done, Aliya," I told her.

"Now we just have to find the college he graduated from," she said. "I'm going to tour college websites on my iPad in bed."

Oops, I told myself. I hadn't checked on my possibles yet. Well, tomorrow morning was surely soon enough.

"Then when we find the college, maybe your friend Edgar could get us a list of the graduating class," she said excitedly. "At least then we'd have, oh, fifty or sixty possible suspects."

"Yup," I said. "Instead of the big fat zero we have now. Great work. Good night, now. Get some sleep."

And then, I thought, punching Edgar's number on my phone, we might be able to correlate the graduation class's names with the owner of the black RAM, as Miranda had suggested. If Edgar could find the truck's owner, that was. Maybe, just maybe, we'd get lucky.

"Edgar," I said, surprised when he answered his phone. "You're awake. Still."

"Databases never sleep, sweetie," he said. "I'm wandering in the thickets of one as we speak."

"Sounds uncomfortable," I told him. "I have a simple request for you, though. Another foray into the British Columbia Insurance Corporation's vehicle database."

"Ah," he said. "Child's play. Do you have the plate number?"

"Well, no, not exactly," I said. "To be truthful, not even approximately. I have one digit from the end of the plate. It might be a seven. Or it might be a one. And the make of the vehicle. A black RAM 3500."

"Hmm, quite a large truck. And not exactly a common one, either, so you might get lucky. I'll get on it as soon as I can. But that will be as soon as —"

"As soon as you wander back from the thicket of your present database," I said. "I know, I know. You're a busy guy." I was too tired for our usual back and forth. "Let me know as soon as you know anything, okay? Name and address would be super."

"Tut-tut," he said. "Don't be catty. And just so you know, I'm still in, ah, negotiations for the owner of that phone number you require. I'll be in touch."

"Okay, Edgar," I said, ending the call.

I tossed my sweatpants in the direction of my rocking chair and lay back on my bed, almost too tired to crawl under the covers. Things were moving, albeit at a snail's pace, it seemed. As soon as Aliya, or I, or Miranda identified the dog thief's alma mater, I'd call Edgar again and ask for the graduating class list. Maybe he'd have a phone number and a name for me by then. And maybe the names would all match up — truck owner, college graduate, cell phone owner. And lastly, maybe, just maybe, he'd have found an address. An address at which we could visit the dog thief and reclaim Beatrice. Now wouldn't that be terrific? Ha, I told myself. Things rarely worked out that neatly, in my experience. Still, wasn't it necessary to hope? After all wasn't it that thing with feathers, that perched in your soul, and . . . and . . . fooey. The rest of the quote eluded me. I was too tired to search my mental database for it.

"*Raff*," opined Trey from the depths of my bedclothes.

"I couldn't have put it better myself," I told him, snapping off my bedside light and snuggling into my flannel sheets. "Good night, guy."

TUESDAY

CHAPTER 14

I had just climbed out of the shower and was drying the condensation from my bathroom mirror, glancing critically at my face in the process — longish face, grey eyes, wavy brown hair, with a raffish white swoosh over one temple courtesy of a chunk of flying metal door from my last case — when my phone buzzed.

"For crap's sake!" I yelled. "Can a girl not even have privacy in her own bathroom?" Then I looked at the number. Ro. *Uh oh. Not good.*

"What's up, kiddo?" I asked, a sinking feeling in my stomach. Who calls at seven in the morning anyhow?

"Izzy's freaking out," Ro said. "The dog thief called and told her there'll be no video today or any other day. He wants the money Thursday morning. They'll make the transfer then, he says. He wanted to do it today, but Izzy convinced him she didn't have the money from her car sale yet. So it'll be Thursday. I listened to the call — she put hm on speaker. He's in one very shitty mood. Something must have happened, I'm guessing. Can you —"

"Come by? Sure. I'm just getting dressed. I have to gather my wits, then I'll be there. Can you calm Izzy down?"

"I'll try. I was going to take her out for breakfast as soon as we'd seen today's video of Beatrice, but now . . . well, now she's pacing."

"Hmm. Do what you can. Some calming herbal tea, maybe. I'll be there as soon as I'm able. Oh, and have Izzy send me the call, assuming she taped it. I want to listen to it. And Ro? How are you? How are your wounds?"

"Ha," she said. "I'm okay. The dog bite hurts like hell, but I'm keeping it clean, as Nurse Ratched instructed. And I haven't had to take any of those serious drugs we picked up. Distracting Izzy is helping me keep my mind off my wounds, as you call them. We've been playing *Fortnite*. I thought she'd like that, given her military background."

"Does she?"

"She loves it," Ro said. "I'm afraid I've led her into evil ways, though. Did you know she wants to work with veterans who have PTSD and need service dogs? I think that's great. Training the dogs really appeals to her, she says. She wants to work for the group that gave her Beatrice. I thought we could pay them a visit. That would be a good distraction. But she's too agitated today."

"Understandable," I said. "How about you? Are you missing class?"

"No. I don't have classes on Tuesdays. I'm supposed to be writing a paper, though. I'm kind of doing research while Izzy's playing *Fortnite*."

"Thanks, Ro," I said. "You're a good egg."

In my bedroom, I pulled on jeans, a heavy pale blue turtleneck — the weather outside looked grey and iffy — found clean socks in a drawer, jammed my feet into sneakers, then I was ready for the day. Following the wonderful smell of coffee brewing and something baking, I made my way to the kitchen where Aliya, dressed in purple plaid pyjama bottoms, an oversized mauve sweatshirt, and sporting a medium-serious case of bed head, was buttering bread for Tris's lunchtime sandwiches. I poured myself a mug of coffee and was about to sit at the kitchen table when Aliya handed me a knife and an apple.

"Cut this into quarters, will you?" she said. "I'm trying to keep an eye on the quiche in the oven and make Tris's lunch at the same time. I'm not great at multi-tasking." She yawned. "And I'm kind of beat."

"Quiche?" I said, joining her at the kitchen counter. "Did you bake? I'm impressed."

"No," she said. "Well, yes, but not today. Last week. I made three quiches and froze them." She yawned again. "Wow. Excuse me."

"Maybe I should make that lunch and you should go back to bed. Late night in the book cover design department?"

She shook her head. "No. Once I got started running down my list of college websites, I decided what the heck, why not look at all of them? I figured you and Miranda would have other things to do and might, well, forget. So I did it. I'll be okay. I just need some more coffee."

Fooey. She was absolutely right. I hadn't exactly forgotten — just told myself last night that I'd do my part first thing in the morning. And then Ro had called, and, okay, yeah, I'd forgotten.

"*Mea culpa*," I said. "I did forget. I got an early phone call from Ro. There's panic *chez* Izzy. Understandably. The dog thief won't be sending a video. He wants the money Thursday morning."

"You're kidding!" she said. "But we don't know where he is or who he is. We need more time!"

"Well, we won't be getting it." I quartered and cored the apple, wrapped it, and put it in Tris's plastic lunch box, adding a couple of chocolate chip cookies from a plate on the counter and a few cheese sticks from the fridge.

"Do you think kids really eat their own lunches?" I asked her. "Or do they trade around? I was a bad kid. I traded my lovingly-made egg sandwiches for yummier things like American cheese slices. Velveeta, I think. Frankenfood. I loved cheese. Hated eggs. Fortunately, other kids thought egg salad was exotic."

However, Aliya wasn't to be distracted by my tales of schoolgirl lunchtime misadventures. She shook her head and took a seat at the table. "I found the college," she said. "North Island Technical Institute. Their school color is kind of unique. Not a bright Kelly green, more a muted, dusty green. Definitely the green of the dog thief's sweatshirt. Anyhow, NITI is a rather specialized place. They train veterinary assistants. And other kinds of medical assistants — phlebotomists, dental assistants. Fortunately, NITI is not a big college. The list of that year's graduates can't be long. But we don't have time to check out every single name. And when we get it, we have nothing to check the list against!"

I poured another mugful of coffee. "You're right, we don't. Not yet," I said. "It's maddening. But right now, I'm going to my office to call Edgar. Maybe, just maybe, he's pried something loose. Oh, can you take Tris to school this morning? You'll have to detour and pick up Dani on the way. Tris will show you where she lives." When she looked at me curiously, I said, "We're saving her from a creep on the bus. I'll explain later. Oh, and I'm not sure I can get the girls from school this afternoon."

"Just let me know," Aliya said. "I can do it if you can't."

"Okay, thanks," I told her. "And remember, it's Tuesday. Tris has some kind of after-school story-writing class that she's started attending, so she won't be ready until four or so."

"Of course I remember!" Aliya exclaimed. "I'm excited that she might want to become a writer. Maybe even another Margaret Atwood. But what about Dani?"

"Dani goes to writing class, too," I said. "The two of them are joined at the hip." I looked at my watch. "I'm thinking I need to call Miranda now. So if I don't get back for breakfast, will you hug Tris for me? And will you wrap up a couple pieces of quiche? I need to take one as a peace offering for getting Miz Blake out of bed so early."

In my office, I looked at my phone and saw that Izzy had forwarded the dog thief's call. I listened. It was the usual blather, delivered through the spooky voice-changing app, which I'd expected. What I hadn't expected, though, was that the call originated from a different number than the last call. I shrugged. Edgar had explained that phone numbers could nest inside each other much like Russian dolls — people could have several numbers, but there was one that was the 'real' traceable number. I'd let Edgar know about this new number and hope it meant nothing.

Much to my surprise, when I tried to get Edgar, I got his voice mail. Hmmf. Well, it was first thing in the morning — the little twerp had probably just gone to bed. I'd long ago given up trying to figure out Edgar's diurnal rhythms: he was up when most people were down, and vice versa. I left a message asking him to please find a list of the North Island Technical Institute's two thousand and four graduating class, and email it to me. I also urged him to make renewed efforts to persuade his colleague at BC Telecom or wherever to cough up the dog thief's *real* phone number . . . and the address associated with his credit card account. I put in a plea for the owner of the black RAM 3500 also. Finally, I gave him the phone number from today's early-morning call to Izzy. I hoped I didn't sound too desperate, but I was beginning to feel that way. Overwhelmed, too. Then I put in a phone call to Miranda.

"Mmf," she said. "Miz Yeats. It's so . . . early."

"It is," I agreed. "But, quoting you from Sunday: 'Houston, we have a problem.'"

She groaned. "Not another one."

"Afraid so," I said, and described the contents of Ro's phone call.

"Shit," she said pithily. "So we only have two more days, not three. What the hell's the rush, I wonder?"

"Good question," I said. "Something's upset him, though. I can't think he's caught wind of the fact that we're on his trail."

"Oh, he might have," Miranda said. "Connie already put the video on our Facebook page and tweeted it to everyone who follows us. The video and the plea for Beatrice's whereabouts have already been retweeted over a thousand times. Half the city, it seems, knows that a veteran's PTSD dog is missing. The outrage is almost palpable. Maybe the dog thief's seen the video. If so, he knows that someone's breathing down his neck."

"That would explain the accelerated timeline," I said. "Anyhow, Aliya found the dog thief's college, and I have Edgar working on a list of graduates. But unless we have something to match the list to —"

"We're just spinning our wheels."

"Unfortunately, yes. So I thought we'd better get spinning early this morning," I said. "I'm on my way. And while I'm en route I wondered if you'd give some thought to the threat in the extortionist's note."

"Which threat? That vile BS about Sinjar?"

"No. His threat about sending Beatrice to a fate worse than death. Bad ends for animals — that's more your department than mine. Can you scratch your head about this? All I can think of is that he'll abandon her up-island in the forest or sell her to the proprietor of a junkyard who'll make her live at the end of a chain." I sighed. "You know, I've been thinking . . . while we're waiting for information from Edgar, it might be helpful to work this puzzle from the other end also."

"From the other end? What do you mean?"

"Well, we're focusing on the dog thief. On identifying him and finding him. But do we really care about him?"

"Only insofar as he's the guy who has Beatrice," she said. "Oh, after we find Beatrice, he needs to get his butt kicked — by us and by the RCMP — but no, we don't care about him right now."

"Exactly," I said. "What if we could figure out this fate worse than death crap, and where it might take place. That might just be a figure of speech, an idle threat, but it might not. If he has something specific in mind, a plan, maybe we could — oh, I don't know," I broke off in frustration.

"Figure out what it is and thwart him. Get ahead of it. Sure, I can think of a couple of fates worse than death. Way worse than abandonment up-island or guarding junked cars. Hell, yes, we can talk about them. I'll throw on some clothes and unlock the side door to The Sanctuary. Just come on in."

"And here's something else that's been bothering me," I said. "Has the dog thief really thought through the logistics of the exchange? We talked a bit about this before and you mentioned money mules and wire transfers to Nigeria. Seems outlandish. But maybe no more outlandish than having Izzy leave a backpack full of cash or gold Canadian Maple Leafs in a crowded Starbucks or a remote ravine, or some ridiculous spy-novel scenario like that. I really don't get it, Miranda. He's made no mention of what form the money is to take: cash, a wire transfer, gold, Bitcoin. Cash seems way too risky — think exploding dye capsules or GPS trackers — and a wire transfer can be traced. Well, the cash can, too, if he wants, say hundred-dollar bills. Every bill has a serial number. We'd catch him sooner or later."

"Not to mention that the backpack-full-of-cash type of exchange rarely ends well. For the extortionist or the victim."

"That's a cheery thought," I said.

"Sorry," Miranda said. "It's the dirty rotten truth. We need to keep it from Izzy, though."

"Or not," I said. "At some point, if things look dire, we'll have to tell her."

"Yeah, we will. Okay, I'm going to get dressed. See you in a bit."

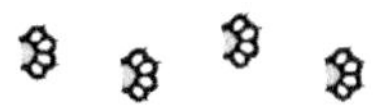

Fortunately, the weather held as I turned north out of Oak Bay, past U Vic, and onto the Pat Bay Highway. I was in a sufficiently filthy mood — all I needed was rain to tip me over the edge. Dark clouds the size of small islands scudded across a vanilla-colored sky, but so far they were keeping their precipitation to themselves. A short drive brought me to the little fir-lined road leading to Miranda's Sanctuary, and I turned in and parked, my optimism at a low ebb. If we couldn't pull this together soon, well . . . it didn't bear thinking about. All the psychotherapy Izzy had done, her hard work on PTSD, her physical therapy, her hopes for a halfway normal future . . . all down the drain because some greedy jerk thought he could score easy cash intimidating a veteran. It made me seethe, and I muttered a few calming words, trying to bring my blood pressure down.

My phone buzzed as I was about to get out of the car. *Edgar. Thank God.*

"You won't be entirely happy with me, sweetie," he said.

"Okay," I grumbled. "Tell me the part I *will* be happy about, Edgar."

"Well, I have the dog thief's phone number and I do have a name, but the address on the account is a post office box. In Sidney."

"Dammit. Okay, let me have the information," I said.

"The owner of the phone is Mohammed Saleh, and —"

"Him!" I yelled. "We're right back at Daesh again!"

"Daesh?" Edgar asked.

"Saleh is one of two guys on the RCMP's watch list who I decided to pass on because I assumed they were Arabic speakers. And Elizabeth Metheny assured me that the extortion note was written by a native English speaker. I guess she was wrong . . . or I was wrong . . . or . . . oh, for crap's sake," I trailed off in frustration.

"In any event, here's Saleh's post office box," he said. "Fourteen twenty. The main post office on Beacon Street in Sidney. Then, as a favor to you because I came up empty on his home address, I did a little exploration of a certain federal database and took a look at the address that Mr. Saleh listed on his box application. This is fairly specialized work, and I only do it for certain clients," he said, falling silent. I waited for him to continue, then realized, oh, for heaven's sake, he wanted praise. Edgar, Edgar.

"I can't believe the things you can turn up," I said, my admiration only partly feigned.

He sniffed. "Yes, well. This *was* more than moderately difficult."

"Edgar, I might kiss you," I said. "So you found his home address?"

"Indeed. It seems Saleh lives at an address in Sidney. Fern Street, number thirteen oh two."

"Sidney," I said. "So far from Victoria. I wonder why."

"Who knows, sweetie," he said. "But here's the bad news. The new phone number you gave me, the number the dog thief called from this morning, is a burner. It's not traceable. Probably he bought it at the local Kwik Mart for cash, and had them activate it for him."

"Shit," I said.

"Indeed," Edgar said. "My guess is that your boy Saleh is too nervous to use his own phone. And if he calls again, I bet it will be from a burner also. Maybe the same one. It hardly matters."

"Yeah," I groaned. "Miranda and I figured something's spooked him. But at least we have an address. You're one in a million, Edgar."

"Hmmf," he muttered, sounding almost embarrassed. Heavens, I thought. I didn't think Edgar could be embarrassed by flattery. Ah, well.

"I'm still working on the graduating class list you asked me for," he said. "I'll send that shortly. And the owners of black RAM 3500s. So that's it for now. Call me if you need anything else."

In Miranda's office, I surprised her in the act of hanging up her navy windbreaker. She looked bright and cheery — cream-colored sweatshirt with The Sanctuary's name and logo on the front and faded jeans. When I told her the results of my phone conversation with Edgar, she raised an eyebrow.

"The Saleh and Amad show," she said sarcastically. "I wondered if there weren't two people involved. One with the phone, taking the video, and one holding the newspaper up in front of Beatrice. So we are dealing with Daesh after all. I'd persuaded myself that we weren't. I'm truly disappointed in the RCMP. If these guys are hinky enough to merit surveillance, the Force needs to work harder on keeping their addresses up to date."

"No kidding," I said. "But I'm sure the Daesh guys aren't exactly eager for the RCMP to know where they are. Anyhow, Saleh made this morning's call from a burner phone. It's not traceable. Fortunately, he made the original call from his own phone, so Edgar was able to use that to get an address. Although he had to hack Canada Post's database to get it."

"A burner phone," she said, shaking her head. "He definitely knows we're onto him. I don't like it."

"Me neither," I said. "Want to go to Sidney?"

"You bet," she said. "We'll take the van, okay? Just in case we find a certain Labradoodle who needs rescuing. We're going to find these guys," she said confidently. "And if they're not there, well, I have faith that you have Plan B up your sleeve. You always do."

"Yeah?" I said, touched by her faith in me, and not wanting to admit that my sleeve was empty today.

"Yeah," she said. "So let's go."

CHAPTER 15

A quaint little seaside town at the northern end of the Saanich Peninsula, Sidney reminded me a great deal of Oak Bay before it was 'discovered.' Nestled on the edge of the Salish Sea, it has splendid views to the east of the Gulf Islands, the San Juans, and Mount Baker on the U.S. mainland. A town of about 10,000, it boasts an aquarium, a marina, the world-famous Butchart Gardens, a six-bookstore enclave called 'Booktown,' art galleries, terrific cafés, half the electric cars on the island, and the Swartz Bay Ferry Terminal, about a five minute drive north. It seemed an unlikely spot for the dog thief to claim as home, given that his previous address was an empty lot in downtown Victoria, but hey, what did I know.

As we drove north toward Sidney, the sea on our right, I realized that I felt . . . freer. Lighter. The Victoria traffic congestion was really getting to me. As was the construction of apartment complexes, businesses, strip malls, and, God help us, skyscrapers. It was damned depressing, all this paving paradise to put up parking lots. Fortunately, we left that behind as we drove north, and I felt my tight shoulder muscles relaxing.

"Trees," I said to Miranda. "Oaks. Evergreens — the murmuring pines and the hemlocks. Acres of salal. Thank God. Must Victoria keep bloody growing? Why does becoming Silicon Valley North have to mean deforestation? And deforestation means loss of bird and animal habitat, which is already happening. Are we proud of that? I think now and then of escaping up-island to, oh, Nanaimo. But it's gotten to be a pretty big place, too. Sidney is small and tidy. Perhaps I'll amend my relocation fantasies and consider Sidney."

"I didn't know you were dissatisfied with Oak Bay," Miranda said, sounding surprised.

"Yeah, I am. It's just come over me in the last year or so. You're lucky," I said, "living out of the city on your acreage. You'll never have a strip mall in your front yard. Or a bar. Jeez, the day the village council allowed that craft beer place to open up right around the corner from me on Oak Bay Avenue was the day I started thinking about Nanaimo. It didn't help that the beer joint got listed in all the tourist brochures, either. And there isn't enough parking. The patrons' cars overflow onto our street every night. Carp, carp," I said. "But I'm thoroughly sick of it."

"Well," Miranda said. "In that case, I have something to show you."

"Yeah?" I said.

"Later," she said mysteriously.

"Let's see if Saleh and Amad are where Edgar claims they are," I said. "Then, if they aren't, I think we need to brainstorm. There's a pretty nice café on the dock — the Seahorse Café — and we might get some breakfast there. Oh, and I promised Ro we'd drop in and talk to Izzy on our way back. But I think I'd like breakfast first."

"Do I hear pessimism in your voice?" Miranda asked.

"Oh, maybe a tad," I said. "I mean, these guys can't be world-class criminal masterminds, but we seem to be two steps behind them. The empty lot, the accelerated timeline, the burner phone . . ."

"Well, let's keep our fingers crossed," Miranda said. "First, Fern Street. Then the Slough of Despond."

"The Slough of Despond?" I said. "Isn't that one of my lines?"

"It is," she said, "but I've been hanging around you for so long it might as well be one of mine."

"Such an impressionable young lass," I tut-tutted. "Sad."

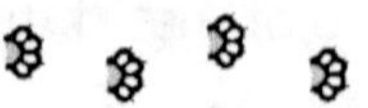

Sometimes I hate it when I'm right. The Fern Street address wasn't an empty lot, but it was an empty house. Through the curtainless front windows we could plainly see the furnitureless interior. I refrained from swearing while Miranda drove up in front of the modest, grey-painted bungalow and parked.

"No chain-link fence," she said. "No green grass, black truck, or white sign. And no Beatrice."

"Fooey," I said. "According to Edgar, this is the address that Saleh used on his post office box application. So he was here at one time. I'm beginning to feel like Ahab chasing the damned white whale. But I wonder . . ."

"You wonder what?" Miranda asked.

"The house next door. Probably someone's at home." I pointed to an elderly grey Toyota. "There's a car in the driveway. Neighbors usually like to blab — remember Audrey? Maybe this batch would like to blab about Saleh and Amad, their improperly parked cars, their loud radios, their yapping hounds, their dope-smoking on the patio, their wild parties. Whatever. Besides, they owe me money and I'm a little ticked."

"They owe you . . ." Miranda said, puzzled. Then, "Oh, I get it. Go for it. I'll stay here. Two of us might seem like a tag team."

After a knock and a brief wait, a pleasant-looking twenty-something young woman answered the door, auburn hair in a bun on top of her head, brown eyes curious. She zipped up her red sweat jacket and asked, "What can I do for you?"

"Hi," I said, offering my hand. "I'm Maud Gonne. I'm looking for the guys next door. I must have just missed them."

"Daphne," the young woman said, smiling, opening the door and shaking my hand. "Daphne Hammond. I'm about to go to work, so I just have a minute to talk. But, yeah, they moved out about a week ago."

"Darn it!" I said with feeling. "You wouldn't know where they went, would you?"

"Nope," she said. "They moved out one day when I was at work. I came home and the place was empty."

"Did they leave a forwarding address? For mail and so on? Stray packages?" I asked, hardly daring to hope.

Daphne shook her head. "Nope. In fact, Mohammed told me that he and Aziz were leaving. They sold all their stuff — had a big garage sale. He said they're not coming back. To Canada, I mean. So they're probably in a short-term rental while Mo finishes up at his work."

"I guess so," I said. *Mo, indeed.* "Any idea where they were planning to go?"

Daphne screwed up her face in concentration. "Mmm, yeah, but . . ."

"Iraq?" I guessed.

"That's it!" she exclaimed. "How did you know?"

"Just a lucky guess," I said. "Say, I wonder what they did with their dog."

"Dog?" Daphne said, frowning. "They never had a dog. Because Aziz is a Muslim. They think dogs are unclean. Mo — I don't think he was a Muslim, y'know, even though he has a Muslim name — Mo works with dogs, although of course he never brought any home."

"Aziz can be a bit of a pill," I ventured, testing the waters, betting Daphne wanted to gossip further.

"Yeah," she agreed. "But not Mo. He's really kind of sweet. And under that dumb blond beard, pretty good-looking. Like a regular Canadian. He might've dressed like a Muslim, but I don't think he was one. I mean, he even had a beer with me now and then when Aziz had gone to the mosque. And I never heard Mo speak Arabic. Maybe he was converting or something and Aziz was, like, his teacher?"

I was thunderstruck. Was Saleh actually a *Canadian*? I was about to try another tack when Daphne spoke up.

"What do you want with them, anyhow?" she asked.

"Well, Mo — Mohammed — owes me money," I invented. "I bought his dog or someone's dog and he hasn't handed it over. He either owes me the dog or the money I paid for it."

"Huh," Daphne said. "Well, maybe Mo's keeping it at his work. I don't think he'd rip you off. He's a nice guy."

I almost stopped breathing. "You don't happen to know where he works, do you?"

"Sorry, no. But, hey, do you want to leave a phone number?" she asked. "He has to come back."

"He does?"

"Uh huh. He left some big dog carriers in our garage. He needs to bring the truck from work to get them, he said."

I hardly dared hope. "The black one? The RAM?"

"Yup."

"Do you have a pen?" I asked. "Let me leave you my number."

She disappeared into the house and came back with a pen and a piece of paper.

As I scribbled my number for her, I said, "When he comes back, will you call me? I need to talk to him and I don't want him running off with my money, leaving me with no dog. It's probably just a misunderstanding."

"Sure," she said. "I can do that."

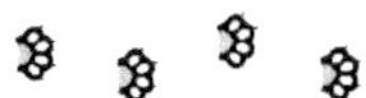

"Thank God for blabby neighbors," I told Miranda as we waited at the Seahorse Café for our food to arrive. "According to Daphne, Mohammed has a 'dumb blond beard,' looks like a Canadian, drinks, doesn't speak Arabic, drives his employer's truck sometimes — the black RAM — and works with dogs. And he's sweet and good-looking."

"Probably sends half his paycheck home to his mother, too," Miranda said wryly.

I snorted. "He wrote that extortion note, dammit. 'We are Daesh,' 'Long live the fighters.' What a pile of BS. Is he really with Daesh? Sweet, my Aunt Fanny."

Miranda frowned. "If only the neighbor had been able to cough up where he works."

"Or where he's living now. She said she thought the two of them were in some short-term rental while they're waiting to skip the country," I said.

"With Izzy's ten thousand dollars."

"Yeah. I guess the Islamic State won't reward them with seventy-two virgins apiece — I think that's reserved for jihadists who get offed and go to Paradise — but I bet they get more than an atta boy for bringing that much money to the cause."

"If we can find them, the RCMP will step in in a heartbeat," Miranda said. "Raising money here in Canada to send, or take, overseas to Daesh is one of the *verboten* activities."

"Yeah, but remember what we promised Mac."

"I do," she sighed. "We rat them out to the RCMP — or to Mac — *after* we find Beatrice. And now that we know, or think we know, that they're getting ready to flee to Iraq, God help us, the RCMP can just watch the airlines and pick them up at the airport."

"Right."

The breakfast we had ordered — scrambled eggs and hash browns for me, huevos rancheros for Miranda, and lots of toast and jam — arrived at that moment, and we cleaned our plates and sat back in our chairs. This was a dandy small café, I thought. Not too large — a few booths, maybe a dozen small oak tables and chairs — plenty of greenery, big windows, murmured conversation, the *whoosh* of the espresso machine, wonderful cooking smells. Heck, maybe I'd have breakfast here once in a while if I were to move from Oak Bay, which, I realized, was something I thought about more and more. Sometimes things don't become real until you talk about them with another person. Well, maybe I'd made my relocation yearnings real by airing them with Miranda.

Over second cups of coffee, Miranda said, "Want to consider that 'fate worse than death' stuff? I've been thinking of the things that might mean."

"Oh?" I said.

"Uh huh."

"Okay. Tell me. What are some of these fates?"

"Dogfighting for one," she said, looking at me evenly. "Beatrice would make a dandy bait dog. She's gentle and trusting. Not at all aggressive."

"Jesus, Miranda," I said, putting my head in my hands.

"Sorry," she said. "But you asked."

"What else?" I asked.

"Ending up in a lab, the subject of some cruel and unnecessary experiment. Or having her fur harvested for trim on clothing. Or maybe just being sold on Kijiji for whatever her breed will bring. After all, our guys need pocket change for when they get to Iraq, right?"

"Okay, which of these fates can we check out?"

"Let me call Connie and get her to watch Kijiji and Craigslist for anyone offering Labradoodles for sale. That will short-circuit one of the fates we're worried about."

"Next?" I asked.

"There's a fur dealer in Chinatown," she said. "He has a little factory. Makes cat- and dog-fur trimmed jackets, then exports them to China. We can check and see if he's been offered Beatrice."

"For God's sake," I said. "Is that even legal? Buying a dog for . . . that?"

"Sadly, yes," she said.

"But why would your fur dealer tell us anything?"

Miranda smiled, baring her teeth. "Let's just say he owes me a favor from when he stepped in it with the RCMP several years ago. Ditto the dog-fighting guys up-island. In fact," she said, "I think I need to take a little drive."

"Up-island?"

"Yeah. Probably by myself." She grimaced. "The dogfighters aren't exactly a friendly bunch. But one of them . . . well, one of them was just a kid. For some reason, he got to me. And I never did think he'd gone completely to the dark side. I offered him the chance to walk away from the arrest that was imminent for the dogfighting ring. I told him he needed to move to civilization, get a job, and stay away from his damned dogfighting friends."

"Oh?" I asked. "How did that work out?"

She waggled her hand. "He's trying. Calls me up now and then for moral support. Unfortunately, the arrest fell apart, and the dogfighters just reconstituted themselves in another location. He can't quite break things off with them, he says. One of them's his brother. Family's hard to walk away from, I guess, even if that family's engaged in doing something despicable. Anyhow, I figure he could find out, if he doesn't already know, if the dogfighters have Beatrice. Or are about to get her."

"God, how awful," I said.

"Yeah," she said glumly, staring out the window. "Just about the last thing I want to do with my life is to revisit dogfighting hell. But for Beatrice and Izzy, I'll do it."

I couldn't think of anything commiserative to say, so I said nothing.

Miranda continued, "Connie can call the fur dealer in Chinatown and remind him of his, ah, indebtedness to me. She'll remember the episode all too well, and I'm certain that if she presses him, he'll tell her if he's been offered a dog resembling Beatrice. If this is one of the 'fates worse than death' that the note was referring to, Saleh would've had to make some overtures. The fur dealer, dogfighters, labs . . . something. The fur guy is just a businessman. He doesn't want more trouble with the law. I don't think we need to show up there. The kid associated with the dogfighters . . . he's a little more problematical. Anton is his name. I'm not sure if he's still working at that job I rustled up for him or if he's gone back to dogfighting. So I need to pay him a visit. And if he has gone back to dogfighting," she set her lips in a grim line, "as soon as I find out about Beatrice, I'm going to kick his butt."

I thought about this for a minute. "Do you feel okay visiting Anton by yourself?"

"Okay as in safe?"

"Yeah."

"Sure," she said. "Perfectly safe."

I wasn't as sure about that as Miranda seemed to be, but it was her call. "Okay," I said. "I have a little job to do while you're up-island." I looked at my watch. Ten o'clock. "Stores ought to be open by now. I need to make a few calls to pet stores, then go pick something up. I've just thought of this while we've been eating."

"Want to share?" Miranda asked.

I frowned. "I need a GPS pet tracker. I plan to tape it up inside one of those big dog carriers Daphne said Mo left in her garage. I'll put the app on my phone. Then, when he comes for them — assuming he does — we can track them. To where he works. And cross our fingers that's where he's stashed Beatrice."

"God, yes," Miranda said. "We're running out of wheres. She wasn't here in Sidney, and I doubt if she's in Saleh and Amad's rental. That leaves . . . Saleh's work, wherever that is. Or . . ."

"Or the back of Anton's scuzzy garage waiting for the dogfighters to come get her," I said gloomily. "Mohammed may already have gotten rid of her."

"That's what I'm going to find out," Miranda said. "Once we've eliminated the Chinese fur dealer and the dogfighters, we'll know something. We'll know where she *isn't*. Then, if your pet tracker idea works, we may know where Mohammed has taken the carriers. If we're lucky, Beatrice will be there, too."

"Agreed," I said. "So we divide and conquer. Drop me back at The Sanctuary? I need my car. I'll go get the pet tracker, stick it on one of the carriers, then pay Ro and Izzy a visit. I'm overdue there. Also, I need to ask some questions of the strip-mall businesses across the hedge from Izzy's and Audrey's apartments. Someone might just have seen something."

"Why don't I join you at Izzy's?" Miranda asked. "Talking to Anton shouldn't take long — half an hour up there and back. Then I can give you a hand with the strip-mall businesses. Let's get a couple of coffees to go. I'll call Connie, then we'll be on our way."

CHAPTER 16

At Animal Crackers, on the main drag in Sidney, I parked out front, then hurried inside, hopeful that the salesperson I had talked to on the phone really did have the GPS tracker I wanted. The door tinkled shut behind me and I walked into a pet supplies store crammed to bursting with cages, carriers, leashes, collars, cat trees, dog beds, fragrant bales of cedar shavings for small animal bedding, racks of pet clothing, bins of toys, and a center aisle whose shelves were lined with more varieties of canned food and kibble than I imagined could exist.

An enthusiastic brown and white Corgi hurried to meet me, a squeaky toy in his mouth.

"Hi, are you Kieran?" asked a plump, dark-haired woman dressed in jeans and a denim shirt with a red Animal Crackers logo on the left chest pocket. She came out from behind the front counter and shook my hand. "I'm Sandy Greene," she said, pushing a wing of hair back behind one ear. "I own Animal Crackers. We don't sell many of the trackers you described. They're expensive. But we do have a few in stock. I got them out for you. They're here behind the counter. Three different models. If you tell me what you need the tracker for, maybe I can help you choose."

The Corgi followed us hopefully as we headed back behind the front counter, chomping his squeaky toy now and then.

"Go lie down, Milton," Sandy told him kindly. "We'll play later. Dogs," she said to me apologetically.

"No problem," I said. "I have cats. They're just as bad." Although they weren't. No self-respecting cat would be caught dead carrying a toy around, begging for playtime and treats. Really.

"So here are the trackers," she said. "Two are good over short distances — a mile for one, seven miles for the other — but this one is virtually limitless." She picked up one of the trackers and handed it to me. It was plastic, about two inches by two inches and shaped like a paw, with a little hook to fasten it to a collar.

"Heavy," I said, hefting it in my palm.

"A little, yes," she said. "This one is better for dogs than cats because of the weight. But if your dog takes a hike and ends up in, oh, Edmonton, as long as he's within range of a cell tower, it's worth its weight in, well, anything. The GPS app will tell you exactly where he is. You can use Google Maps to blow up the location on your phone and pinpoint it down to the street number."

"Sounds good," I said. "How about battery life?"

"Seven days," she said. "Then you just pop it into one of your computer's USB ports and recharge it."

"Well, I only need it to hold a charge for a day, maybe two. Is it charged now?"

Sandy nodded. "Yes. I use it for demonstration purposes."

"Can I buy this one?" I asked. "I need to hurry off to attach it to . . . the item I need tracked."

"Oh. Then you don't intend to put it on your dog's collar?"

"No, I have something else that needs tracking."

She gave me an odd look and I decided to spin a little story. God knows, I couldn't tell her the truth — she'd be horrified. Canadian Extremist Travellers, the RCMP, jihadists, stolen dogs, extortion, fates worse than death. If I weren't in the middle of all this, I might not believe it myself.

"Someone stole property from a friend of mine," I said. "I volunteered to get it back. But so far the thief's been eluding me. I know where he's stashed what he stole, and he's due to come get it soon. I thought if I attached the pet tracker to the property, I could track him to his home, call the police, and they'd catch him with the stolen goods. I need to recover what he stole for my friend, but the thief needs to pay for what he did, too," I invented.

"Crime and punishment," Sandy said, clearly interested. "A little amateur detective work. Well, the tracker would work for that, too," she said.

I decided to embellish my story a bit more, as Sandy seemed a sympathetic soul.

"I just can't find this guy," I said, shaking my head. "It's very frustrating."

Sandy nodded, brown eyes concerned.

"Apparently he 'works with dogs.' Probably locally. But I don't know Sidney very well."

"You know," Sandy said thoughtfully, "if he 'works with dogs' here in Sidney, or someplace close by, there are only so many possibilities."

"I wondered about that," I said. "What in heck does 'works with dogs' mean anyhow? Where? A pet supplies store, a vet's, a groomer's, a dog walker's business? They would all fit."

"Hmm, yes," Sandy said. "Or doggie daycare? Maybe a breeder?"

"Maybe," I said. "I thought I'd just sit in my car and search Google. Then start making calls. I have to do something while I'm waiting around for him to pick up the stolen property."

Sandy said, a conspiratorial smile on her face, "I know most of the dog-related businesses around here. Many of us run ads together — I've got a pretty good list. Google doesn't index them all, and even some of the places in the Yellow Pages have gone out of business. And others never took out an ad. I could let you have my list. It would definitely save you some time."

I raised my eyebrows. "That would be terrific."

"I'll need a few minutes to go print it," she said.

"And I need to go tape the pet tracker to the stolen property," I said. "Why don't I do that, then come back for your list? Is there a hardware store close by?"

"Just at the end of the street," Sandy said. "Here, let me go online and register the tracker for you. You can put the app on your phone when you get back. Then you'll be able to trace the tracker from your phone, or call up the tracker company's website on your computer at home."

While I waited, Sandy registered the tracker at the company's website and sent the app to my phone. "Here's your user name and password," she said, writing them on the back of a business card. "It's all set up. And if you like," she said, "you can use my office to make phone calls when you come back. I'm happy to help."

I was genuinely touched. Perhaps I ought to amend my jaded view of people, I thought. They don't *all* live down to my expectations. "That's very generous of you," I said. "I'll take you up on that offer."

At 1304 Fern Street — a grey-painted bungalow the twin of Mohammed and Aziz's — Daphne had gone to work. Or I hoped she had. At any rate, the elderly grey Toyota was no longer in her driveway. I parked my car in front of Mohammed's former rental, then walked across the brown, crunchy lawn and around the far side of the house, hesitating when I reached the weedy, overgrown backyard. I looked apprehensively over to Daphne's house, but everything seemed quiet. No lights were showing. I walked down Daphne's driveway to her garage, a quiver in my stomach — the quiver I always felt when I was about to break the law. Still, there was no help for it today. I decided not to try to heave up the overhead garage door, but instead to investigate the side door which faced Saleh and Amad's yard. I tried the knob, and to my surprise, it turned. And then I was inside Daphne's garage. One small window in the far wall, plus a window in the door through which I had just entered, provided a pitiful amount of light, but enough for me to see what I needed to see. The interior of the garage was pretty neat — the floor swept, the walls free of cobwebs. Along one wall was a broom, a lawn mower and two bicycles — oops. Did Daphne have a roommate? I wondered. I hoped not. Along the other wall was a set of metal shelves with garden tools, bug spray, bamboo stakes, tomato cages, fertilizer, and other things you might use in the garden if you believed you had a green thumb. I harbored no such belief. My thumbs, both of them, were decidedly black.

Against the back was a cairn of three off-white dog carriers, with the letters PROPERTY OF E.A.R. printed in black on their sides. I ground my teeth in frustration. What was E.A.R. anyhow, and why in hell couldn't the establishment have thoughtfully spelled out its name for me? I kneeled down in front of the dog carriers, fished the pet tracker and duct tape out of one pocket of my jacket, ripped off a length of grey tape, lay on the floor with my head and shoulders inside one of the carriers, and taped the tracker firmly to the roof of the carrier. There, I told myself. Now, come get the damned things, Mohammed.

Back at Animal Crackers, I sat in my car for a moment checking the tracker app on my phone and was reassured to see it blinking as Sandy told me it would. Just because I'm a little paranoid, I tapped on it and a map opened up, showing me with a red diamond the street location of the tracker. I swiped the diamond and the little map enlarged showing Fern Street as well as the neighboring streets. Good.

"Here's the list," Sandy said as I walked back into the shop. "Go on back — take a left at the humungous pile of dog kibble — and you'll find my office. I left my computer on for you in case you need to use it."

Milton showed me the way into Sandy's office, and I took a seat at her desk, phone in hand, prepared to make my way down her list. I noted that there were several dog breeders, an artist who came to one's home to do portraits, a dog behaviorist, a dog trainer, a poop scooper, a maker of homemade doggie treats, a knitter of dog sweaters, an author of dog mysteries, a pet tag maker, and several other dog-related businesses. No E.A.R. None of them seemed quite right, but I dutifully started phoning. After half an hour, I'd finished the list. No one named Mohammed worked at any of the businesses, although the dog artist and the knitter would have to get back to me after they picked up their messages.

"Fooey, Milton," I said, leaning back in Sandy's chair, looking around dispiritedly. On the wall was a large poster advertising 2017's Dog Days of Christmas fundraiser — a bazaar featuring a bunch of local doggie businesses, including Animal Crackers, that had joined forces to sell goods and services to the community for the benefit of local dog nonprofits. The corporate sponsor was Hill's Science Diet. "Hmmf," I muttered, betting that Hill's had given away hundreds of trial packets of dog kibble and attracted dozens of new customers, which was, of course, the point of their sponsorship. Don't be cynical, Kieran, I told myself. As well as good PR, the bazaar seemed like a kind-hearted, charitable effort by local dog-related businesses. My gaze traveled idly down the poster to a row of photos along the bottom depicting the nonprofits that would benefit from the Dog Days.

"What?" I yelled, sitting up straight in Sandy's chair, startling Milton out of a snooze in his doggie bed. There in the middle of the row of photos of representatives of dog nonprofits — smiling people with dogs in their arms, standing in front of vans or their rescue establishments — was a photo of a low, unattractive cinder-block structure with a blue metal roof. That wasn't what made me leap out of Sandy's desk chair and rush over to the poster, though. Nope, it was the green lawn, the chain-link fence, the white sign with faded lettering, and the black pickup truck in the parking lot. Damn. I was seeing the backdrop for Mohammed's video of Beatrice.

With an apology, I vaulted over Milton's doggie bed and hustled out of the little office.

"The poster?" Sandy asked as I hurried up to the front counter, explaining about the poster on the wall of her office. "Oh, *that* poster. It's a few years old. The Dog Days event took place just before I bought Animal Crackers. I don't know the names of the nonprofits that benefitted from the bazaar. And we didn't repeat it, so . . ."

I groaned. "Could we find out who they are?"

She frowned. "Well, I'm pretty sure Hill's put the poster together and paid for its printing. I could ask Brad, our Hill's rep. Or one of the other businesses. Greg Sammons, the poop scooper, for instance. I know him pretty well. Sure, I can make some calls for you." She looked at me, clearly intrigued. "Did you find a clue in the poster? Maybe where your thief works?"

I tried not to giggle. A clue indeed.

"Maybe," I said, part of me regretting that I couldn't tell this perfectly nice woman the truth. "Thanks a million. The photo I'm interested in is right in the middle of the bottom row. It's the cinder-block place behind the chain-link fence. The one with the blue roof."

"All right," Sandy said. "I'll start phoning right away. Someone will know. I'll go back to my office."

My phone buzzed. Ro.

"Say, are you —"

"Coming over?" I said, finishing her question for her.

"Yeah. Sorry to be a nag, but Izzy's literally in the closet and I don't know what to do for her. She's sort of buried herself in a nest of pillows and blankets — I guess that's where she went when she had flashbacks to the Griffon accident, before she got Beatrice. If it were me, I wouldn't want to be closed up in a small dark space with no way out, but what do I know? Maybe it's comforting."

"Must be," I said. "Flashbacks . . . I don't know what to do either. Did anything specific happen to set her off?"

"Oh yeah. The dog thief called again. Apparently, he's decided how he wants to be paid. Izzy freaked out after that."

"Ah," I said. "So how does he want to be paid?"

"One-ounce Canadian Maple Leaf gold coins. He told Izzy to go to her bank, get them, then put them in a black backpack. He was very precise about that."

"But the exchange is still on?"

"Yup."

"I don't suppose he said anything about where it was to take place?"

"Nope. The call was just about the gold coins and the backpack."

"Okay," I said. "I'm in Sidney right now, but I can be on my way in a minute. As for Izzy, maybe just sit outside the closet and talk to her. Let her know someone friendly is there. Say, Ro, did you guys eat?"

"No. I thought while I was waiting for you that I might sneak out and pick something up, but I'm glad I didn't. Izzy would've been alone here when the phone call came in."

"She needs to eat," I said. "And so do you. This is stressful enough without starving yourselves. Just as soon as I thank someone who's been a great help to me here, I'm leaving for Izzy's. I'll pick up some food on my way there. Be there in twenty minutes."

CHAPTER 17

On the drive from Sidney back into town, I picked up coffee and an assortment of sandwiches at Sandwich Express, then had to fight down a serious case of the screaming meemies. I'd put Aliya, Edgar, Miranda, and now Sandy to work ferreting out information, but I really did need some of the pigeons to come home to roost. Right now, I had too few facts, and the ones I did have were adding up to a big fat zero. Oh, I had a name, Mohammed Saleh, but so far he was proving damned elusive. There were only really three questions to be answered — well, and a host of secondary questions — and I was nowhere close to answering them.

One, where the hell was Beatrice? Once Miranda returned from up-island, I fervently hoped we'd be able to cross dogfighters off our list. And once Connie reported in about the fur dealer, maybe we'd be able to eliminate that fate worse than death also. Assuming so, what did that leave? The place in the Dog Days poster, the place that looked a whole lot like the backdrop for the video Izzy had been sent of Beatrice? Was that E.A.R.? And was that where Mo 'worked with dogs'? That crummy cinder-block building? What fate worse than death could await her there?

Question number two: was Mo, that sweet guy, really planning to return for the dog carriers? A man who would write an extortion note designed to scare Izzy half to death with that disgusting Sinjar reference, and terrify her that Beatrice was going to meet some unimaginably horrid fate . . . did I really think someone like that was going to thoughtfully return three dog carriers as if they were overdue library books? He may have told Daphne that was his plan, but was it? My clever pet tracker idea might well prove to be a bust.

And question number three: where was Mohammed? Right now. At work? Or at home in his short-term rental, packing his socks and underwear in preparation for leaving the country? And how the hell did he think he was going to get his gold coins out of B.C.? He'd have to take several connecting flights to get to Iraq, if that's where he and Aziz were going, but he sure as hell wouldn't be able to fly with the coins. So that eliminated the Victoria airport and left what . . . driving across the U.S. border at Blaine, Washington, where he would risk a car or a luggage search? Nope. My candidate for Mohammed's border crossing was the BC Ferries from Sidney to Anacortes, Washington. The last time I'd taken one of the ferries, there was only a cursory customs and immigration check — a couple of questions and an ID check right in the ferry line. I didn't even have to get out of my car. Then, once Mohammed was in the U.S. with all that gold, maybe he'd be joined by the rest of his cabal of jolly jihadists who could high-five each other about ripping off the evil female Griffon pilot to advance the holy war against the infidel. Then they could divide up the loot and figure out how to get gold coins one by one out of the U.S. That's what I would do. But then, I wasn't a criminal mastermind, was I?

Ro met me at Izzy's front door, took the bag of food from me, then pointed to the hall leading to the bedrooms.

"She's back there," Ro said. "I was thinking . . . could she have an emergency session with her therapist? I'm worried about her. She's awake, but she has shrieking fits. Not crying fits . . . more like muffled screaming from anger and frustration. Fury, I guess. But what about medication? Does she have anything for emergencies? Xanax maybe?"

"Let me go back and talk to her," I said. "Sit down and eat something. How's your leg?"

"Oh, it's all right. It's my arm that's aggravating. It's itchy under the cast. But I'll survive." Ro grinned. "That'll teach me to try my hand at sleuthing. I'll leave that to you in future."

"Ha," I said.

In Izzy's bedroom, I saw that she had emerged from the closet and was now wrapped in a comforter on her bed. Her eyes were closed and she seemed to be sleeping. I thought this was a good sign. I pulled her bedroom door mostly closed and went out to the kitchen to join Ro.

"Can you tell me any more about the phone call?" I asked Ro. "Did she record it?"

She shook her head, hastily swallowing a bite of her sandwich and washing it down with coffee. "No. He took Izzy by surprise. Apparently, he just said to get the coins and the black backpack and wait for further instructions tomorrow. I heard Izzy try to ask him a question, but I think he just hung up on her." Ro looked at me curiously. "Are you going to tell her to do it? Get the coins?"

"Certainly not," I said. "The black backpack, yes. I was hoping you could go out shopping for one. But the gold, definitely not."

Ro relaxed. "Good. I knew you'd have a plan for that."

I restrained myself from laughing. A plan for that? We'd see.

"Did Izzy take her phone into the bedroom with her?" I asked.

Ro shook her head. "No. It's over there on the kitchen counter."

I fetched her phone and took a look at the last call — the number was the same as the call from the dog thief's burner phone. I snorted. Paranoid but consistent.

"Any help?" Ro said.

"Nope," I told her. "Same burner phone as last time. We won't catch him that way."

"What *do* we know about him?" Ro asked.

"Not very bloody much, Ro. His name is Mohammed Saleh. He 'works with dogs,' according to his neighbor. Maybe at a place called E.A.R.," I said, explaining the crates. "Until a few days ago he was living in Sidney, but he and his jihadist buddy Aziz Amad moved. So, not only do I not know where he works, I have no idea where he's living. His phone calls come from burners." I grimaced. "Mr. Elusive."

"So are we at a dead end?" Ro asked, sounding worried.

"Only temporarily," I said with more confidence than I felt. "Aliya, Edgar, and a woman I met in Sidney are asking questions for me. My experience has been that if you turn over enough rocks, something useful often scuttles out. My only concern is that it scuttles out in time. Brother, I wish Izzy had gone to Mac sooner. Ah well." I sighed. "If Izzy is going to sleep for a while, I think I'll go across the street and pop through the hedge. I want to find out if the convenience store owner has any videotape of the area behind his store in the wee hours of the morning."

"Good idea," said Ro. "I'll keep an eye on Izzy."

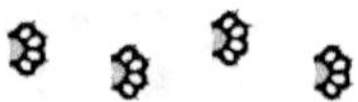

At the back of the convenience store, in the little parking lot, I hesitated. Maybe I didn't need to go bother the owner. A young guy in jeans, a black long-sleeved T-shirt with a green cannabis leaf on it, a red knitted wool cap with earflaps, and dark-rimmed glasses was busy breaking up cardboard boxes and tossing them into a dumpster. He tossed in one final box, then sat down on the store's back steps and took a rolled joint out of a pocket of his jeans. Must be break time, I figured.

"How's it going?" I asked.

"Going okay," he said, rolling his cigarette between his fingers in preparation for lighting up.

I held out my hand. "I'm Kieran Yeats. I'm an investigator looking into a theft that occurred about a week ago from one of the apartments on the other side of the hedge. I was wondering: does the store owner have a video camera that records this little lot at night?"

The kid shook my hand. "Gavin Cook," he said. "Nah, Ajay doesn't have a camera. But I bet you're investigating the weird drone guy." He lit his joint, took a toke, then offered it to me.

"Gorilla Glue," he said, blowing out smoke. "Great for relaxing."

Lordy, I thought, taking the joint and pretending to take a puff. Marijuana — I hadn't smoked it since my university days . . . except it was illegal then. How times have changed.

"The drone guy?" I asked Gavin, handing him back the joint.

"Yeah. About two weeks ago, a guy started showing up late at night. Well, early in the morning. I was coming in to work at four that week. I have a weird study schedule," he explained. "I'm a U Vic student. Anyhow, the guy drove an old beat-up brown Honda. Parked it over there by the hedge. Every night he'd drive up, get the drone out of the back of his car, and launch it." Gavin took another puff. "I figured he was taking pictures of someone in one of the apartments across the street, you know, maybe a girlfriend cheating on him."

"Hmm," I said. "Did you talk to him?"

"No," Gavin said. "I figured it was better if he didn't see me. I didn't want any trouble. So I hung out behind the dumpster until he took off. A drone at four in the morning?" He shook his head. "It was too weird."

"Could you see . . . was the guy wearing a green hoodie?" I asked, pretty certain of the reply I'd get.

"Green, yeah. A kind of murky green, but green. Every night. The same hoodie. How did you know?"

"Investigator's intuition," I said, smiling.

Gavin nodded. "That's cool. Was it drone guy who stole something?"

"Yup."

"So he was, like, using his drone to scope out the place he was going to rob?"

"Something like that," I said.

"Bummer," Gavin said with feeling.

"Yeah. Say, you didn't happen to notice a license plate, did you?"

"Nah," Gavin said. "I just kind of chilled behind the dumpster, reading, until the guy left. Ajay keeps his back lights on all night." He took another puff, then carefully stubbed the joint out on the side of the dumpster, fished a piece of foil out of his jeans, wrapped the joint in the foil, then put it back in his pocket.

I sighed. Well, nothing was going to crawl out from under this rock, despite what I said to Ro.

"Say, do you want a Coke?" Gavin asked. "Ajay provides all the sodas I could ever want. He's a pretty good boss. Lets me come in whenever I can to do the recycling. I'm going inside to get a Coke. I could get one for you, too."

I smiled. "No thanks, Gavin. I need to get back to . . . investigating."

"Good luck," he called as I crossed the parking lot and walked back through the laurel hedge to the little cul-de-sac. "Hope you catch him."

As I was opening the gate to Izzy's front yard, I realized I'd left my phone in my car. As I went to fetch it, it buzzed. Miranda.

"Hey, you," I said. "What's up? How's Anton?"

"The little bastard!" Miranda erupted. "I thought I'd scared him into giving up dogfighting. But no. He's been using the garage where he works as a place to stash the dogfighters' bait animals. I retrieved one very scarred, very frightened Black Lab cross, a Beagle who isn't in much better shape, a Border Collie with chewed ears, and a couple of chihuahua mixes who may not make it. Also a scared-out-of-her-mind mother cat and a litter of kittens I had to load into a cardboard box. The dogfighters must have been answering those 'free to good homes' ads again," she said in disgust. "Won't people ever learn?"

"A cat and kittens?" I said. "What would dogfighters want with them?"

"Don't ask," Miranda said. "You don't want those images in your head. Anyhow, I'm just leaving The Sanctuary — I dropped the animals off there. Connie, several volunteers, and our vet are taking care of them."

"No Beatrice, I take it?" I said, relieved.

"Nope."

"Do you think Anton's telling you the truth? About Beatrice?"

"Well, we had words about that," she said. "I had to beat on him a little. But I think he's being straight with me."

"Sorry things turned out like that with Anton," I said. "I know you were trying to help him."

"Yeah, I was. But no more." She snorted. "Please give me a pill and make me lie down if I ever suggest that I can keep some kid out of jail. Anyhow, about Anton. I turned him in to the Sidney cops for animal cruelty. With a side order of assault. On me. They'll come by the garage and pick him up. He may be able to wiggle out of the animal cruelty charge by ratting out his brother and the other dogfighters. And I haven't decided how vigorously I'm going to press charges against him. But in any event, I've washed my hands of him."

"Did you get pictures of the animals? Especially the injured ones?" I asked, the prosecutor in me coming to the fore.

"Yup. Emailed the photos to the police when I made my statement, too. All that took longer than I would have believed possible. So I'll be along. Need anything?"

"No," I said. "I'll see you when you get here."

CHAPTER 18

As I climbed the steps to Izzy's front porch, my phone buzzed again. I didn't recognize the number. A pigeon coming home to roost?

"Miz Yeats?" said a voice I recognized as Sandy's. "Greg — the man with the poop scooper business — ID'd the photo on the poster that you were interested in. The building with the blue roof in the middle of the bottom row."

"Yes?" I said eagerly.

"Yes. He's pretty sure that it's a small shelter just north of the airport, out toward West Saanich Road."

"Wow," I said. "Remote."

"Yes," Sandy agreed. "It's called Evergreen Animal Rescue. I've never heard of it but that doesn't mean anything. Oops," she said, as I heard the front door of her shop tinkling. "Customers. Got to go."

"Thanks a million, Sandy," I said.

I dithered on Izzy's front porch, thinking furiously. Evergreen Animal Rescue. E.A.R. A shelter. Why hadn't I thought of shelters? So that's where Mohammed worked with dogs, where the carriers belonged. And undoubtedly where the video of Beatrice was shot. But was either Mohammed or Beatrice there now? And hadn't I heard that shelter's name before?

I stepped inside the apartment. Ro was working on her iPad at the kitchen table, a cup of coffee at her elbow. I sat down across from her.

"The other night Miranda went off on a rant about pound seizure shelters," I said. "She said that you, she, and Connie had visited several, and that you were making great headway with one of them."

Ro nodded. "Yeah, we are. Connie and Miranda are talking persuasion and philosophy; I'm talking money. In my opinion, the shelters' reluctance to abandon their seizure status is really all about money. I've been working with the director of one of the shelters — the one that seems most amenable to learning other ways to raise money besides handing over animals to labs whenever they run short of cash." Ro shook her head. "It takes work, though. Planning. Examining programs. Balancing income and expenses. Budgeting. The director — Barbara Davidson — isn't used to doing this. But I'm having some success."

"Which shelter is it, Ro?" I asked.

"Evergreen Animal Rescue," she said. "They have a terrible adoptions track record, but they want to improve. It's as if their collective imagination has deserted them. Heck, I can think of at least half a dozen offbeat and successful adoption strategies, all learned from Miranda. Anyhow, when the end of the month comes, the poor animals they've taken in — the ones that didn't get adopted by random people wandering in to look at them — off they go to whichever research project or biological supply house will pay money for them. Those shelters, the so-called pound seizure shelters, they're nothing more than conduits to the labs. Or worse." *So, that was the 'fate worse than death,'* I thought. *What do the wags say? 'Giving your body to science while you're still in it?' Cute, Mohammed.*

"Damn," I said.

"Damn?" Ro asked.

"Yeah. I think that's where the dog thief stashed Beatrice. At least, that's where the video was shot. The little turd probably works there."

Ro's eyes opened very wide. "I've been there three times. The last time was a few weeks ago. I don't recall seeing anyone who might look like . . ."

"A jihadist?"

She blushed. "I was going to say anyone who might look like anyone other than a regular Canadian. Whatever that is. I never did see any of the animal care people, though. The kennel cleaners and so on. I just met with Barbara in her office. So he might well have been there. Not that I'd have known what he looks like, anyhow." She gave me a worried look. "Are you going there?"

"Yup. Right now. Where is this place?"

"Take the Pat Bay Highway and keep going north of the airport. North of the ferry terminal, too. Turn west on Resthaven Road. It turns into John Road. The shelter is on John Road."

I stood up. "Okay. I'd better go."

"Miranda?" Ro said.

"She was checking with some dogfighters, up the peninsula," I said. "Just making sure they didn't have Beatrice. They didn't, but they had some other animals — bait animals, she called them — and she removed them. They sound in pretty bad shape. Anyhow, she dropped them at The Sanctuary, and she's on her way here. I'm not going to wait for her, though. I'm too antsy. This is the first lead we've had and I don't want to blow it. Will you tell her where I'm going? She can call me. We can rendezvous at Evergreen. And with any luck, surprise Mohammed, and reclaim Beatrice."

"Do you think so?" Ro asked, looking hopeful.

"My fingers are crossed," I told her.

I sped out of Izzy's cul-de-sac, cursing that ahead of me was the constipation of late afternoon Victoria traffic which I'd have to navigate on my way to the Pat Bay Highway and points north. At the stop sign on Izzy's corner, a yellow Jeep turned into the cul-de-sac. Miranda. She pulled up beside me and rolled down her window.

I noticed that she had the beginnings of a monster black eye — her left eye was mostly closed, the skin red and puffy. There was a long scrape on the left side of her face, her hair looked a fright, and she had a split lip that had been only hastily taken care of. In fact, she was dabbing at it with a handful of paper napkins.

"You look like you've been wrestling grizzlies," I commented. "Is this the side order of assault you were referring to?"

"Yeah," she said. "I didn't wait to clean up. Thought I'd do it at Izzy's. What's up?"

"I'm on my way up north to Evergreen Animal Rescue," I said. "It's where Mohammed shot the video."

"No kidding," she said. "Well, if we're lucky —"

"The little shit will be there. And with any luck, so will Beatrice. We'll just pick her up. No need to wait for this bogus transfer on Thursday."

"You and me both," she said. "I'll pull in behind you. Let's not worry about leaving one of our cars. Just go."

I drove through stop-and-go traffic to the Pat Bay Highway, Miranda right behind me. I wasn't at all sure that Mohammed would be at work, given that he must be getting ready to flee the country, but it was certainly worth a drive back up north to check things out. If this was where he'd stashed Beatrice — hiding her in plain sight among the other dogs at the shelter — it had been a good plan. Then, I guessed, if Izzy didn't pay up, he'd just allow Beatrice to join the ranks of the other Evergreen dogs bound for whichever lab Barbara saw fit to sell them to this month.

Traffic was moving even more sluggishly as we drove past Cedar Hill Cross, past Elk Lake, and approached the wide spot in the road known as Keating. Then, traffic stopped. Ominously, I noted that there was no traffic at all on the left-hand side of the highway. What the hell? I was just about to get out of my car to see if I could peer down the road a little when a call came in from Aliya.

"It's Tris!" Aliya said, sounding hysterical. "I've lost her!"

"What?" I said, my stomach in free fall. "Calm down, Aliya. What do you mean you've lost her?"

"Well, I picked her and Dani up from story-writing class, drove Dani home, drove Tris home, set her up with her homework and a snack at the dining room table, and went downstairs to get my iPad. When I came back up, she was gone."

"And she's not in her room, or outside at her bird feeders, or —"

"No! I've looked! She's nowhere!"

"Well, she's somewhere," I said. "And I've got an idea where that somewhere might be. Look, I'm stalled in traffic on the Pat Bay Highway —"

"Oh, it's been on the radio that there's a major accident north of Keating. A log truck jackknifed and lost its load. Several cars were involved — people were actually *crushed*, Kieran. Emergency vehicles are on their way from Sidney. And a giant crane's been commandeered from one of the log harvesting companies to turn the truck back over and clean up the log mess. It'll be hours before all that's cleared away."

"I'm in the middle of it," I said. "I'll turn around and come back into town. Miranda and I have a lead on Beatrice, but she's going to have to go check it out by herself. I'll be home as soon as I can get there. And don't worry, Aliya. This isn't your fault. If it's anyone's, it's mine."

"Your fault? So you might know where she is?"

"I might." *Oh, yes, I might indeed know where Tris is*, I thought. And when I found her, then what? A little metaphorical neck-wringing? Shaming? Harsh words? Yelling? Grounding for life? I hadn't had to administer punishment to Tris, and I realized I didn't have a clue how to do it. Nor did I want to. Motherhood 101 was a class I never attended. Well, maybe I'd think of something useful on my drive back to town.

I walked around the rear end of my car to Miranda's Jeep. She'd found a towel and a bottle of water and was dabbing at her soon-to-be black eye and her split lip, looking in her rearview mirror and grimacing. I explained that Tris had gone AWOL and Miranda raised her eyebrows.

"What?" she said. "That doesn't sound like Tris. Do you have any idea where she's gone?"

"I do, actually," I said. "Remember the story I told you about Dani and the creepy old guy on the bus?"

"Sure. Oh, no. You don't think —"

"Uh huh, I do. Listen, a kid who'd hold an air pistol on that loser Peter when he was about to shoot me, then threaten to cut off her classmate's testicles for bullying Dani . . . well, I don't think the creepy child-molesting guy has much of a future."

"When you put it like that, yeah, you'd better go get her," Miranda said. "Crap. I thought *we* were going to devise a suitable punishment for the old guy. Right after we wrapped up the Beatrice affair."

"We were. But I guess it didn't happen fast enough for Tris. I certainly didn't keep her in the loop regarding our plans."

"Plans," Miranda snorted. "Did we have plans? I remember talking about making plans, but —"

"Nope. We put making plans on the back burner. Really, we've been kind of busy hunting down Mohammed. But I guess what happened to Dani started to eat at Tris. Maybe I should have checked in with her. Reassured her that we hadn't forgotten about justice for her friend." I kicked at a clump of earth at the side of the road in frustration.

"Okay, let's think," Miranda said. "Where is she likely to be?"

"Riding the bus looking for him. What I hope she *isn't* doing is riding the bus with her air pistol."

Miranda whistled. "Is it locked up?"

"Yeah, in the gun safe with my thirty-eight. But you know kids. Clever little devils."

"Okay," Miranda said. "You definitely need to hustle back to town and short-circuit Tris's vigilantism. I can go up to Evergreen."

"You're a mess, girlfriend," I said. "First Ro, now you . . . this case is kicking our butts."

"I got beat up worse than this the first time I got on my Musical Ride horse," she said, smiling crookedly. "The divine Arabella. She didn't like me. Threw me into a fence and galloped off. But we worked things out." She looked past me at the stalled traffic. "We both have to get around this mess."

"Where in hell are we anyhow?" I asked, looking back at the line of cars that had come to a halt behind us. "I don't often come up this way."

"Head back south," she said. "Turn off the highway at Lochside. Be careful — the road twists and turns. But it'll take you past the University to Cordova Bay. Then you can take the coast road back to Oak Bay."

"I feel awful leaving you to go on another dog chase by yourself." I was about to add something pithy when my phone started pinging.

"Oh for cripes' sake!" I yelled. "It's the damned pet tracker. Mohammed's come back to Daphne's and picked up the carriers."

"That's good, right?" Miranda said. "He's going to take them back to Evergreen, so I'll intercept him there. Grab him, grab Beatrice. It'll all work out."

"Maybe," I said. "But what if he's taking the carriers somewhere else? What if he's going to load Beatrice into one of them and go . . . to his crappy short-term rental? What if he's as nervous as we are?"

"In that case, I'll follow him," Miranda said. "So here's what we're going to do. Give me your phone."

"Give you my —"

"Your phone. I'll need it to track the carriers. I'll head up to Evergreen, and if Mohammed — or the pet tracker — takes off for parts unknown, I'll follow. Maybe we'll get lucky. Maybe we can wrap this up tonight. Reunite Beatrice with Izzy."

"Maybe," I said doubtfully. "But '*the best-laid plans*' and all that —"

"Oh, nuts to Robbie Burns," she said. "Even though he was a Scot, his famous lines are all downers. C'mon, Miz Yeats," Miranda said. "You're stalling. Your phone will be safe with me."

I handed over my phone, not liking the naked feeling I got as Miranda took it from me.

"You're going to owe me for this," she said, tut-tutting in feigned annoyance.

Feigned or not, I immediately felt guilty. "Okay," I said. "What do you have in mind?"

"Dinner. Connie's having dinner with Robert, Jimmy's former owner. Ro's taking care of Izzy — I assume she, or you, isn't letting her starve. But

I'm starving right now, and I sure don't want to cook dinner. And I might only have one eye to see out of soon. But I *could* manage a meal with sympathetic friends . . . if someone picked up some food while I was busy chasing jihadists, Labradoodles, and pet carriers."

"I'll get Aliya to pick something up," I said. "I have no imagination left. It's being occupied picturing the trouble Tris might be getting into."

"I hear you," Miranda said. "You go ahead and get turned around. I'm going to look for a way past this traffic jam — I think there's a gravel road just off to the west. Then I'll drive around this mess and continue north to Evergreen. If I need to talk to you, I'll call Tris's phone."

"Okay. I know you'll take Beatrice back to Izzy's but what will you do with Mohammed?"

"Don't ask," she said. "Maybe I'll truss him up like a Thanksgiving turkey and toss him in the back of my Jeep. Then call Sylvie. But first things first. Get going, Miz Yeats," she said. "Your daughter the Junior Crimestopper may be making a citizens' arrest as we speak."

"Knowing her, it's likely to be something worse," I muttered, hoping like hell that I was wrong.

CHAPTER 19

Tris and Dani's private school did not have a bus, but there were two Oak Bay city buses that passed by the school late in the afternoon — one at three-fifty, just after normal classes were dismissed, and one at five-fifteen, when after-school classes, such as story-writing, let out. I bet Tris had sneaked out of the house and caught the five-fifteen bus, hoping to catch the creepy old child molester as he rode the bus looking for Dani. What Tris intended to do once she'd found him, I had no idea. But first things first.

I decided I needed to park my car somewhere along the bus route and just get on the damned bus. Then I could apprehend Tris and we could go somewhere quiet and have a nice little chat about how she scared Aliya and me half to death. The creepy old guy must be pretty confused by now, I figured, because yesterday and today, Dani hadn't been on the bus. Would he still be riding it, hoping Dani would return? I had no idea. But I bet Tris would be on the five-fifteen bus this afternoon, though, looking for him as he was looking for Dani.

I followed the bus for a bit, wondering what Tris might be up to, and if she would get off at any of the stops, but she didn't. I really didn't know if she was even on the bus, but it seemed like a good possibility — I couldn't imagine where else she might have gone. I found myself getting incandescently angry at the creepy old guy who saw a little kid riding the bus alone as prey, as an invitation to act out his sexual fantasies. I bet that Dani might have even enjoyed her bus trips before the old guy zeroed in on her. The route was straight up Oak Bay Avenue from the Marina, through the village and past the quaint shops with their Tudor-style storefronts, Dogwood trees resplendent with white blossoms, overflowing flower baskets hung from streetlamps, little tables and chairs on the sidewalk under green awnings. Altogether a very pretty ride. Damn him anyhow for spoiling it for her, I thought, although I still maintained that kids as young as Dani shouldn't ride the bus alone.

I passed the bus, looked ahead for a place to park, found one at the curb, then stepped out onto the sidewalk. I was about twenty yards from the bus stop where quite a few people were waiting inside a little kiosk. The bus glided in to the curb, and I walked down the sidewalk toward it, intending to join the crowd at the kiosk and board the bus. I was thinking how feeble my plan was — simply to grab Tris before she did something dire — when the front door of the bus opened, and Tris hurried out holding her phone, hopping from the last step onto the sidewalk. My heart contracted a little — she looked so damned small and vulnerable, no matter that she was dressed in a tough black T-shirt with a snowy owl on it (with the words ALWAYS GIVE A HOOT in red underneath the owl), black cargo pants, and black skateboarder's sneakers. She was a skinny, curly-haired little blond kid with a heart as fierce as a tiger's. *Oh Tris*, I thought in despair, *what am I going to do with you?*

I was just about to start up the sidewalk toward Tris, but decided to hold off for a minute. Something or someone had made her apprehensive. With a furtive look behind her, she hurried away, her attention on her phone. But whoever it was she had been looking for didn't exit from the front door of the bus — he exited from the back door and walked purposefully toward her, grabbing her while her attention was on her phone. The people waiting to board the bus had gotten on, the bus's doors had closed, the bus had pulled away from the curb . . . and on the sidewalk, an emaciated old guy with lank grey hair and a face full of stubble, shabby jeans falling off skinny hips, and an oversized, frayed black nylon jacket had wrapped Tris in a bear hug. I broke into a run.

"Hey!" Tris yelled, but he clamped a hand over her mouth. That's how easily child abductions happen, I told myself. When no one's watching, just grab the kid, hold her mouth shut. And then? And then anything, I told myself bitterly. Except not with this kid, and not today.

The old guy dragged Tris behind the bus kiosk, across the sidewalk, and toward a side street. "Give it to me!" I heard him say as he muscled Tris around the corner.

"Go to hell!" I heard Tris say in a muffled reply. Then I rounded the corner, and saw Tris rip one of the old guy's hands away from her mouth as she struggled to free herself from the grip he had on her upper arm.

"Get off me, asshole!" Tris yelled. She stepped back hard on one of his feet, making *him* yell this time.

"Brat," he hissed, giving her a couple of good whacks on the side of the head. "Give me that damned phone. I'll —"

"— you'll what?" I asked. I reached past Tris, grabbed the old guy by his shirt collar, and lifted him off his feet.

The old guy let go of Tris's arm and she stumbled away from him. "Kieran!" she called out in amazed relief.

By this point we were all standing in the little doorway of a closed-up shop, and I turned the old guy around and pushed his face into the weathered wood of the door. "Do you beat on little kids very often?" I asked him in contempt. "Why do you want her phone anyhow?"

"Because I took his picture!" Tris yelled. "That's why he's mad! 'Cause now Dani can ID him to Mac. He's not going to get away with what he did."

"I don't know what you're talking about," he said, half turning. "Who the hell's Dani?"

I shoved him hard up against the door and held him in place with one hand as I felt for his wallet in the back pocket of his jeans. It was there and I flipped it open and looked at his driver's license. Andrew Summers. I wondered how long his rap sheet was, and how many times he'd been interviewed — if not arrested — for child molestation. Actually, I hated that expression. Child molestation indeed. If we wanted to describe crimes properly, as we should, what he did to Dani was, in British Columbia common law legalese, 'sexual assault of a child.' A felony. No more wimpy 'molestation.' That was an expression left over from the days when we were willfully ignorant, when we didn't want to believe that children as young as two could be raped by penises or fingers or bottles or screwdrivers, and that dear old grandpa or uncle or the nice babysitter from across the street could be guilty of such things. Andrew Summers could be looking at fourteen years in jail for only one instance of sexual assault on Dani. How many had there been? She'd have to tell us. With any luck, Summers would spend the rest of his life in jail.

"Tris, do you have Mac's number in your contacts?"

"Uh huh," she said.

"Call him," I said. "Tell him we've apprehended a sexual assault suspect named Andrew Summers who needs to be escorted to a cell in the Oak Bay jail."

Tris took out her phone and punched Mac's number. "We got him, right?" she asked me, pausing, a note of worry in her voice. "He's not going to get away, is he? He is going to jail?"

"We got him," I told her. "And he's definitely going to jail."

"No, wait," gibbered Andrew Summers. "Just wait. I didn't . . . I can't be . . . don't . . . oh, just let me go, why don't you? Nothing really happened. The kid's all right."

"This kid?" I said. "Her name's Tristan, not kid. And you did beat on her. I don't imagine her head feels very good where you whacked her. I imagine we'll be pressing charges against you for that. I think that's called assault. Oh, and you also abducted her."

"Oh, c'mon," he wheedled. "Please? I'm . . . not well. Sometimes I don't know what I'm doing."

"No deal," I told him. "Even if you hadn't hurt her I'd be turning you in for what you did to the other kid. Her name's Dani, by the way."

"The other . . . ohhh," he said, breaking into tears. "I didn't hurt *that one*. I just —"

"Shut the fuck up," I said to him. "You have no idea what you did to her." *Poor Dani. She might well have nightmares for years from those bus rides with Andrew Summers. Or maybe not.* I thought I'd read somewhere that kids' trauma could be mitigated if they saw that the law took their complaints seriously, punished perpetrators swiftly, and most important, were supported throughout the ordeal by their parents. I was certainly going to support Tris. As for Dani? Well, there was only so much I could do.

"I got Mac," Tris said, putting her phone back into her pocket. "He says he's coming."

Summers wept steadily now and Tris looked at him in disgust. "Why are *you* crying?" she said. "It's *my* head that hurts, and it's Dani you scared. So why are *you* crying?"

"He's scared, too," I told Tris. "He's probably done to other kids what he did to Dani. Those other kids' parents might have pressed charges against him, and he might even have gone to jail. He doesn't want to go back there."

"Oh, you don't know," he wailed. "I can't go back." He slid down the door and was now sitting at the ground with his head in his hands. "I can't."

"You just might," I told him. "You should've thought about that when you picked out that cute little girl with shiny black hair and the pink backpack. Made her touch you." I shook my head. "Too bloody bad."

I caught Tris looking at me. "But why is he so scared?" she asked. "Were people mean to him in jail?"

I thought for a moment. Well, it didn't hurt for her to know some of the truth. "There's a pecking order in jail, Tris. Even felons think that some crimes are pretty horrible. Men who hurt kids, well, they're at the bottom of the barrel. Bad things often happen to these men in jail."

Tris thought this over. "Okay, but later, when these guys get out of jail — like Mr. Summers — why do they keep on hurting kids? Jail doesn't fix them?"

Good question, I thought. I said, "No, jail doesn't fix them. It just keeps them off the streets and away from other kids they might victimize."

Tris put her hands in her pockets and looked down at the blubbering Andrew Summers. "So why do people do that kind of thing anyhow? What he did to Dani?"

"They're grown-up bullies, Tris. Remember Peter, the guy who set your arm on fire when you lived with the old dog man?"

Tris set her lips in a grim line. "Yeah."

"And Nigel, from last year? The boy whose, um, private parts you were going to cut off?"

"Uh huh," she said, looking sheepish.

"Well, bullies start out like Nigel. Picking on little kids like he did with Dani. Heck, Peter probably started out like Nigel when he was a little kid, too. Bullies always find somebody younger, somebody weaker, somebody different, somebody who can't fight back. Then they torment them. Later, when they're older, some of the Peters and Nigels get even more warped. They see . . . prey."

"Like wolves," Tris said.

"Worse," I said. "Wolves kill cleanly and kill because they need to. These guys . . ." I fell silent. I didn't dare tell Tris what I believed, what I'd learned from the words of a seventeenth-century opera as a trio of witches sang in delight: *'From the ruin of others our pleasures we borrow.'* Translation: *We kill happiness because it pleases us.* That was too hard a concept for a nine-year-old.

"Why do they do what they do? That's the sixty-four-thousand-dollar question, Tris. Psychologists have been trying to figure out for decades why people want to hurt other people. And recently, because women won't let men get away with it anymore, why men want to hurt and degrade women. We might have to talk to Helen about that."

"Helen? Dr. Mikita?" Tris asked.

"Uh huh," I said. "She's good at thinking about tough things."

Helen Mikita was my upstairs tenant, a U Vic lecturer in the psychology department. Her field was anthrozoology, the emerging field of animal-human relations, but she was always up for a discussion of the question Plato's students asked him: 'Tell us, teacher, how are we to live the good life?' And the corollary of that question: 'What is a bad life?' Studying philosophers' writing about their search for virtue, or *arete*, had consumed many of my undergrad hours. As had the study of evil, or ponerology. Indeed, learning that Helen was a hybrid philosopher/psychologist had cemented her lease application for my upstairs suite. Helen and I had finished off many a bottle of wine late at night listening to music in her little apartment as we debated whether Diogenes — the cynic philosopher who searched Athens holding up a lantern so he could see citizens' faces clearly — could ever have found the honest man he sought.

"Okay," Tris said solemnly. Then, "Am I going to have to talk to Mac about *him*," she said, gesturing to Andrew Summers. "Or do you do that 'cause you're the adult?"

"I imagine Mac will want to talk to you," I said. "Are you okay with that? Or the department has special interviewers who talk to kids."

"I don't need a special interviewer," she said. "I'm not scared to talk to Mac. But I'll have to tell him that I disobeyed you, won't I?"

I smothered a smile. Good. I won't have to drag a confession of wrongdoing out of Tris. She'd volunteered it. Somewhere in her past, she'd acquired a moral foundation. "Yeah, that will probably come up," I said. "But I wouldn't worry too much about it right now. You and I can talk about it later."

"Okay," Tris said, subdued, looking up as a white sedan with a blue and gold swoosh, and the words Oak Bay Police on the side, pulled up at the curb. "Here's the cruiser."

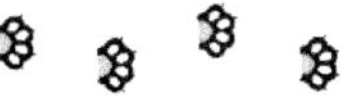

The Oak Bay Police indeed had their protocol, and Tris disappeared into the kids' interview room with Erin, Mac's detective partner, a thirty-something woman with frizzy brown hair, kind hazel eyes, and a sunny smile. I got a glimpse of the room as the door was closing — a cheerful pink and green painted room with a forest scene on one wall, a rainbow on another, stuffed animals in bins here and there, and a couple of kid-sized tables and chairs with crayons and drawing paper on the tabletops.

After I gave my statement, I found Mac in his office and settled back for a chat.

"I was thinking that Tris might call Dani and tell her how cool and painless the interview was," I said. "She might be more amenable to coming in and making a statement if Tris tells her it was okay."

Mac raised his eyebrows. "That seems like a good plan," he said, smoothing his moustache, a tell that attested to worry.

"What's up, Mac?" I asked.

He sighed. "We haven't done well with Mr. Summers. He's a bloody great menace but the courts seem to have been lenient with him. I looked up the terms of his release — counseling, volunteer work at a food bank, and no contact with children. He knows that. His family — yes, he has one — knows that. We know that. Yet . . ." He fell silent.

"You seem depressed, old friend," I said.

"Och, it's that we'll try him again, some ambitious defense attorney will plead for a reduced sentence due to his age, a jury will feel sorry for him, he'll be incarcerated for a year or two, then turned loose and the same thing will happen all over again with another Dani or another Tris."

"Discouraging, isn't it?" I said with a bitter laugh. "Tris wanted to know why Mr. Summers keeps on hurting kids, why jail didn't fix him."

"Ah," Mac said.

"In fact, she wanted to know why men like him want to hurt kids at all. I told her we'd have to consult our in-house psychologist, Helen Mikita." I shook my head. "Brother. I hope Tris will have forgotten the question by dinnertime."

Mac sat back in his chair, fiddling with a pen, brushing imaginary wrinkles out of his tie, trying not to ask the question that I was sure was in the forefront of his mind. I decided to reassure him.

"We're working on it," I told him.

"It?" he asked.

"Finding Beatrice. We think we know who took her — a guy named Mohammed Saleh. Is he a Muslim? He's a blond Canadian, if we can believe the neighbor." I shrugged. "I guess he found the Anglican church unfulfilling and converted to Islam."

"A Canadian wrote that extortion note?" Mac asked in disbelief.

"Apparently. Hard to believe, isn't it? I guess even blond Canadians can get radicalized and join Daesh. Imagine the hero's welcome he'll get when he brings his cell — or whatever his group of homies is called — ten thousand dollars. Anyhow, I had some luck, and we think we've tracked him to his workplace — an animal shelter just west of Sidney. We believe Beatrice might be there."

"An animal shelter?" Mac asked.

"Well, it's a pound seizure shelter," I said. "Lost pets come in the front door then go out the back door to labs or biological supply houses. Not much adopting goes on at Evergreen. We believe he stashed Beatrice there after her abduction. Probably he had in mind that if Izzy didn't pay up, Beatrice would be on her way in the next shipment of dogs to whichever mainland lab needs them. A true fate worse than death. Miranda's gone to pay them a call and," I looked at my watch, "right about now might be talking to the director." I thought it best to just leave things at that. Did I think that Miranda was going to waltz into the shelter and waltz out with Beatrice? No, I didn't. Oh, it was possible, but I didn't think it likely. Nothing else about this case had worked out — why should Beatrice's retrieval from the shelter be straightforward?

"So this might be over tonight?" Mac asked.

"It might be," I equivocated. "I have to contact Miranda and see what's happening. She has my phone," I told him. When he looked surprised, I said, "Don't ask."

Mac smoothed his moustache again. "Mr. Saleh . . . I'd like to talk to him before you turn him over to the RCMP. I'd like to understand the kind of mind that would write that note."

"I think several of us — including the RCMP — will be talking to him," I said. "I'd like to understand the note-writing, too. According to my forensics linguistic expert, he's a native English speaker. And Miranda's RCMP source says he's an Extremist Traveller, not just a Canadian who got bored with the Anglican church and switched to Islam. He's been in and out of this country, associating with people on the RCMP's watch list. Hell, *he's* on their watch list. I'd like to know how disillusionment with Canadian life led him to embrace the ideals of Daesh — a group that now recruits members from around the world, that slaughters civilians, that summarily executes soldiers and rival militants, that takes hostages for ransom, that kidnaps women and girls to use as sex slaves. I'd like him to tell me how that came to appeal to him, and how Izzy and Beatrice fit into all this. It seems as though something happened to Mr. Saleh. I'd very much like to know what that something was."

"Knock, knock," Erin said, sticking her head into Mac's doorway. "I've finished

taking Tris's statement. She even emailed us Andrew Summers's photo. That's a scrappy kid," she said in admiration. "I left her in the interview room with some vanilla pudding and a book."

"I'll go get the little investigator," I said to Mac. "I'm not at all happy with her. Things turned out well enough, but they could have turned out very badly. If I hadn't been there when Summers started beating on her for her phone . . . well, we're going to have words about that." I got up and started for the door. "Thanks, Mac," I said.

"Thank *you*," he said. "For working so hard to recover Beatrice."

"Well, we don't have her yet," I said. "Soon, though. I'll be in touch."

I walked thoughtfully down the hall to the interview room to pick up Tris and discuss what on earth possessed her to get on that bus and look for Summers. Dammit, she'd never disobeyed me. Not once in the nearly two years she'd been living with me. What was I going to say to her? I sighed. I had a strategy in mind . . . but would it work?

CHAPTER 20

"Want to go for a drive?" I asked Tris as we pulled out of the little brick police station's parking lot. "Maybe just down past the Marina — the east side of MacNeil Bay. There's a neat little maritime meadow called Kitty Islet. We could sit there for a bit and look at the ocean and chat."

"Are there kitties?" Tris asked.

I laughed. "I asked that question, too, when I first came to Victoria. I just found out the answer lately. No kitties. Apparently, the islet is named for the pirate Arthur Catt. Or for the feral cats that used to hang out there."

"A pirate. Cool," Tris said. Then, as I drove down Oak Bay Avenue to the ocean, she commented in a low voice, "You were really mad at that man, Mr. Summers, weren't you?"

I listened carefully — Tris often broached difficult subjects by coming at them obliquely. She might get around to asking me if I was mad at *her* after we discussed Andrew Summers, but I'd have to let her make her own way into that.

"I was, Tris. Maybe madder than I've been in a long time. He hurt you, and he hurt Dani in a different way. He's probably hurt lots of little girls. So, yes, I'm plenty mad."

Tris said, "Is Dani going to have to go to the police station and give a statement?"

"Yes. Erin will be calling her parents," I told her. "You know, Mac and I were thinking it might help Dani if you could talk to her."

"Yeah?" Tris said.

"Yeah. You could tell her about your experience giving a statement. Let her know that it wasn't scary."

Tris nodded. "Sure. I could do that. Because it wasn't scary. Erin's a nice lady. Should I call Dani now?"

"Why not?" I said. "You can talk while I drive us to Kitty Islet."

Tris chattered away to Dani while I turned onto Beach Drive and drove around the Marina to Kitty Islet. A tiny, comma-shaped marine park, it boasted concrete steps and a walking path that led to a rocky shoreline. I parked where we could see the ocean clearly — I didn't think we wanted to walk out onto the little spit as the weather was rapidly deteriorating. An ambitious wave-ruffling wind had come up, and far out at sea, a peach-colored sun was headed for the horizon, trailing streamers of orange and gold.

"Pretty," Tris said.

"It is," I agreed.

My strategy? I'd decided that Tris and I would just sit here until it dawned on her that she needed to talk to me about this afternoon's escapade. Without prompting from me. I was certain that particular approach wasn't in any of the parenting books, but I'd decided I'd just clam up and see what would happen.

"Dani says she'll talk to her mother and father and they'll call Mac. She says she isn't scared now that the old guy is in jail. So that's good," Tris said.

Tris hummed a little, put her phone away, looked appreciatively out at the ocean again, then looked over at me. I said nothing. We watched the disappearing sun paint the sky a few more luscious colors — cantaloupe, butterscotch, tangerine — then Tris sighed. "I guess you're pretty mad at me, aren't you?" she said.

At last. The mad talk. Good. "Well, I'm a little upset," I said. "I wouldn't say I was mad, though. Mostly I was alarmed, Tris. You scared me. You scared Aliya, too. And Miranda." She started to say something and I shushed her. "No, just listen for a minute, then you can talk.

"In my previous job, I saw dozens of Andrew Summerses, Tris. He's not only a scary old man but a dangerous old man, too. He may seem feeble, but he was strong enough to drag you down that side street. I think he would've done more than whack you a few times across your head if you'd been there with him alone. He knew exactly why you were taking his picture. Tris, what you did was brave, but it was foolish. Do you understand why?"

"Because he was bigger than me. And stronger." She looked over at me, clearly hoping she was saying the right thing.

"Partly. I'm going to make a confession, but you can't tell anyone, okay?"

"Okay," Tris said. "Cross my heart."

"When I have something risky to do, something dangerous, something that might mean I'll get clobbered, I don't go alone."

"You take Miranda, right?"

"Or someone helpful," I said. "Like Lawrence, or Ro, or Aliya. There's no shame in being cautious. Miranda and I hadn't had time to develop a plan to put an end to Mr. Summers's bus-riding, but whatever plan we came up with, we'd agreed we'd execute it together. We try to have each other's back."

Tris shifted uncomfortably in her seat. "That makes sense," she said. "But, Kieran . . . well . . . I did call you. But I didn't get you."

"You . . . did?" I thought furiously. What the hell? How had I come to miss Tris's call? Then I remembered. I'd left my phone in my car when I went to talk to Gavin, behind the convenience store. Dammit. It was just my luck that she'd tried to call me then.

Tris continued. "I was really worried that Mr. Summers would stop riding the bus because he'd realize that Dani wasn't on it. And then he'd get away. So I thought that if I got on the bus and took a picture of anyone who looked like the guy Dani described, it would help your investigation. It didn't seem risky."

Help my investigation indeed. I didn't know whether to hug her or . . . or what? Wring her skinny neck? "That was a terrific idea," I told Tris. "A brilliant inspiration, really. But . . ."

"But it was risky. I needed someone to have my back, right?" she said.

Ai yi. No, Tris, that's not what you needed. "I think it would have been better if we could have talked about your idea," I said. "I wish I hadn't missed your call."

"I knew you were busy with your case," she said. "And I didn't think taking his picture would be a big deal."

"Oh, Tris," I said, wondering what I should say now.

"I didn't realize you'd be scared about what I did," she said. "And Aliya. And Miranda. I'm sorry. I guess I should have waited to talk to you. But I was afraid —"

"— that Summers would get away."

"Yeah," Tris said, sounding miserable. "I screwed up, didn't I?"

Fooey. This little chat hadn't turned out at all the way I thought it might. I'd missed the kid's call. She was afraid Summers would just disappear. What else was she to do but take matters into her own hands? At least she knew she ought to talk to me first in future.

A gust of wind shook my car and Tris said, "Whoa! Storm coming!" as we looked out at the ocean together. A group of six cormorants, skinny black necks extended, skimmed the tops of the waves, as if in flight from something. Sure enough, in less than a minute, a rain squall pocked the ocean, turning the waves choppy and driving the birds onto the rocks, where they hunkered down, plainly miserable. In the west, a single eerie ribbon of lemon-colored sky on the horizon marked the end of the day. As Tris had suggested, there'd be a dandy storm tonight. Time to go.

"So am I grounded forever?" Tris asked mournfully. I was sure she was fretting that there'd be no more Saturday afternoons working in Lawrence's shop folding T- shirts, no more photo shoots, no more story-writing classes. All the things she enjoyed.

"No, Tris. I don't believe in grounding," I said. "I wouldn't want to take away things you like to do."

"Oh," Tris said, clearly surprised. "Well, I *could* do extra chores," she offered. "Clean the catboxes twice a day. Take out the recycling."

"Nope."

Tris looked at me, puzzled. "Then what?"

"Let's just agree that when you think you need to do something dire, something drastic, you'll talk to me first. And we'll figure out how to get it done. You might need someone to have your back. Or you might need to pass the something dire a little higher up the food chain. To me or Miranda."

Tris nodded her head enthusiastically, visions of being grounded forever or doing my evening catbox duties clearly disappearing from her head.

"I had a thought, though," I said. "If you'd reached me, we could have talked about what you intended to do. So . . . to avoid this kind of thing in future, I need to modify *my* behavior, too."

"Yeah?" Tris asked.

"Yeah," I said. "I need to be better about my phone. I missed your call when I left my phone in the car, and I was so preoccupied with what I was doing that I didn't check my calls when I got back."

"Oh," Tris said.

"So I need to do better. I need to check my phone for calls more often." I looked at her shrewdly. "Maybe we could have a deal about this."

"Hmm, okay," Tris said. "I'll talk to you before I do anything weird and you can check your phone more often. Is that fair?"

"Sounds fair to me," I said.

Tris nodded. "Should we shake or something?"

"Maybe a pinky swear," I said, holding out my little finger. "What do you think?"

"Okay," she said, grinning, proffering her pinky also.

"You know what this means," I said.

"A promise," Tris said.

"Yeah, but a special kind of promise," I said. "In Vulcan it's called *yubikiri*. It's the highest of all promises. An unbreakable oath."

Tris's eyes got huge. "Vulcan?"

"An ancient language," I told her, tongue firmly in my cheek.

"What does that mean, though, *yubikiri*?"

"*Pinky cut off*," I said. "So be sure."

Tris swallowed. "Oh, I get it. Whoever breaks the promise gets their pinky cut off."

"Yup."

"Okay," Tris said. "I'm swearing to talk to you first instead of just going off to do possibly dangerous things, and you're swearing to be better about your phone. Even when you're involved with a case."

We twined little fingers and said simultaneously, "Swear."

"Now, pass me your phone, my Sproutlet. I need to call Miranda. She has my phone. I should check in with her and let her know that we're on our way to pick up Chinese food. She's coming to help us eat it," I confided in Tris.

"Chinese food? Miranda? Yay!" Tris said, grinning, pulling out her phone, evidently delighted. I didn't know which fact pleased her more — another take-out dinner or the presence of Miranda, one of Tris's favorite people. I'm sure she was looking forward to more talk about the Musical Ride and whether becoming a Mountie or an ornithologist would be the wiser career move.

The mad talk had turned out better than I feared. And now Tris and I had shared a pinky swear. That meant I'd better turn the volume up on my phone and find an appropriate ringtone if I wanted to keep *my* finger. *Yubikiri* indeed. I knew watching all those old *Star Trek* episodes would come in handy someday. Gene Roddenberry had had quite an imagination, and Mr. Spock intoned *yubikiri*, whatever it meant, so well.

CHAPTER 21

"How are the wilds of West Saanich?" I asked, when Miranda answered her phone.

"You don't want to know," she said, sounding testy. "My wonderful side road for points north apparently got washed out in the winter rains, so I had to search for another route. I found one, but that got me to the shelter too late to intercept Mohammed. He does or did indeed work there, and, as we thought, he simply stashed Beatrice there with the rest of the dogs. No one even noticed — except a blabby kennel cleaner named Brent. He apparently knows everything that goes on at the shelter and gave me quite an earful. I'll fill you in when I see you. Anyhow, Beatrice was gone when I got there, whisked away by Mo, no doubt."

I groaned. "What about the pet tracker?" I asked. "Could you follow it?"

"It worked like a charm until I got up around Deep Cove," she said. "Then . . . the signal stopped. I called the company that makes the tracker and they say there must be something jamming it."

"Oh, for God's sake, will we ever catch a break with this case?" I yelled. Only the presence of Tris short-circuited a Vesuvius of bad language on my part.

"Really," Miranda said. "Anyhow, I'm going to circle around what I think the problem is — a bloody great cell tower, a Coast Guard station with forests of antennae, and what I'm sure is the upper peninsula's power station

— and see if I can't pick up the signal again. Too much metal, according to the tracker people. If I can, I'll call you and we'll figure out how to rescue the Labradoodle. If not, well, hell, I'll just give up. For tonight, anyway. We can work on Plan C over dinner."

"Sounds good," I said. "Tris and I are just on our way to get Chinese food."

"Hmm, I gather the prodigal daughter came to no harm?"

"Thankfully, no," I said, looking over at Tris. "Come on along when you're able. Or call me and we'll figure out how to do some Labradoodle-rescuing."

"Ha, yes," Miranda said. "Rescue. It can't come too soon for Izzy, I bet. Or for us."

※　※　※　※

"Do you think I should call Aliya?" Tris asked when I handed her back her phone.

"That might be a good idea," I told her. "Let her know you're safe. Maybe tell her that we're bringing dinner and that Miranda's joining us."

"Okay," she said. As we pulled out of the little parking lot at Kitty Islet, I reached over and ruffled Tris's hair.

"You were a brave kid," I told her.

"I was a lucky kid," she said seriously. "You were there. If you hadn't been . . ."

"Yeah, well," I said a little self-consciously. Then, "Hey, I've got a riddle for you."

"Yeah?" she said, brightening. We often tried to out-riddle each other, a game I thoroughly enjoyed. "Bet I get it right away," she teased.

"We'll just see about that, missy," I told her. "Here goes. Katie's mother has four daughters. The names of three of the daughters are April, May, and June. What is the name of the fourth daughter?"

"Easy," Tris scoffed. "It's July."

"Nope," I told her.

"Nope?" she said, surprised. "Oh, then it's March."

"Nope," I told her again.

"Hmm," Tris said. "February? August?"

"Nope."

"I guess I'm going to have to think about this," she said.

I grinned. "Let me know when you've got it."

She looked over at me. "Oh . . . no fair . . . it's a hard one, isn't it?"

"Pretty hard."

"And there's a trick to it, right?"

"Nope."

"'*Katie's mother has four daughters,*'" she repeated to herself, looking thoughtfully out the window. "'*The names of three of the daughters are . . .*' Darn it," she said. "I don't get it."

"You will," I said. "Just keep thinking about it."

"I'm going to ask Miranda," she said confidently. "She'll know. She knows just about everything."

Back at home, on the little table beside the door leading to Helen's upstairs suite, was a bottle of wine with a note on it.

I won this in the Saltspring Spring Fling 10K. Want to come up and drink it with me tonight? I'll be back around 9. I have something to discuss with you.

Helen

Wine and a discussion. Hmm. I put the bottle of wine in the kitchen, wondering what could be on Helen's mind.

In the dining room, Aliya had set Tris up with her homework and was delivering a scolding. I didn't interrupt. Tris had heard how her adventures had affected me; she deserved to hear how they had affected Aliya also.

"See this face?" Aliya said, pointing to her frown.

"Uh huh," Tris said, looking worried.

"This is my mad face," Aliya said. "It's also called *stink eye*, from the Hawaiian. You do not want to see Aliya's *stink eye* again."

Tris's mouth trembled and a tear rolled down one cheek.

"Now, see this face?" Aliya said, pointing to her smile.

"Uh huh," Tris said.

"This is my glad face. You want to see that a lot."

Tris nodded.

"Okay," Aliya said, enveloping Tris in an enormous hug and planting a kiss on the top of her head. "No more going AWOL, all right? Now, French irregular verbs. Oh, I get it. That's why you ran away, right?" Aliya teased. "Verb avoidance."

Tris sniffled a little, drying her eyes on her T-shirt sleeve, giving Aliya a tentative smile.

"Kieran, Edgar called me when he wasn't able to get you," Aliya said. "He wants you to call him." She frowned a bit. "Did something happen to your phone?"

"No," I told her. "Miranda has it. I put a GPS tracking app on it, and Miranda's, well, tracking. We hoped it would lead us to Beatrice. But something's jamming the signal. Miranda will tell us all about it when she gets here."

Behind Tris's back, Aliya shrugged her shoulders, pointing to Tris, shaking a finger, pantomiming "Was my scolding okay?" I gave her a thumbs-up. After all, Aliya had three younger brothers. If anyone knew how to read youngsters the Riot Act, it was Aliya.

I put the containers of Chinese food in the oven to keep warm, poured two

fingers of Method and Madness Irish Whiskey, took it into my office, flipped on my lamp, and sat down with my feet propped up on my desk. I wondered what Edgar had dug up. Something useful, I hoped. Trey had finished eating his grain-free Tuna and Mackerel Dinner in Gravy and had followed me into my office, insinuating his portly self onto my lap, making me juggle my whiskey glass, the receiver of my landline phone, and his soft, warm bulk.

"What's up, big guy?" I asked as he settled down, licking a paw. "I've been neglecting you. I'm sorry. This case will be over soon and we can spend more time reading ourselves to sleep. I know we're only halfway through *The Way the Crow Flies* by Ann-Marie MacDonald. Her background is a lot like mine, did you know? We graduated from the same university, our fathers were in the military, we spent a number of years overseas, and we came home to the same southern Ontario town. Coincidental, right? Anyhow, I'd like to get back to her book. And then there's Billy Collins. We promised ourselves we'd improve our minds and read some of his poetry."

"*Raff,*" he said.

"Remember the one we started listening to on YouTube? You liked it even though it was about a dog. Or maybe because it was about a dog. We'll listen to more of it tonight," I told him. I sat back in my chair, scratching Trey's ears, thinking I should call Edgar back, instead feeling thwarted, aggravated, depressed, and, yes, tired. Ha, I thought. Not half as tired as Miranda must be, struggling back from adventures in West Saanich. I gave Trey's chin a scratch, drank a little more whiskey, then punched Edgar's number on my speed dial.

"At last," he said. "The phoneless investigator returns."

"Don't start with me," I told him. "It's been a long, miserable day fraught with frustration and failure."

"Well, sweetie, I'll tell you right off the bat that I'm about to add to your frustration," he said. "I've emailed you the NITI class list you wanted."

"And?" I said eagerly.

"Your boy Mohammed is not among the graduates."

"Not —" I was momentarily speechless. "Did he graduate the following year? Two thousand and five?"

"Alas, no," Edgar said. "I went back two years and ahead two years. No Mohammed. But in any event, I've emailed you the names for two thousand and four, as you asked."

"Huh," I said, not knowing what the hell to make of this. "But he's evidently proud of his graduation ring. I can't see why he'd wear it if it isn't his. And he wears a green hoodie associated with the place he works — Evergreen Animal Rescue. He seems like a guy attached to things — class rings, hoodies — that proclaim he belongs. Or belonged."

"I had better luck with the black RAM," Edgar said. "It's owned by a woman named Barbara Davidson."

"She's the director of Evergreen Animal Rescue," I said. "So that solves that mystery. Mohammed works at Evergreen and drives the RAM sometimes."

"But he didn't graduate from NITI as you thought he did," Edgar said.

"Dammit," I said, more to myself than to Edgar. "I need to think all this over, Edgar. I don't need to keep you on the phone, though. Let me look at my email. I'll call you if I have questions."

"I'll be here, sweetie," Edgar said.

I hung up and sat back in my chair, Trey purring on my lap. "Nuts," I told him as my printer spat out the list of 2004 NITI grads. Trying not to disturb Trey, I pulled the list out of my printer tray, looking for Saleh, in case Edgar had missed it. Nope. No Mohammed Saleh. Or Aziz Amad, either. Aggrieved, I was about to wad up the list and toss it in the direction of my wastepaper basket when a name caught my eye. The name right after James Taverner and Irene Templeton.

Louis Tremblay.

"Holy shit!" I exclaimed, sitting up straight, dumping Trey unceremoniously onto the floor. Louis Tremblay, Louis Tremblay . . . that was Izzy's brother's name. What the hell was going on here?

CHAPTER 22

"**O**w, Miz Blake," I said, looking closely at Miranda's face as she hung up her jacket on the coat tree. Her lower lip now sprouted two uncomfortable-looking sutures where Anton had slugged her, and her about-to-be black eye had been cleaned up, but was pretty much closed.

"After driving round and round, trying to put the cell tower, the power station, and those damned marine antennae behind me so I could pick up the GPS signal, I gave up," she said. "We'll need to use your computer — or Aliya's, since she has that whopping great monitor — and Google Maps to look at a blowup of the spot where I lost the signal. It was on the road to Deep Cove. I figured we'd work on that after dinner. Then, on the way back here, I passed an Urgent Care clinic," she said cheerfully. "They must have been trolling for business because they had a sign out front that said: *'Hurting? Boo-boos fixed ASAP.'* My lip hurt like hell and wouldn't stop oozing, so I thought, why not? After the not-very-busy staff sewed it up, they gave me a pain shot. Probably what the ER gave Ro. So, as they say, I'm feeling no pain."

I looked at her closely. "You seem a little goofy to me," I said, "but I'm glad you visited the clinic. You looked somewhat ragged earlier."

"Yeah, I'm getting a bit long in the tooth for fisticuffs with twenty-year-olds. Say," she said, lowering her voice, "how did things go with your wandering daughter? You found her, I take it?"

"I did," I said. "Right after *she'd* found the creepy old child molester on the bus, took a picture of him, and damned near got herself abducted."

Miranda whistled softly. "I'm sure you and she had a heart-to-heart afterwards."

"Oh, yes," I said. "It was second only to the heart-to-heart Aliya dispensed a little bit ago. Tris has learned the meaning of the word *stink eye*."

"A little *stink eye* often makes a lasting impression," she said. "I'm not long on punishment, but sometimes being given hell is useful. Let me say hi." She walked through the living room and leaned against the dining room doorframe.

"Irregular French verbs?" she called to Tris.

"*Oui*," Tris said. Then, "Miranda, *je suis désolée de t'inquiéter*. Really, I am."

"Hmm," Miranda said, crossing her arms and looking sternly at Tris. "*Très bien. J'accepte tes excuses*."

"Are we still friends?" Tris asked timidly.

Miranda grinned. "You betcha. Who else can I talk to about the Musical Ride?"

Tris gave her a feeble smile, then said, "We have Chinese food."

"I think I heard a rumor about that," Miranda said. "I'll just talk to Kieran for a bit, then we can all tuck into a nice big plate of General Tso's chicken."

"General . . . no, Miranda," Tris said, looking at me in confusion. "We got all veggie dishes."

"Just fooling," she said, winking. "Back to those verbs, kid."

Tris grinned and bent over her homework.

"Why don't we eat now?" Aliya said. "I hear you two might want to use my big monitor. What's up?"

After Miranda explained about losing the GPS signal up around Deep Cove, Aliya nodded. "There's not much in the way of civilization there. I had to visit a client up that way a few weeks ago. She lives on her boat at the marina. I had to take some photos for her website. It's pretty remote."

A worrisome thought struck me. "When I was concerned about the dog thief trying to get on a plane with the ten Maple Leafs, I concluded that he'd never risk flying. He'd drive across the border. But what if, instead, he's headed for the marina and a boat? There are hundreds of places he could put in on the Washington shore. Maybe he's smarter than we think."

"And maybe he's not," Miranda said. "I think he's had a run of really good luck. But luck is fickle. I think it's our turn now."

I nodded. "Okay. Let's get a Google Map for Deep Cove. Aliya?"

"Sure," she said. "Why don't we eat first, get the dishes cleared away, see a certain young person tucked up in bed with a book, then go downstairs?"

"Hmmf," I said, giving Tris a stern look. "I'm afraid I'll want to tie a certain young person's leg to the bedpost to be sure she doesn't get a wild hair to go sleuthing again."

"Guys, I'm right here," Tris said, closing her French grammar book. "I can hear you just fine. I promise, I won't go anywhere. Kieran and I did a pinky swear."

"You better not, short stuff," Miranda said. "Any more shenanigans and Connie won't share with you photos of what's just arrived at The Sanctuary."

"Just arrived . . .?" Tris asked eagerly. "What? Is it kittens?"

"It might be," Miranda said coyly. "You could call her in a while. She has a dinner engagement, but she should be back, oh, around eight. So assuming you haven't gone walkabout —"

Tris shook her head vigorously, "I've *told* Kieran I won't go anywhere! Our swear was a *yubikiri* swear."

"Ah," Miranda said, giving me a quizzical look. "That's pretty serious. No one wants *yubikiri*."

Tris nodded.

"Then . . . if you're sure . . . Connie'll send you the photos. Just give her a call. Okay?" Miranda told her.

"Okay!" Tris said excitedly, hopping down from her chair and gathering up her books. "I'm going to get cleaned up for dinner. Is it time to set the table, Aliya?"

"Just about," Aliya said. "Go wash up. I need to do some work on the salad."

"Who would have imagined the power of kittens to modify behavior?" I said. "Volunteering to set the table no less."

"It's called bribery," Miranda said, taking some cutlery from its drawer in the kitchen and setting four places. "We all have our currency. Tris's just happens to be kittens."

"And nuthatches," I said, "and owls, and turkeys and goldfinches . . ."

"And fear of *yubikiri*," Miranda said. "By the way, what is *yubikiri*?"

"Don't ask," I said as Aliya handed me four plates. "It's Vulcan."

Miranda raised an eyebrow. "Vulcan? As in *Star Trek* Vulcan? Dr. Spock and all that?"

"*Mister* Spock," I tut-tutted. "You descendants of Braveheart can be such philistines."

Once the dishes had been cleared away, and Tris had been installed in bed with the latest book in the *Warriors* cat-adventure saga, Miranda, Aliya, and I made our way downstairs.

"Read it and weep," I said, brandishing the piece of paper I'd brought with me from my office.

Aliya looked at me curiously, as did Miranda.

"I heard from Edgar," I said. "The NITI class list?"

Aliya nodded. "Uh huh?"

"Here it is," I said. "Unfortunately, our guy Mo is not on it."

"What?" Miranda said. "Not . . . then who the hell was I following?"

I passed her the list. "Look at the Ts. Taverner . . . Templeton . . ."

"Louis Tremblay?" Miranda said incredulously. "Wait . . . Louis freaking Tremblay? Izzy's brother? Born again as Mohammed Saleh? *He* took Beatrice?"

"Maybe grab two chairs, Kieran?" Aliya said. "Miranda looks as though she might fall over."

I set up folding chairs in front of Aliya's desk and Miranda collapsed into one.

"I'm . . . beyond shocked," she said.

"Izzy's brother?" Aliya said. "I don't get it. He took Beatrice, wrote that note, made the phone calls and . . ."

Miranda put her head in her hands in evident frustration, muttering something that I didn't quite catch. Finally she sat up, smoothing her ruffled hair. "Kieran, how do we look at the pet tracker report?"

"Scoot over and let me use the computer," I said to Aliya as I called up the pet trackers' website and entered my user name and password. Up popped a record of Miranda's pursuit of the dog carrier.

"Here's where the carrier left Evergreen," I said.

"And here's where I picked it up," Miranda said. "I followed it to about here," she tapped the screen, "which is where I lost it."

"Wow, that's miles from the shelter, Miranda," Aliya said. "Look — the signal stopped just . . . here. Now, let's see what's around there." She switched to satellite view and we watched roads, rooftops, ocean, and acres and acres of dark green forest spring into view. "This is Chalet Road," she said. "There's a Life Flight International helipad, the Coast Guard station, a marina, *ooh-la-la* a fancy French restaurant — who'd have guessed it up there — a beach, a bunch of dilapidated boathouses, some falling-down cabins, and that's it."

I pointed to the map. "What about Land's End Road, just up the coast a little more? There's a bed and breakfast up there. At least according to this map there is. And after that . . . an entire unspoiled forest."

"I don't know if the bed and breakfast is open, though," Aliya said. "It's a little early in the season."

"Screw it," I said. "Let's just phone them."

"Number?" Miranda asked, phone in hand. Aliya found it, read it to her, and we waited while the number evidently rang and rang. "Nope," Miranda said.

"Crap," I said. "He needs a place for the night. One night. Two at the most."

"And a place that will let him have a dog," Miranda said.

"Unless he leaves her in the car."

Miranda raised her eyebrows. "A car? According to Brent, the kennel cleaner at Evergreen, Louis took the black RAM. Beatrice was in a carrier in the truck bed. So I guess Louis — or Mo, as he's called at Evergreen — could just leave her in the carrier."

"He could," I said thoughtfully. "But I wonder where the beat-up brown Honda is? Is he just going to abandon it?"

"The Honda?" Miranda asked.

I explained about my chat with Gavin behind Ajay's convenience store and his description of Louis unloading the drone from a Honda in the little parking lot at night.

"Well then, my guess is that the Honda is still at Evergreen," Miranda said. "I didn't see it, but I wasn't looking for it. He must have switched vehicles."

"Which means he has to go back to the shelter tomorrow from wherever he is. With Beatrice. Probably in the morning. He has to switch vehicles again. Load Beatrice into the Honda, ready to make the exchange. Beatrice for the Maple Leafs."

Miranda leaned back in her chair, looking up at the ceiling. "So he's in the black RAM. Where's he going? Somehow I don't think he'll spend the night in the truck, snuggled up to the back door of the French restaurant, so —"

"So where *is* he?" Aliya asked.

"Where does Barbara Davidson live?" I asked. "I'm having trouble believing she doesn't know anything about this. Oh, not the theft of Beatrice and the attempted extortion, but Louis's using the RAM to do dodgy animal deals."

"North Sidney," Miranda said.

"Fooey. That lets her off the hook," I said. "He's certainly not going to drive back to Sidney. If he was going to stay with her, he'd have gone there in the first place. He wouldn't have had to go wandering around Deep Cove." I thought for a minute. "You know, he's not wandering. Except when he made a stop, which was maybe to let Beatrice out to pee — he's driving straight for . . . somewhere. He knows where he's going."

"Barbara Davidson," Miranda muttered balefully. "Not tomorrow, but soon . . . I need to have a chat with that lady. She was the biggest holdout for our No Pets In Research coalition. Just couldn't make up her mind to commit herself to running a shelter that wasn't a seizure shelter."

She continued. "I never did get it. How can you run a shelter, and be committed to animal rehab and rehoming, when you sweep the place clean of unadopted animals every month? The undesirables, the not-quite-pretty ones, the behavior challenges. Just move them on. Whoever will pay her for them. Evergreen . . . it's nothing more than a conveyor belt to a researcher's lab." She fell silent and I realized how deeply pound seizure hurt Miranda. She might talk tough, but underneath the blather was a vulnerable soul.

"It is horrible," I said, wanting to validate Miranda's ire but also to distract her from imagining a vanful of frightened animals bound from Evergreen to the ferry docks and a mainland lab. "But right now we have to figure out how to find Beatrice. I don't think we want to wait to accost Louis on the road outside Evergreen tomorrow morning. I think we need to figure this out tonight. Or at least I do. Anyone who's had enough of this, please bow out."

"I'm in," Miranda said.

"Sutures and all?" I asked her, trying to make light of the fact that she might very well feel like hell. I felt guilty. First Ro and now Miranda had been laid low by this case.

"Sutures and all," she said.

"Count me in, too," Aliya added.

"Thanks, you two," I said. "So . . . I wondered if it might be helpful to think about Louis. Maybe something in his past, or something that Mac might have said, might be helpful."

"Well, here's some history," Miranda said. "Mac and I go back quite a way. I remember him telling me that just after Izzy graduated, got her wings, and received her assignment to the Griffon Squadron and Operation IMPACT that Mac kicked Louis out of the house. I recall his talking about that even years later. He still feels guilty. Mac's a very sweet guy and what he had to do upset him greatly. It wasn't so much the music-playing, the dope-smoking, and the lying-in-bed-all-day reading that dumb book that finally soured Mac on Louis. It was the kid's refusal to go see his sister get her pilot's wings. That's what ended his patience with Louis. Mary's patience, too.

"Apparently Louis has, or had, an outsized case of Izzy envy. It started when the kids lived at home, as these things do. But Louis never got over it, never, well, developed a self that he or anyone else could be proud of. He was a jerk from an early age — skipped classes, pilfered stupid, meaningless things from stores, never finished school, and finally ended up in jail in Toronto when he and a friend stole the electronics gear out of a plane on the Air Force base. He served a year for that.

"Then, later, after he'd screwed himself at Mary and Mac's and was asked to leave, Mac said Louis just wandered away — low-level jobs, marijuana, bad friends, more jail." She shrugged. "But there's a lot more to the story, I guess. It's been, what, over twelve years since Louis was kicked out of Mac's house. In that time, apparently he got himself straightened around, attended NITI, got a job at Evergreen."

"And then he became Mohammed," I said. "Something happened. Something profound, I imagine."

"Profound? Ya think?" Miranda said, sarcastic.

"Yeah, I do. Louis Tremblay, someone who never fit in, who lived his whole resentful life in his sister's shadow, found a group to belong to. A group that valued him. He shed his loser Canadian persona and became Mohammed Saleh, got radicalized — probably in reverse order — and converted to Islam. And he discovered a way he could really fit in with his new friends — bring them a nice little pot of money."

"And punish his sister in the process," Miranda said. "Steal her dog, frighten her with that terrifying Sinjar reference, make her clean out her bank account."

"Ruin her," I said thoughtfully, thinking of the lines of that opera I was so devoted to: *'From the ruin of others our pleasures we borrow.'* "What a guy. Eventually, after he became a real jihadist, he traveled to Iraq, attracting the RCMP's attention and got put on their watch list. He's not nobody now, is he?"

"Nope," Miranda muttered.

"I'm just wondering," Aliya said. "If we had known right off the bat . . . say, yesterday, that Mo wasn't Mo, that he was Louis, that he was Izzy's brother, would that have helped us? Should we have studied the video more closely?"

"I don't think so, Aliya," I said. "Look, we got two great pieces of information from that video. That class ring which led us to NITI. And the video itself, which was how I recognized Evergreen from a photo in that Sidney pet supply store. Louis was truly careless to have taken the video practically in the front yard of Evergreen. I don't think identifying Beatrice's abductor as Louis, though, would have made any difference."

"I agree, Kieran," Miranda said. "We would still have been sitting outside that house in Sidney; you would still have put the pet tracker in the dog carrier; I would still have driven halfway to Land's End following it. We would have known Louis was Louis a day earlier, but . . ." She shrugged.

"We just need Beatrice," I said. "The RCMP can have Louis. Undoubtedly the Force has psychologists who can wring out Louis's brain like a water-soaked sponge. They can document his journey from loser to jihadist," I said.

"Right," Miranda said. "We get the dog, the RCMP gets the dog thief. Louis Tremblay." She snorted in derision. "He can call himself Mohammed all he likes, but in my opinion, he's a jealous little mope who couldn't bear to see his far more able sister succeed. What happened later, how he came to be Mohammed . . . maybe it's the lateness of the hour or the headache I'm developing, but I find I don't give much of a rat's ass about it. I know Mac will want to know, Sylvie will want to know, but me . . . nah."

I sighed. "It's sad, but I really don't care a lot either. However, here's something we do need to ponder."

"Yeah?" Miranda said.

"Do we — or Mac, as he's really our client — tell Izzy that her dog wasn't taken by some rogue jihadist, but by her *brother*? And that it was Louis who wrote that ugly extortion note?"

"Brothers," Miranda said contemptuously. "Mine were a piece of work. After my mother died, they took the injured birds I rescued out the back door. No more trips to the vet to indulge soft-hearted seven-year-old animal-loving Miranda. My oldest asshole brother put one of my broken-winged birds out of its misery by tossing it in the back flowerbed and stepping on its head. I called him a shit-eating wanker for that. Aunt Connie grounded me for a week, but it was worth it. But Louis," she said, coming back to the present and shaking her head, "he's in a league of his own."

I said, "I've been asking myself if I would want to know that *my* brother had insinuated rape, planned to devastate me by taking away my beloved dog, was okay with the thought that I'd imagine her torture every day of my life, and was thrilled that I had to impoverish myself to pay the ransom? If I were Izzy, I wouldn't want to drag this knowledge along with me through the rest of *my* life.

"So I think we need to be kind here," I said, "try to figure out what would cause Izzy the least distress. She doesn't need to know who the extortionist is — she's had enough pain in her life. Oh, I suppose someday she might come to know his identity, but I figure Louis will be in prison by then."

I continued, "And another thing, Louis might well be in prison for a good long while. Extortion is usually thought of as a crime against property, but when you take into account the threat of bodily injury — and the Sinjar reference certainly applies here — and the fear that accompanies it, extortion is more than just a property crime. Anyhow, we can leave sorting out the legal tangle to the RCMP. Right now we're back to the problem at hand. Where the hell are Louis and Beatrice and how can we find them?"

"You know, I just thought of something that might help," Aliya said diffidently.

"Great," I said. "What?"

"I'm not sure if it will pan out, but it might," she said. "I have to make a phone call."

"Okay," I said, mystified. Then, "Let's go upstairs," I said to Miranda. "I think we need coffee and I need to say goodnight to Tris. She's probably swooning over Connie's photos of kittens."

"I'll make coffee," Miranda said. "Why don't you go to see Tris, and Aliya can make her phone call."

On the way upstairs, Miranda said, "*Yubikiri*?"

"Oh, hush," I told her. "It's a *Star Trek* thing. Somehow I don't think the show was a favorite of yours."

"*Au contraire*," she said. "I hung on Uhura's every word. But I don't recall anyone saying anything about *yubikiri*."

"Poetic license," I told her. "Go make coffee."

CHAPTER 23

"It's Katie, isn't it?" Tris said, as I sat beside her on her bed. "The fourth daughter. It's a kind of trick because you think it's so easy and that the next daughter ought to be July, but she's not. The answer is in the question," she said knowledgeably, closing her book and putting it up on her headboard. "The riddle talks about Katie's mother. So one of the daughters has to be named Katie, right?"

"Hmm, did a certain retired RCMP constable help out a little?" I asked.

"Well, just a little," Tris said. "Miranda told me the answer was in the question, and once she said that, I thought it over again, and got it."

"Good work," I said. "Say, how was story-writing class?"

"Interesting," Tris said. "I never realized writing a story took so much planning."

"Planning?" I asked.

"Yeah. Our instructor — she's a published author, y'know — told us the secret of a good story."

"There's a secret?"

"Uh huh. She says every story is about someone who wants to do something or get something or be something . . . and what gets in the way to make it hard for her."

"Ah," I said, "the struggle."

"Yup. So we're in the pre-writing stage of planning," she told me. "We're thinking of our character and what she wants."

"And *your* character?" I asked her. Jeoffry hopped up onto the end of Tris's bed, stretched mightily, then came purring to lie beside her. She snuggled down, one arm around him.

"A little girl," Tris said. "She's maybe ten. Or eleven."

"Ah. Does she have a name?"

"Not yet," Tris said.

"You'll think of one," I told her. "Maybe Katie."

Tris giggled. "Or April. Or May."

"What does the little girl in your story want?"

Tris frowned. "Oh, well, she wants to take all the birds someplace where they can be safe. We've learned in school that climate change and defor-estation is killing birds. But what if there was a place, like another world, where they could go? What if my character knows about this other world and is, well, searching for a way to get into it? Like maybe there's a magic doorway that she has to find. Anyhow, once she finds it, she has to figure out how to open it. Then, when she does, all the birds can fly through. They could wait out the bad times there," she said, her voice a little husky.

"Wow," I said, genuinely impressed. "That sounds like quite a story." I didn't tell her my own private thoughts, though — that it was way too late. For birds, for animals, for us. That the bad times couldn't be waited out.

"I wish there was such a place," Tris said, hugging Jeoffry. "Then the birds and animals wouldn't have to die. We could send them away and just . . . bring them back later. When climate change is fixed."

I cleared my throat, fussing unnecessarily with her comforter, wanting to tell her something optimistic, but found I didn't have a hopeful word to say. "Sprout — Miranda, Aliya, and I will be working downstairs in her apart-ment. Just wanted you to know."

"Okay," she said, yawning.

I turned off Tris's reading lamp, thinking about the little girl in her story, the one who wanted to take the birds and animals someplace safe. Of course the little girl was Tris. I remembered from my one and only writing class, the instructor's telling us that whatever character we wrote — a saint, a bank robber, a ballerina, an ax-murderer — we were always writing ourselves. That upset me so badly that I never went back to writing class. Perhaps I'd been in denial about my ballerina self.

I could hear Miranda and Aliya talking in low voices, sipping coffee at the kitchen table, clearly waiting for me. But as I'd sat talking to Tris, an idea had come out of nowhere. It seemed pretty outrageous, even to me, but before I ran it by Miranda and Aliya, I needed the answer to a question. I stepped into my bedroom, sat on the end of my bed, and pulled out my phone.

"Mary," I said, as Mary MacLeish, Mac's wife, answered her phone. "It's Kieran Yeats. Don't say my name. I don't want Mac to know I'm calling."

"Oh, no need to worry, dear," Mary said. "He's out on the garage refinishing a bookcase. I'm curious. Why do you not want him to know it's you?"

"It's the case I'm working on," I said. "He's pretty close to it."

"The Izzy and Beatrice case, of course," she said calmly. "He has been fretting about it, but I knew once he contacted you and Miranda, that you two would have things well in hand."

"Well, we're trying," I said. "We need to check something out, and I don't want Mac to play the role of the cavalry and come charging over the hill."

"Ah," Mary said. "Yes, he does confuse himself with the cavalry now and then. How can I help?"

"On Sunday when I was talking to him, Mac told me that when you asked Louis to leave all those years ago, you let him stay in your fishing cabin up north. Am I remembering this correctly?"

"Yes," Mary said.

"Can you tell me where this cabin is? And if you still own it?"

"Well, the cabin is on the beach, near Deep Cove, on an almost nonexistent road rather optimistically called Beach Access Road. Are you familiar with the Deep Cove area?"

"No, but we've got the satellite view up on our computer."

"Might I ask why you're interested in the cabin?" Mary wanted to know.

I decided to tell her the truth. She was the calmest, most sensible person I knew — the chances of her shrieking and rushing out to the garage for Mac were minuscule.

"Mary, we think Louis took Beatrice. And he may have taken her to your cabin."

"Oh, no," Mary said. After a moment she added, "Very well. I'll tell you how to get there. Proceed up Chalet Road, past that nice French restaurant, past the fork with Tatlow Road. You'll come to a narrow, barely paved road called Moses Point Road. Chalet Road changes names there and becomes Land's End Road which continues up around the end of the peninsula."

"Moses Point Road. Okay, I recall seeing that on satellite view," I said.

"Turn left on Moses Point Road. It dead-ends at a tiny dirt road called Beach Access Road. It won't have a sign, but . . . it's there."

"Is your cabin the only one there? On the beach?"

"No. There are several others, none in very good repair. We're number six. Last time we were there, oh, a couple of years ago, two of the five neighboring cabins were in very bad condition. Collapsing roofs. Crumbling docks. I really think the owners have forgotten about them. The cabin looks out on the Saanich Inlet and really, it's not a very attractive place. The beach, such as it is, is shingle. We bought it because it was remote and the cabin was inexpensive. There's no landline. And no Wi-Fi. Mac wanted peace and quiet. Initially, he thought he might repair the cabin's dock. But that seemed too much of a job — all that sawing and hammering and dragging building materials from the city. And when he thought things over, he decided that he really didn't want to sit on a dock and pretend to fish. He liked his Adirondack chair on the beach just fine. But then he got promoted, weekends started becoming not his own, and we just found it harder and harder to get away. You understand, I expect."

"Unfortunately, I do," I said.

"I won't ask you any questions about . . . about your progress with the case," she said, "and mum's the word from me — I won't let anything slip to Mac — but you'll keep us posted?"

"Of course we will. I know how worried you two must be about Izzy. Thanks, Mary."

As I was talking with Mary on the phone, Trey came muttering into my bedroom and hopped up on the bed, giving me an inquiring, golden-eyed look.

"Not just now. A little later," I told him, holding up the bedclothes. "You can go ahead if you like, though. I'll be a while. Or you can go across the hall and snuggle with Tris and Jeoff."

"*Yang*," he said agreeably, disappearing under the covers.

In the kitchen, Aliya and Miranda were drinking coffee and chatting. I poured myself a mugful.

"Let's go back downstairs," I said. "I'm in the throes of plan formulation. We need to look at the Deep Cove area on your monitor again, Aliya."

"Thank heavens one of us has a plan," Miranda said. "Perhaps it's the fact that I was sucker-punched by Anton this morning, but I don't seem to be able to put two and two together. Or three and —"

Aliya gave Miranda a worried look. "Do you need a Tylenol? Or something stronger? I think I can find something."

"Maybe a bit later," she said. "Things are starting to hurt that didn't before. Let's hear Kieran's plan, and then I might have to avail myself of your drugs, depending on what they are."

"I'm sure one of us has something," I said. "But let's go back downstairs. Aliya, we'll need Deep Cove on satellite view again. Let's grab more coffee, too."

When we got back downstairs and were arranging ourselves in front of Aliya's desk again, something occurred to me. "Aliya," I said, "earlier you mentioned you had an idea, but you had to make a call."

She nodded. "Remember I said my client lived on a boat at the marina near Deep Cove? Well, she's a friend as well as a client, so I didn't feel too bad about asking for a favor. I asked her to drive to the French restaurant, and take a look in the parking lot. I remembered one of you said Louis probably wouldn't be snuggled up to the back door of the restaurant."

"And?" I asked.

"No black RAM," Aliya said. "My friend even drove up to the Coast Guard station and the Life Flight lot also, just to see if there were cars still parked there after hours." She shook her head. "There weren't. No RAM there either."

"Ha! Okay, so we know where he isn't. But we might be able to nail down where he *is*. I just got off the phone with Mary MacLeish. Apparently Mac and Mary own a cabin on the beach," I gestured to the monitor. "Specifically, right here." I found Moses Point Road, then traced Beach Access Road to the beach. "Mac told me on Sunday that when he kicked Louis out of the house those years ago, he let the kid stay at the beach cabin. I think Louis remembered it. I think it's his bolt-hole."

Miranda bent forward to look at the monitor. "That's just north of where I lost the tracker signal. He may be there right now. Damn," she said. "We need eyes up there."

"We do," I said. "So I started thinking . . . why wait for Louis to load Beatrice into the RAM and come back to Evergreen? Why not get a jump on him? See what's going on up there at Mac's cabin early tomorrow morning? Very early tomorrow morning. And maybe we could ask Lawrence if we can use his drone."

"Ah, an eye in the sky would be perfect," Miranda said. "Aliya? You're the chief drone-driver. What do you think?"

Aliya frowned. "Well, Lawrence has a new drone. Lots more bells and whistles than the old ones. It was fabulously expensive — has a range of about three miles, a twenty-five-minute flight life, an HD video transmission system, a 4K camera. Lawrence wants to use it for panoramic real estate projects. He even has three projects booked. But the search for Beatrice — that would be its maiden voyage. I bet he'd be thrilled for us to use it. One, it's a good cause, and two, it would give us a chance to get the bugs worked out."

"Whew," I said. "When you started talking about Super Drone, Aliya, I thought we'd have to do some arm-twisting."

"No. Lawrence is just very insistent that my brother Samir never puts a hand on the new drone. He's already lost two," she said, rolling her eyes. "One in a fish pond, and the other in the Inner Harbor."

"I wonder how he still has his job," I muttered.

"Sometimes I wonder that, too," Aliya said. "Anyhow, I'm certain that Lawrence will want to help."

"Okay," I said. "I'll give him a call."

"Maybe hold off for a few minutes," Miranda said. "I've been thinking about Louis. And Beatrice."

"Anything specific?" I asked.

"Well, yes," Miranda said. "If it were me, and I had a valuable piece of property that I was going to trade for ten thousand dollars, well, I think I'd put it in a safe place."

"Meaning?"

"Louis is already a little suspicious, right? He got another burner phone, he moved the timeline up, he doesn't intend to send another video, he moved out of the place he was renting with Aziz, he's not driving his own car, and we're pretty sure he's hidden himself away in Mac's cabin. Again, if it were me, I wouldn't take my most valuable asset, my bargaining chip, with me. I'd have it stashed in a location separate from where I'm spending the night."

"Huh," I said. "Never thought of that."

"Great," Aliya said. "So now we have two problems. We can use the drone to look for Louis at Mac's cabin, but where will we look for Beatrice? I doubt if she's just in a cabin down the beach. Or in her carrier in the back of the RAM."

"I doubt that, too," I said. "But I do agree with you, Miranda. According to the tracker, Louis made only one stop on the way from Evergreen. And that was for about three minutes, out in the middle of nowhere. Probably for Beatrice to pee. So where in hell did he stash her? And wherever it is, it has to be north of where the pet tracker lost him. He didn't make any stops before that."

"Well, we may need help to answer that question," Miranda said, grinning.

"No shit, Sherlock," I said. "What kind of help do you have in mind?"

"Four-legged," she said, still grinning.

"Four —"

"A dog, Kieran. A dog with a fabulous nose. A retired RCMP sniffer dog."

"Holy moley," I said. "Max."

"Yup, Max."

CHAPTER 24

"**S**ure," Lawrence said. "If Miranda thinks Max can do it, then . . . sure."

I'd already broached the subject of using the new drone, and he'd agreed immediately. As long as Aliya drove it, which I assured him she would. Then I aired the matter of Max. I wasn't sure how Lawrence would react. If dogs have nine lives, like cats, Max was definitely on his ninth, and Lawrence was very protective of him.

Lawrence had adopted Max, a Belgian Malinois, from Miranda's shelter several years ago. As an RCMP sniffer dog, Max – and his nose – was a Vancouver Island legend. But tragedy struck the day he, his handler Duncan, and their squad raided a drug house. Masks were handed out, but in a great stroke of bad luck, Duncan inhaled a minute quantity of fentanyl before he could get a mask on properly, passed out, and died of a seizure in the drug house's makeshift lab, amid the pill presses and baggies of white powder. Max also got a snootful of fentanyl, but it fortunately didn't kill him. Squad members carried the unresponsive dog out to one of their cars and raced him to the vet hospital where he barely survived. He was given a medal and a plaque by the mayor and had his fifteen minutes of fame on a feel-good TV special about crime-fighting canines. Then, ignominiously, he was packed off to Miranda's Sanctuary with a miserable case of canine PTSD, where he lived in Miranda's office under her desk. He was mourning

Duncan, and his interest in the world was zero . . . until the day Lawrence and I dropped in to meet with Miranda, on our way to another case. As the three of us sat talking, Max came out from under Miranda's desk, sniffed Lawrence's shoes carefully, put one paw on his knee, looked into his eyes . . . and it was all over. Lawrence likes to say that Max adopted him that day.

"He's still a pretty good finder," Lawrence volunteered. "Samir and I hide things around the shop and get him to go sniff them out. The kids — Samir and Aliya's little brothers — and I take him to the park and play hunt and fetch games with him there, too. So he's been keeping in practice. What would he be searching for?"

"Another dog," I said. "A Labradoodle. Beatrice. She was stolen by a nutjob jihadist wannabe named Louis Tremblay. Long story. But we're pretty sure he has her up near Land's End. We want to use the drone to find Louis, and Max to find Beatrice. Louis is probably holed up in Mac's old fishing cabin, so once we've used the drone to establish that for sure, we can call for help to winkle him out of there."

"Help?"

"Miranda's RCMP contact. Sergeant Desjardins. Sylvie. She and her squad will come and pick him up. But Beatrice? I'm worried."

"You don't think she's with Louis at the cabin?" Lawrence asked.

"No, we don't think so. Louis wants ten thousand dollars for her safe return. We're worried that he's stashed her someplace extra safe — where, we have no idea. That's the aggravating part of this."

"Hiding her someplace away from the cabin is pretty smart, though," Lawrence said. "That's what I'd do. She's his bargaining chip, right?"

"Right. And we want to take that advantage away from him. Our plan, feeble though it is, is to find her first, get her safely stowed away in Miranda's van, then call the RCMP, who'll be coming along Chalet Road behind us."

"Gotcha," Lawrence said. "Max will need something to get a scent from. Do you have something?"

"How about Beatrice's dog bed? Miranda can talk to Ro, and ask her to bring it here in a plastic bag, all sealed up to keep in the smells," I told him.

"So I guess once Ro drops off the bed, we'll be set. I was thinking we ought to leave, oh, around four? Sunrise this time of year is seven-ish. That will give us plenty of time to get there and get set up. If you want to look up our destination on a map, use Google's satellite view and look at the intersection of Moses Point Road and Beach Access Road, just south of that French restaurant."

"Oh yeah, I vaguely know where that is," he said. "I'm Googling as we speak. Okay . . . got it. It's pretty remote, isn't it? That road, Beach Access, do we know if it's passable?"

"I'm not sure," I said. "Mary implied it was pretty primitive."

"So we should assume it's barely passable," he said. "Once we get up there, we'll figure things out."

"Yeah," I said, "but before that —"

"Beatrice. Don't worry, Kieran. She's the priority. And Max will find her."

I didn't tell him that I had my fingers crossed, but I did. What if Max was out of practice? What if we were wrong and Louis had dropped Beatrice off somewhere closer to town. With his partner in crime Aziz? Or at the spot where the pet tracker stopped for three minutes? Or . . . oh fooey.

I said, "I thought you, Aliya, the drone, and Max could ride in your Range Rover. Miranda and I will take her van. Ro's bringing a sweater of Izzy's — Izzy is the dog owner — to comfort Beatrice on the way home."

Ever cheerful and optimistic, Lawrence said, "A veteran Griffon pilot, jihad, a kidnapped PTSD dog — this sounds like quite the story. I'm looking forward to hearing the whole thing. After the rescue, that is."

"Okay," I said. "See you at my place around four."

Ro had come and gone, leaving the plastic-bag-wrapped dog bed, and a navy sweatshirt that Ro swore Izzy had just taken off, having worn it for parts of four days. Lotsa good smells. Ro had also left a black backpack, as Louis had specified. However, instead of the gold Canadian Maple Leafs, it contained a volume of *The Rubaiyat of Omar Khayyam* which I had added from my library. My copy was about the same heft as ten one-ounce gold coins. A nice touch, I thought. Louis might even want to read Omar's musings in prison, if the RCMP let him have the book. I thought about one of the stanzas of *The Rubaiyat*:

> *And, as the Cock crew, those who stood before*
> *The Tavern shouted — "Open then the Door!*
> *"You know how little while we have to stay,*
> *"And, once departed, may return no more."*

Indeed. The brevity of life . . . and the fact that once it's over, it's over. Well, Louis could peruse the entire *Rubaiyat* in prison, and think about the botch he'd made of his life. The Door certainly wouldn't be opening for him again. I found myself unable to feel a single iota of sympathy.

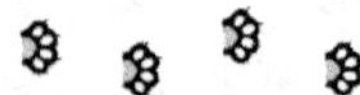

"How about four as an ETD?" I asked Miranda, who was wrapped in a fluffy blue throw on the futon in my office. We'd decided that it made no sense for her to go home only to sleep for an hour or two, then come back here while we assembled our team. I had an assortment of clean socks and underwear; a drawer full of complimentary toothbrushes and tiny tubes of toothpaste, courtesy of my dental hygienist; at least a dozen sample bottles of shampoo, conditioner, mouthwash, and lotion; a linen closet with plenty of clean towels and facecloths; and a bottle of Tylenol ER if Miranda's sutured lip continued to bother her.

"Sounds fine," she said, yawning, putting her phone down on the floor beside the futon.

"Tell me about tracking dogs?" I asked Miranda, perching on a corner of my desk. I didn't want to get too comfy — I still had to go upstairs to talk with Helen Mikita. "I understand they're terrific with scent trails, but Max wouldn't be tracking Beatrice on the ground. If we can believe what Brent the kennel guy at Evergreen told you, Louis took off with her in a carrier in the bed of the RAM. The only place she might have touched the ground is that three-minute gap of time when the RAM stopped."

"Tracking is misunderstood by civilians," Miranda said. "A little history: did you know that bloodhounds used in Scotland in the seventeenth century were known as *slough dogs*? Why? Because the constables used them to track outlaws through the sloughs. Anyhow, that's where the word sleuth came from. Thought you'd like to know how your newly adopted profession got its name." She winked.

"Really?" I said. "How disappointing. And here I thought we sleuths were descendants of Holmes, reasoning our way to elegant solutions in cozy, smoke-filled rooms, not traipsing through muddy ditches, peering at the hind end of a dog."

"Another romantic myth shattered," Miranda said. "Anyhow, about tracking. Many Malinois, including Max, are trained to do air scenting. And they're good at it. Better than Shepherds. The Force tends to prefer Malinois to Shepherds. They're smaller, more agile, more talented, have fewer health problems and, if possible, are more intense. They never give up."

"Air scenting?" I said. "Never heard of that. How does that work?"

"Well, microscopic particles — skin cells, dander — are shed by canine or human bodies at a rate of about forty thousand per minute. Some fall to the ground, but about fifty percent stay airborne. A dog can track a scent footprint to footprint, by following the highest concentration of ground particles, or they can track through air scenting — sniffing those particles that are still in the air. And some particles stay airborne for hours. In fact, a trained search dog can detect a mere three particles of scent per trillion particles of air. There was a case about ten years ago in which a child was abducted by automobile in Salt Lake City. A Rottweiler trailed her by air scenting and led police to her location over forty miles away."

"Okay, I'm sold," I said. "I know Lawrence and Samir play with Max to keep his tracking skills up, but I was thinking that you probably know more about serious tracking."

"Oh, maybe a little more," she said. "I even thought about becoming a dog handler, but, well, other things intervened. However, I've been out on a few searches. So you're thinking that you and I ought to track with Max while Lawrence and Aliya use the drone? We find the dog; they find Louis?"

"Well, yes and no," I said. "I really want to keep them out of harm's way. Maybe after we find Beatrice, and they establish that Louis is at the cabin, that's good enough. We could call Sylvie and her team to play cleanup. How does that sound?"

"It sounds good to me," she said. "But we have to be prepared to improvise if things go pear-shaped, though. Say if Louis makes a run for it."

"Pear-shaped?"

"An old RCMP term, bequeathed to us from the Brits. It really means, well, if things go to hell."

"Oh, how comforting," I said. "If things go pear-shaped, let's just let the jerk run. Where can he go? Down the beach? There's nothing to run to. We'll have Beach Access Road blocked off with Lawrence's car and your van. So he won't be able to get away in the RAM. Maybe Sylvie and her squad will feel like a foot race early in the morning."

"Or maybe not," Miranda said. "I just had a discouraging thought. What if Louis has a boat stashed at the cabin? It's not beyond the realm of possibility. I mentioned this to Sylvie and she reassured me that the Force has a patrol boat stationed at Nanaimo. It will probably leave around midnight. Plans are to anchor off the beach, in Saanich Inlet, just in case. Sylvie tells me that she's pretty interested in talking to Louis. Or Mohammed. He's been out of the country one too many times, and been involved in one too many shady activities. This attempted extortion of Beatrice is the end of the road, Sylvie says."

"Brother, I hope he's there," I said. "We'll look like the boys who cried wolf otherwise."

"I'm confident that's where he is," she said. "Beatrice?" She waggled a hand and shook her head. "Her I'm not so sure about."

I looked at my watch. "I have to go upstairs and talk to Helen for a bit," I said. "I've left a small pile of things for you on the hall table by the bathroom. Personal grooming aids, socks and underwear, drugs."

"Drugs?" She raised an eyebrow.

"Nothing serious. Just some Tylenol ER. And if you want something soothing to ease you into slumber, well, there are chamomile teabags in the cupboard."

"Say, I just had a thought," Miranda said, unlacing her sneakers. "Doesn't Tris need a ride to school tomorrow?"

"Oh, Lord, yes," I said. "Aliya will be busy."

"How about Connie?" Miranda suggested. "I don't think she'd mind. And you certainly don't want Samir to play chauffeur."

I shook my head in horror. "Nope. He's way too . . . flighty. He might misplace her on the way to school. I know Lawrence likes him, but there's no way I could trust him with Tris. Should I call Connie?"

"Why don't you let me?" she said. "I know she was a bit miffed when she had to sit out our adventures the other day. I think I need to do some soothing."

"Okay," I said, "soothe away. I'd better go. Why don't I check in with you when I come back from talking with Helen? You might have more thoughts about tomorrow's early-morning escapade."

"Ha," Miranda said. "Or I might be snoring."

"Indeed you might be," I said. "Maybe take a Tylenol for your lip and chill out. I'll poke my head in when I come back."

"Better make it decaf," I said to Helen as she took a container of coffee out of the fridge. "Or something made from leaves and twigs." I explained my latest case, including the fact that Miranda, Aliya, Lawrence, and I needed to leave in the wee hours of the morning for points north.

Helen whistled, spooning decaf into her coffeemaker. "Sounds exciting. And potentially dangerous. But all your cases do," she said, "sound exciting and dangerous."

"I don't see the potential for rough stuff with this case," I said. "We're just going to pick up a dog, then call the RCMP to pick up the dog thief."

"Uh huh," she said, giving me a level look. We both took seats at her kitchen table, and I waited for her to come to the point of this late-night meeting. Fifty-ish and blue-eyed, with curly, prematurely silver hair and a mouth that liked to smile, Helen was a fitness nut. Tonight she was wearing black jeans and a grey souvenir sweatshirt with the winged foot logo of the Island Running Club in gold, and NORTH ISLAND MARATHON 2012 in white underneath it. Her anthrozoology classes at U Vic were always oversubscribed, as hundreds of students apparently wanted to debate the ethics of eating chihuahuas as opposed to chickens. An author as well as an academic, Helen had written four immensely readable books. *Kitten Soup* — a provocative title if there ever was one — was her best-seller.

"So I've been offered a job," she said. "At that new school just west of Sidney. North Saanich College. They have some very interesting programs planned. They're billing themselves as a bastion of the arts and humanities . . . sort of a counterpoint to all the high-tech courses, and indeed colleges, that are proliferating."

"Arts and humanities," I said. "Do they think they can stay in business? I thought every kid wanted to learn to code. Or build websites. Or do computer graphics."

"Apparently not every kid," she said.

"Hmm. And you would be doing what . . . teaching psychology? Or anthrozoology?"

"The latter," she said. "People's inconsistent behavior toward animals; our desire to live the Mowgli dream of blissful kinship with our four-footed brethren, and our equally powerful desire to use, eat, or experiment upon them; climate change and species extinction. It's potentially exciting. I can plan my own courses."

"Courses?"

She nodded. "Two courses. Maybe three."

I thought I heard some hesitation in her voice and wondered if I ought to pursue it. "You sound a trifle ambivalent. Is it the money?"

"No, that's acceptable," she said. "I wouldn't be making what I'm making at U Vic, but my books are selling well, so I'm not terribly concerned about the salary. And I'd put my books on the reading lists. Classes and classes of built-in readers. An author's dream."

"You still sound a little hesitant," I commented. "What's up?"

"Rents," she said. "Rents are impossible here in Victoria, and they're not that much better up north. I'd sure as heck hate to leave here, Kieran. This has been a perfect rental for me, and you've been a great landlord. But the commute from here to there would be too aggravating."

"I hear you," I said. "Miranda and I drove up to Sidney earlier today. I have to confess that I didn't unclench my shoulders until we'd left the clutter and traffic of Victoria behind. Ahhh, trees. So much more satisfying to the soul than the ever-burgeoning condo developments. Although the firs and hemlocks are going to have to duke it out with the condo developers, I'm afraid."

"Unfortunately," Helen said.

"So here's a confession," I said. "I had, oh, I guess you'd call it an epiphany this morning."

"Sounds serious."

"Pretty serious," I agreed. "The relocation bug bit me. I hadn't realized it, but moving out of the city must have been on my mind for quite some time. As I sat eating breakfast with Miranda at a little café by the water in Sidney, I thought, *I could live here.*"

"Ah," she said. "Bitten."

"So . . . maybe hold off on signing a lease up north." I took a deep breath and blurted out, "I'm thinking of selling this place and moving up the peninsula. I haven't even started looking yet, but leaving here, well, it's a mighty attractive prospect. The traffic, the building boom downtown, the sacrifice of trees for parking lots —" I fell silent.

"Joni Mitchell was right," Helen said sadly. "You don't know what you've got till it's gone."

"Exactly," I said, sighing. "I'm beginning to feel smothered here, Helen. And depressed about so-called progress, trading oaks for asphalt. I hadn't realized just how sad I am until this morning. But because I suddenly have this wild hair to relocate doesn't mean the rest of my family longs to live among the pines and poplars. I haven't mentioned this to Aliya yet. Horrors! She might want to stay in town." I groaned. "I can't imagine how I'd get along without her. Quite apart from what she does for Tris and me — she's Tris's nanny and tutor as well as our cook and housekeeper — I'd miss the heck out of her. I've grown quite fond of that young woman."

"You might be surprised," Helen said. "I think she's more devoted to you and Tris than she is to Oak Bay. Besides," she chuckled, "she'd have to win the lottery to afford a comparable rent."

"There is that," I said. "I may be deluding myself, but I sure hope she'd want to come along. And you, too. Depending on what I can find, of course."

"Count me in," she said. "Classes wouldn't start for me until the fall. I'll have to sign a contract with North Saanich pretty soon, which I intend to do even if I have to live in a motor home at the Land's End Campground."

"I think that would be pretty grim in winter," I said, laughing. "As soon as this case is over, I'll start looking."

"Have you mentioned this to Tris?" Helen wondered.

"Nope," I said. "But I'd better do that soon. I don't think she's particularly attached to this house, but you never know. At least she wouldn't have to change schools. Oak Grove is a private school. No geographical restrictions. And she loves it there."

The coffee had finished brewing and Helen poured decaf for both of us. I took a sip, then sat back, hands clasped behind my head. We sat in companionable silence for a few minutes, then Helen said, "Your case. A jihadist. A homegrown one, too. Fascinating." She shook her head. "One wonders how that happens. Online, we hear. In chat rooms. Or on the dark web." She turned her coffee mug around in her hands, clearly thinking.

"I know almost nothing about your case," Helen said, "only what you've told me. But there are so many inconsistencies in the brother's behavior . . . well, they speak pretty loudly to my psychologist's mind. And that note . . ."

"Miranda and I have been trying to ignore him and his motivation," I said. "Dwelling on it would just be a distraction. We've been fixed on locating Beatrice. Frankly, any sympathy I might have had for poor Louis, the lost soul, evaporated when I realized he's written the extortion note." I'd re-counted to Helen the contents of the note and she'd been appropriately appalled.

"It's so ugly," Helen said. "The Sinjar reference especially." She was quiet for a moment, then said, "Have you ever read Thomas Harris's novel *The Silence of the Lambs*?"

"Sure," I said, puzzled.

"Well, Hannibal Lecter — he's a psychiatrist, you may recall — says a very interesting thing about the book's kidnapper and murderer. 'Read Marcus Aurelius,' he tells FBI agent Clarice Starling. 'Of each particular thing, ask: What is it in itself? What is its nature?' Clarice is a little out-matched intellectually, but he asks her to consider, 'What does he do, this man you seek?' Well, she bumbles around trying to come up with an answer, so Lecter tells her. 'He covets. That's his nature. And how do we begin to covet, Clarice? Do we seek out things to covet?' Again, Clarice is intellectually outgunned, but Lecter helps her. He says, 'We begin by coveting what we see every day.' I wonder," Helen said, "if Louis doesn't have a serious case of coveting."

"That makes sense," I said. "All this jihad nonsense . . . I was thinking at one point that he just wanted to *belong* to something bigger and more powerful than himself. Find a tribe, a cause. But now I think it's not ideological with him, but intensely personal. He's eaten up with envy or jealousy or covetousness, whatever you want to call it. Of his *sister*. Oh, for heaven's sake. Did he . . . want to *be* Izzy? To be, what, a Griffon pilot?"

"You won't know until you talk to him, if you get a chance to do that," Helen said. "But I expect it's quite complicated. I expect he wanted and wants to be Louis, but a Louis he himself could like, and a Louis other people could admire."

"I see. Like people admired Izzy's accomplishments. Her competence and courage."

"Exactly."

"Well, the RCMP's psychologists will figure him out," I said. "It's sure not my job. I'm no shrink. My reaction to all this is, frankly, boo-hoo. I'm tired of giving men — or badly grown-up boys — hall passes for crappy behavior. I'm but a simple-minded gumshoe. A sleuth." I told Helen the derivation of the word sleuth and she threw back her head and laughed.

"Anyhow, I'd better go downstairs and try to get some sleep," I said, getting up from the table. "Four a.m. will be here before I know it. Ugh. Thanks for the decaf. We'll save that bottle of wine for another night," I said winking.

"Do keep me in mind on your upcoming real estate adventures, will you?" Helen said. "I'm actually quite eager to leave all these newly paved parking lots and rediscover Joni Mitchell's paradise."

"I will," I said. "You can count on that. Right now, however, this sleuth needs to get a few hours' sleep."

WEDNESDAY

CHAPTER 25

"Let's stop here for coffee," I suggested to Miranda, and she pulled her van into Tim Horton's Donuts, a 24-hour eatery and coffee shop located just off the Pat Bay Highway. We were on our way out of town, headed north. Lawrence's Range Rover pulled in behind us, and when we'd gone through the drive-through, I motioned for Miranda to park. Lawrence pulled in beside us, and I said to Miranda, "I'm having a serious case of the heebie jeebies. I just want to make sure everyone's okay." Miranda rolled her eyes, but I ignored her and walked over to Lawrence's car.

"Everyone all right in here?" I asked. Aliya nodded and gave me a thumbs-up. Lawrence seemed pretty well put together for this ungodly hour of the morning — sandy hair neatly combed, a pale grey turtleneck, black cords. But his worried blue eyes behind rimless glasses betrayed him, as did his pro forma smile. Heck, he might be even more nervous than I was, I thought. "How's Max the Wonder Dog?" I asked, peering into the back of the Range Rover where Max was safely stowed in his crate. He gave me a quiet "*Ruff*," at the mention of his name.

"He's a little restless," Lawrence said. "He knows something's up. I have treats for him for when this is all over. He can smell them. He gets treats after he's successfully tracked down one of his toys when we hide them in the park, so he's pretty excited."

"Okay, just to recap . . . we're going up the Pat Bay Highway to 17-A. We'll take that to West Saanich Road, turn off onto Tatlow Road, then —"

"— turn onto Chalet Road," Aliya said. "Then we look for Moses Point Road and Beach Access Road. Got it," she assured me, patting my arm.

"Okay. Half an hour," I said. "See you there."

"Everyone okay?" Miranda asked as I climbed back into the van.

"Yup."

"You okay?" she asked, pulling out onto the highway.

"Nope," I said.

"You former attorneys," Miranda tut-tutted. "Worry, worry, worry."

"Whereas you former RCMP types never turn a hair in dicey situations, I suppose."

"Grace under fire," Miranda replied.

"That's one of the things I'm worrying about," I said.

"What? Grace?"

"No, fire."

"Ah," said Miranda. "As a matter of interest, did you bring your .38 with you?"

"Yes. Reluctantly," I said.

"Good," she told me. "Because I don't have my nine-millimeter. I chose napping on your futon over going home, snoozing for fifteen minutes, grabbing my gun, and coming back to get you."

"Oh, fine," I said testily. "So I'm the designated shooter? You know how I hate guns."

"I do. But you've managed well enough in the past, haven't you?"

"Not really," I said. "Remember, in our first case together, I got my gun taken away from me by a malevolent drug addict. Tristan saved me from getting my head blown off with my own gun. Not my proudest moment."

"Hmm, yeah," Miranda said.

"And in the next case, crap, I gave my gun away to the bad guy."

"True. But he was incapacitated, if I remember correctly. Caught under a loading bay door with a fire raging at his feet. You gave him your gun to let him shoot himself as opposed to burning to death."

I said nothing. Guns, fooey. But sometimes shooting — or at least brandishing a weapon — was necessary. An investigator friend of mine, Caitlin Reece, called her Smith and Wesson .357 'the irresistible voice of reason.' So far my .38 hadn't done much reasoning. At Mac's urging, I bought the blasted thing and took a pistol course after Lawrence and I had been attacked gathering evidence against a horse abuser who had whacked me with a two by four and broken my arm. I sometimes look back on that afternoon and wonder what I would have done if I'd come armed to that muddy pasture. Would I have shot the raving, two-by-four-wielding horse guy or just brandished the gun and tried Caitlin Reece's approach? No way to know. So, I'm sure guns have their place, but I just wished mine was not the only gun on this particular junket.

As if she were privy to my thoughts, Miranda said, "We probably won't run into any rough stuff. Louis is just a dognapper with ideological pretensions."

"It's nice of you to try and reassure me, but we actually know almost nothing about him. I didn't ask Edgar to dig around in his past, more fool I. We need to remember that he wrote that extortion note, whose purpose — apart from telling Izzy how much money to assemble — was to terrify her with the reference to Sinjar. He's not on the RCMP's watchlist for no reason," I said as the lights of Victoria faded behind us and we drove steadily into darkness. Miranda's headlights illuminated the road ahead and the huge sentinel-like evergreens on either side of the highway.

Miranda said, "Here comes the turn to West Saanich Road." We drove along in silence for a bit longer, then she asked, "Still have that feeling?"

"Yeah. I've been thinking about William Stafford's poem 'Travelling through the Dark,'" I said. "It's about a man who has a choice to make on a dark road in the middle of the night." I sighed. "It's not about a potential dog rescue, or the confrontation of bad guys. It's about the duty we owe to other people. But it's speaking to me this morning."

"Oh?" Miranda said. "Which part?"

"The line where Stafford says, 'I thought hard for all of us.'"

"Ah," she said. "You feel responsible for Lawrence and Aliya."

"I do," I said. "I'd just like to keep them out of harm's way. I've been thinking —let's send them back to town with Beatrice once we find her. We can transfer Beatrice and her carrier — assuming we find it when we find her — into the Range Rover. They can deliver her to Izzy's."

"Makes sense," Miranda said. "That way they won't have to stick around longer than necessary. We can get Aliya to launch the drone and see what's going on at the cabin while we track with Max. She can give us a report."

"That ought to work," I said.

"Whew," Miranda said. "I was afraid there for a minute that you'd get all wibbly and start quoting more William Stafford to me. Or worse, your famous forbear."

"Philistine," I groused.

"Want to hear a story?" Miranda said. "It might take your mind off what-ifs."

"Sure," I told her.

"I've had a windfall. Or rather The Sanctuary had a windfall. An elderly donor, Deirdre Ryan, went to an assisted living facility on the mainland. She's not been doing well for many years and finally accepted that she needed help. She has MS. It's been harder and harder for her to get around. Anyhow, she left us ten acres, or four hectares if you're a metric maven. It's close to our present location."

"Holy smokes, Miranda!"

"Yeah. She really wanted to leave it to us for a feral cat refuge. She has a big heart, as is common among cat lovers, but a small deficit in the good-sense department." She shook her head. "I don't want to be glib about a serious problem — animal collecting. It's much more than a deficit of good sense. I've known a few animal collectors — cat hoarders — and they're often sweet, kind, and generous. But just as often, they're psychologically fragile and oh-so-anxious about their rescued animals. Sadly, many rescuers have abuse in their past. So I shouldn't be so dismissive. Anyhow,

Deirdre had been letting cats move in and live there over the years. Of course, two cats led to fifty cats, and that's when she called us. We've been working with her to bring the population down. Her head understands that it's better for cats to live in homes than live in the woods, even her woods, but her heart tells her that wild and free is best."

"I'm glad she came around to your point of view," I said. "Wild and free is not necessarily best. Your philosophy on ferals makes a lot of sense."

"Yup. Find them jobs," she said. "Stables, barns, farms, warehouses for the hardcore ferals. Shops, libraries, and bookstores if they can be socialized, and many of them can. And finally, some of them make lovely full-of-purrs house pets. You just have to work with them."

"Warehouse cats," I chuckled. "Like Vlad." Vlad, my big black feral who'd been left to me by a client, had lived unhappily on my enclosed back porch for years. When I met Miranda, I took advantage of her Rodent Ranger Program and sent Vlad to work catching mice in a wildflower seed warehouse. He was now the poster boy for the program. A photo of him lying in his cushy cat bed in the warehouse manager's office graced The Sanctuary's Rodent Ranger brochure, and only I knew that Vlad's ferociously toothy expression was really a satisfied grin.

"So you talked Deirdre out of her feral colony refuge idea?"

"Oh, pretty much," Miranda said. "I think she just wanted reassurance that we'd do the best thing for the ferals she's cared for over the years. She had a vision about fencing in the property, getting the cats all altered, and trying to keep them contained. But when we went over the cost, she saw the idea wasn't feasible."

"Have you signed the papers?"

"Yeah, we've signed."

"Wow. So you own the property?" I asked.

"Well, the organization does, but yeah. We own it."

"Now you have an embarrassment of riches. What a problem, right? What will you use it for? A dog ranch? I recall your saying a while ago that you needed more room for the dogs at The Sanctuary."

"Actually, Connie and I have been talking about moving the dogs on to other rescue organizations and just, well, working with cats. Cat overpopulation is a huge problem on the island. All the humane groups acknowledge it, but no one is stepping up to take the lead and tackle the problem. I have visions of . . . well, anyhow, I have a plan for that."

"Big changes for you," I said. "And maybe you'll sell the property. Every rescue group needs money. And if you have plans for new projects . . ."

"Hmm, maybe. But we won't be listing it on the open market, though. Deirdre and I talked about that and she doesn't want it chopped up for condos or some wealthy person's hideaway or a development of ticky-tacky houses. I have to drop in to the property this afternoon," she said. "Our volunteers are rounding up the last of the ferals. Cat-catching, as Connie calls it. We've been taking them in batches to Zee's, then bringing them to The Sanctuary to spend some time in the reception area and my office. They need to get used to people."

"Good idea," I said.

"Anyhow, want to see the acreage?" she continued. "Maybe you'll have some ideas about what we could do with it. How to repurpose it from its present state as a former unofficial feral cat colony."

"Sure, I'd like to see it," I said. "I bet it's fabulous. So much land."

"It's pretty darned nice. Forest and meadows, a little lake in the middle of it. An old but nicely renovated farmhouse that Deirdre lived in for years. Even a garage that she had remodeled into a guest house."

"We could pick up some lunch and go look at your windfall when we're done here," I said. "I'd like that."

"I thought you might," she said. We drove along in the dark in silence and after a bit Miranda asked, "Whatcha thinking? Feeling better?"

"Some," I said. "I'll feel even better once we have Beatrice safely stowed away."

She slowed the van, looking for the turn onto Moses Point Road. Lawrence's Range Rover followed.

"There," I said. "On the left. That break in the trees. Those salal bushes at the side of the road have been driven over. Recently. I'd say the RAM definitely came this way."

Miranda turned left onto the narrow road, bumping along through some serious ruts, but suddenly, at the intersection of Beach Access Road and Moses Road, we found a vehicle parked. In our way. A white SUV with POLICE in blue lettering across the back bumper.

"What the hell?" I muttered as Miranda came to an abrupt stop and killed her lights.

A dark figure exited the SUV and walked quickly back toward us.

"The SUV's interior lights are off," I said. "Any idea what this is all about?"

"I'm afraid I might," Miranda said. To my amazement, she hopped out of the van and walked toward the dark figure that now stood in the road ahead of us. To my even greater amazement, they shook hands, hugged, and began a conversation, peppered with many hand and arm gestures. The moon provided just enough light for me to see that the dark-clad figure was a youngish woman, dressed in boots, heavy black canvas fatigues, a black bulletproof vest, a black baseball cap with POLICE on the front of the cap in white, and the letters RCMP/GRE above the POLICE lettering. An assault rifle was slung over one shoulder. I ground my teeth. The RCMP. Just who we didn't need up here. At least not yet.

Miranda shook hands with the RCMP officer again, and came back to the van. "We have to go back to Chalet Road," she said. "Text Lawrence to meet us there, before he follows us in here."

"What's up?" I asked, texting. "Was that Sylvie? Your RCMP contact?"

She nodded, looking over her shoulder as she put the van in reverse.

When we reached Chalet Road, Miranda drove the van onto a wide spot on the shoulder and killed her lights. "We'll wait here for Lawrence," she said, her lips set in a grim line. "To answer your question, yes, that was Sylvie. This operation got away from her, she said. Her team leader decided they needed to go pick up Mohammed and Aziz, as well as some of the other Extremist Travellers, before they flee the country. Apparently, the powers that be in the Force were appalled that the guys Ro found — the IED-makers — were so far along with their bomb-making efforts. They don't want to make a similar mistake with Mohammed and Aziz. Whatever they're planning, whatever they need the ten thousand dollars for — the RCMP wants to know about it. Sylvie didn't have time to phone me about the RCMP's change of plans. But she convinced the team leader to wait for us here and let us know what's going on."

"That's not much help," I said. "If there's going to be rough stuff, what about Beatrice? Crap. This is just what we were trying to avoid."

"I know," Miranda said. "But we're not likely to get much more cooperation out of them."

"This is shaping up to be a FUBAR," I said. "We don't even know if Beatrice is there at the cabin. And we won't know until Max tells us." I ran a hand through my hair in frustration. "For that matter, how the hell did the Force even find Mac's place?"

"Public records, I expect," Miranda said. "Once they knew the cabin belonged to Mac, it would have been easy to find the location."

"And they figure Aziz is there, too?"

She nodded. "Yeah. So . . . unless he figured out how to get up here on his own, Louis must have picked him up somewhere along the way. Brent at Evergreen didn't mention that Louis had someone else with him when he took off with Beatrice."

"Of course," I said. "The place where the tracker stopped for three minutes. We thought Louis was letting Beatrice out to pee. I bet he was reconnecting with his buddy Aziz. Taking him to the cabin. So they're both there?"

Miranda nodded. "Sylvie thinks so, but of course, they have no way of knowing. They're going in to arrest them, oh, pretty much right now."

A gunshot came from the direction of the cabin and I jumped, startled.

"Uh huh," Miranda said, wincing. "I guess Louis and Aziz are declining to be arrested." She checked the rearview mirror. "Lights. Must be Lawrence and Aliya. Oh hell, you can blame me for this FUBAR. I told Sylvie about Louis and Aziz and our plans a while ago. I figured —"

"Hey, it's okay," I said. "You're not responsible for Sylvie's superiors thinking they need to scoop up Mohammed and Aziz." I'd no sooner spoken these words than we heard another shot from the direction of the cabin. Muttering something I couldn't hear, Miranda stepped out of the van, and I followed, motioning for Lawrence to park behind her. She and I both walked back to the Range Rover — I gestured for Aliya to roll down her window.

"Problems," I said, trying to project calm. "There's a gunfight going on at Mac's cabin."

"What?" Aliya asked, eyes wide.

"The RCMP and Louis," Miranda said. "At least. Maybe Louis's buddy Aziz also."

"Oh, no!" Aliya said. "Beatrice. What if someone *shoots* her? Accidentally, of course, but —"

"Let's hold a good thought," I said. "Miranda spoke to Sylvie. She said they'll be on the lookout for Beatrice."

Indignant, Aliya had more to say. "If the Mounties make a mess of the cabin —sorry, Miranda — then we have to hope that we don't find Beatrice dead," she said heatedly. "Or find that Louis has stashed her someplace he won't tell us about. Just to be a butthead!"

"Hey, hey," Miranda said soothingly. "First, we're going to find Beatrice alive. Second, it doesn't matter if Louis tells us or doesn't tell us where she is. I'd take bets on Max's nose over Louis's malevolence any day, Aliya. Wouldn't you?"

Mollified, Aliya nodded.

Hearing his name, Max scratched a little on the side of his crate. *I'm ready, guys*, he seemed to be saying. *Let's go.*

"Well, if we have to wait for the RCMP to conclude, how about some food?" Lawrence said. "I got my thermos filled at Tim Horton's. Tea. I bought doughnuts, too. Bring your paper cups and jump in. Might as well drink tea and eat doughnuts while things cool off. After all, how long can it take?"

CHAPTER 26

How long could it take?

Well . . .

Three hours later, we'd drunk Lawrence's tea, eaten the doughnuts, listened to the local oldies station (I now had America's 'A Horse with No Name' lodged firmly in my brain), admired the blood-red sunrise, checked our phones for messages . . . and finally the RCMP's white SUV came bumping down Chalet Road. The vehicle slowed to a stop as it approached us, and Miranda got out of the Range Rover and walked around to the SUV's passenger side to talk with Sylvie. A minute later, she came back to join us.

"Louis and Aziz are over there in handcuffs," she said. "They look mighty disgruntled. Sylvie says the team can hardly wait to get back to town so they can dig into the laptops and phones they confiscated." I looked over at the SUV. A young bearded blond face looked back at me from the near passenger-side window, a melancholy face with sad brown eyes. Louis, I guessed.

"Beatrice?" Aliya asked, her priorities straight. Fooey on Louis and Aziz and their electronics.

Miranda shook her head, looking apologetic. I understood this must be hard for her — Sylvie was a former colleague, and evidently still a friend.

"They didn't find her. Sylvie says she made it a point to do a careful search. But alive or dead, no curly-haired beige dog."

"Bet she didn't look as carefully as we will," Aliya said confidently. "What about the law, Miranda? If it's a crime scene, the RCMP might not want us there."

Miranda shot me a meaningful look and I thought, Oh oh. She doesn't think we're going to find Beatrice there. But she doesn't want to say so to Aliya.

"Oh, I don't think we need to let a few strips of crime tape deter us," Miranda said. "The RCMP will understand. Lawrence, want to drive down to the cabin and park? I think it's time we put Max on the case. What do you think, Kieran?"

"I agree," I said with feigned cheerfulness, joining Miranda in this charade. "Let's see what he can find."

When Lawrence let Max out of his crate, he stretched luxuriously, evidently overjoyed to be released, then hopped down, sniffed the tires of the Range Rover, lifted a leg on one of them, and finally pawed at Lawrence's leg. *Okay*, he seemed to say. *What's the game today?* Lawrence kneeled down, hugged him, then looked at us for guidance.

The four of us — five including Max — were standing on a little rise overlooking Mac's cabin. Indeed there was a strip of yellow crime-scene tape stretched across the makeshift driveway, but following Miranda's lead, we were evidently going to ignore that. A small, cedar-shingled structure badly in need of paint, the cabin overlooked a beach hardly deserving of the name. True, the tide was out, but the so-called beach seemed to be nothing but miles of mud and driftwood. As Mary had told me, the neighboring cabins were in even greater need of repair — missing roof shingles, a sheet of plywood tacked over a window, a collapsed deck.

"Give me a hand?" Miranda asked me. Together we walked back to Miranda's van, opened the back, and took out the plastic bag that contained Beatrice's bed. I hoped her smells had marinated sufficiently for Max to get a good whiff.

Lawrence snapped a lead onto Max's collar, and walked him around to a spot on the driveway behind the RAM and the Range Rover. Miranda and I were waiting there with Beatrice's doggie bed, and held it out to Max. He lowered his head into the bed, took a long sniff, then looked up at Lawrence.

"*Such*," Lawrence said, pronouncing the word *zoo-ch*.

"It means seek," Miranda said to me.

"Ah," I replied, my attention on Max, who was busy, head lifted, scenting the air. He trotted past the Range Rover to the black RAM, put his paws on the tailgate, where Beatrice's now-empty dog carrier sat in the pickup's bed, then gave one "*Ruff*," and sat down. I guessed that was how Max had been trained to tell his handler he'd found something. As indeed he had. He'd found the source of that delicious smell.

"*Braver Hund!*" Lawrence said to Max, handing him a treat that he took from a baggie in his jacket pocket, giving him a hug. "Freeze-dried chicken," Lawrence said, a little embarrassed. "Max's favorite."

"*Braver Hund* . . . good dog?" I asked Miranda, who nodded.

"So we know that Beatrice was once in this carrier," Aliya said despondently, hands in her jeans' pockets. "Big deal. Now what?"

Max crunched his way through his chicken treat, licked his chops, then looked up, clearly ready to play more hide-and-seek games.

"Now Max searches for more of that wonderful smell," Miranda said. "Lawrence, do you and Aliya want to take him to the cabin?"

Lawrence nodded, and he, Aliya, and Max ducked under the crime-scene tape, and went down the little path to the cabin.

After the three of them had disappeared into the cabin, Miranda and I stood in silence looking out to Saanich Inlet. Ghostly body-sized columns of fog had risen from the water and swayed eerily in a little breeze that had come down the inlet.

"Revenants," I said.

"Hmm?" Miranda asked.

"The fog shapes. Revenants. Creatures called back from the dead to haunt the living."

"Good grief, you're full of cheer this morning," Miranda observed.

"Oh, well," I said, sighing. "Anyhow, I think you're as pessimistic as I am that Max will find Beatrice in the cabin. Or on the deck. Or under the dock. Or in one of the cabins next door."

"Yeah, I'm right there in the pessimism pit with you," Miranda said. "But I thought it best for morale that we ask Max to try."

"Ha," I said. "Whose morale? Max's?"

"Nope. Lawrence and Aliya's."

"Hmm," I said.

"Any ideas?" Miranda asked.

"Well, one, but it might be only a D-minus idea."

"Yeah? Let's hear it," Miranda said.

"Just north of here . . . along the beach . . . what if we get Aliya to send the drone north along the water's edge? Not as far as that bed and breakfast or the Coast Guard station that we saw on Aliya's monitor. But there might be beachfront cabins or boathouses there that we don't know about. Then, if anything looks promising, we can take Max up there. Get him close for a sniff."

"We could do that," Miranda said. "The peninsula gets pretty primitive north of here — just shingle beach and miles of tall evergreens. Land's End is a good name for it. But, yeah, the drone might spot something useful, someplace that Louis might have stashed Beatrice."

"You seem doubtful," I said.

"I'm trying to think like Louis," she said. "As it turns out, you were right about him. He did get spooked, and feeling spooked must have led him to execute his own Plan B." She looked north up the beach and shook her head. "I really don't think so. But let's have Aliya search the beach and nearby forest by drone anyhow. We might find, oh, a cozy clearing with a humble woodcutter's hut —"

"— and a kettle of tasty stew cooking over an open fire, with a kindly white-haired granny stirring it, and Beatrice gnawing contentedly on a bone by the fire." I snorted.

We looked at each other. "Not bloody likely," she said.

I kicked at a clump of sea grass, thinking. "You know, the more I think about it, I don't think Louis drove any further north than this cabin," I said.

"Really?" Miranda said, surprised. "What makes you think that?"

"Where is there to drive *to*? As you say, it's pretty primitive up there."

"Yup, pretty much," Miranda said.

"So do we seriously think he drove north a mile or two and tied her to a tree and left her overnight? And why stash her so far away? He's expecting — was expecting — to call Izzy this morning, arrange a meetup, collect Beatrice, make the swap, and disappear."

"Go on," Miranda said.

"So I'm arguing against my own let-us-go-north idea. I think Louis's plan was something like this: stash Beatrice somewhere away from the cabin, yet someplace close by. Maybe someplace he would have to pass on his way *south* to drive into town and meet up with Izzy. It's not logical that he would stash her in some inconvenient spot that would take him out of his way on the fateful morning of the swap."

"What's just south of us?" Miranda said. "I guess we need Aliya's iPad to call up Google and get a satellite view. There's always that French restaurant. Maybe he left her, oh, in the parking lot or behind the garbage dumpsters."

"I have a better idea," I said. "Why did Louis stop the RAM anyhow? Originally I figured he stopped to let Beatrice out to pee. Then I figured he probably stopped to pick up Aziz . . . but I've changed my mind. No, the place where the pet tracker stopped for three minutes . . . I think Louis dropped Beatrice there. And I think she may still be there."

"You could be right, Miz Yeats," Miranda said.

"I could be, Miz Blake. I need to get into my pet tracker account and look at recent history. Then we can figure out exactly where the RAM stopped. And if I'm wrong . . ."

"Then we go north," she said glumly. "After all, the dog has to be *some-where*. What you propose makes a lot of sense. First we'll go south, and ask Max to lead us to Beatrice."

If she's there, I said to myself, crossing mental fingers.

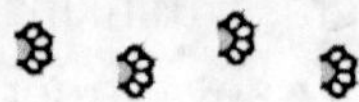

"What the heck is *that?*" Aliya asked, guiding the drone in and out among the trees in an extensive stand of softwoods. All five of us were sitting in the Range Rover in a little pullout on Chalet Road, just past that swanky French restaurant whose name I could never remember. I'd checked the map on my pet tracker account, and right about here was where the tracker indicated that the RAM had stopped for three minutes.

The 'that' Aliya was asking about was row upon row of carefully stacked wood — dozens of cords of it piled neatly four feet high and eight feet long, back among the alders.

"A woodlot," I said. "I bet the restaurant owns it. They need cut wood for their fireplaces. A roaring, air-polluting fire makes meals so much more enjoyable, right?"

Aliya nodded, frowning, concentrating on driving the drone.

"Look there," I said, pointing to an image on her iPad, something the drone was seeing from about twenty feet high as Aliya maneuvered it in and out among the leafless trees. "Just ahead. There's a barricade with a sign on it. Can you take the drone down so we can see what the sign says?"

"Sure," Aliya said, maneuvering the drone into position as we crowded around, Miranda and I peering over her shoulder, looking at the iPad's display.

PRIVATE PROPERTY — NO TRESSPASSING
ASK FOR KEY AT RESTAURANT

"Private property," she tut-tutted. "Kieran?"

Recalling Miranda's cavalier attitude toward the yellow crime-scene tape, I took a similar approach. "Are we going to let little things like a discouraging sign and a locked barricade deter us? I think Max needs to go take a sniff in there. Lawrence? Can you get him on his lead?"

"Sure can," Lawrence said, before getting out, fetching Max from his crate and attaching his lead again. Miranda let Max sniff Beatrice's bed once more, then Lawrence said, "*Such*," and led Max across the road and into the woodlot while we followed. Max put his nose to the ground, then found several spots among the alders to be very sniff-worthy.

"She was here," Aliya said excitedly. "Max smells her. You were right, Kieran."

I said nothing as Max followed what was clearly a scent trail among the piled-up cords of wood. True, she probably had been here, but maybe Max was smelling the sent trail she had left last night, when Louis had stopped here for three minutes. Maybe Louis really had let her out here to pee. Maybe that was what Max was smelling. Beatrice's latrine. Who knew?

"*Ruff*," we heard from just ahead of us, a narrow makeshift walkway between the stacked cords of wood.

"He's found her," Aliya said happily as the three of us scrambled after Lawrence and Max. We hurried around the corner of one of the stacked cords to find Max, nose to the ground, sniffing intently at a giant pile of unstacked wood. I noted, however, that he didn't sit down as he had when he found Beatrice's carrier in the back of the RAM. So was she here or not?

"Max isn't quite sure," Miranda explained quietly. "I think he's overwhelmed by Beatrice's scent. Louis must have walked her back and forth in here looking for the best place to leave her."

As we watched, Max transferred his attention to a haphazard pile of alder trunks about fifteen feet long and six feet high stripped of leaves and small branches, lying on the ground evidently awaiting their turn to be cut up into cordwood.

"*Ruff*," Max said again. But as before, he didn't sit down, just gave a "*Ruff*" to let us know that he'd scented Beatrice. Before I could ask what all this meant, Aliya spotted a rope tied to one of the alder trunks. Or part of a rope.

"Oh, no . . ." Aliya said rushing over to the rope and picking it up. "It's been . . . shredded, right in the middle!"

Max looked up at her and said definitively, "*Ruff*."

"Oh, Max," Aliya said in disappointment. "She was here, but I guess she chewed through her rope and escaped. You're right, but you're wrong."

"*Braver Hund*," Lawrence said sadly, offering Max some pieces of freeze-dried chicken, petting him fondly. Max chomped the chicken, but pawed insistently at Lawrence's leg. "*Ruff*," he said again.

"Max . . ." Lawrence said, clearly at a loss for what to do.

I tapped Miranda on her shoulder and cocked a thumb in the direction of the higgledy-piggledy pile of cut wood ready to be stacked into neat cords, just six feet away, the first place where Max had given a '*Ruff*.'

"Let's think this through," I said as she joined me. "Louis must have walked Beatrice all over this woodlot, looking for the best place to tie her up. And poor Max is smelling all of those places. That pile of alder trunks with the rope, the place where Max is signaling — I bet that's the freshest scent. It's evidently where Louis left her."

"Yeah," Miranda said. "But she's not here now, dammit. After she chewed through her rope, she probably ran off. She might be halfway to Victoria by now."

"Or maybe not," I said. "I want to check something out." Only half-hopeful, I lay down on the soggy, wood-chip-covered ground and peered into the dark recesses at the base of the untidy pile. Was it possible? I wondered, sticking my hand into the darkness under the cordwood, feeling around. "This little hidey-hole goes back quite a long way," I said. "In fact —"

Something licked my fingers.

"Holy crap," I whispered to Miranda, withdrawing my hand. "Get some chicken."

She hurried back around the stack of felled alder trees and returned in a jiffy. Kneeling down beside me, she put a piece of freeze-dried chicken on my palm. Slowly and carefully, I reached back into the darkness. I had one instant of atavistic dread, telling myself that a slavering, toothy beast did not lurk there in the dark ready to shred my hand, and then the tentative lick came again. I opened my fingers and whatever was hiding in there gently took the freeze-dried chicken.

"Beatrice," I whispered, recalling Audrey's description of how Louis the Green Man had seduced the dog a couple of nights ago. With treats. "You little chow-hound. Come on out," I said quietly. "Izzy needs you."

Nothing. All was quiet in the land under the woodpile. Maybe I was wrong. Maybe a slavering, toothy, freeze-dried-chicken-loving beast really did live there. Maybe Beatrice —

"I'll get Lawrence's whole baggie of chicken," Miranda whispered. "She might need more persuading."

"Come on, Beatrice," I coaxed. "Come on, girl."

Just then, a kind of rustling came from under the woodpile and, alarmed, I withdrew my hand.

"Got the chicken," Miranda said, kneeling beside me again, opening Lawrence's baggie and passing me another piece. Then she whispered hoarsely, "Holy smokes."

A curly, brown-colored dog face appeared in the place where I had withdrawn my hand.

"Beatrice, I presume," Miranda said.

I offered the dog another piece of chicken, which she took gently from my hand.

"Okay, girl, you're going to have to work for the rest," Miranda said, standing up and taking Max's leash out of her back pocket. I guessed she'd asked Lawrence for the leash when she'd gone back for the chicken. Good thinking.

"You feed her, I'll get the leash on," Miranda said. "Okay?"

"Okay," I agreed, holding out another piece of chicken.

Beatrice slowly eeled out from under the woodpile, and stood there, looking around uncertainly. I knew Max, Aliya, and Lawrence were probably watching, and I mentally telegraphed them to stay away. I didn't want anything to spook Beatrice.

"Don't worry, kiddo," I said softly. "We're going to take you home to Izzy."

I continued to offer chicken, Beatrice continued to eat, and very, very slowly, Miranda bent down and attached Max's leash to her collar.

"Gotcha," I said, relief making my knees feel weak. "Gotcha."

CHAPTER 27

"**H**oney, I'm home!"
I called out my usual empty-house greeting as I closed the front door behind me. This was the cats' cue to sing out a welcome and, amazingly, they often did.

"*Mraff,*" my portly grey cat, Trey, called to me from the living room sofa where he had made a nest in the mohair throw I keep there for emergency snoozes.

"*Frrtt,*" said Jeoffry, who was curled up beside him.

"*Mraff,* yourselves," I said, tossing my jacket and baseball cap at the coat tree in the hall. "I'm bushed. I'm thinking about a shower and some shut-eye. If anyone's interested, they can join me. For the shut-eye."

I wandered into the kitchen, thought about some soothing chamomile tea, decided it was too much trouble, poured a glass of orange juice, then yawned my way into my bedroom where I sat on the end of my bed, contemplating undressing. Suddenly that seemed like an overwhelming effort, as did the shower. So I kicked off my sneakers, pulled my sweatshirt over my head, bundled it and my jeans together, and tossed them onto the rocking chair in the corner. Then, still dressed in my T-shirt, socks, and underwear, I crawled under the covers. Sighing in sybaritic comfort, I closed my eyes, expecting a pleasant slide into sleep, but found instead an unexpected wakefulness.

After a few minutes, I rolled over on my back and stared at the ceiling, wondering in the words of the Anglican Church's Morning Prayer, if I had 'left undone those things which we ought to have done.' Hmm. Was a small mental review in order? Well . . .

Lawrence and Aliya had delivered Beatrice to an overjoyed Izzy. Ro had phoned to tell Miranda and me that she and Izzy were bathing, fluffing, and brushing Beatrice, and that Izzy couldn't stop crying but Ro figured they were tears of happiness so that was okay, wasn't it? I assured her it was. Mac was thrilled when I called him to report that Beatrice was back with Izzy. Miranda was rounding up humane traps and a couple of volunteers to drive over to her new property for some cat-catching — I'd come later. Connie would fetch Tris and Dani from school. There were no loose ends to tie up. So why couldn't I sleep?

Trey jumped up on the bed beside me, and I hugged him close, wrapping us both in my comforter.

"Have you come to debrief me?" I asked him. "Evidently I have a few questions I need to contemplate before I fall into the arms of Hypnos."

Trey yawned.

"Hmm, okay. Here's one that's been bothering me. Why didn't Beatrice run away after she'd chewed through her rope? Why did she hide in the woodpile? Miranda expected her to be halfway to Victoria. Thoughts?"

Snores.

"Well, I wondered about that, and figured she was probably scared to death. I mean, Louis tied her to those alder trunks and left her there — exposed, no place to shelter. No food. I think she got spooked and headed for the first hidey-hole that she could fit herself into."

More snores. I pulled the comforter up under my chin.

"But why did Louis do that, you may ask — leave her tied there? It seems awfully careless. After all, she was a ten-thousand-dollar dog. Ideas? No? Well, maybe he got distracted when Aziz showed up. After all, Aziz doesn't like dogs. Maybe he didn't want to share the cabin with one. Or . . . heck, we'll never know. And what about the covetous Louis? Do we tell Izzy about her brother's role in this tawdry little drama? Or leave it to Mac? After all, she's his niece. I'll have to think on that."

I tucked the snoring Trey under one arm, and rolled over into a sensible sleeping position, which for me was a fetal curl.

"Despite my saying I don't, I do wonder about Louis," I murmured to Trey. "What kind of guy gets a certificate as an animal technician then goes to work for a pound seizure shelter? Most people in rescue and rehab are appalled at pound seizure shelters. Was Barbara Davidson kicking back to Louis some of the money her shelter received for sending animals on to labs? Did Louis have a financial incentive to find animals for the shelter? It's all very confusing. We may never know what motivated Louis. Is he just covetous, as Helen explained? Or is it worse than that? Is he malevolent? Like the witches in Henry Purcell's opera? The ones who cackle about getting pleasure from people's pain? Was it like that with him? Ruining Izzy would give him a thrill?"

Trey gave my elbow a tentative lick. I got it. *Stop talking, human.*

"One last thought," I told him. "Remember what's-his-name Rumsfeld south of the border? One of the more odious Bush flunkies back in the last century? No? I really don't either, just his comment about knowing. It's either mighty profound or mighty silly. Remember, he said:

> *'There are known knowns; there are things we know we know. We also know there are known unknowns, that is to say we know there are things we do not know. But there are also unknown unknowns.'*

"So we may never know what makes Louis tick. He may have to stay an unknown unknown for us. And maybe it doesn't matter. Miranda can ask questions about him when she goes to Evergreen to have a chat with Barbara. Or not. So that's it, I guess. Oh, apart from my copy of *The Rubaiyat* that I stuffed inside the black backpack. I think it's in the Range Rover. I kinda want it back. Thanks for listening."

I checked to see that my phone's ringer was turned off. It was. I intended to sleep until two or three in the afternoon — I had an alarm set — and didn't want an unexpected call to wake me. I'd agreed to pick up a late lunch for Miranda, Aliya, and me while we apprehended ferals on Miranda's new property. The place must be teeming with cats, I guessed, as Miranda had asked Aliya, too, to come and help. Apparently, every pair of hands was needed. I'd order sandwiches for three, I figured. Or four. Or five. Miranda had mentioned volunteers might be helping also. But right now I needed to close my eyes.

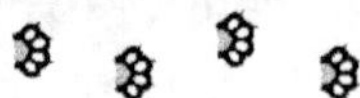

My alarm warbled at three o'clock. "Fmmf," I mumbled, disoriented and thick-headed. Middle-of-the-day naps do not agree with me. My mouth felt as parched as the nameless desert in 'A Horse with No Name,' and I had the beginnings of a thumping headache. Trey had deserted me, so I tossed the comforter aside, sat on the edge of the bed for a minute, then went on into the bathroom. A hot shower made me feel more or less human, as did clean clothes, and I wandered into the kitchen following the wonderful smell of . . . coffee?

I found a note on the kitchen counter next to the coffeemaker.

See you at Miranda's new place! Wear your grubbies, she says. Apparently we're cat-catching. Thought you might need coffee.

Aliya

Touched by Aliya's thoughtfulness, I poured coffee into my travel mug, found my jacket and baseball cap on the coat tree, and headed out to my car. The bag of Subway sandwiches was ready for me, and after I picked up the food, I decided I'd take a small detour down Beach Drive to admire the ocean and the marina on my way north. Traffic was snarled at the intersection of my street and Oak Bay Avenue, and I found myself once again fuming in frustration. For heaven's sake . . . what was this? Toronto? Perhaps it was time to pick up a real estate paper, maybe in Sidney, and start investigating homes for sale.

As I drove past the Oak Bay Marina, I checked out the boats, wondering if my friends from Oregon were still tied up at their slip, or if they'd gone back over the border to spend some time at their farm in the Willamette Valley. I knew where their boat, *The Catspaw*, was berthed, but I couldn't spot it in the forest of masts. They must still be at their farm, I thought. Or adventuring on the high seas. Ah, the life of retired nomads!

Mid-afternoon. The pewter grey ocean was uncharacteristically still, but here on the coast we're rightly suspicious of ocean calm. A storm brewing? Possibly. The sun, which had risen in such glory this morning, now hid sullenly behind mountainous clouds the color of a day-old bruise. I hoped the inclement weather would hold off for Miranda's cat-catching project.

Looking for the little road that Miranda had described to me, and the sign that said RYAN, I turned off the Pat Bay Highway and continued down a narrow gravel road flanked by frothy pink-blossomed apple trees. On either side of the road, beyond the apple trees, were astonishing, vibrant, multicolored riots of wildflowers — blue cornflowers, yellow daisies, red poppies, pink foxgloves, purple lupin . . . and about a dozen other colorful species whose names I didn't know. But what really drew my attention were the oaks that, in groups of four or five, dotted the meadow. Garry oaks. Thriving Garry oaks. I stopped my car and just stared. Less than ten percent of the Garry oak ecosystems remained in the world but here, on Deirdre Ryan's property, were magnificent stands of trees, still leafless, but tall and healthy-looking. I continued thoughtfully down the road, which turned a little to the left, skirting the verge of dark, tall, mysterious evergreens that lay beyond the meadow. The forest proper. I felt embarrassed that I couldn't tell the firs from the cedars or the spruces from the hemlocks. And what about the pines? I bet Deirdre could identify the trees, I thought, feeling sad again that she'd had to leave such an astonishing place.

The road ended at a spacious, white-painted, two-story farmhouse with a wraparound porch clearly meant for sitting and enjoying summer evenings. What luxury, I thought, fantasizing about a soft spring evening, the sun edging toward the horizon somewhere behind the cedars (or firs or pines), a gentle wind ruffling the wildflowers, a couple of white wicker chairs, Tris with a mug of hot chocolate, immersed in *The Golden Cat* (Book Two of Tailchaser's adventures), me with a glass of Method and Madness and Mary Oliver's *A Thousand Mornings*, Albinoni's *Adagio in G Minor* wafting from the living room speakers . . . ah well.

Seeing two vehicles approaching, I pulled off the road to let The Sanctuary's dark blue van and their old beat-up white one pass. I didn't recognize the young women driving but they waved and I waved back, figuring these might be the last of Miranda's volunteer cat-catchers. Finding a parking spot behind Miranda's yellow Jeep, Connie's black Honda and Aliya's green Nissan Leaf — the gang seemed to be all here — I stepped out of my car and stood there quietly for a moment, drinking in the woodland silence. The air was cool. And fresh. And smelled somehow . . . green.

"Kieran, you're here!" Tris called, coming around a corner of the farmhouse, mud plastered on the front of her T-shirt. "Isn't this place cool?"

"It's very cool," I agreed. "Did Connie bring you to help with cat-catching? And by the way . . . you have two yellow leaves in your hair. And mud on your nose."

"Oops," she grinned, plucking the leaves from her hair, then brushing at her nose. "Yeah, Connie brought me. She's gone to Zee's with Selene and Bianca and the last of the cats. But, you have to see something," she said, a look of wonder on her face. "C'mon, I've been waiting for you!" She held out her hand and I took it, letting her lead me around the farmhouse and into the woods.

"Back here," she whispered as we forced our way through waist-high huckleberry and laurel bushes. "We have to be quiet now. There's a kind of lake just beyond those green bushes over there. The ground is a little yucky, but we have to crawl."

Crawl through the mud? Only for you, my Sproutlet, I thought. Only for you.

She dropped to the ground and I followed, crawling with elbows and knees to a stand of salal bushes. We lay together on the cold, gooey ground, and Tris parted two of the bush's branches. Sure enough, in front of us was a small lake about the size of a basketball court, fringed with cattails, a tiny island no larger than a Volkswagen smack in the middle of it.

"Look!" she whispered excitedly.

"Ohhhh," I replied. Because on the island, half hidden by a holly bush, was a Canada Goose. Just . . . sitting. And in the water beside her was another goose, swimming. "Tris, they're so beautiful. I bet that's the female on the island, sitting on eggs. And the one in the water, that's probably the male. He's guarding her. They mate for life, you know."

"Do they?" Tris said. "Eggs. So there'll be baby geese. Wow. I wonder what they'll look like. Fuzzy chickens?"

We wriggled backward until we reached a place where Tris figured we could stand up without spooking the geese. She tried to brush mud off the front of her T-shirt — a dark blue one with a colorful assortment of songbirds on it and the lettering EASILY DISTRACTED BY BIRDS in white — and failed.

"More mud," she said. "Sorry."

"Mud, shmud," I said, brushing at my own clothes. "No problem. We'll just toss your shirt and pants in the washer along with mine. Our sneakers, too. Seeing those geese . . . that was really something. Thanks for showing me. Did you know, Canada geese are my favorite birds?"

"Really?" She looked up at me, smiling conspiratorially. Then her mood turned serious.

"Kieran, the babies when they hatch, will they be okay here?"

"The goslings? Sure they will. The parent geese scoped out this place. They decided it's safe, so the little ones will be okay. They'll hatch in about a month, and stay here with mom and dad goose, learning all the things they need to learn — swimming, bug-catching — until they can fly away."

"Who flies away?" she wanted to know, her voice quiet. "The big geese?"

All of a sudden I realized what she was asking. Her Canadian Army father — the dad goose — flew away to Afghanistan and was killed giving covering fire to his unit fleeing a firefight. Her mother — the mom goose — died when a drunk driver ran a stop sign and hit her car. Next stop on the abandonment train was her grandmother, who just keeled over one day from a heart attack. Then came the old dog man (Tris's grandfather) and his despicable son, Connor, and his druggie pals. No wonder she was worried about the little geese. They were proxies for her own abandoned self. Brother.

"Well, I think they all fly away," I said.

"Together?" she asked.

"I'm pretty sure," I said, hoping like hell I was right.

"Okay, that's good," she said, but I doubted if this particular worry had been put away. *Oh, Tris. Why did I ever assume it had?*

"Everyone's starving," Tris said, changing the subject. "Selene and Bianca and Connie will be back from Zee's pretty soon. Aliya said you'd have sandwiches?"

"I do," I said, my voice a little husky. "A late lunch for Miranda's volunteers. And her. And me. And Connie. Probably Aliya, also. What about you, though? You probably had lunch at school, so I'm sure you don't want anything to eat," I said with feigned seriousness.

"Nah," Tris replied, grinning, "I can always eat."

"Thought so. You're on that see food diet, right?" I teased.

"What? We don't eat —"

"Seafood. I know. It's the other see food diet. You know, see food, eat food."

"Yuk, yuk," Tris said, rolling her eyes. "Sometimes you are sooo corny."

"I am," I said unrepentantly. "Kieran the Corny. C'mon. You can help me with the sandwiches. They're in the car."

As we were carrying the bags of sandwiches up the front porch steps, she said, "I saw something else today. When Selene and I were going to get the trap she'd set. A kind of path through the forest. I asked Miranda and she said it was a deer trail." Tris looked at me, eyes wide and shining. "Do you think there could really be deer here?"

"O ye of little faith, of course there are deer here," Miranda said, appearing in the farmhouse doorway, holding it open for us as we carried the food into the kitchen. "In fact, I saw three just a while ago. A doe and two fawns. The fawns are so young — they still have their spots. Part of that deer trail is right here." She pointed out the kitchen window.

"No way," Tris said, excited, handing her bag of food to Miranda and hurrying over to the big kitchen window overlooking the forest. She pressed her nose to the glass, probably searching for those spotted fawns.

"So," Miranda said to me, "get any shut-eye?" She'd changed out of the sweatshirt she'd been wearing earlier today which was, admittedly, a bit bloodstained from her misadventures with Anton. Now she was dressed in a black turtleneck and jeans, her navy windbreaker thrown over a white plastic chair in a corner of the kitchen. Her banged-up face looked a little worse — her stitched lip was puffier, her black eye almost swollen shut.

"Oh, a little," I said. "I'm not a good daytime sleeper. I feel weird."

"You and me both," she groaned, motioning for me to put the bags I was carrying down on a table in the corner. "We brought in a table and chairs," she explained, pushing aside a couple of clipboards and a handful of pens. "The volunteers have been keeping track of ferals sighted and ferals removed. Bianca has photos, too. Very organized. I think we've got them all." She looked around the kitchen. "So we can close up shop here soon. Aliya's outside, I think."

"Nope, Aliya was upstairs," a voice called from the hall. "Nice bathroom," she said to Miranda. "In fact, that whole upstairs seems newly renovated. I was looking around. I'm nosy," she whispered to me.

"Deirdre had quite a bit of remodeling done a few years back," Miranda said. "She was hoping she could age in place . . . even thought about hiring a caregiver who could live here and help her. Thus the second bathroom and a little kitchen upstairs. But her deteriorating health got the better of her." She put her hands in the pockets of her jeans and looked around the kitchen a bit regretfully. *That seems odd*, I thought. *Regret? Or just sadness*

that her friend Deirdre had to leave this place she evidently loved. Hmm.
"Want a tour of the farmhouse?" she asked me. "I've been thinking more seriously about what you said when you wondered if I'd sell this place. And, well, I just might."

"Really?" I said, my interest piqued. "Sure, let's have a tour."

Aliya joined Tris at the kitchen window. "Want to come with me and look for those fawns? Kieran and Miranda are just going to poke around the house."

Tris looked at me. "Can I?"

"Sure," I said. "You can look for snake balls, too."

"Snake balls?" Tris said, cocking her head skeptically. "You're teasing, right?"

"Nope," I told her. "It's a spring thing. Snakes sometimes mate in, well, balls. Dozens of them coiled and slithering around each other."

Tris shook her head. "Snake balls. Weird, but cool. I love snakes, y'know. Most people don't, but I do. Aliya, if we see one, I want to take a picture of it for science class."

"Snake balls," Aliya said, shuddering. "C'mon, Tris."

CHAPTER 28

After Aliya and Tris had left, Tris talking Aliya's ear off about fawns and geese and snakes, Miranda said, "Hey, let's go see the upstairs renovations. Deirdre did a great job. I wouldn't mind living here myself."

Oh-ho, I thought. Is that what this is all about? Miranda wants to move to here, to this property . . . but she thinks she should sell? Is she conflicted? Is it an ethical thing? I shrugged, deciding I'd just follow her lead. Let her bounce ideas off me if that's what she needed to do. For some reason she wanted me here. To look at the place with her? And maybe hear my thoughts? Okay. I could do that.

When she was sure we were alone, Miranda turned to me. "Fooey. I'm not good at beating around the bush," she said. "I found something here a few days ago that just, well, blew me away. I've been hanging onto it until I could bring you here and show it to you."

This sounds mysterious, I thought. But I think I get it. She wants to move here and is going to ask my opinion. Of course I'll be supportive. Who wouldn't want to live here? She can sort the legal niceties out with The Sanctuary's attorney. But what is the something she found that blew her away?

"Stay right here," she said, holding up one finger. "I have to go down to the basement for a minute."

"Okay," I said, mystified.

When she returned, she was carrying a piece of weathered white wood, about eighteen inches long and nine inches high. On one side, something — a word, a name — had been hand-lettered. The lettering must have been done a while ago as it was faded and barely legible.

Miranda held the sign up in front of her, a grin on her face. "Can you read it?" she asked.

"If I squint," I said, doing just that. "One word. Hmm. It starts with an i. Maybe a capital i?" And then it hit me. The word was INNISFREE. "Oh my God, it's the Yeats poem," I exclaimed as Miranda handed me the sign. "'The Lake Isle of Innisfree.' I have to sit down."

Innisfree. In Loch Gill, County Sligo, Ireland . . . the place to which my famous great-uncle had longed to return, a place where he'd spent idyllic childhood summers. Sickened by the hustle and bustle of modern life, Yeats said that one day as he was walking in Fleet Street, in London, he happened to pass a shop with a fountain outside. He stopped, and the tinkling of water transported him back to Innisfree, to his childhood, and he realized how much he longed for the peace he once knew in Loch Gill. He went directly home and composed the poem, which is, arguably, one of the English language's most poignant poems about longing for the natural world. It's certainly one of my favorite Yeats poems.

"How the heck did you know I was fond of that poem?" I asked.

Miranda chuckled, leaning against the kitchen wall. "Remember the night you, Mac, and I went to The Snug and got a little blithered? The night Mac sang 'A Scottish Soldier,' I sang 'Caledonia,' and you recited the Yeats poem?"

"Mercifully, no," I said. "God, I'm surprised we weren't thrown out. Can you sing? I didn't know you could sing."

She laughed. "More like drunken caterwauling. We were a great hit. Well, not the Yeats, sadly. Seems the Snug-goers are into maudlin patriotic songs from the old country, not poetry. But Mac and I got enthusiastic rounds of applause. And others joined in. It was a lively evening." She shook her head. "Amazing what passes for entertainment in the dead of winter on

Vancouver Island. Anyhow, you recited 'The Lake Isle of Innisfree,' cried in your beer, and I had to drive you home."

"And you remembered," I said. "So Deirdre, who was evidently a good Irish Colleen, and a Yeats afficionado, named this place Innisfree and even had a sign made to remind her of the poem. That's what blew you away — finding the sign."

"Yup."

"And the cat-catching was a ruse."

"Yup."

"You wanted me to see this place, fall in love with it, and then, when you showed me Deirdre's sign, you figured I'd swoon and the deal would be sealed."

"Yup," she said again, her grin slipping just a little. She was probably saying to herself, Oops. What if I'm wrong? What if Kieran doesn't want the property? I decided to put her out of her misery.

"Well, I have to tell you," I said, making my face stern, then letting my own grin show, "you're right. I swooned. I love it. Who wouldn't love it? I want it. But how can we make that happen? Deirdre . . . you said she was fussy about who might want to buy it."

Miranda waved a hand in the air. "I already talked to her. And," she said, "now that it belongs to The Sanctuary, I get to be fussy, too. The back of this property backs up to land The Sanctuary already owns."

"Really?" I said. "So we'd be neighbors. Separated by several hectares, but still neighbors. As Tris would say, cool. But, let's come down to earth, girlfriend. I have no idea if I can afford Innisfree. I have equally little idea about what my house in Oak Bay is worth."

Miranda nodded. "Quite a lot. A house not quite as nice as yours one street over sold for more than a million. I, um, happened to take a look at the real estate section of the newspaper. Basically you'd be swapping properties. The Oak Bay house for, well, for Innisfree."

"A million dollars," I said, beyond amazement. "I had no idea. Of course, I'll have to talk to Aliya. She might want to stay in town."

Miranda shook her head. "I doubt it. She's been unhappy about the bus-yness in Oak Bay, too. I think she'd be okay with moving north."

"Interesting," I said. "Coincidentally, I had a chat with Helen last night. She's going to be teaching just north of Sidney at that new college and wanted to tell me she was considering a move. Something closer to the new college. I said I'd been thinking of moving north myself; she said she'd be happy to tag along. That leaves Tris, though. I wonder what she'll think?"

"Are you kidding?" Miranda said. "Between the fawns and the snake balls and the deer trail? And who knows what else she'd find here?"

"She already found something else." I chuckled. "Geese. Well, goslings, once they hatch."

Hearing car door-slamming noises outside, Miranda said, "Must be Selene and Bianca back from Zee's. Connie, too. Let's eat. Oh, you might want to have this." She reached into her back pocket and pulled out a business card. "Someone you can talk to about this property," she said. "Peggy Molloy. She's The Sanctuary's attorney. One of her partners handles real estate transactions. You'll like them. They have a ginger office cat named Justice," she said, grinning.

I took the card. "Hmm," I said. "It seems I might have to go seeking Justice."

※　※　※　※

"So you like this place, do you?" I asked Tris as we were in my car, turning from Innisfree onto the highway. A little breeze ruffled the boughs of the apple trees, and blossoms swirled in the air, falling like an improbable blizzard of pink snowflakes.

"Oh, yeah," Tris said enthusiastically. "But I was going to ask you . . . about the geese."

"Uh huh?"

"Well, can we come back and check on them? The babies? You know, see how they're coming along. I guess no one lives here, so we wouldn't be disturbing anyone."

276

I smiled. "I think we could do that."

"You said they'd hatch in about a month?"

"Yeah. But we ought to check before that, don't you think? We don't know how old the eggs are."

"Oh," Tris said. "I didn't think about that. They might be twenty-nine days old. They might be just about ready to hatch. So . . . could we come tomorrow?"

"I don't see why not," I said, taking a breath. Then, "Tris . . . what would you think about moving here?"

Tris looked at me as if she'd just won the lottery. "Move here?" she squeaked. "As in *live here*?"

"Yeah. I'm getting pretty fed up with the busyness in Oak Bay. And the nightly singalongs at that craft brewing place around the corner. Plus the fact that the patrons park on our street and block our driveway. Helen and Aliya have to leave their cars way down the street."

"So . . . how would this work?" Tris asked, thoughtful. "Could I still go to my same school?"

"Sure. Why not?"

"And we'd take the cats?"

"Of course!" I exclaimed. "They're part of our family, right?"

"Right. But what about Helen? And Aliya?"

"Well, fortunately, there seems to be plenty of space. There's a remodeled garage attached to the house, and the upstairs has been renovated. Deirdre, the former owner, wasn't very well. So she fixed it up, thinking she'd get someone to live there and help her out. But that didn't happen. She moved to a retirement home in Vancouver."

"Oh," Tris said. "She must have been sad to leave. But she could come to visit if she wanted, couldn't she? Or I could email her photos of the geese and the wildflowers so she didn't feel so bad. But, Kieran, could we *really* live there?"

I took a deep breath, hearing the longing in her voice, realizing I was about to cross the real estate Rubicon. "I don't see why not. Once we make up our minds, it's just paperwork," I said, shuddering about all the details — a realtor, listing my house, showing it, cleaning, moving. Ai yi. Still, I'd have Peggy and Justice to help organize things. "We just have to decide if we want to do it, Sprout. Simple as that," I said. "So you think things over, okay?"

"Okay," she said solemnly. "Wow. Can I tell Dani? I could call her when we get home."

"Sure you can," I said. "Say, let's drive by the ocean on the way back to Oak Bay. What do you think? We might see orcas."

"Yeah," Tris said excitedly. "You know, Miranda told me the orca pod that's in trouble, J pod, well, they had a calf. A new baby orca. Maybe we'll see it."

"We'll sure look for it," I said, turning onto the coast road. "I'll stop at that little overlook."

Tris hummed a little, looking out at the ocean, then said, "Can we sing? That song about the place with two cats in the yard?"

I was always happy when Tris wanted to sing. To my surprise, she'd proven to be as fond of the oldies as I was. More importantly, songs had become a kind of communication between us. When she was worried or upset, she sometimes asked to hear songs that reflected feelings she couldn't easily express. So I paid attention to her song choice. At other times, though, she was just a kid, wanting to sing silly songs. I wondered which it was this time.

"Two cats in the yard? You want to turn Jeoff and Trey out in the meadow with the poppies when we move?" I asked in mock horror. "It's a pretty safe property, but —"

"No, silly," Tris said. "I just really like that song. And the place, would be, you know . . ." she trailed off. Thinking she had something else to add, I waited, but she was quiet.

"Sure," I said, a little puzzled, hunting through the songs on my iPod. The song 'Our House' by Crosby, Stills, Nash and Young was an odd choice. It was a love song. But what the heck. Weren't there many kinds of love? So maybe it wasn't such an odd choice . . . and it was Tris's choice. Innisfree would be Tris's and my house. And Jeoffry's and Trey's. Our house.

I started the song playing and when Crosby, Stills, Nash and Young made their way into the chorus, Tris started to sing. After a few seconds, I joined her.

Our house is a very, very, very fine house
With two cats in the yard,
Life used to be so hard
Now everything is easy, 'cause of you.

We warbled together to the end of the song, giggling at the la, la, las and I wondered: was it the thought of *our* house as opposed to my house that Tris wanted me to know? A place that we'd discovered together, a place that could be hers as well as mine? Or was there something else in those lines, something that Tris couldn't speak aloud, something that she let others speak about for her. I wasn't certain, but maybe it didn't matter. Maybe the same line was speaking to both of us. 'Now everything is easy 'cause of you.'

Indeed it is, I thought, swallowing the lump that had, unaccountably, formed in my throat.

Indeed it is.

The Lake Isle of Innisfree

I will arise and go now, and go to Innisfree,
And a small cabin build there, of clay and wattles made;
Nine bean rows will I have there, a hive for the honey bee,
And live alone in the bee-loud glade.
And I shall have some peace there, for peace comes dropping slow,
Dropping from the veils of the morning to where the cricket sings;
There midnight's all a glimmer, and noon a purple glow,
And evening full of the linnet's wings.
I will arise and go now, for always night and day
I hear lake water lapping with low sounds by the shore;
While I stand on the roadway, or on the pavements grey,
I hear it in the deep heart's core.

by William Butler Yeats